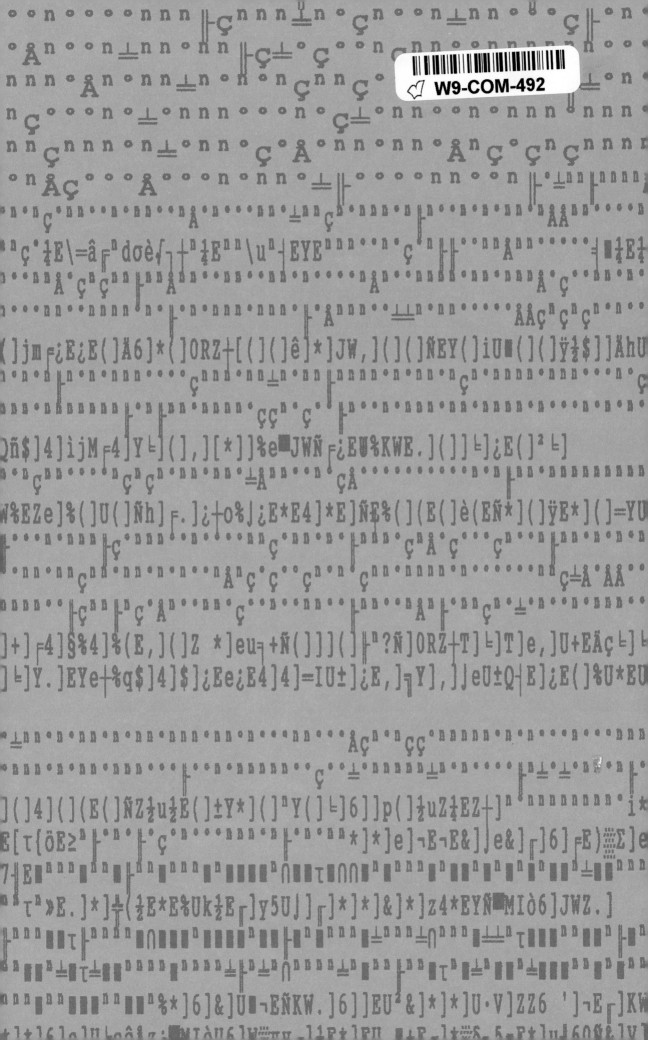

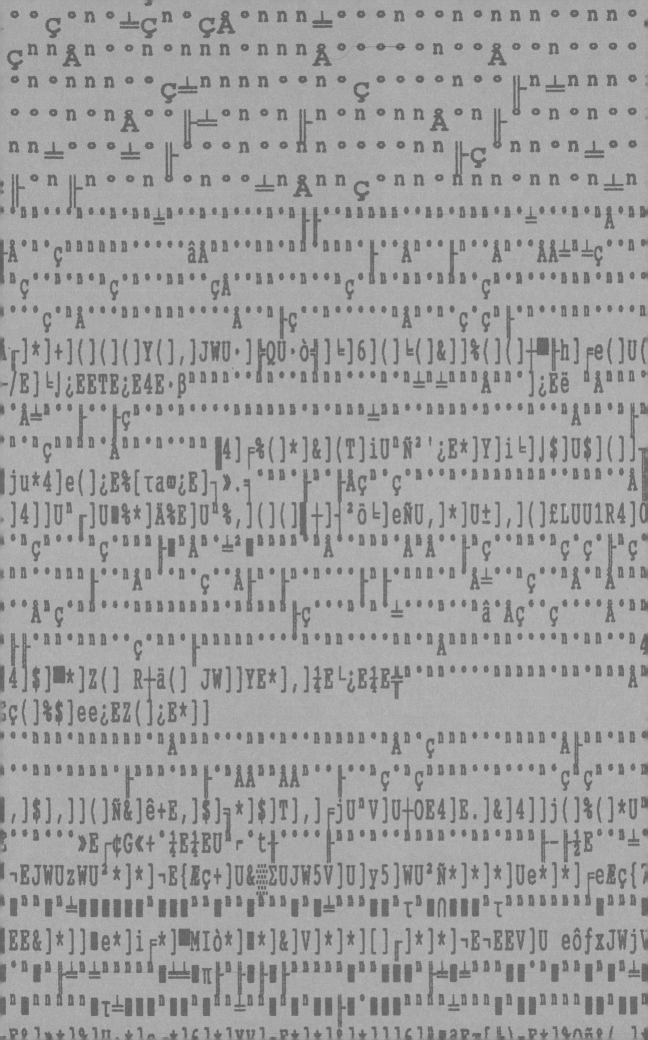

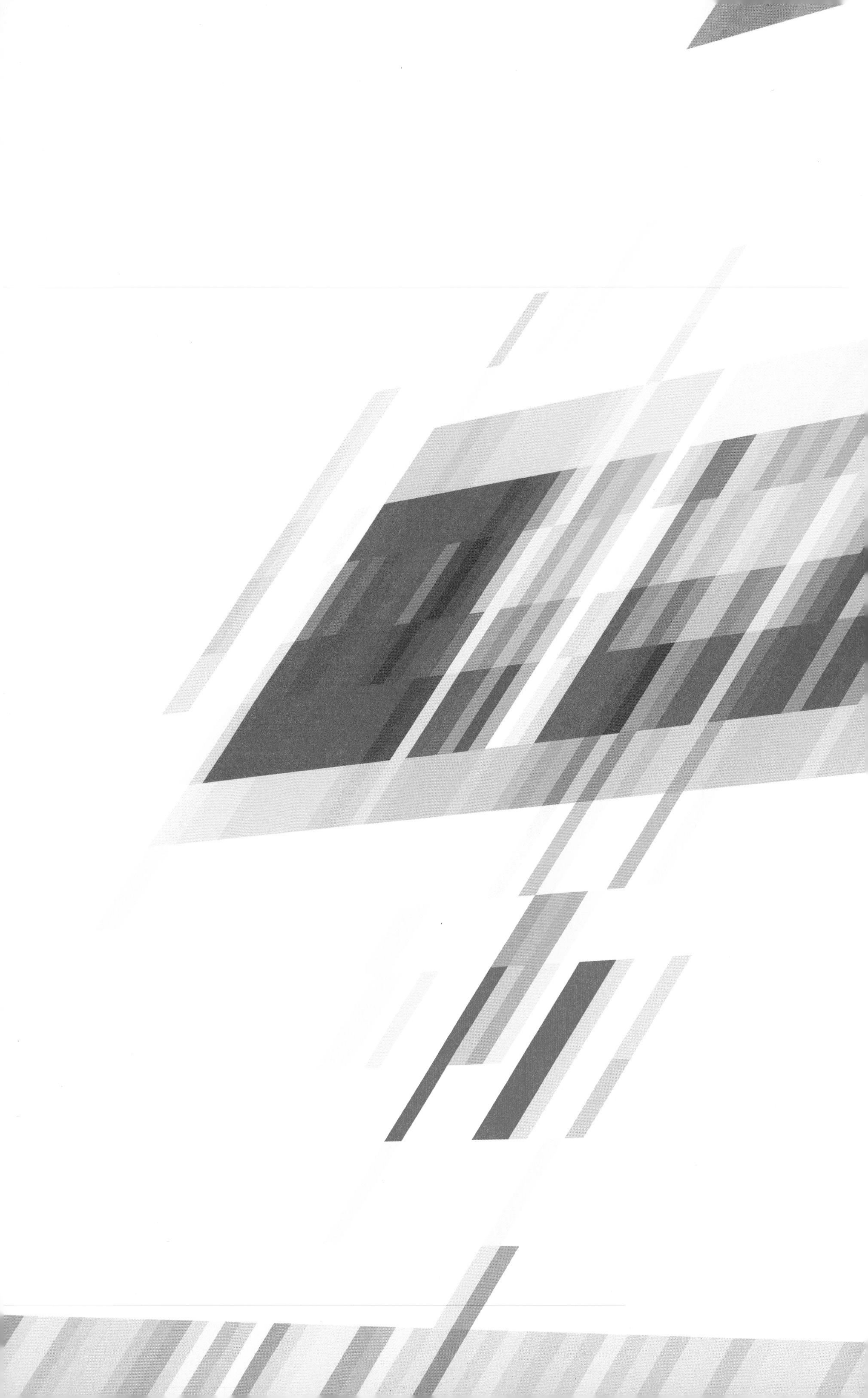

USER

Devin Grayson
John Bolton
Sean Phillips

IMAGE COMICS, INC.
Robert Kirkman—Chief Operating Officer
Erik Larsen—Chief Financial Officer
Todd McFarlane—President
Marc Silvestri—Chief Executive Officer
Jim Valentino—Vice-President

Eric Stephenson—Publisher
Corey Murphy—Director of Sales
Jeff Boison—Director of Publishing Planning & Book Trade Sales
Chris Ross—Director of Digital Sales
Kat Salazar—Director of PR & Marketing
Branwyn Bigglestone—Controller
Susan Korpela—Accounts Manager
Drew Gill—Art Director
Brett Warnock—Production Manager
Meredith Wallace—Print Manager
Briah Skelly—Publicist
Aly Hoffman—Conventions & Events Coordinator
Sasha Head—Sales & Marketing Production Designer
David Brothers—Branding Manager
Melissa Gifford—Content Manager
Erika Schnatz—Production Artist
Ryan Brewer—Production Artist
Shanna Matuszak—Production Artist
Tricia Ramos—Production Artist
Vincent Kukua—Production Artist
Jeff Stang—Direct Market Sales Representative
Emilio Bautista—Digital Sales Associate
Leanna Caunter—Accounting Assistant
Chloe Ramos-Peterson—Library Market Sales Representative
IMAGECOMICS.COM

Introduction

In the late 1990s, we goofed off with multiplayer **Doom II** on the DC Comics office network, shrieking at each other from our offices as we chased Cyberdemons through the corridors of Hell. I'd been greenlit to start running my own projects at Vertigo, and reached out to Devin Grayson, who'd become a top DC Universe writer via her work on **Catwoman**, **Batman**, the **Titans** and **Nightwing**. As a woman writing multiple top titles, she was a rarity in mainstream comics; as a woman in demand for writing major male characters - Roy Harper, Bruce Wayne, Dick Grayson - with exquisite confidence, sexiness and psychological sensitivity, she was even rarer. I was a big fan, and had tried to recruit her to reboot **Swamp Thing**; she'd politely declined. Couldn't take on another big series. Too busy. [I hired this guy she recommended, Brian K. Vaughan, instead. Long story.]

The next time I asked, I offered a creator-owned project of any length. To my surprise and delight, she said yes - and what she wanted to do wasn't, on its face, anything she was known for. Devin proposed a story about a young woman escaping from her troubled everyday life via online roleplaying as a male knight. I'd loved my **Doom II** escapades, I'd been queer since high school and I loved female protagonists; I knew the material, so I said yes. Truth is, I knew it, but had no idea how much I still had to learn from it.

User's original working title was **MUN**. At the turn of the millennium, that was gamer lingo for your offline identity, short for "mundane." **User**, however, is anything but. John Bolton and Sean Phillips' stunning artwork combines with Devin's sophisticated and prescient exploration of online identity to create something that was years ahead of its time and resonates with all its original power today. Look at how John infuses the virtual community with color and depth, while Sean commands Meg Chancellor's world with greys and uniform texture broken only by the seductive glow and color of 2000-era computer screens.

The powerful hallmarks of **User** have found their way forward. Gamers find new expression in virtual bodies, virtual currency, virtual communities. Self-seekers go beyond questioning sexual orientation to challenging fundamental gender norms. This book was way ahead of its time in testifying to an absolute truth: identity cannot be faked. You can try, whether you're trying to play within the boundaries of gender, classic chivalry, or coding, but inevitably, one day, you'll be faced with your authentic self.

Joan Hilty

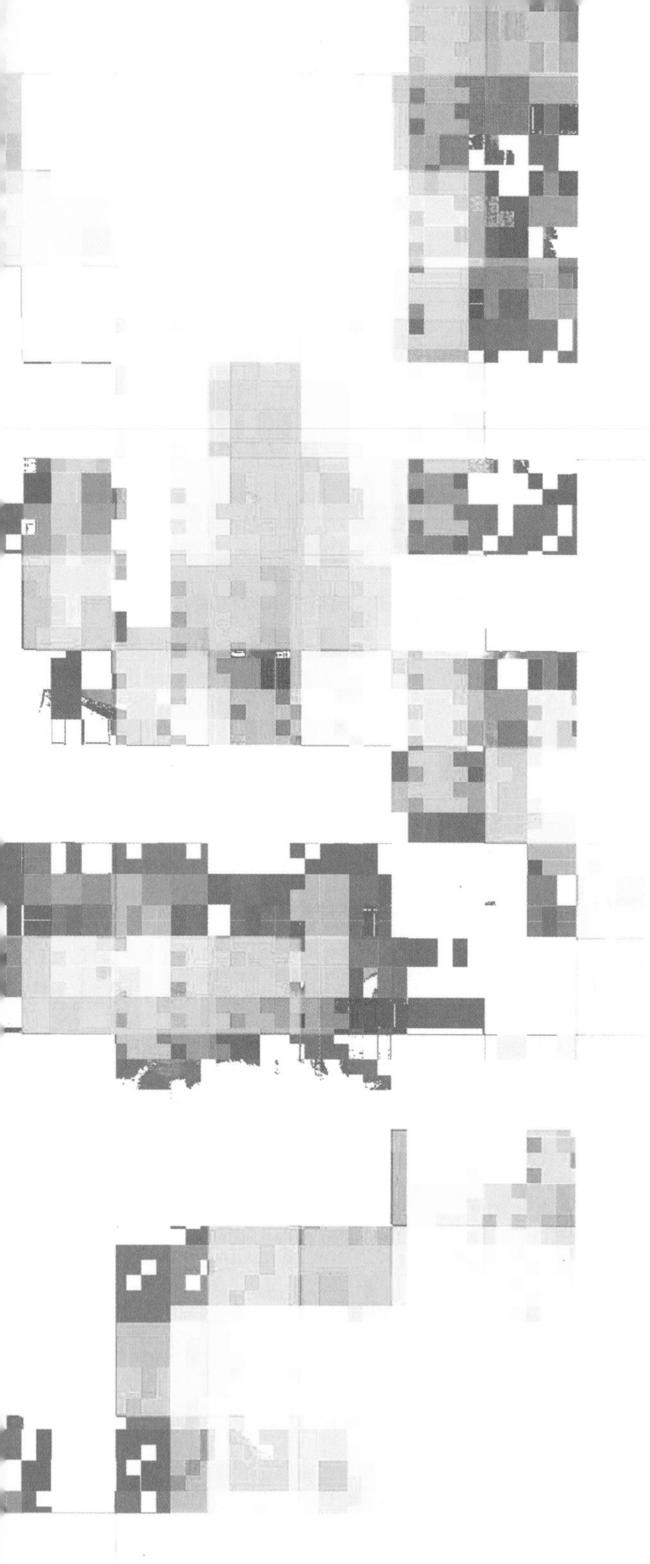

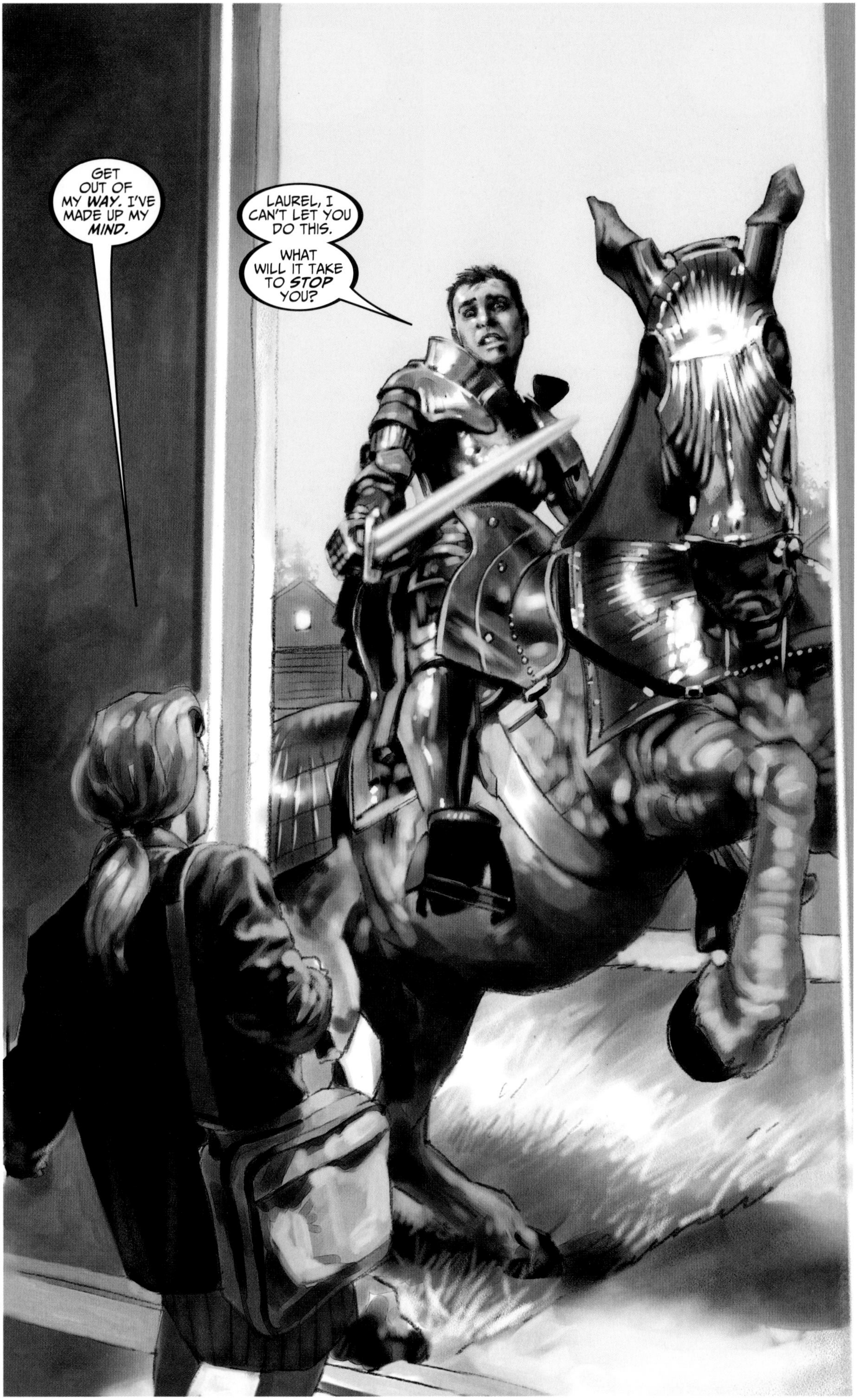
GET OUT OF MY WAY. I'VE MADE UP MY MIND.
LAUREL, I CAN'T LET YOU DO THIS.
WHAT WILL IT TAKE TO STOP YOU?

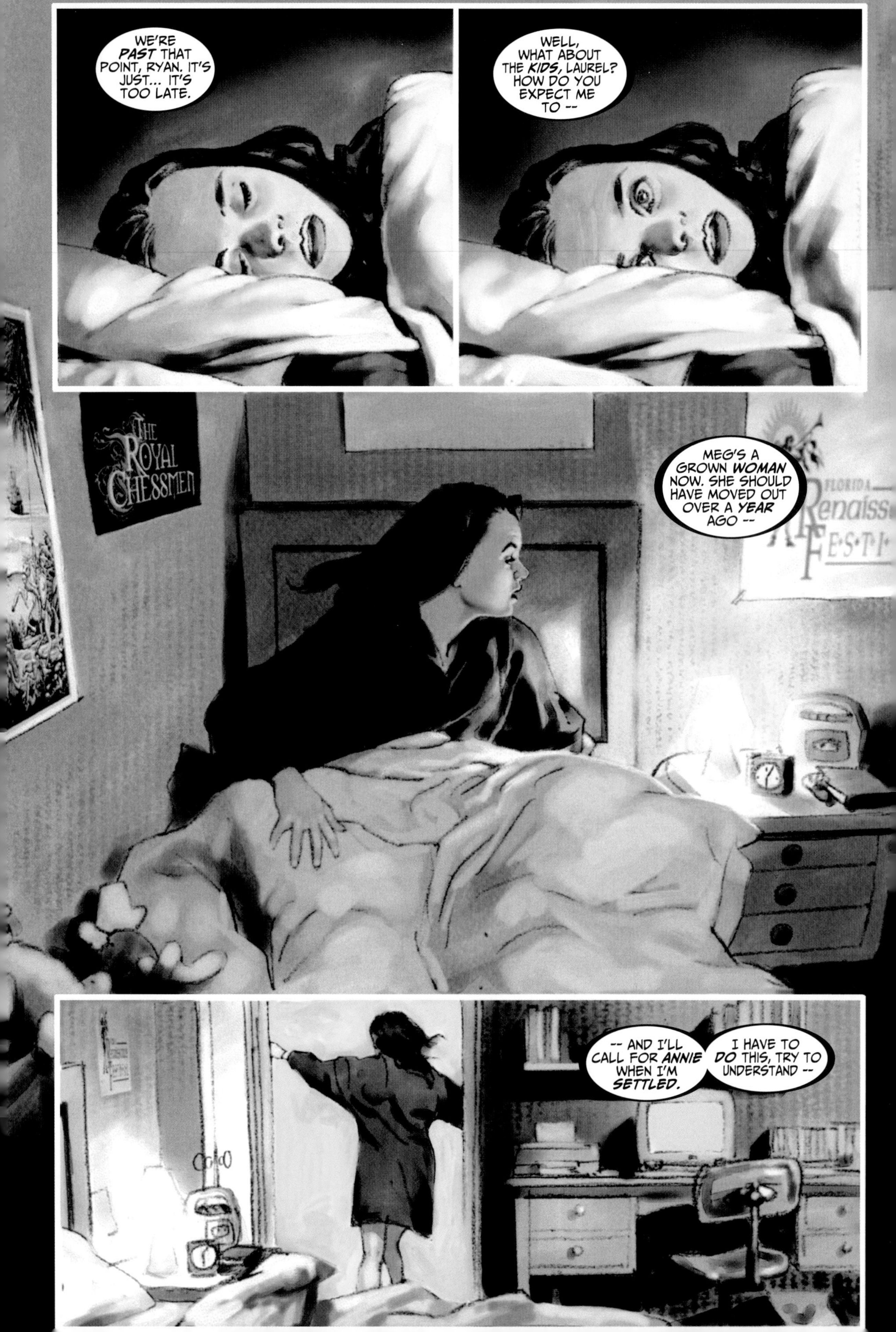
WE'RE PAST THAT POINT, RYAN. IT'S JUST... IT'S TOO LATE.
WELL, WHAT ABOUT THE KIDS, LAUREL? HOW DO YOU EXPECT ME TO --
THE ROYAL CHESSMEN
MEG'S A GROWN WOMAN NOW. SHE SHOULD HAVE MOVED OUT OVER A YEAR AGO --
-- AND I'LL CALL FOR ANNIE WHEN I'M SETTLED.
I HAVE TO DO THIS, TRY TO UNDERSTAND --

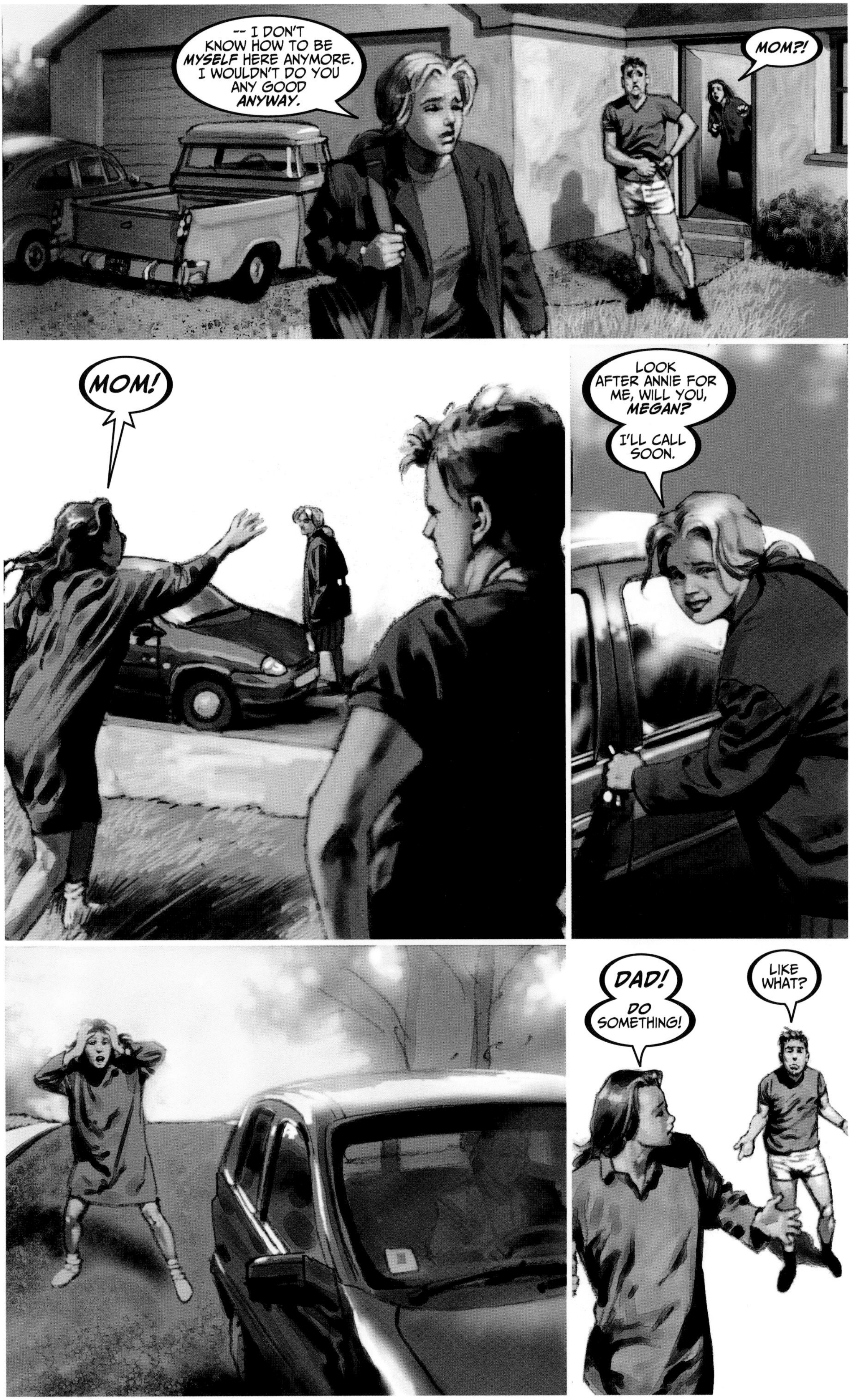
-- I DON'T KNOW HOW TO BE MYSELF HERE ANYMORE. I WOULDN'T DO YOU ANY GOOD ANYWAY.
MOM?!
MOM!
LOOK AFTER ANNIE FOR ME, WILL YOU, MEGAN?
I'LL CALL SOON.
DAD! DO SOMETHING!
LIKE WHAT?

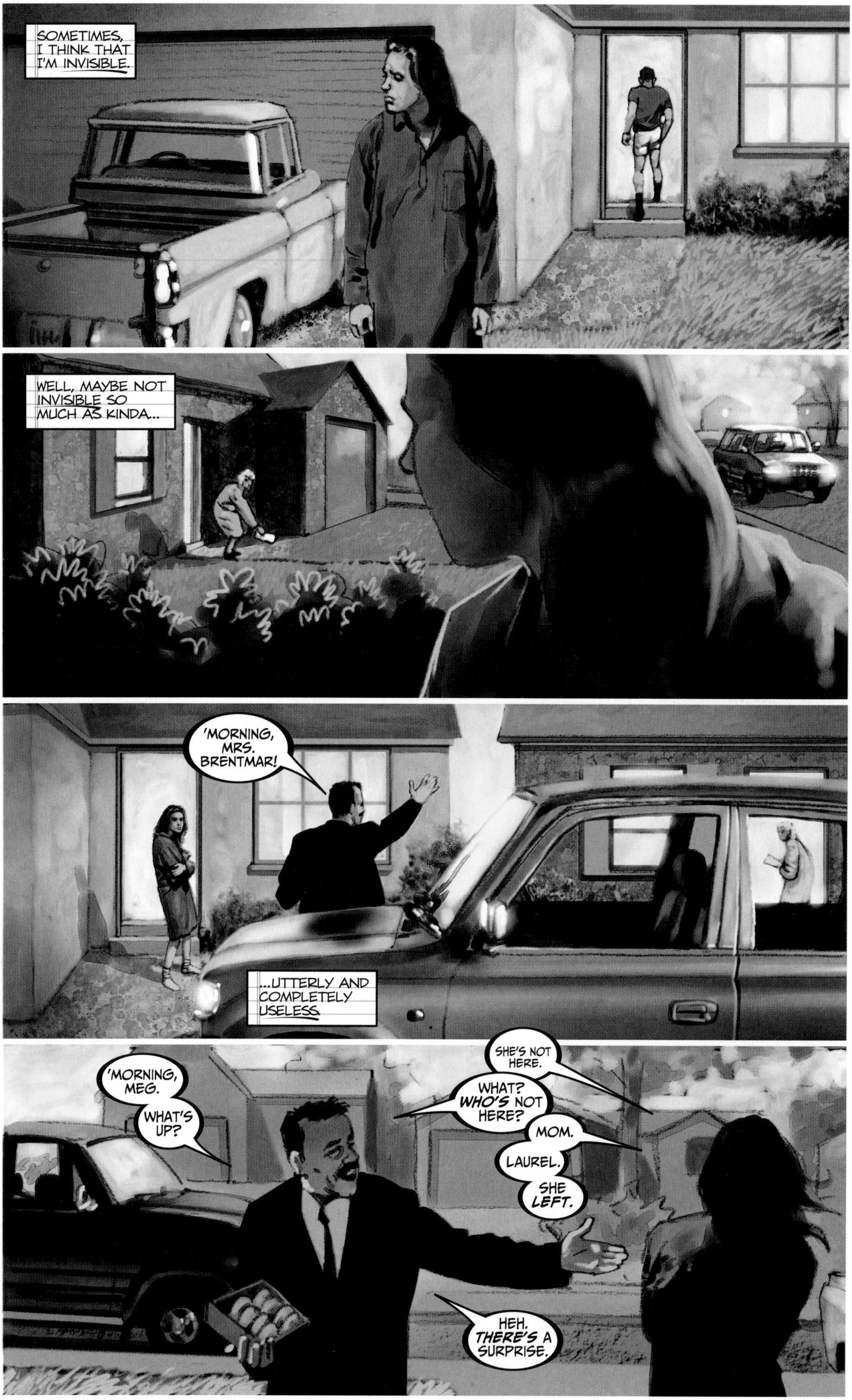
SOMETIMES, I THINK THAT I'M INVISIBLE.
WELL, MAYBE NOT INVISIBLE SO MUCH AS KINDA...
'MORNING, MRS. BRENTMAR!
...UTTERLY AND COMPLETELY USELESS.
'MORNING, MEG.
WHAT'S UP?
SHE'S NOT HERE.
WHAT? WHO'S NOT HERE?
MOM.
LAUREL.
SHE LEFT.
HEH. THERE'S A SURPRISE.

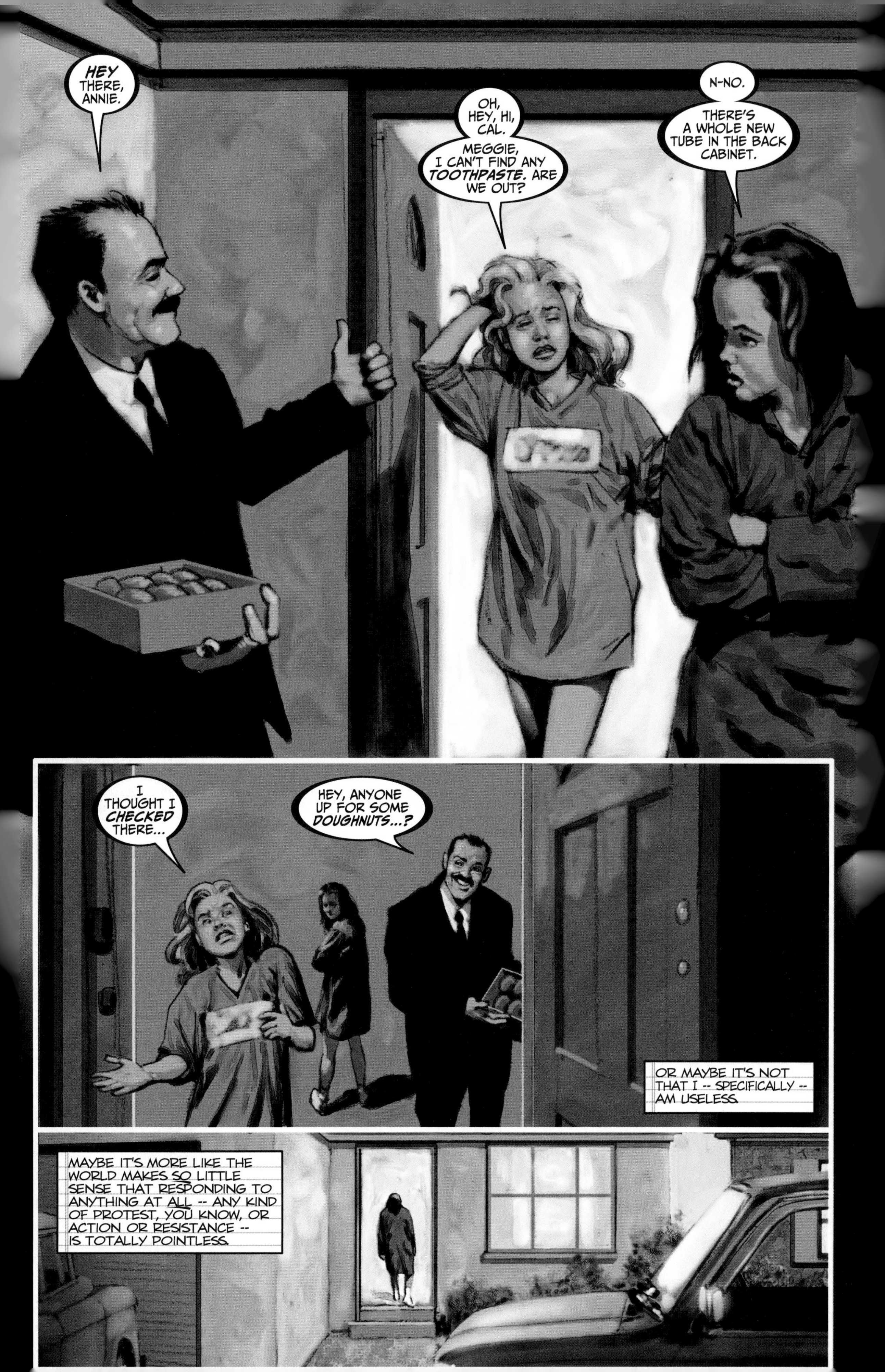
HEY THERE, ANNIE.
OH, HEY, HI, CAL.
MEGGIE, I CAN'T FIND ANY TOOTHPASTE. ARE WE OUT?
N-NO.
THERE'S A WHOLE NEW TUBE IN THE BACK CABINET.
I THOUGHT I CHECKED THERE...
HEY, ANYONE UP FOR SOME DOUGHNUTS...?
OR MAYBE IT'S NOT THAT I -- SPECIFICALLY -- AM USELESS.
MAYBE IT'S MORE LIKE THE WORLD MAKES SO LITTLE SENSE THAT RESPONDING TO ANYTHING AT ALL -- ANY KIND OF PROTEST, YOU KNOW, OR ACTION OR RESISTANCE -- IS TOTALLY POINTLESS.

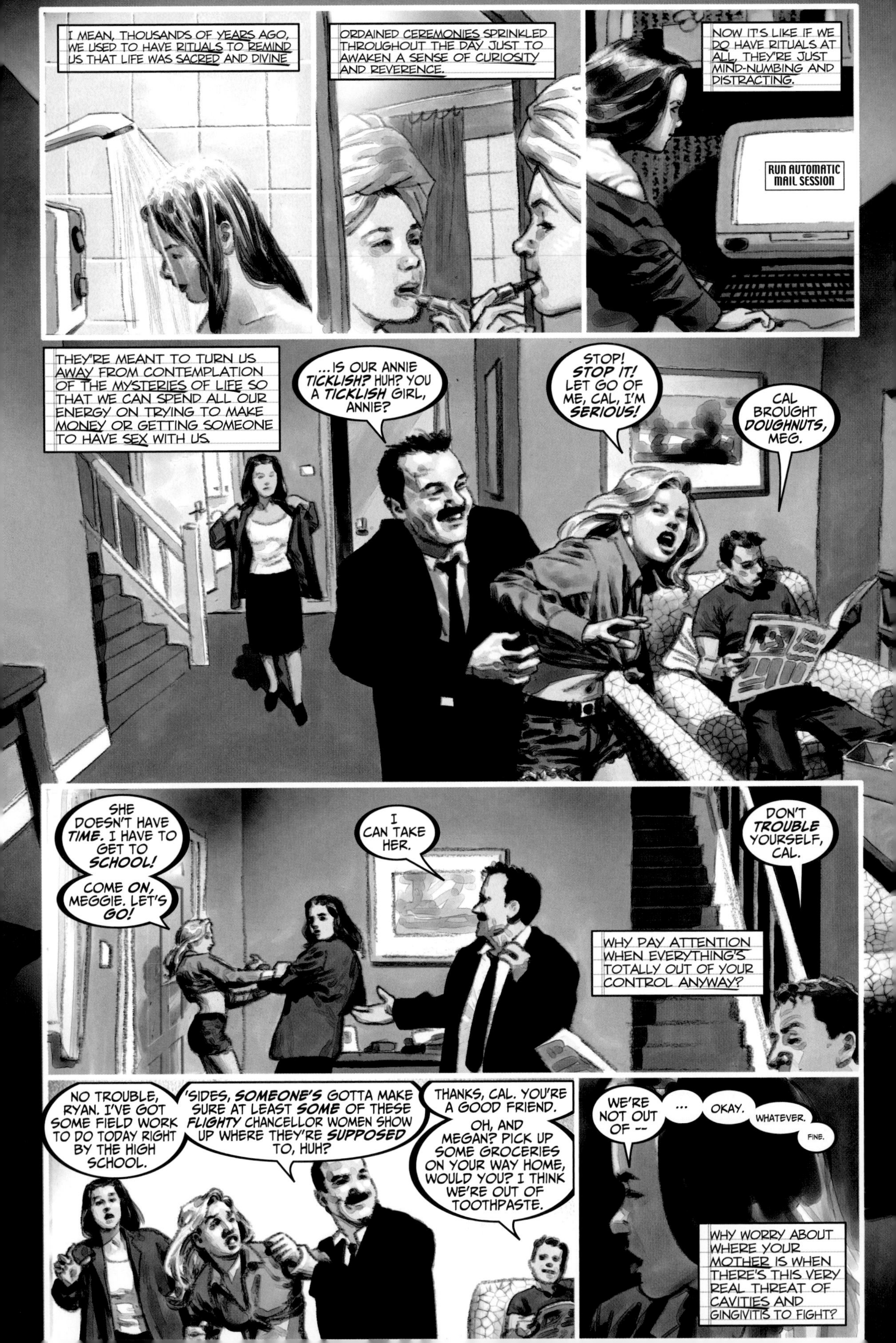
I MEAN, THOUSANDS OF YEARS AGO, WE USED TO HAVE RITUALS TO REMIND US THAT LIFE WAS SACRED AND DIVINE
ORDAINED CEREMONIES SPRINKLED THROUGHOUT THE DAY JUST TO AWAKEN A SENSE OF CURIOSITY AND REVERENCE.
NOW IT'S LIKE IF WE DO HAVE RITUALS AT ALL, THEY'RE JUST MIND-NUMBING AND DISTRACTING.
RUN AUTOMATIC MAIL SESSION
THEY'RE MEANT TO TURN US AWAY FROM CONTEMPLATION OF THE MYSTERIES OF LIFE SO THAT WE CAN SPEND ALL OUR ENERGY ON TRYING TO MAKE MONEY OR GETTING SOMEONE TO HAVE SEX WITH US.
...IS OUR ANNIE TICKLISH? HUH? YOU A TICKLISH GIRL, ANNIE?
STOP! STOP IT! LET GO OF ME, CAL, I'M SERIOUS!
CAL BROUGHT DOUGHNUTS, MEG.
SHE DOESN'T HAVE TIME. I HAVE TO GET TO SCHOOL!
COME ON, MEGGIE. LET'S GO!
I CAN TAKE HER.
DON'T TROUBLE YOURSELF, CAL.
WHY PAY ATTENTION WHEN EVERYTHING'S TOTALLY OUT OF YOUR CONTROL ANYWAY?
NO TROUBLE, RYAN. I'VE GOT SOME FIELD WORK TO DO TODAY RIGHT BY THE HIGH SCHOOL.
'SIDES, SOMEONE'S GOTTA MAKE SURE AT LEAST SOME OF THESE FLIGHTY CHANCELLOR WOMEN SHOW UP WHERE THEY'RE SUPPOSED TO, HUH?
THANKS, CAL. YOU'RE A GOOD FRIEND.
OH, AND MEGAN? PICK UP SOME GROCERIES ON YOUR WAY HOME, WOULD YOU? I THINK WE'RE OUT OF TOOTHPASTE.
WE'RE NOT OUT OF --
...
OKAY.
WHATEVER.
FINE.
WHY WORRY ABOUT WHERE YOUR MOTHER IS WHEN THERE'S THIS VERY REAL THREAT OF CAVITIES AND GINGIVITIS TO FIGHT?

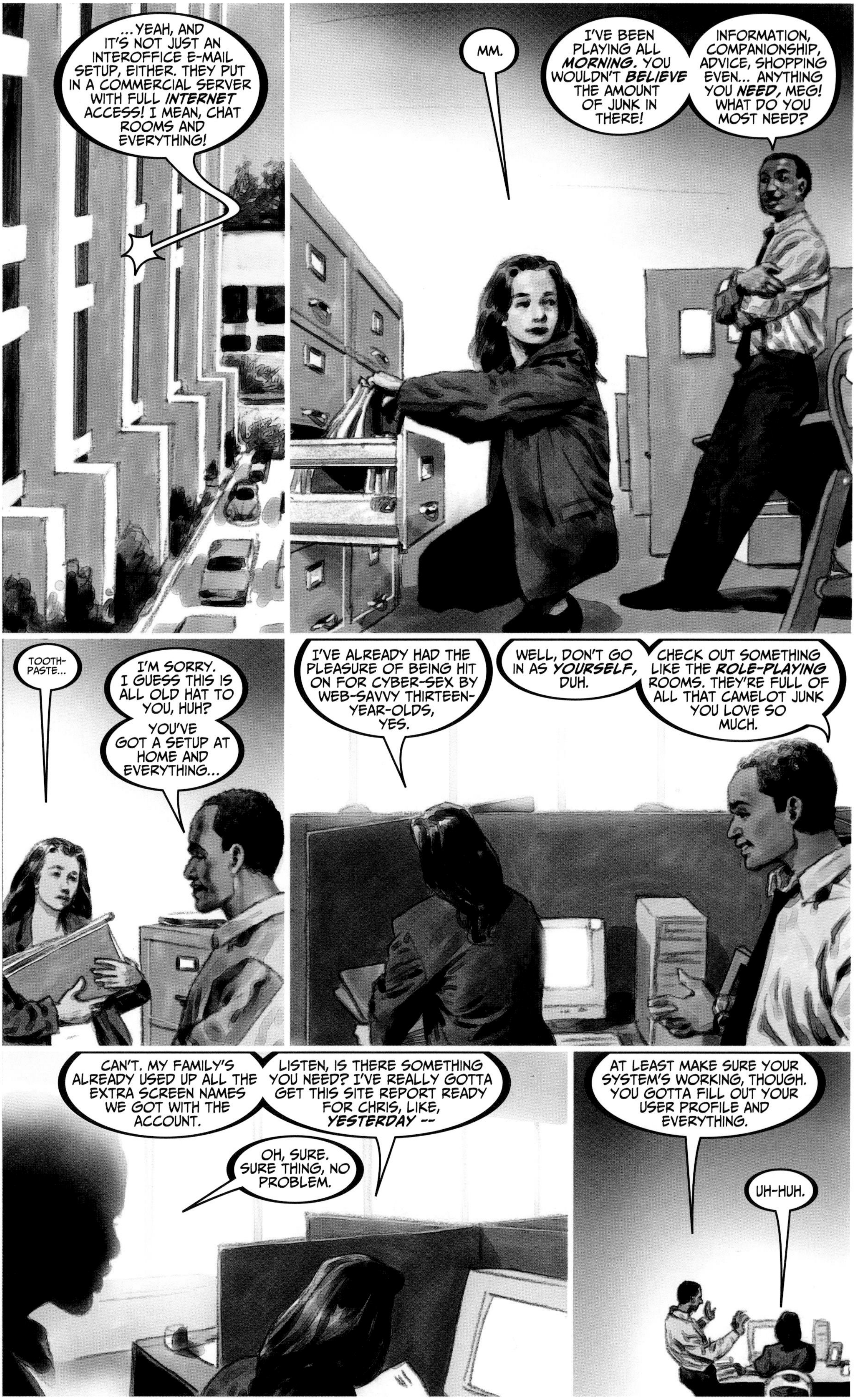
...YEAH, AND IT'S NOT JUST AN INTEROFFICE E-MAIL SETUP, EITHER. THEY PUT IN A COMMERCIAL SERVER WITH FULL INTERNET ACCESS! I MEAN, CHAT ROOMS AND EVERYTHING!
MM.
I'VE BEEN PLAYING ALL MORNING. YOU WOULDN'T BELIEVE THE AMOUNT OF JUNK IN THERE!
INFORMATION, COMPANIONSHIP, ADVICE, SHOPPING EVEN... ANYTHING YOU NEED, MEG! WHAT DO YOU MOST NEED?
TOOTH-PASTE...
I'M SORRY. I GUESS THIS IS ALL OLD HAT TO YOU, HUH?
YOU'VE GOT A SETUP AT HOME AND EVERYTHING...
I'VE ALREADY HAD THE PLEASURE OF BEING HIT ON FOR CYBER-SEX BY WEB-SAVVY THIRTEEN-YEAR-OLDS, YES.
WELL, DON'T GO IN AS YOURSELF, DUH.
CHECK OUT SOMETHING LIKE THE ROLE-PLAYING ROOMS. THEY'RE FULL OF ALL THAT CAMELOT JUNK YOU LOVE SO MUCH.
CAN'T. MY FAMILY'S ALREADY USED UP ALL THE EXTRA SCREEN NAMES WE GOT WITH THE ACCOUNT.
LISTEN, IS THERE SOMETHING YOU NEED? I'VE REALLY GOTTA GET THIS SITE REPORT READY FOR CHRIS, LIKE, YESTERDAY --
OH, SURE. SURE THING, NO PROBLEM.
AT LEAST MAKE SURE YOUR SYSTEM'S WORKING, THOUGH. YOU GOTTA FILL OUT YOUR USER PROFILE AND EVERYTHING.
UH-HUH.

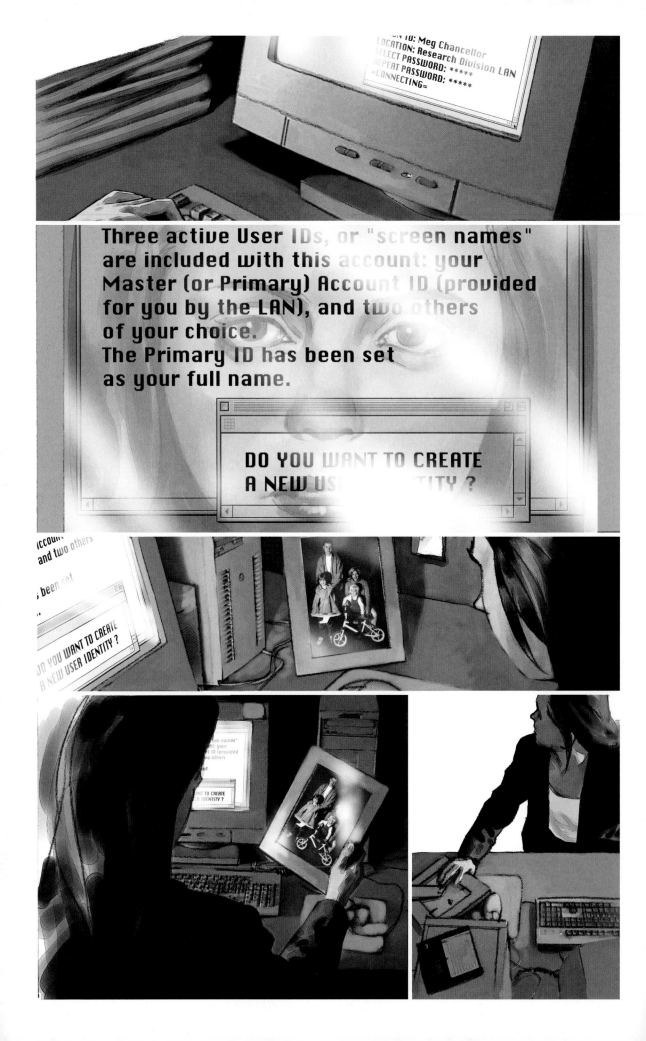

LOGIN ID: Meg Chancellor
LOCATION: Research Division LAN
SELECT PASSWORD: *****
REPEAT PASSWORD: *****
=CONNECTING=

Three active User IDs, or "screen names"
are included with this account: your
Master (or Primary) Account ID (provided
for you by the LAN), and two others
of your choice.
The Primary ID has been set
as your full name.

DO YOU WANT TO CREATE
A NEW USER IDENTITY?

USER
Meg Chancellor
Location: HealthTec Research Division
Tallahassee Office
Position: Research Data Coordinator
Sex: Female
Marital Status: Single
Hobbies: Reading, music, movies
Program Proficiencies: Word, Paradox, Lotus, DOS
Personal Quote: "Is it Friday yet?"

I GUESS PART OF MY PROBLEM, TOO, IS THAT I'VE NEVER HAD A GOOD SENSE OF WHAT WAS "REAL."

LIKE, HOW IS IT THAT A STORY ISN'T REAL, WHEN IT'S MAYBE SOMETHING THAT SOMEONE HAS SPENT YEARS OF THEIR LIFE WORKING ON, POURING THEIR HEART INTO...

...BUT A CUSTOMER SATISFACTION SURVEY THAT NEVER LEAVES THE BUILDING -- NEVER CHANGES ANYTHING AND JUST GETS CRAMMED INTO A DATABASE TO GET MANIPULATED INTO A STRING OF STATISTICS NO ONE CAN READ -- THAT'S COMPLETELY "REAL"?

NEW USER ID:
Location:
Position:
Sex: M
Marital Status:
Hobbies:
Program Proficiencies:
Personal Quote:

OR, LIKE, WHY AM I CONSIDERED A WOMAN JUST BECAUSE OF THIS TOTALLY TEMPORARY BODY THAT WILL GET BURIED AND ROT UP INTO NON-EXISTENCE SOMEDAY...

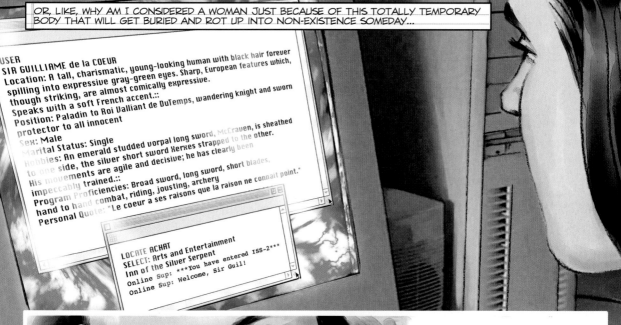

USER
SIR GUILLIAME de la COEUR
Location: A tall, charismatic, young-looking human with black hair forever spilling into expressive gray-green eyes. Sharp, European features which, though striking, are almost comically expressive.
Speaks with a soft French accent.::
Position: Paladin to Roi Valliant de DuTemps, wandering knight and sworn protector to all innocent
Sex: Male
Marital Status: Single
Hobbies: An emerald studded vorpal long sword, McCraven, is sheathed to one side, the silver short sword Xerxes strapped to the other. His movements are agile and decisive; he has clearly been impeccably trained.::
Program Proficiencies: Broad sword, long sword, short blades, hand to hand combat, riding, jousting, archery
Personal Quote: "Le coeur a ses raisons que la raison ne connait point."

LOCATE ACHAT
SELECT: Arts and Entertainment
Inn of the Silver Serpent
Online Sup: ***You have entered ISS-2***
Online Sup: Welcome, Sir Guil!

...WHEN EVERY VOICE IN MY HEAD TELLS ME THAT WOMEN ARE UNRELIABLE, AND... AND FLIGHTY... AND IF YOU WANT TO LEAVE ANY KIND OF MARK ON THE WORLD... YOU'VE GOTTA BE A...

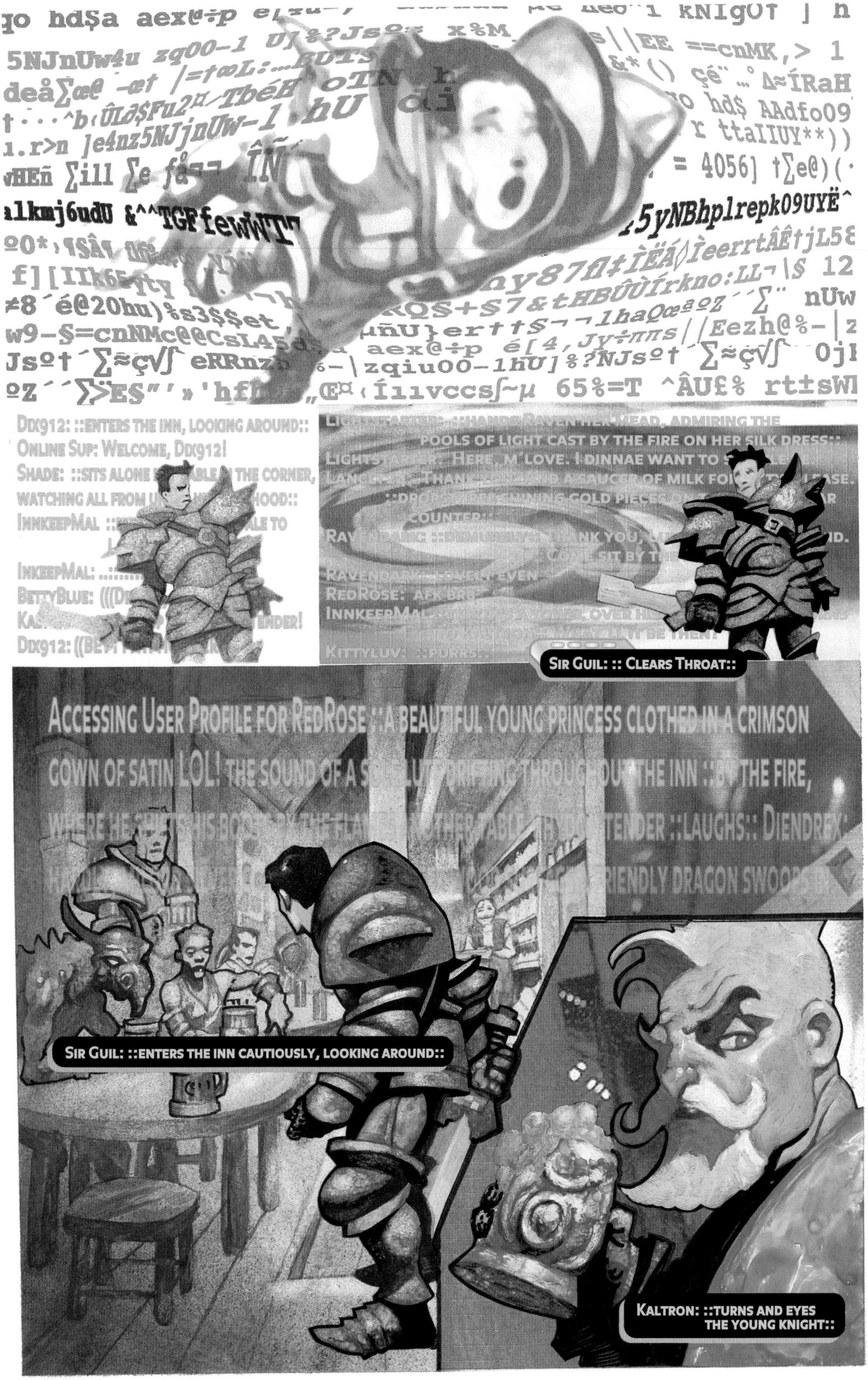

Dix912: ::enters the inn, looking around::
Online Sup: Welcome, Dix912!
Sir Guil: :: Clears Throat::
Accessing User Profile for RedRose ::a beautiful young princess clothed in a crimson
Sir Guil: ::enters the inn cautiously, looking around::
Kaltron: ::turns and eyes the young knight::

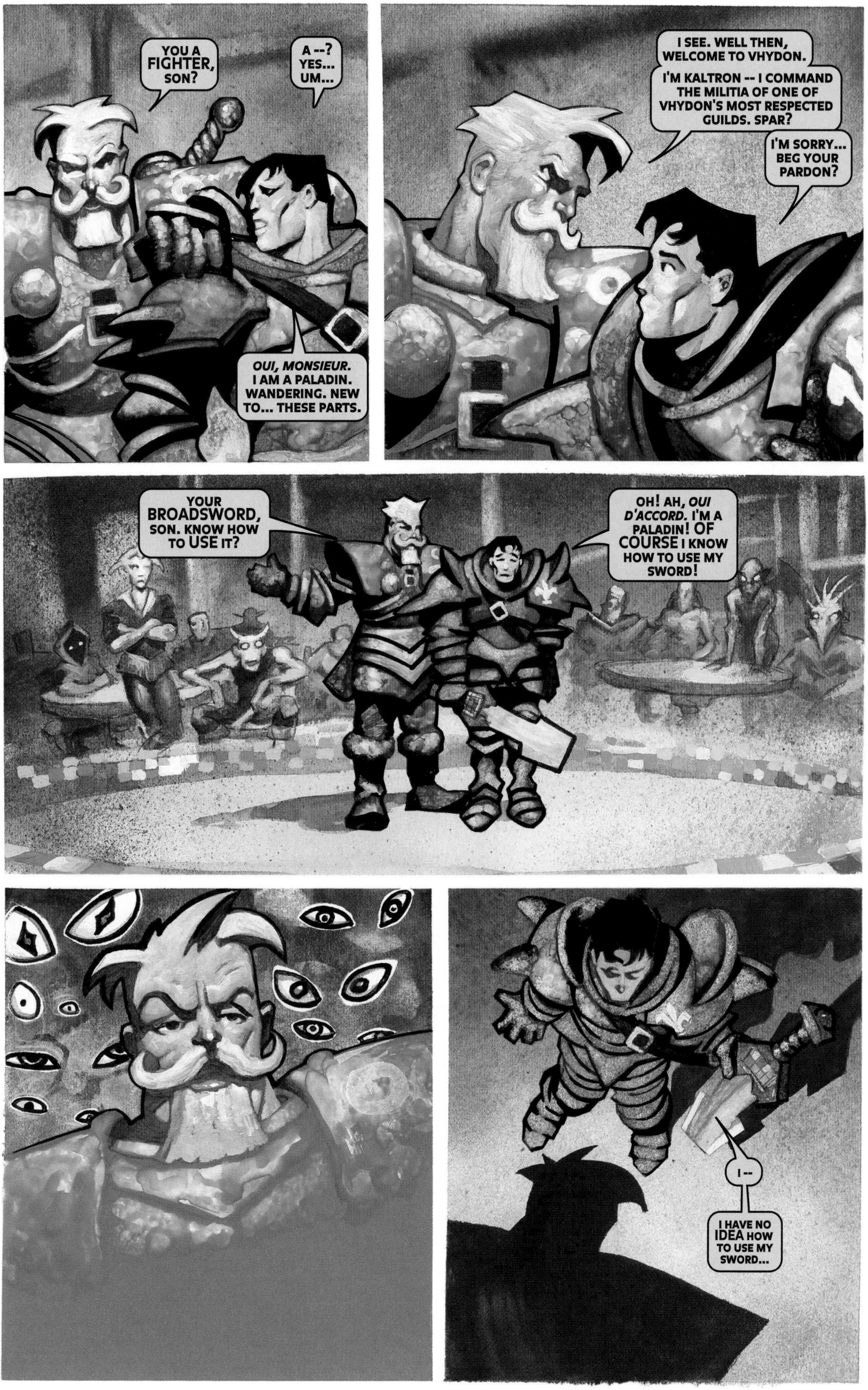
YOU A FIGHTER, SON?
A --? YES... UM...
OUI, MONSIEUR. I AM A PALADIN. WANDERING. NEW TO... THESE PARTS.
I SEE. WELL THEN, WELCOME TO VHYDON.
I'M KALTRON -- I COMMAND THE MILITIA OF ONE OF VHYDON'S MOST RESPECTED GUILDS. SPAR?
I'M SORRY... BEG YOUR PARDON?
YOUR BROADSWORD, SON. KNOW HOW TO USE IT?
OH! AH, OUI D'ACCORD. I'M A PALADIN! OF COURSE I KNOW HOW TO USE MY SWORD!
I --
I HAVE NO IDEA HOW TO USE MY SWORD...

PING

YOU'VE GOT MAIL!

KALTRON: ((DO YOU RP OFFLINE? IT'S REALLY SIMILAR JUST TYPE THE COMMAND//ROLL2D10 TO ROLL. I'LL SEND YOU THE HIT CHART TO SCORE. HOLD ON))

::LEANS IN AND WHISPERS IN THE YOUNG KNIGHT'S EAR::

SIR GUIL: RP?
KALTRON: ((ROLE PLAY. CHECK YOUR MAIL I JUST SENT THE CHART))
KALTRON: ((DON'T WORRY IT'S NOT HARD))

KALTRON: ((KAL'S LOOKING FOR SOLDIERS FOR HIS MILITIA -- IF YOU'RE GOOD KAL MIGHT ASK GUILLIAME TO JOIN))
SIR GUIL: ((OH, OKAY! THANKS! SORRY, THIS IS MY FIRST DAY!))
KALTRON: ((NO PROB))

EMAIL: SUBJ: HIT CHART
DATE: 1/1/99 12:55:05 PM EST
FROM: KALTRON
TO: SIR GUIL

AFTER EACH ANIMATION, MAKE A DICE ROLL TO DETERMINE DAMAGE. FOR A STANDARD 2D10 DUEL:
0-2 = YOU HURT YOURSELF
3-9 = MISS (NO EFFECT)
10-19 = HIT (+1)
20 = HELL OF A HIT! (+2)

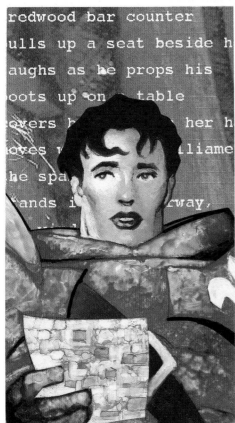

redwood bar counter
ulls up a seat beside h
aughs as he props his
oots up on table
overs h her h
oves Uliame
he spa
ands i rway,

RIGHT.

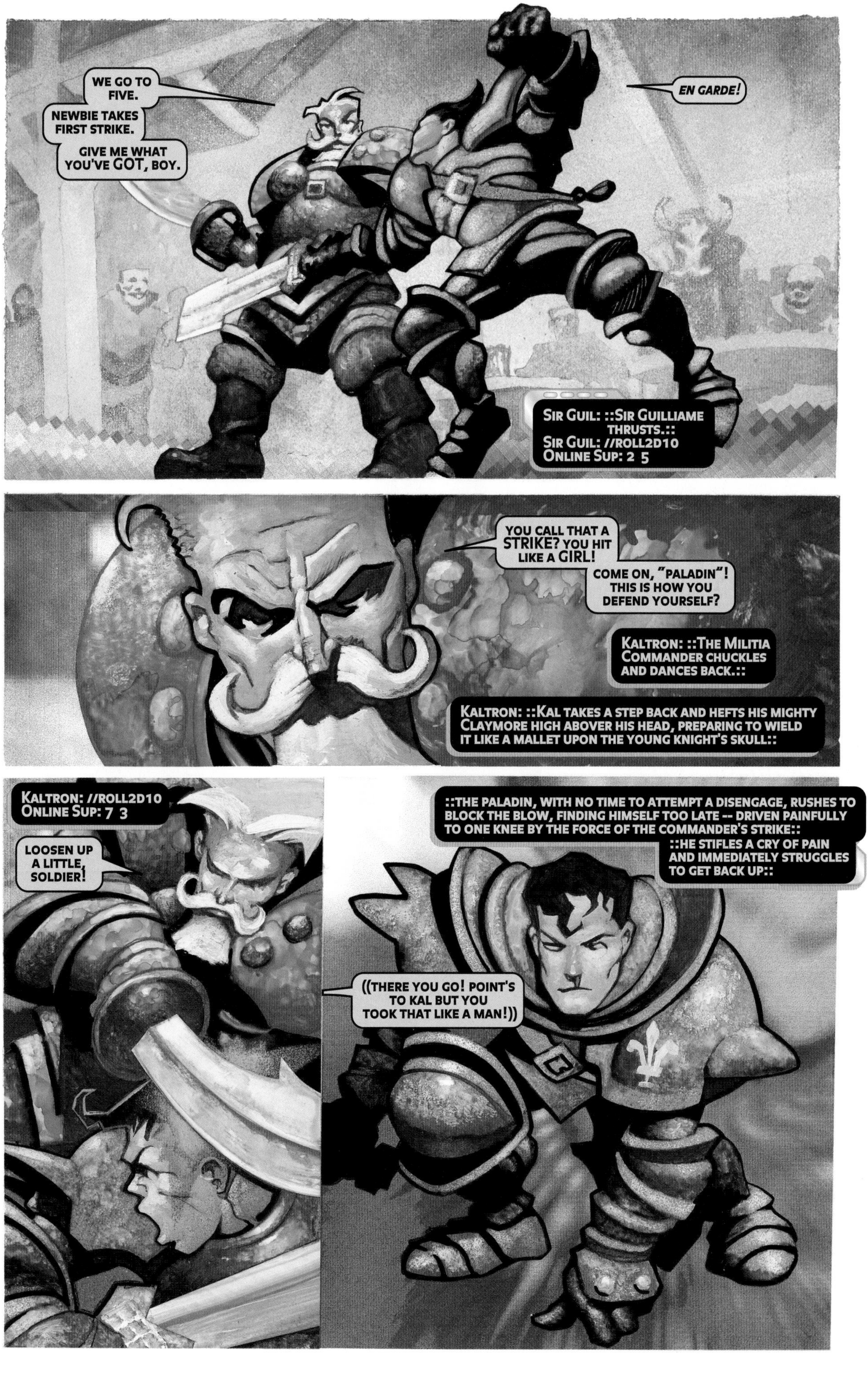
WE GO TO FIVE.
NEWBIE TAKES FIRST STRIKE.
GIVE ME WHAT YOU'VE GOT, BOY.
EN GARDE!
SIR GUIL: ::SIR GUILLIAME THRUSTS.::
SIR GUIL: //ROLL2D10
ONLINE SUP: 2 5
YOU CALL THAT A STRIKE? YOU HIT LIKE A GIRL!
COME ON, "PALADIN"! THIS IS HOW YOU DEFEND YOURSELF?
KALTRON: ::THE MILITIA COMMANDER CHUCKLES AND DANCES BACK.::
KALTRON: ::KAL TAKES A STEP BACK AND HEFTS HIS MIGHTY CLAYMORE HIGH ABOVER HIS HEAD, PREPARING TO WIELD IT LIKE A MALLET UPON THE YOUNG KNIGHT'S SKULL::
KALTRON: //ROLL2D10
ONLINE SUP: 7 3
LOOSEN UP A LITTLE, SOLDIER!
::THE PALADIN, WITH NO TIME TO ATTEMPT A DISENGAGE, RUSHES TO BLOCK THE BLOW, FINDING HIMSELF TOO LATE -- DRIVEN PAINFULLY TO ONE KNEE BY THE FORCE OF THE COMMANDER'S STRIKE::
::HE STIFLES A CRY OF PAIN AND IMMEDIATELY STRUGGLES TO GET BACK UP::
((THERE YOU GO! POINT'S TO KAL BUT YOU TOOK THAT LIKE A MAN!))

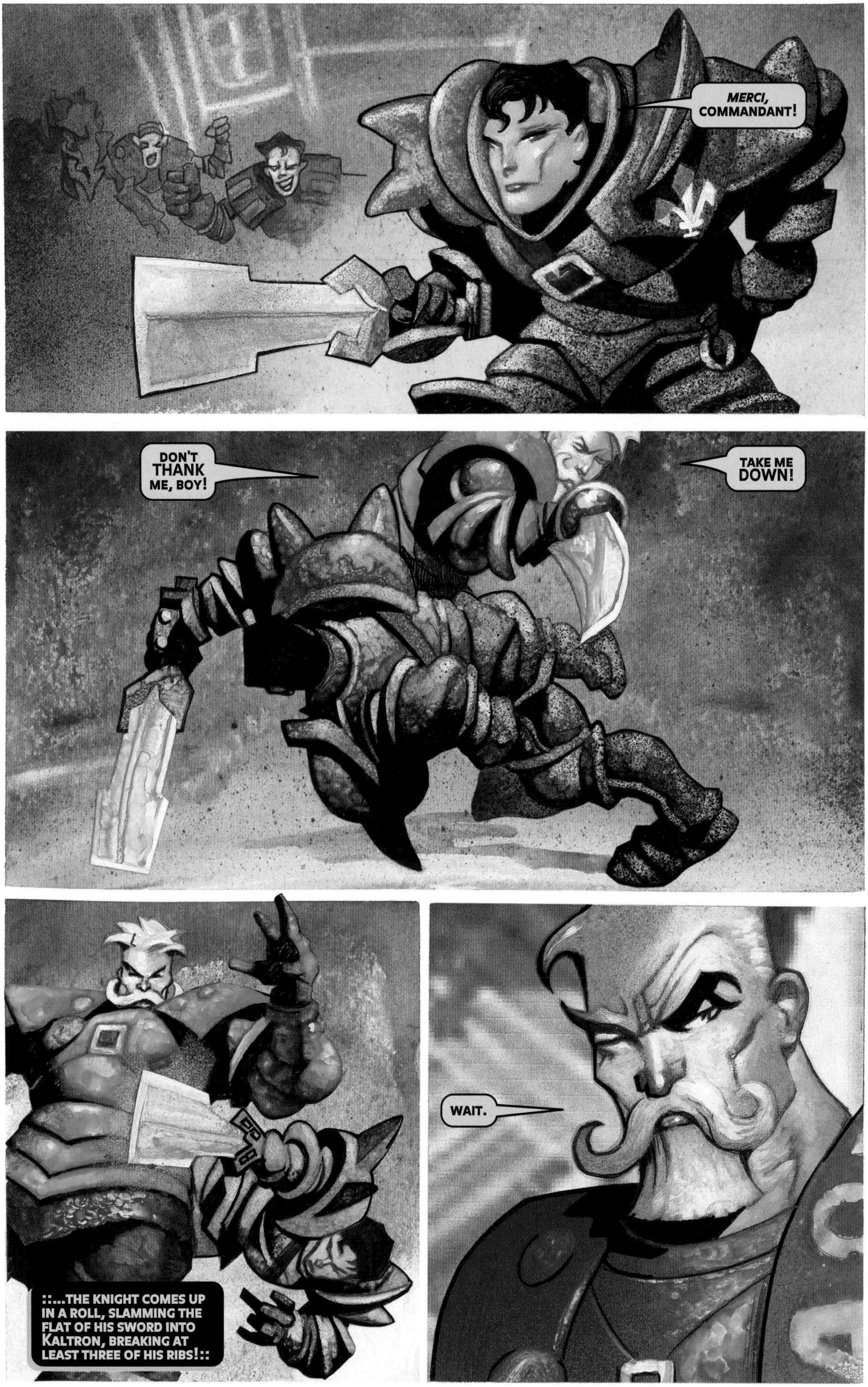
MERCI, COMMANDANT!
DON'T THANK ME, BOY!
TAKE ME DOWN!
::...THE KNIGHT COMES UP IN A ROLL, SLAMMING THE FLAT OF HIS SWORD INTO KALTRON, BREAKING AT LEAST THREE OF HIS RIBS!::
WAIT.

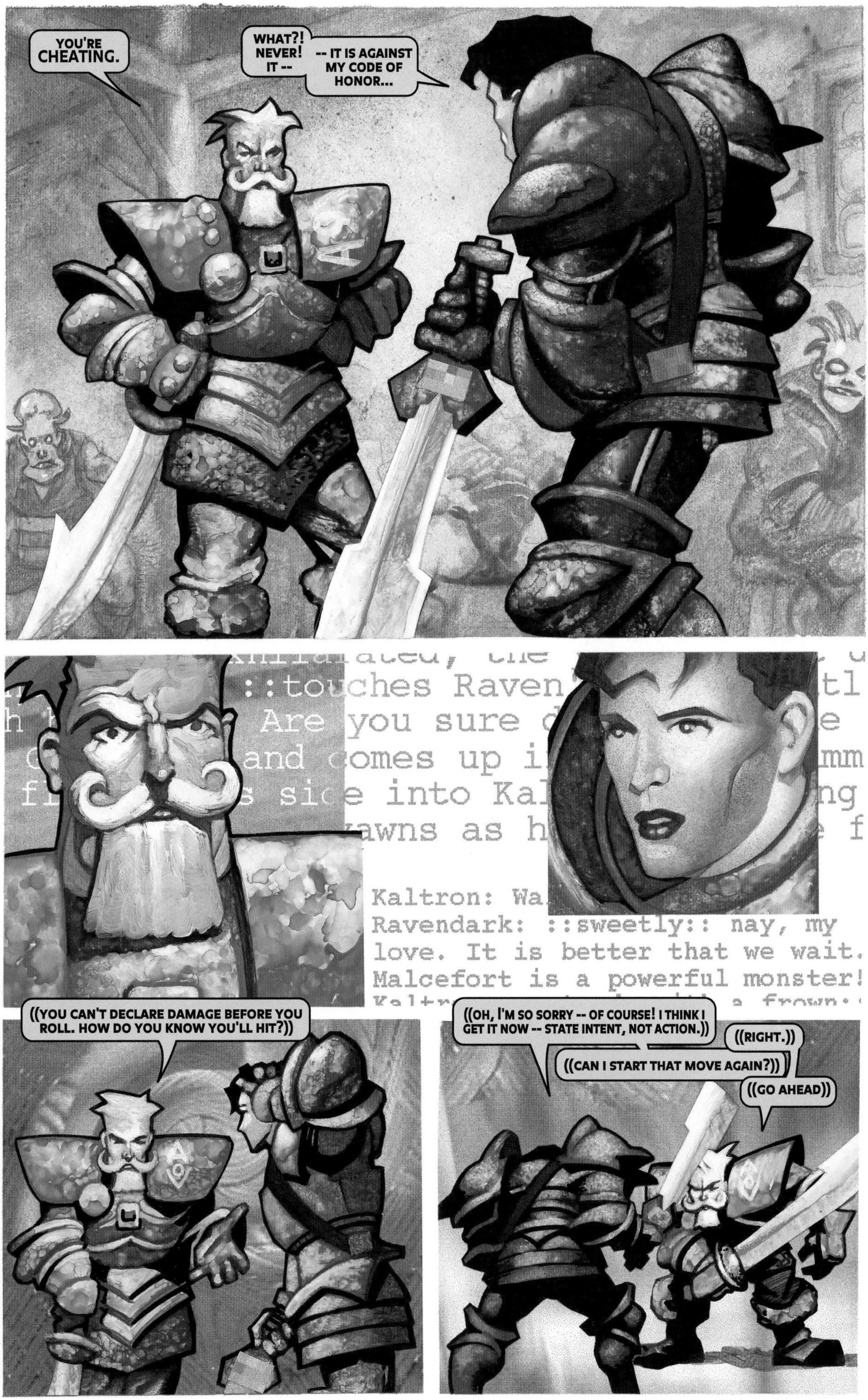
YOU'RE CHEATING.
WHAT?! NEVER! IT --
-- IT IS AGAINST MY CODE OF HONOR...
Kaltron: Wa
Ravendark: ::sweetly:: nay, my
love. It is better that we wait.
Malcefort is a powerful monster!
((YOU CAN'T DECLARE DAMAGE BEFORE YOU ROLL. HOW DO YOU KNOW YOU'LL HIT?))
((OH, I'M SO SORRY -- OF COURSE! I THINK I GET IT NOW -- STATE INTENT, NOT ACTION.))
((RIGHT.))
((CAN I START THAT MOVE AGAIN?))
((GO AHEAD))

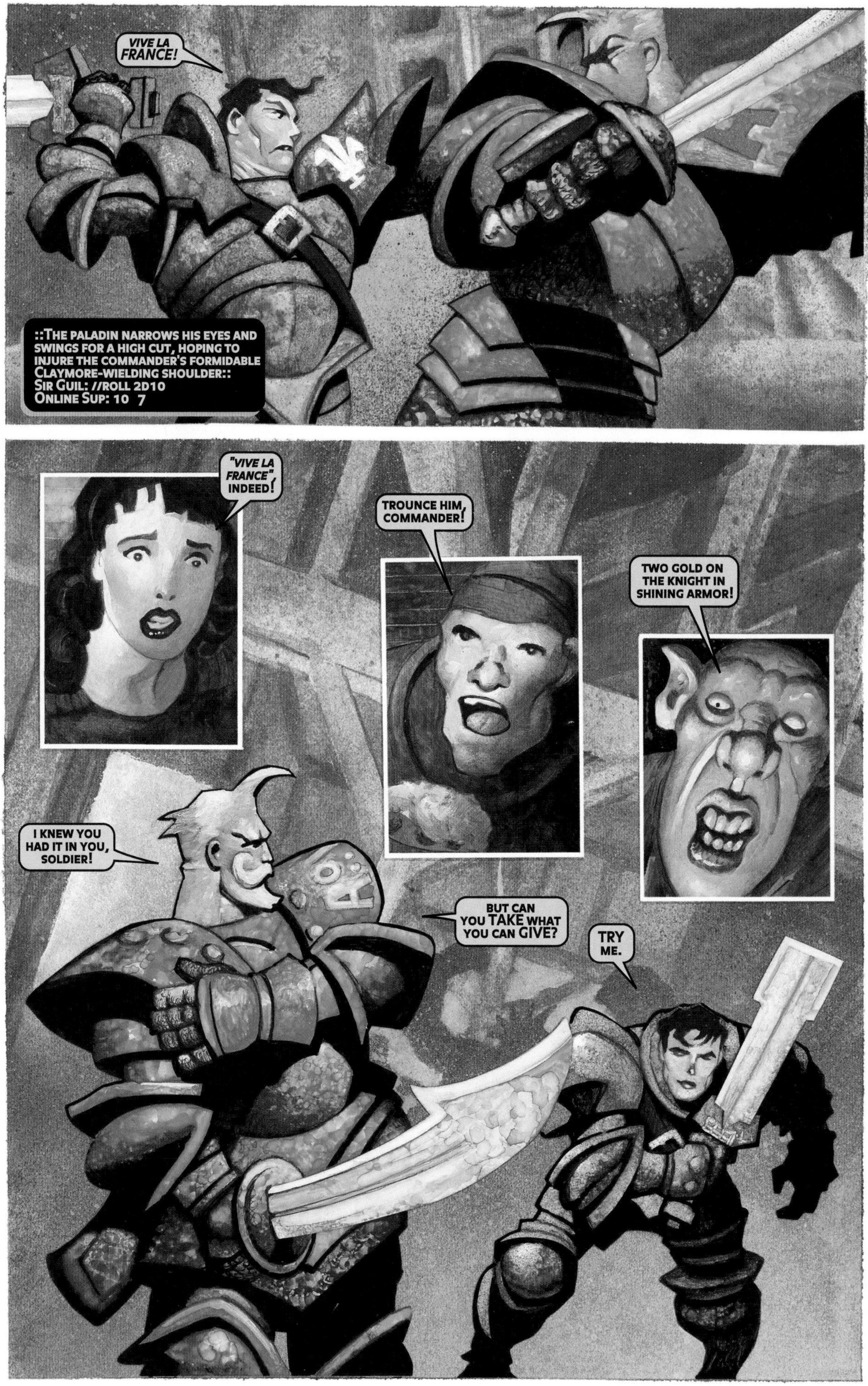
VIVE LA FRANCE!
::THE PALADIN NARROWS HIS EYES AND SWINGS FOR A HIGH CUT, HOPING TO INJURE THE COMMANDER'S FORMIDABLE CLAYMORE-WIELDING SHOULDER::
SIR GUIL: //ROLL 2D10
ONLINE SUP: 10 7
"VIVE LA FRANCE" INDEED!
TROUNCE HIM, COMMANDER!
TWO GOLD ON THE KNIGHT IN SHINING ARMOR!
I KNEW YOU HAD IT IN YOU, SOLDIER!
BUT CAN YOU TAKE WHAT YOU CAN GIVE?
TRY ME.

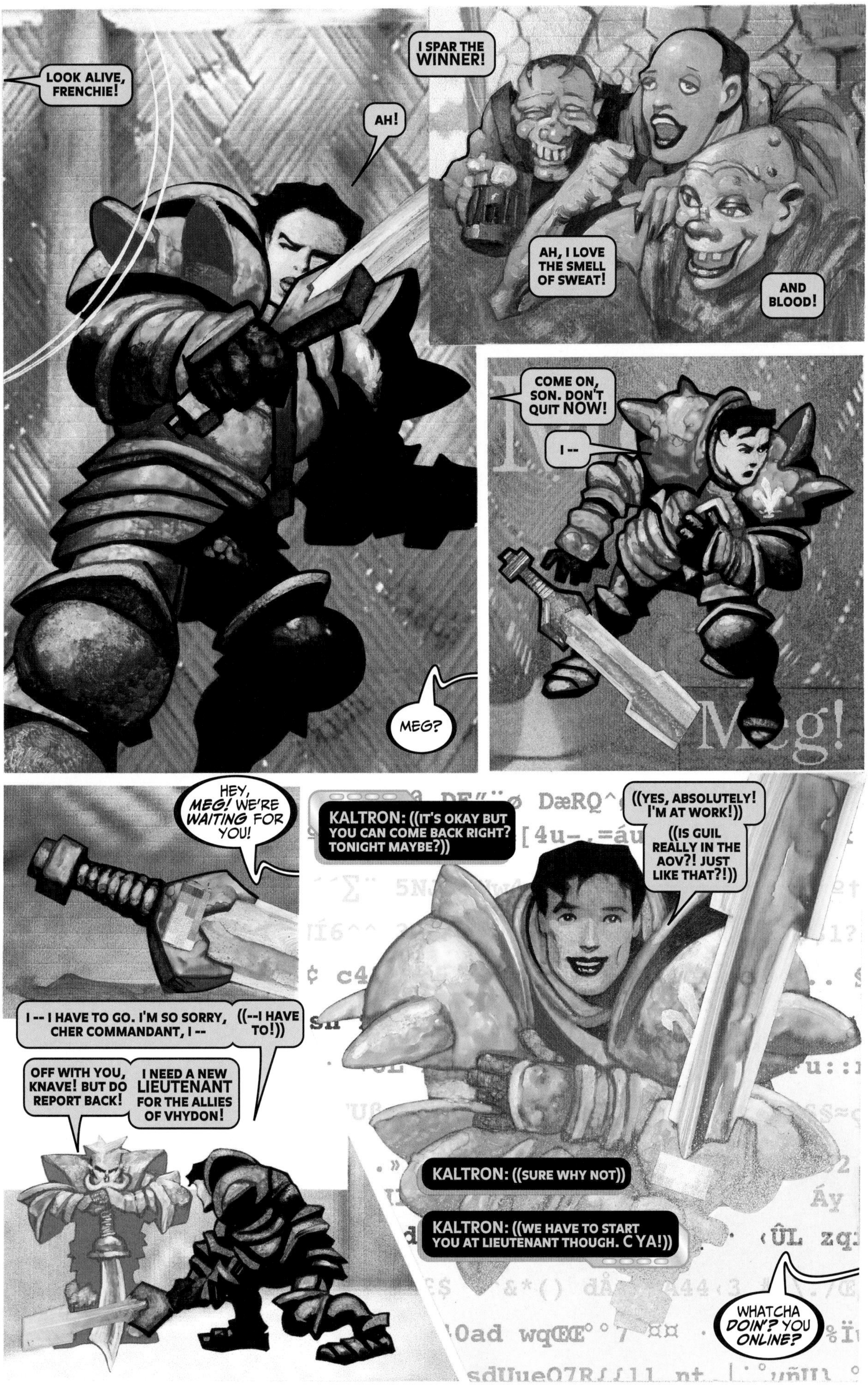
LOOK ALIVE, FRENCHIE!
AH!
I SPAR THE WINNER!
AH, I LOVE THE SMELL OF SWEAT!
AND BLOOD!
COME ON, SON. DON'T QUIT NOW!
I --
MEG?
Meg!
HEY, MEG! WE'RE WAITING FOR YOU!
I -- I HAVE TO GO. I'M SO SORRY, CHER COMMANDANT, I --
((--I HAVE TO!))
OFF WITH YOU, KNAVE! BUT DO REPORT BACK!
I NEED A NEW LIEUTENANT FOR THE ALLIES OF VHYDON!
KALTRON: ((IT'S OKAY BUT YOU CAN COME BACK RIGHT? TONIGHT MAYBE?))
((YES, ABSOLUTELY! I'M AT WORK!))
((IS GUIL REALLY IN THE AOV?! JUST LIKE THAT?!))
KALTRON: ((SURE WHY NOT))
KALTRON: ((WE HAVE TO START YOU AT LIEUTENANT THOUGH. C YA!))
WHATCHA DOIN'? YOU ONLINE?

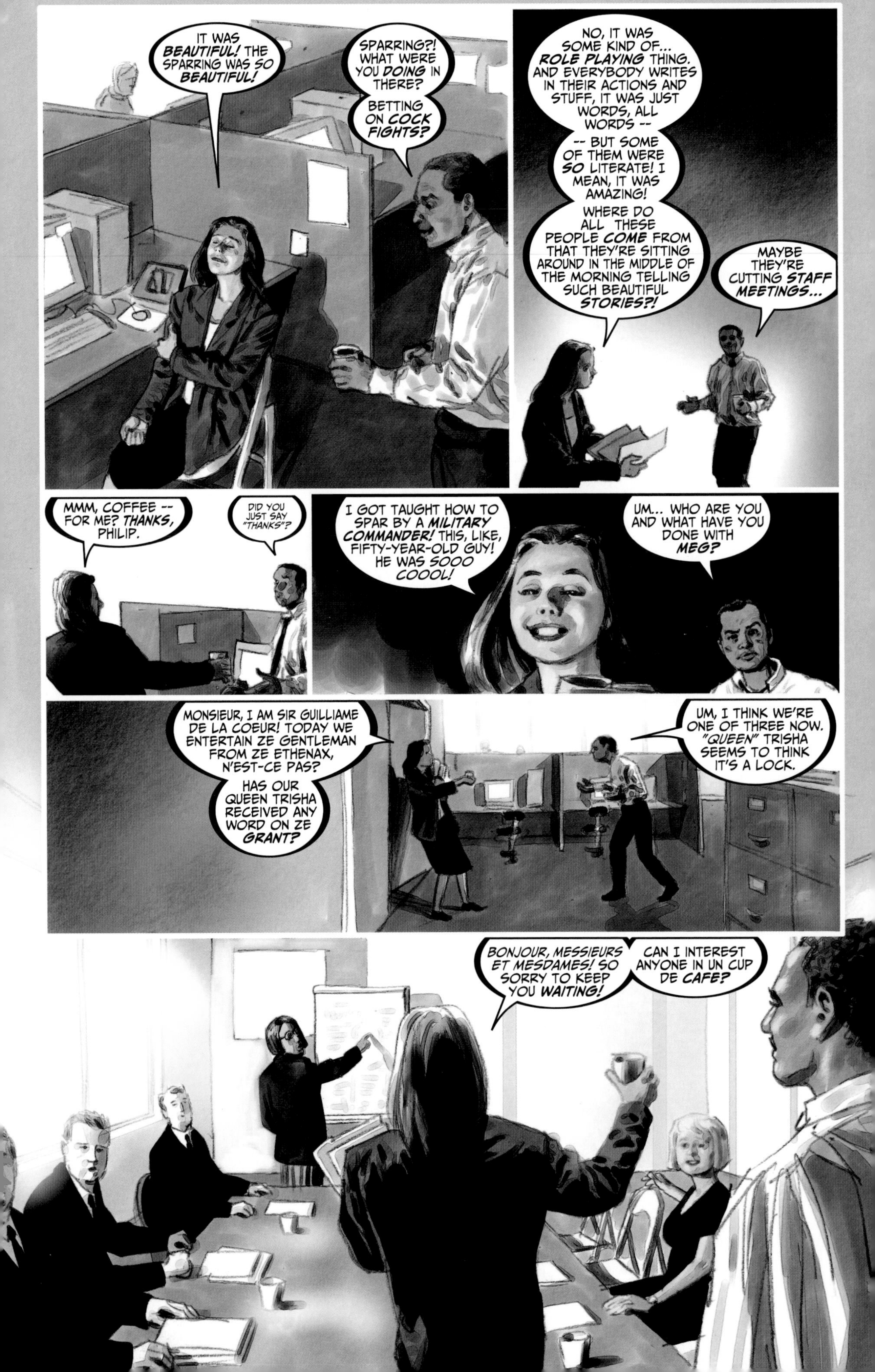
IT WAS BEAUTIFUL! THE SPARRING WAS SO BEAUTIFUL!
SPARRING?! WHAT WERE YOU DOING IN THERE?
BETTING ON COCK FIGHTS?
NO, IT WAS SOME KIND OF... ROLE PLAYING THING. AND EVERYBODY WRITES IN THEIR ACTIONS AND STUFF, IT WAS JUST WORDS, ALL WORDS --
-- BUT SOME OF THEM WERE SO LITERATE! I MEAN, IT WAS AMAZING!
WHERE DO ALL THESE PEOPLE COME FROM THAT THEY'RE SITTING AROUND IN THE MIDDLE OF THE MORNING TELLING SUCH BEAUTIFUL STORIES?!
MAYBE THEY'RE CUTTING STAFF MEETINGS...
MMM, COFFEE -- FOR ME? THANKS, PHILIP.
DID YOU JUST SAY "THANKS"?
I GOT TAUGHT HOW TO SPAR BY A MILITARY COMMANDER! THIS, LIKE, FIFTY-YEAR-OLD GUY! HE WAS SOOO COOOL!
UM... WHO ARE YOU AND WHAT HAVE YOU DONE WITH MEG?
MONSIEUR, I AM SIR GUILLIAME DE LA COEUR! TODAY WE ENTERTAIN ZE GENTLEMAN FROM ZE ETHENAX, N'EST-CE PAS?
HAS OUR QUEEN TRISHA RECEIVED ANY WORD ON ZE GRANT?
UM, I THINK WE'RE ONE OF THREE NOW. "QUEEN" TRISHA SEEMS TO THINK IT'S A LOCK.
BONJOUR, MESSIEURS ET MESDAMES! SO SORRY TO KEEP YOU WAITING!
CAN I INTEREST ANYONE IN UN CUP DE CAFE?

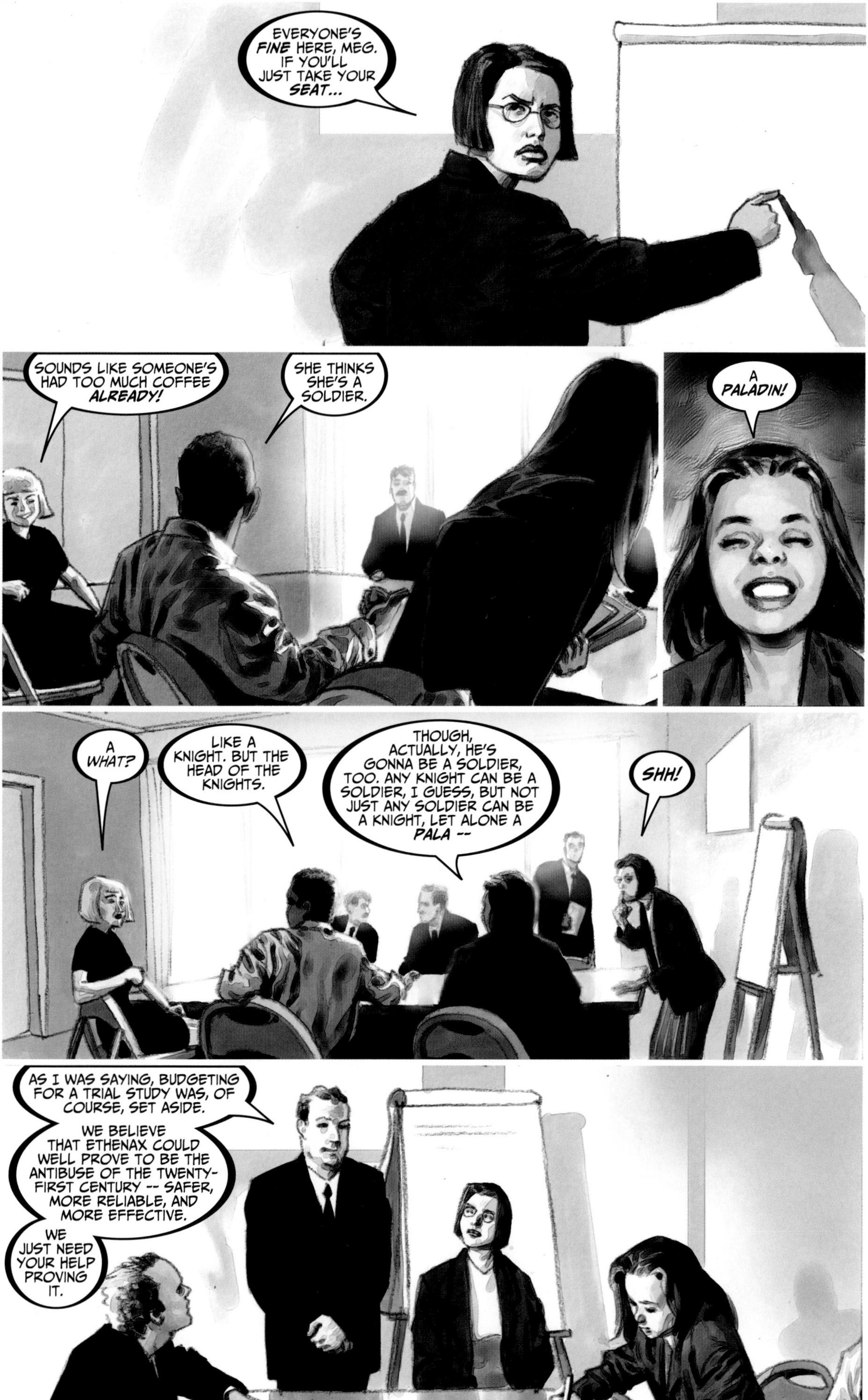
EVERYONE'S *FINE* HERE, MEG. IF YOU'LL JUST TAKE YOUR *SEAT...*
SOUNDS LIKE SOMEONE'S HAD TOO MUCH COFFEE *ALREADY!*
SHE THINKS SHE'S A SOLDIER.
A *PALADIN!*
A *WHAT?*
LIKE A KNIGHT. BUT THE HEAD OF THE KNIGHTS.
THOUGH, ACTUALLY, HE'S GONNA BE A SOLDIER, TOO. ANY KNIGHT CAN BE A SOLDIER, I GUESS, BUT NOT JUST ANY SOLDIER CAN BE A KNIGHT, LET ALONE A *PALA --*
SHH!
AS I WAS SAYING, BUDGETING FOR A TRIAL STUDY WAS, OF COURSE, SET ASIDE.
WE BELIEVE THAT ETHENAX COULD WELL PROVE TO BE THE ANTIBUSE OF THE TWENTY-FIRST CENTURY -- SAFER, MORE RELIABLE, AND MORE EFFECTIVE.
WE JUST NEED YOUR HELP PROVING IT.

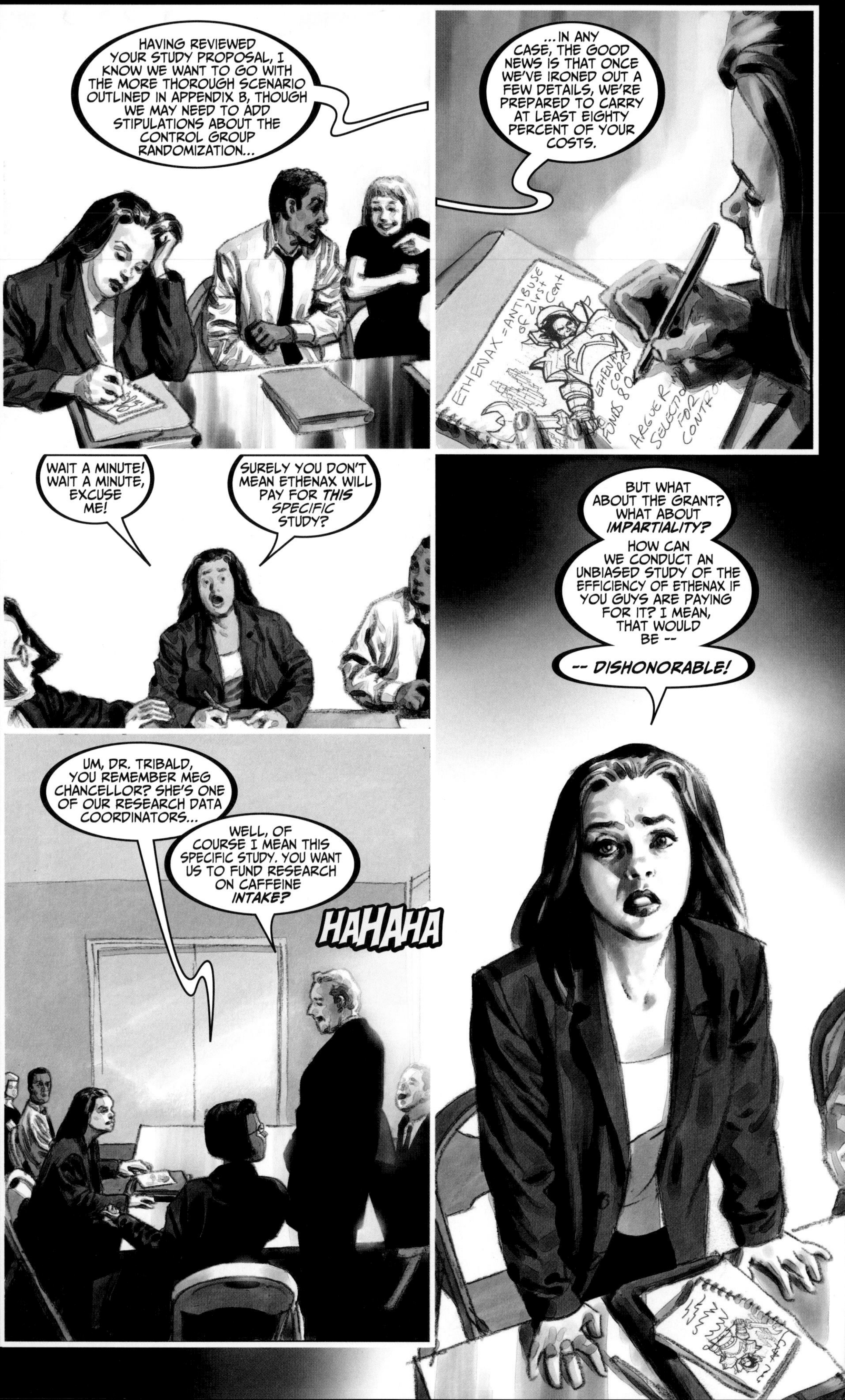
HAVING REVIEWED YOUR STUDY PROPOSAL, I KNOW WE WANT TO GO WITH THE MORE THOROUGH SCENARIO OUTLINED IN APPENDIX B, THOUGH WE MAY NEED TO ADD STIPULATIONS ABOUT THE CONTROL GROUP RANDOMIZATION...
...IN ANY CASE, THE GOOD NEWS IS THAT ONCE WE'VE IRONED OUT A FEW DETAILS, WE'RE PREPARED TO CARRY AT LEAST EIGHTY PERCENT OF YOUR COSTS.
WAIT A MINUTE! WAIT A MINUTE, EXCUSE ME!
SURELY YOU DON'T MEAN ETHENAX WILL PAY FOR *THIS SPECIFIC* STUDY?
BUT WHAT ABOUT THE GRANT? WHAT ABOUT *IMPARTIALITY?*
HOW CAN WE CONDUCT AN UNBIASED STUDY OF THE EFFICIENCY OF ETHENAX IF YOU GUYS ARE PAYING FOR IT? I MEAN, THAT WOULD BE --
-- DISHONORABLE!
UM, DR. TRIBALD, YOU REMEMBER MEG CHANCELLOR? SHE'S ONE OF OUR RESEARCH DATA COORDINATORS...
WELL, OF COURSE I MEAN THIS SPECIFIC STUDY. YOU WANT US TO FUND RESEARCH ON CAFFEINE *INTAKE?*
HAHAHA

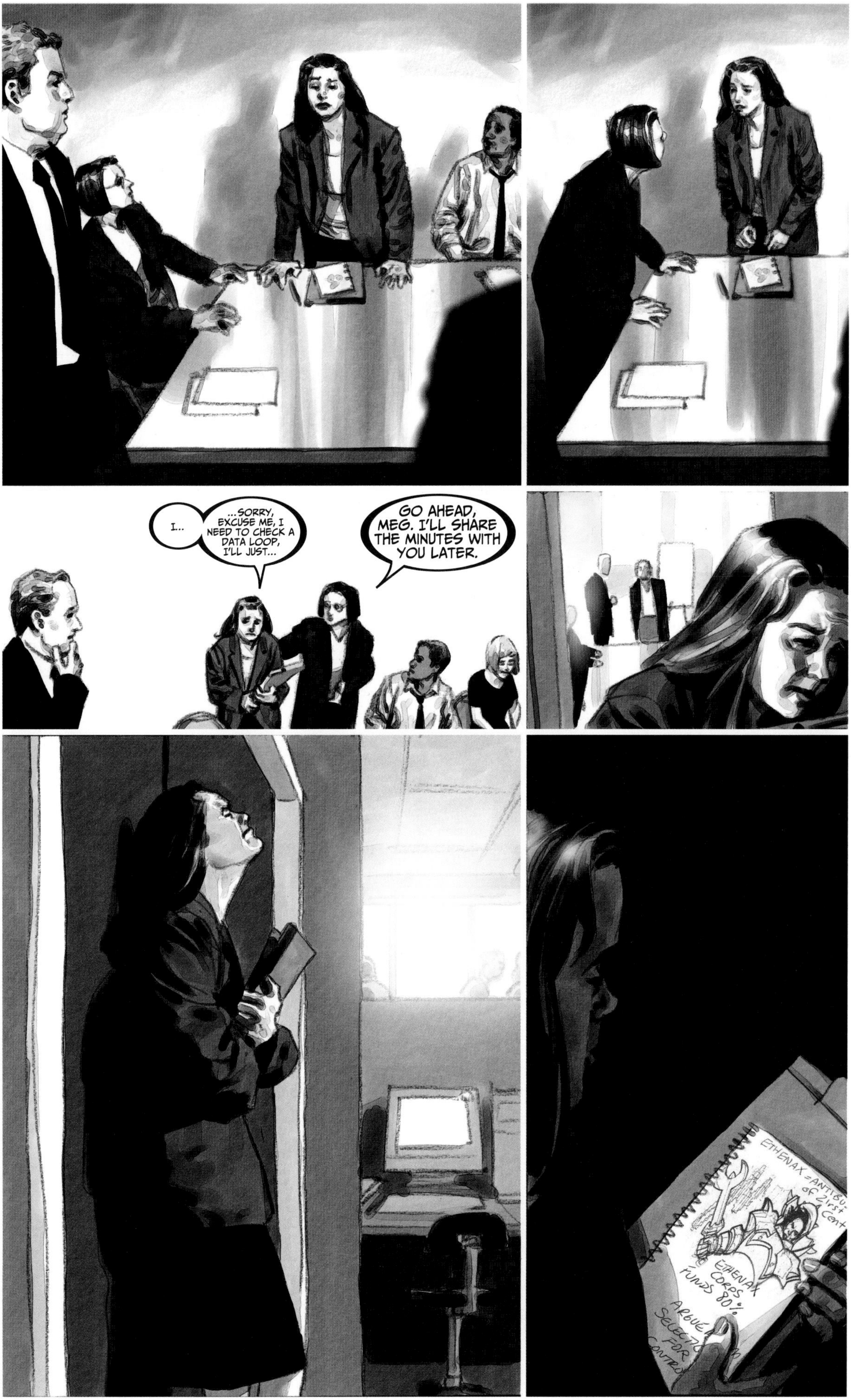
I...
...SORRY, EXCUSE ME, I NEED TO CHECK A DATA LOOP, I'LL JUST...
GO AHEAD, MEG. I'LL SHARE THE MINUTES WITH YOU LATER.
ETHENAX
of
ETHENAX CORPS FUNDS 80%
FOR

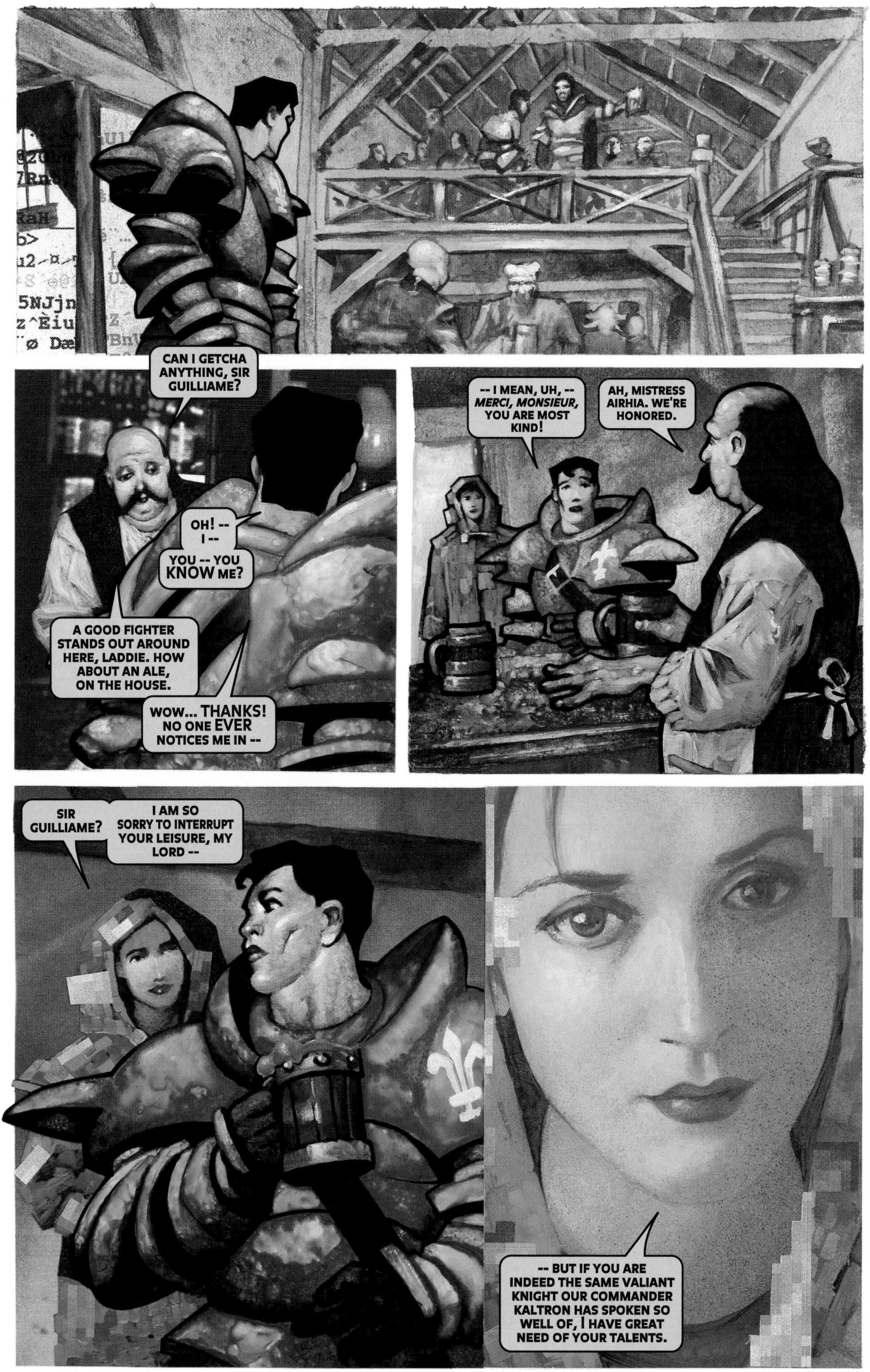
CAN I GETCHA ANYTHING, SIR GUILLIAME?
OH! -- I --
YOU -- YOU KNOW ME?
A GOOD FIGHTER STANDS OUT AROUND HERE, LADDIE. HOW ABOUT AN ALE, ON THE HOUSE.
WOW... THANKS! NO ONE EVER NOTICES ME IN --
AH, MISTRESS AIRHIA. WE'RE HONORED.
-- I MEAN, UH, -- *MERCI, MONSIEUR,* YOU ARE MOST KIND!
SIR GUILLIAME?
I AM SO SORRY TO INTERRUPT YOUR LEISURE, MY LORD --
-- BUT IF YOU ARE INDEED THE SAME VALIANT KNIGHT OUR COMMANDER KALTRON HAS SPOKEN SO WELL OF, I HAVE GREAT NEED OF YOUR TALENTS.

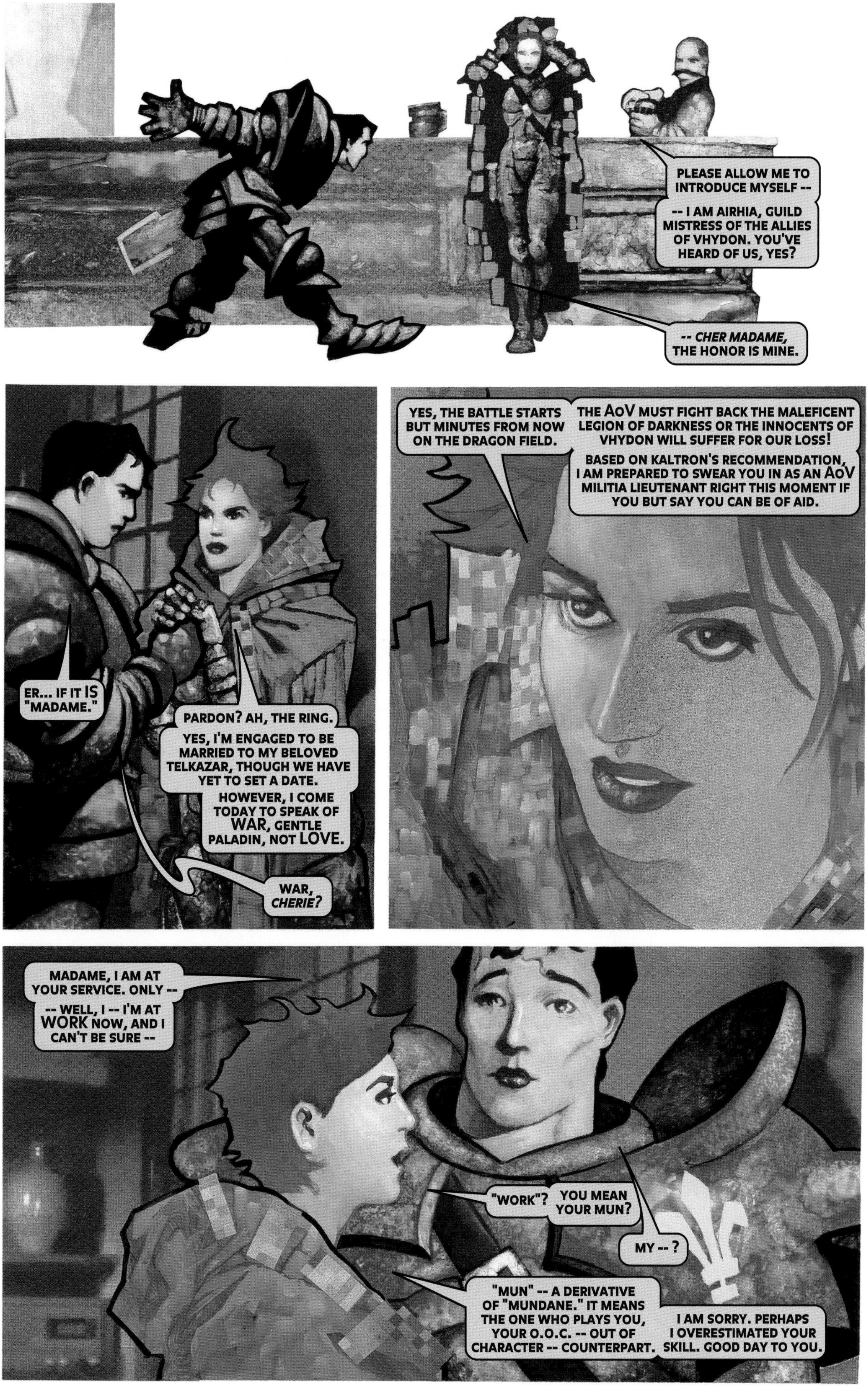
PLEASE ALLOW ME TO INTRODUCE MYSELF --
-- I AM AIRHIA, GUILD MISTRESS OF THE ALLIES OF VHYDON. YOU'VE HEARD OF US, YES?
-- *CHER MADAME*, THE HONOR IS MINE.
ER... IF IT IS "MADAME."
PARDON? AH, THE RING.
YES, I'M ENGAGED TO BE MARRIED TO MY BELOVED TELKAZAR, THOUGH WE HAVE YET TO SET A DATE.
HOWEVER, I COME TODAY TO SPEAK OF WAR, GENTLE PALADIN, NOT LOVE.
WAR, *CHERIE*?
YES, THE BATTLE STARTS BUT MINUTES FROM NOW ON THE DRAGON FIELD.
THE AoV MUST FIGHT BACK THE MALEFICENT LEGION OF DARKNESS OR THE INNOCENTS OF VHYDON WILL SUFFER FOR OUR LOSS!
BASED ON KALTRON'S RECOMMENDATION, I AM PREPARED TO SWEAR YOU IN AS AN AoV MILITIA LIEUTENANT RIGHT THIS MOMENT IF YOU BUT SAY YOU CAN BE OF AID.
MADAME, I AM AT YOUR SERVICE. ONLY --
-- WELL, I -- I'M AT WORK NOW, AND I CAN'T BE SURE --
"WORK"?
YOU MEAN YOUR MUN?
MY -- ?
"MUN" -- A DERIVATIVE OF "MUNDANE." IT MEANS THE ONE WHO PLAYS YOU, YOUR O.O.C. -- OUT OF CHARACTER -- COUNTERPART.
I AM SORRY. PERHAPS I OVERESTIMATED YOUR SKILL. GOOD DAY TO YOU.

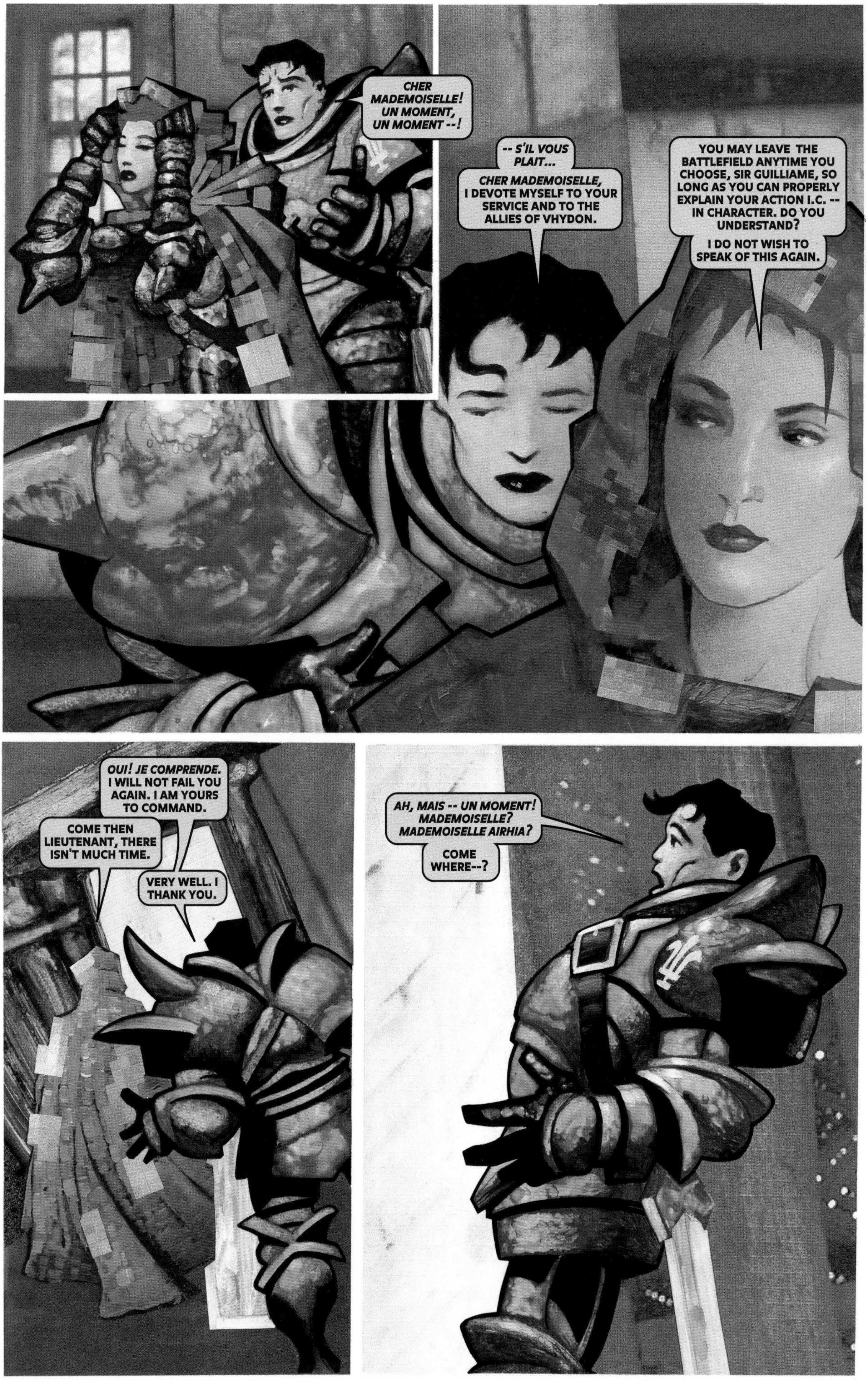
CHER MADEMOISELLE! UN MOMENT, UN MOMENT --!
-- S'IL VOUS PLAIT...
CHER MADEMOISELLE, I DEVOTE MYSELF TO YOUR SERVICE AND TO THE ALLIES OF VHYDON.
YOU MAY LEAVE THE BATTLEFIELD ANYTIME YOU CHOOSE, SIR GUILLIAME, SO LONG AS YOU CAN PROPERLY EXPLAIN YOUR ACTION I.C. -- IN CHARACTER. DO YOU UNDERSTAND?
I DO NOT WISH TO SPEAK OF THIS AGAIN.
OUI! JE COMPRENDE. I WILL NOT FAIL YOU AGAIN. I AM YOURS TO COMMAND.
COME THEN LIEUTENANT, THERE ISN'T MUCH TIME.
VERY WELL. I THANK YOU.
AH, MAIS -- UN MOMENT! MADEMOISELLE? MADEMOISELLE AIRHIA?
COME WHERE--?

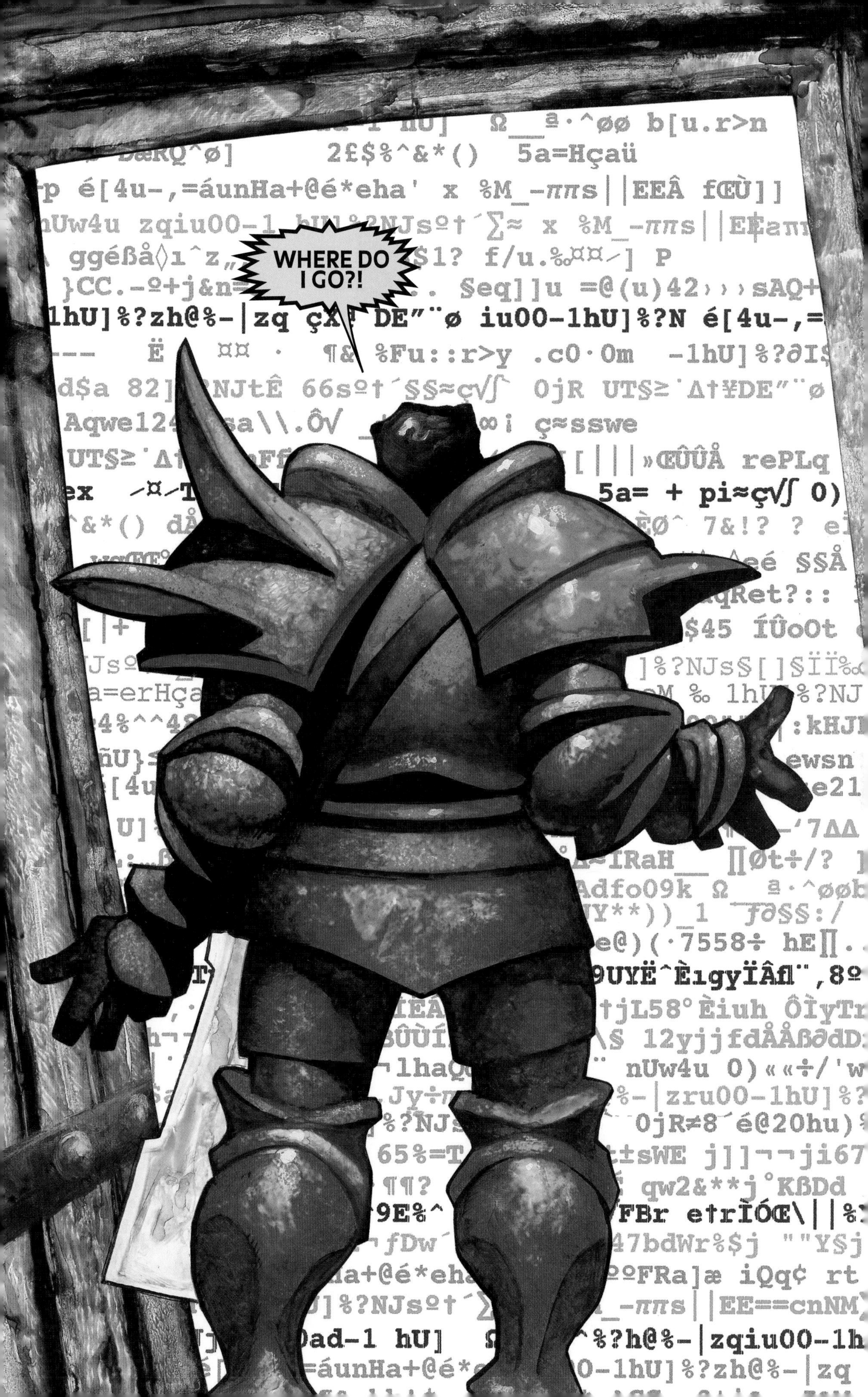
WHERE DO I GO?!

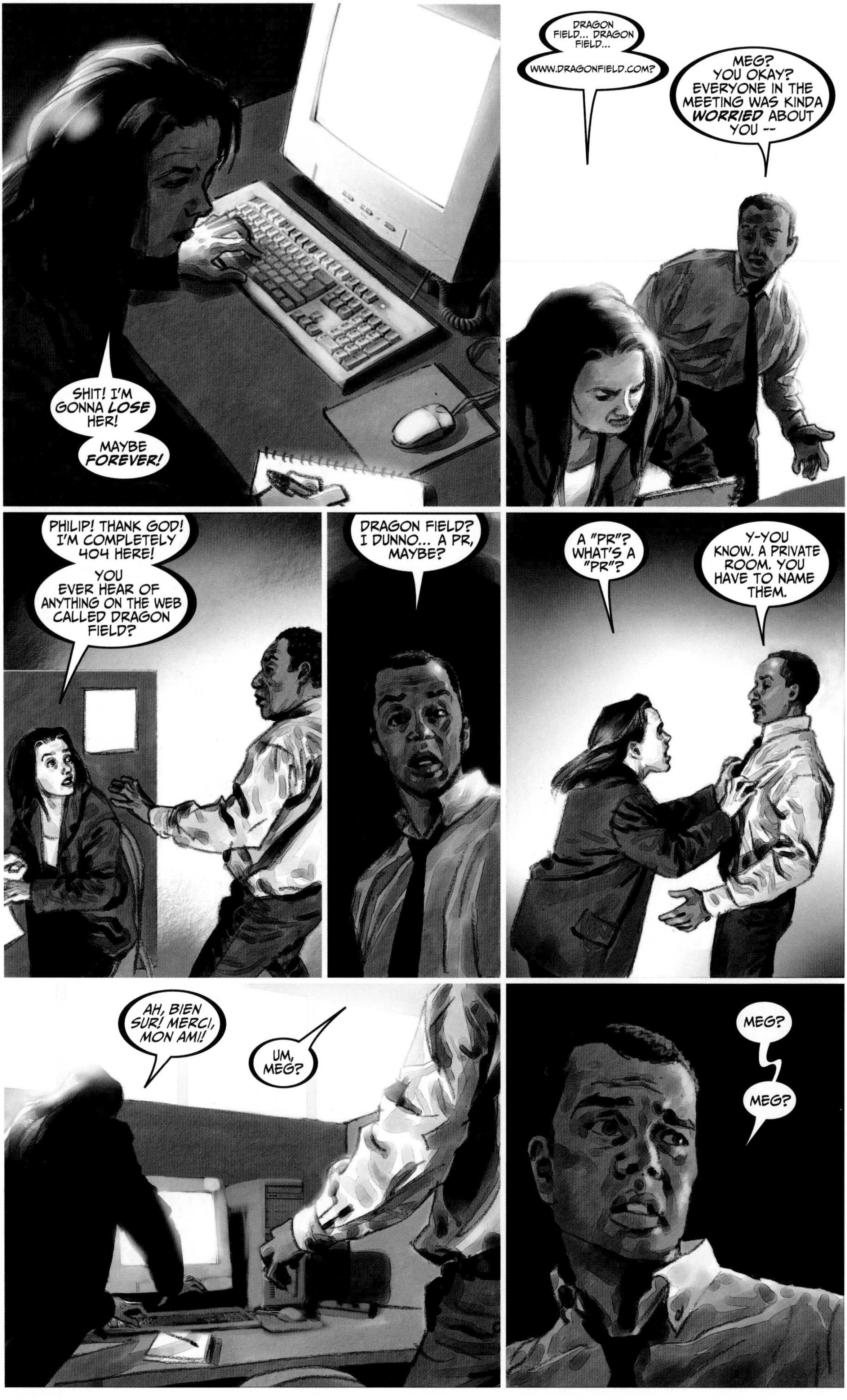
SHIT! I'M GONNA LOSE HER!
MAYBE FOREVER!
DRAGON FIELD... DRAGON FIELD...
WWW.DRAGONFIELD.COM?
MEG? YOU OKAY? EVERYONE IN THE MEETING WAS KINDA WORRIED ABOUT YOU --
PHILIP! THANK GOD! I'M COMPLETELY 404 HERE!
YOU EVER HEAR OF ANYTHING ON THE WEB CALLED DRAGON FIELD?
DRAGON FIELD? I DUNNO... A PR, MAYBE?
A "PR"? WHAT'S A "PR"?
Y-YOU KNOW. A PRIVATE ROOM. YOU HAVE TO NAME THEM.
AH, BIEN SUR! MERCI, MON AMI!
UM, MEG?
MEG?
MEG?

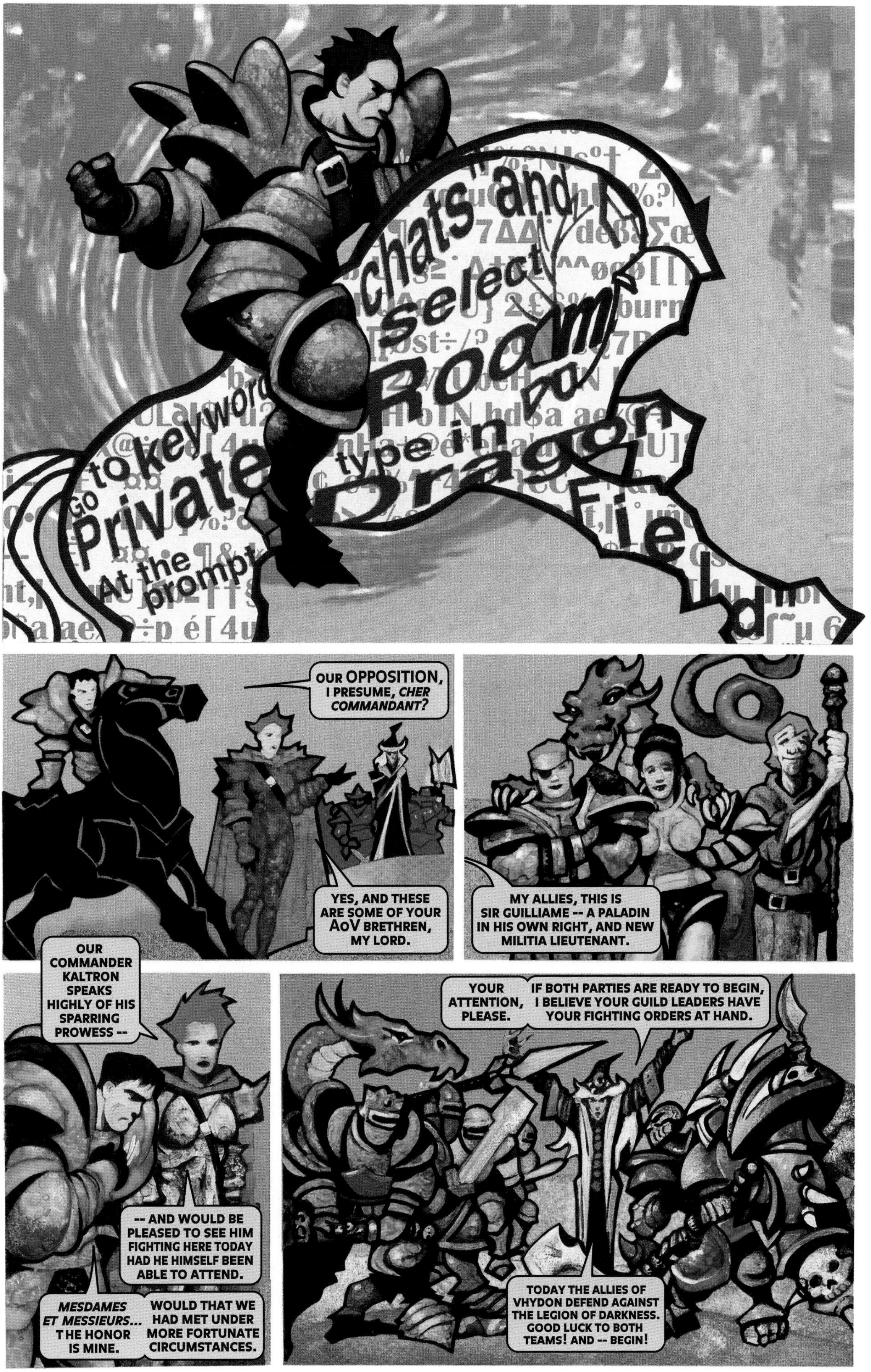
Go to keyword
Private
chats and
Select
Room
At the prompt
type in
"Dragon
Field"
OUR OPPOSITION, I PRESUME, *CHER COMMANDANT*?
YES, AND THESE ARE SOME OF YOUR AoV BRETHREN, MY LORD.
MY ALLIES, THIS IS SIR GUILLIAME -- A PALADIN IN HIS OWN RIGHT, AND NEW MILITIA LIEUTENANT.
OUR COMMANDER KALTRON SPEAKS HIGHLY OF HIS SPARRING PROWESS --
-- AND WOULD BE PLEASED TO SEE HIM FIGHTING HERE TODAY HAD HE HIMSELF BEEN ABLE TO ATTEND.
MESDAMES ET MESSIEURS... THE HONOR IS MINE.
WOULD THAT WE HAD MET UNDER MORE FORTUNATE CIRCUMSTANCES.
YOUR ATTENTION, PLEASE.
IF BOTH PARTIES ARE READY TO BEGIN, I BELIEVE YOUR GUILD LEADERS HAVE YOUR FIGHTING ORDERS AT HAND.
TODAY THE ALLIES OF VHYDON DEFEND AGAINST THE LEGION OF DARKNESS. GOOD LUCK TO BOTH TEAMS! AND -- BEGIN!

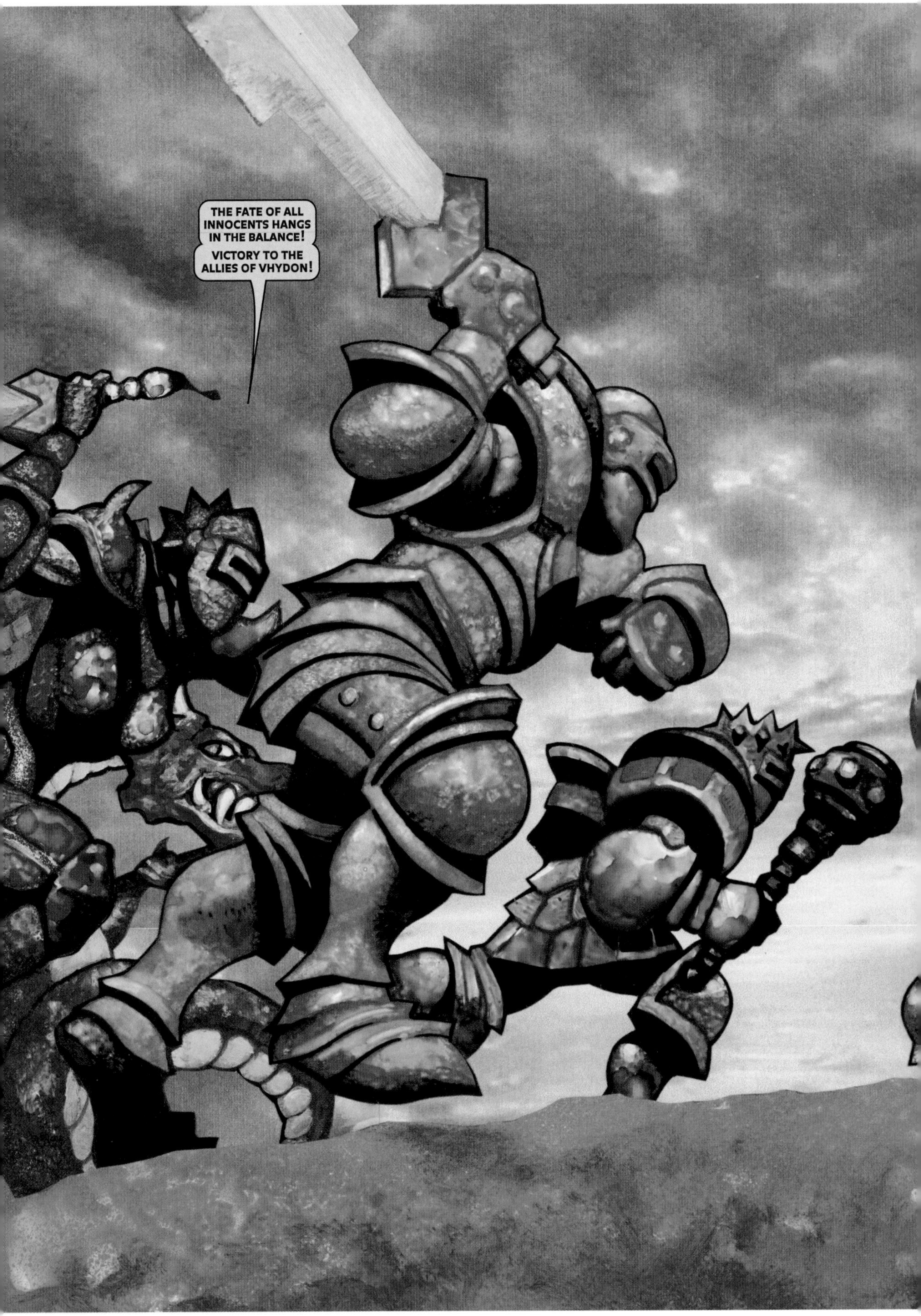
THE FATE OF ALL INNOCENTS HANGS IN THE BALANCE!
VICTORY TO THE ALLIES OF VHYDON!

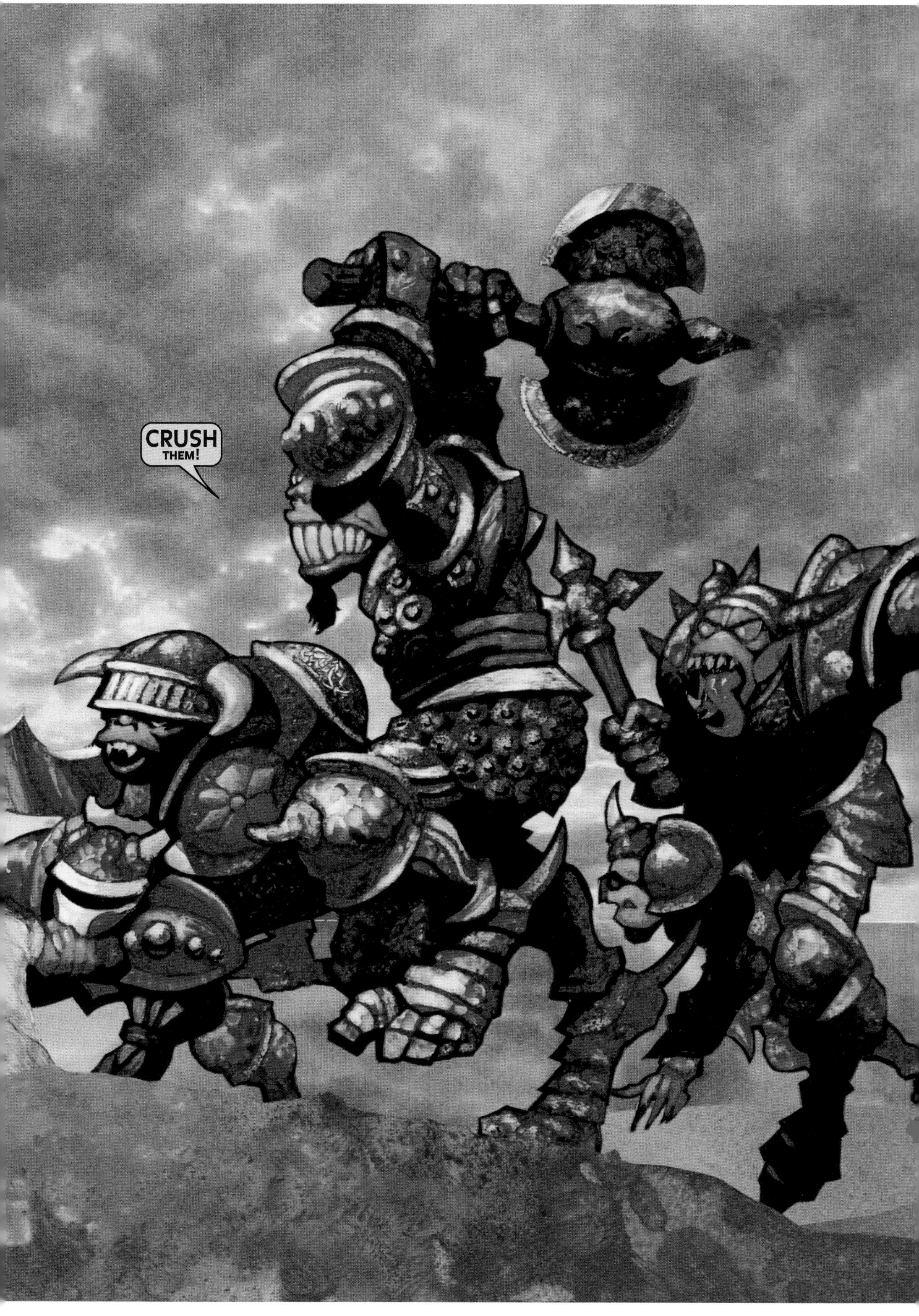
CRUSH THEM!

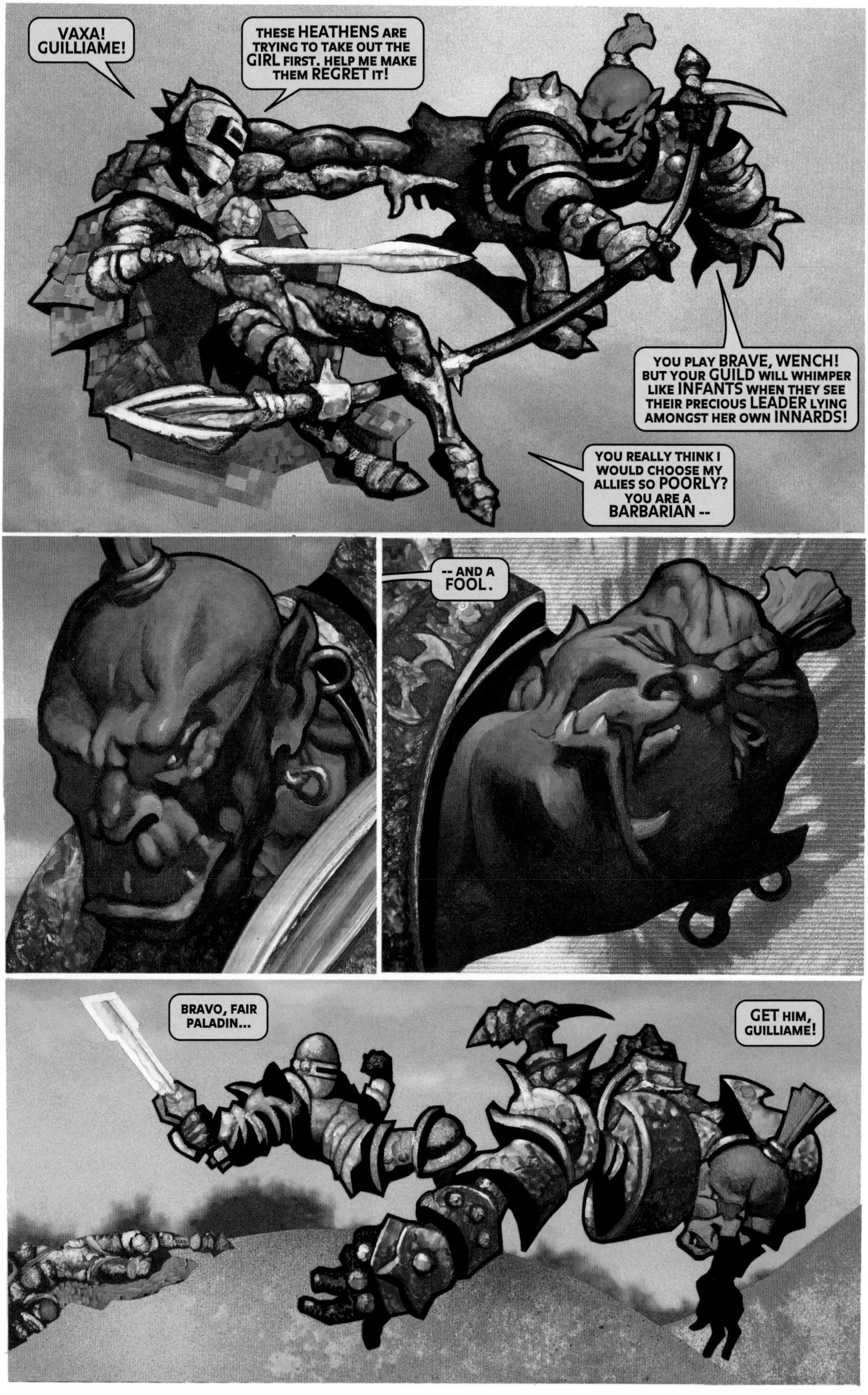
VAXA! GUILLIAME!
THESE HEATHENS ARE TRYING TO TAKE OUT THE GIRL FIRST. HELP ME MAKE THEM REGRET IT!
YOU PLAY BRAVE, WENCH! BUT YOUR GUILD WILL WHIMPER LIKE INFANTS WHEN THEY SEE THEIR PRECIOUS LEADER LYING AMONGST HER OWN INNARDS!
YOU REALLY THINK I WOULD CHOOSE MY ALLIES SO POORLY? YOU ARE A BARBARIAN --
-- AND A FOOL.
BRAVO, FAIR PALADIN...
GET HIM, GUILLIAME!

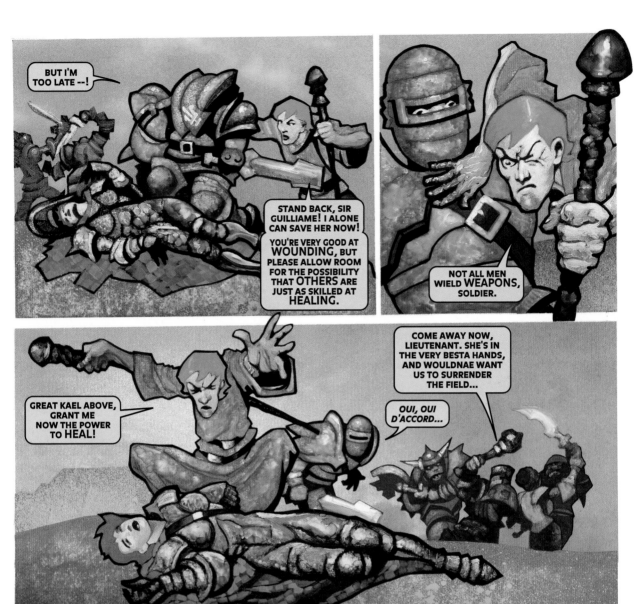

BUT I'M TOO LATE --!

STAND BACK, SIR GUILLIAME! I ALONE CAN SAVE HER NOW! YOU'RE VERY GOOD AT WOUNDING, BUT PLEASE ALLOW ROOM FOR THE POSSIBILITY THAT OTHERS ARE JUST AS SKILLED AT HEALING.

NOT ALL MEN WIELD WEAPONS, SOLDIER.

GREAT KAEL ABOVE, GRANT ME NOW THE POWER TO HEAL!

COME AWAY NOW, LIEUTENANT. SHE'S IN THE VERY BESTA HANDS, AND WOULDNAE WANT US TO SURRENDER THE FIELD...

OUI, OUI D'ACCORD...

BY THE TREE! WHO IS --!

BEHIND YOU!

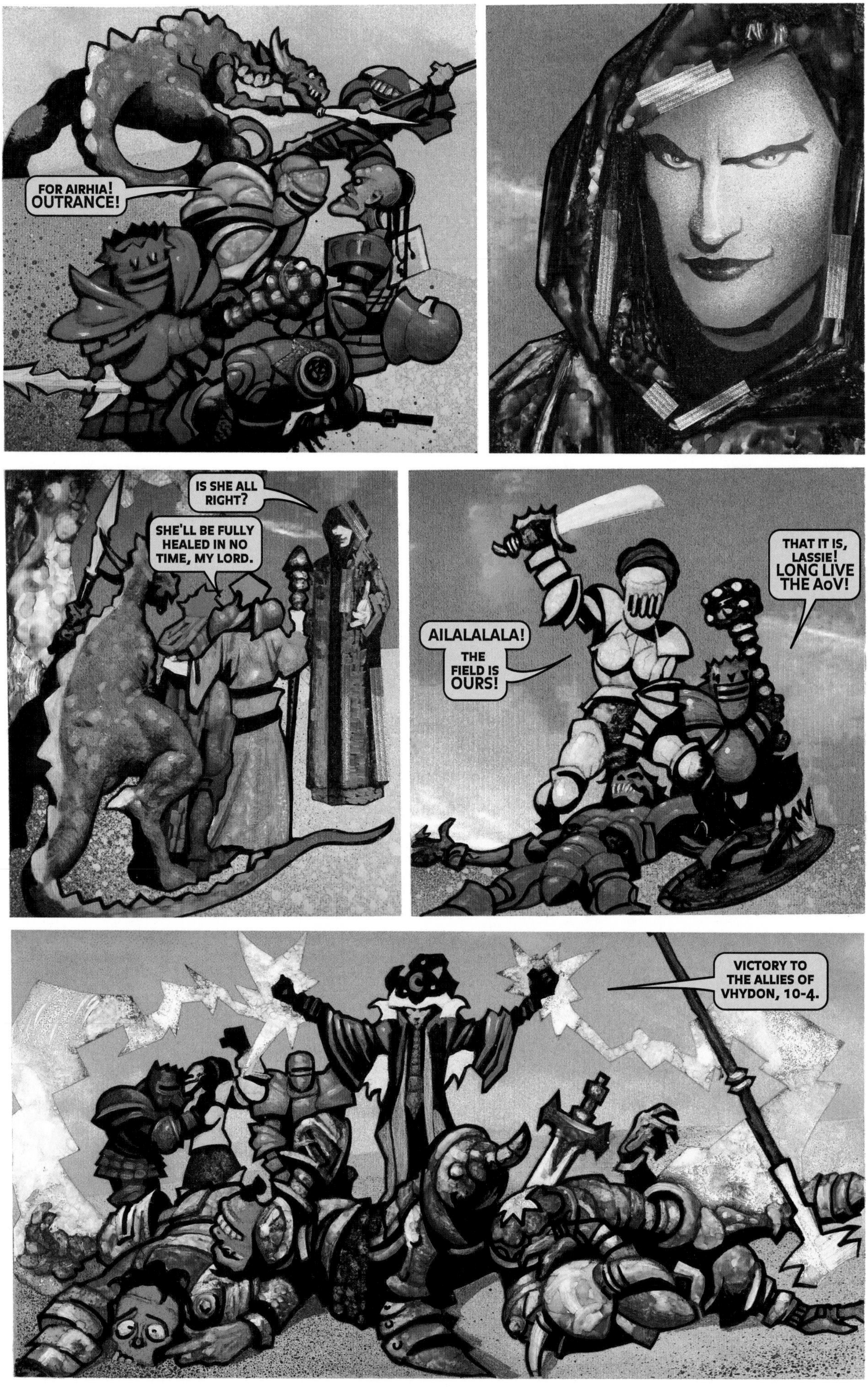
FOR AIRHIA! OUTRANCE!
IS SHE ALL RIGHT?
SHE'LL BE FULLY HEALED IN NO TIME, MY LORD.
AILALALALA! THE FIELD IS OURS!
THAT IT IS, LASSIE! LONG LIVE THE AoV!
VICTORY TO THE ALLIES OF VHYDON, 10-4.

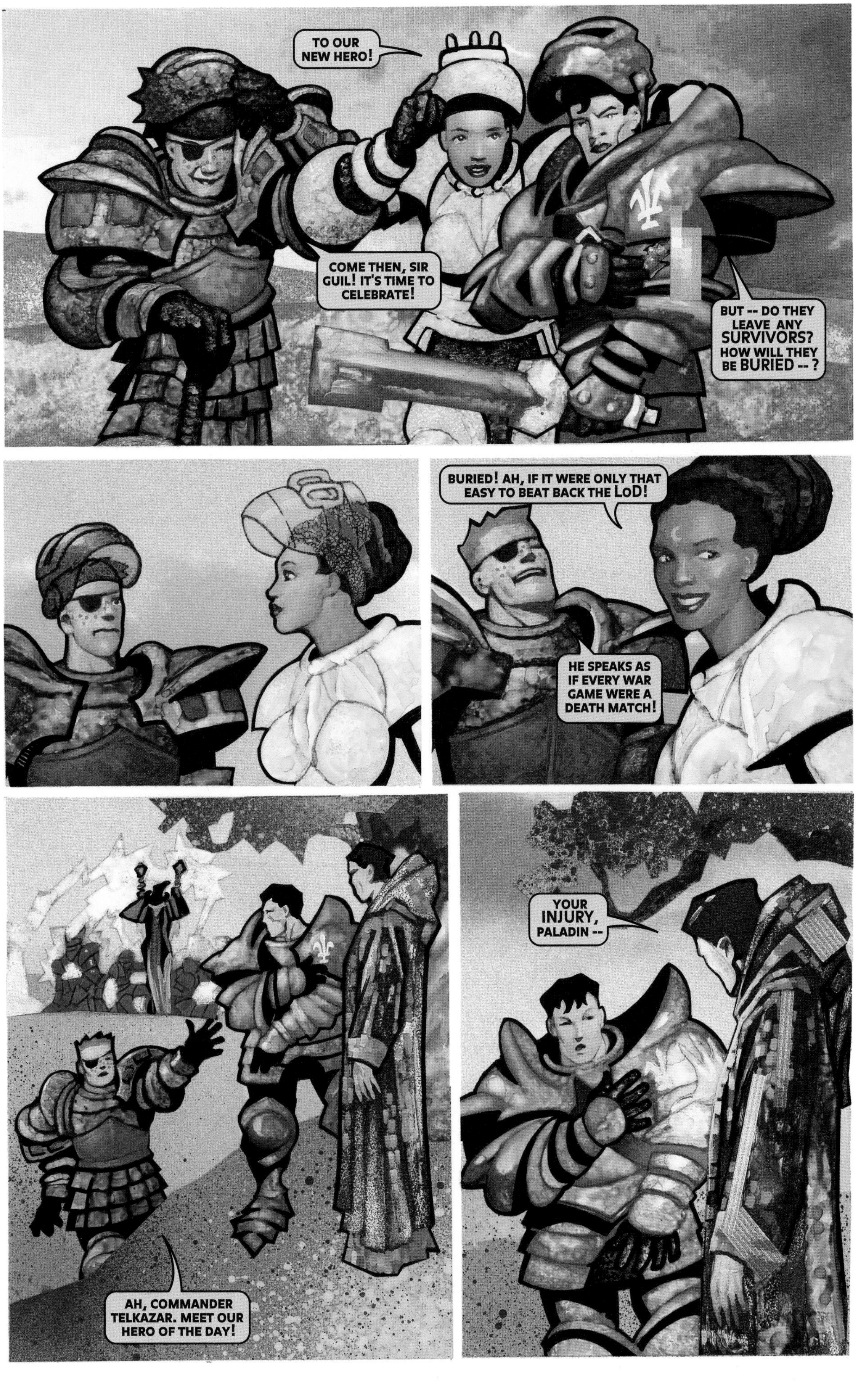
TO OUR NEW HERO!
COME THEN, SIR GUIL! IT'S TIME TO CELEBRATE!
BUT -- DO THEY LEAVE ANY SURVIVORS? HOW WILL THEY BE BURIED -- ?
BURIED! AH, IF IT WERE ONLY THAT EASY TO BEAT BACK THE LoD!
HE SPEAKS AS IF EVERY WAR GAME WERE A DEATH MATCH!
AH, COMMANDER TELKAZAR. MEET OUR HERO OF THE DAY!
YOUR INJURY, PALADIN --

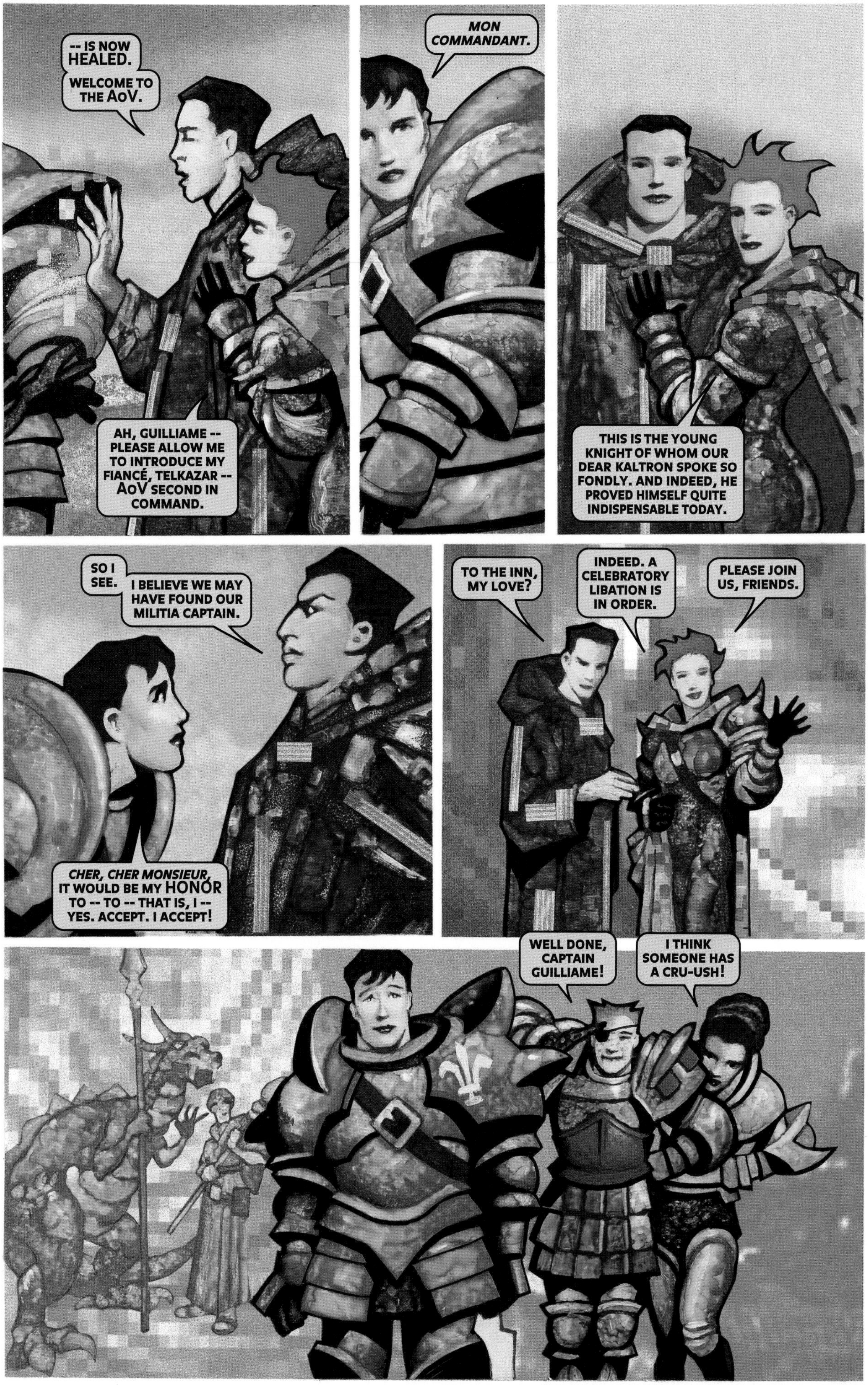
-- IS NOW HEALED.
WELCOME TO THE AoV.
AH, GUILLIAME -- PLEASE ALLOW ME TO INTRODUCE MY FIANCÉ, TELKAZAR -- AoV SECOND IN COMMAND.
MON COMMANDANT.
THIS IS THE YOUNG KNIGHT OF WHOM OUR DEAR KALTRON SPOKE SO FONDLY. AND INDEED, HE PROVED HIMSELF QUITE INDISPENSABLE TODAY.
SO I SEE.
I BELIEVE WE MAY HAVE FOUND OUR MILITIA CAPTAIN.
CHER, CHER MONSIEUR, IT WOULD BE MY HONOR TO -- TO -- THAT IS, I -- YES. ACCEPT. I ACCEPT!
TO THE INN, MY LOVE?
INDEED. A CELEBRATORY LIBATION IS IN ORDER.
PLEASE JOIN US, FRIENDS.
WELL DONE, CAPTAIN GUILLIAME!
I THINK SOMEONE HAS A CRU-USH!

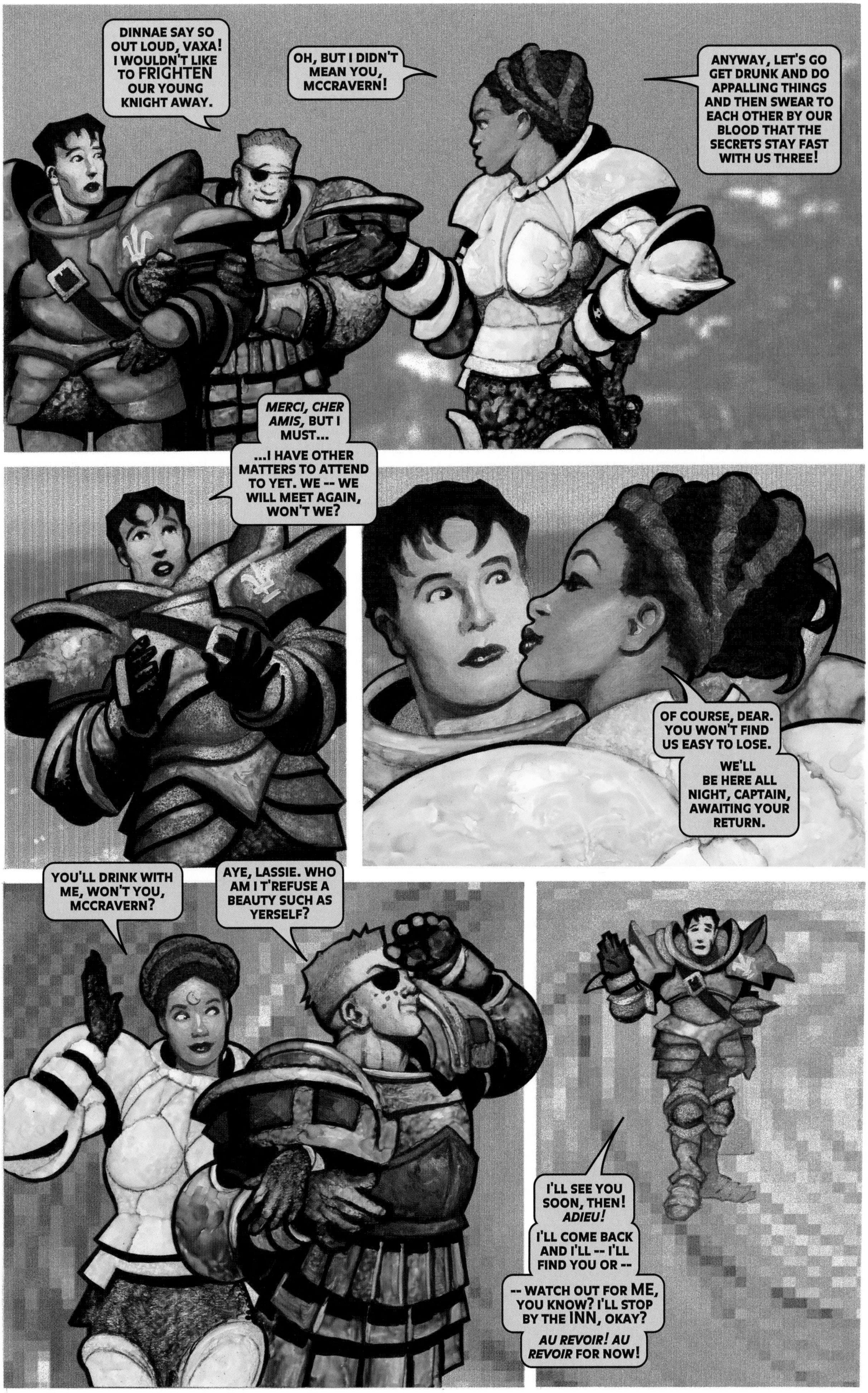
DINNAE SAY SO OUT LOUD, VAXA! I WOULDN'T LIKE TO FRIGHTEN OUR YOUNG KNIGHT AWAY.
OH, BUT I DIDN'T MEAN YOU, MCCRAVERN!
ANYWAY, LET'S GO GET DRUNK AND DO APPALLING THINGS AND THEN SWEAR TO EACH OTHER BY OUR BLOOD THAT THE SECRETS STAY FAST WITH US THREE!
MERCI, CHER AMIS, BUT I MUST...
...I HAVE OTHER MATTERS TO ATTEND TO YET. WE -- WE WILL MEET AGAIN, WON'T WE?
OF COURSE, DEAR. YOU WON'T FIND US EASY TO LOSE.
WE'LL BE HERE ALL NIGHT, CAPTAIN, AWAITING YOUR RETURN.
YOU'LL DRINK WITH ME, WON'T YOU, MCCRAVERN?
AYE, LASSIE. WHO AM I T'REFUSE A BEAUTY SUCH AS YERSELF?
I'LL SEE YOU SOON, THEN! *ADIEU!*
I'LL COME BACK AND I'LL -- I'LL FIND YOU OR --
-- WATCH OUT FOR ME, YOU KNOW? I'LL STOP BY THE INN, OKAY?
AU REVOIR! AU REVOIR FOR NOW!

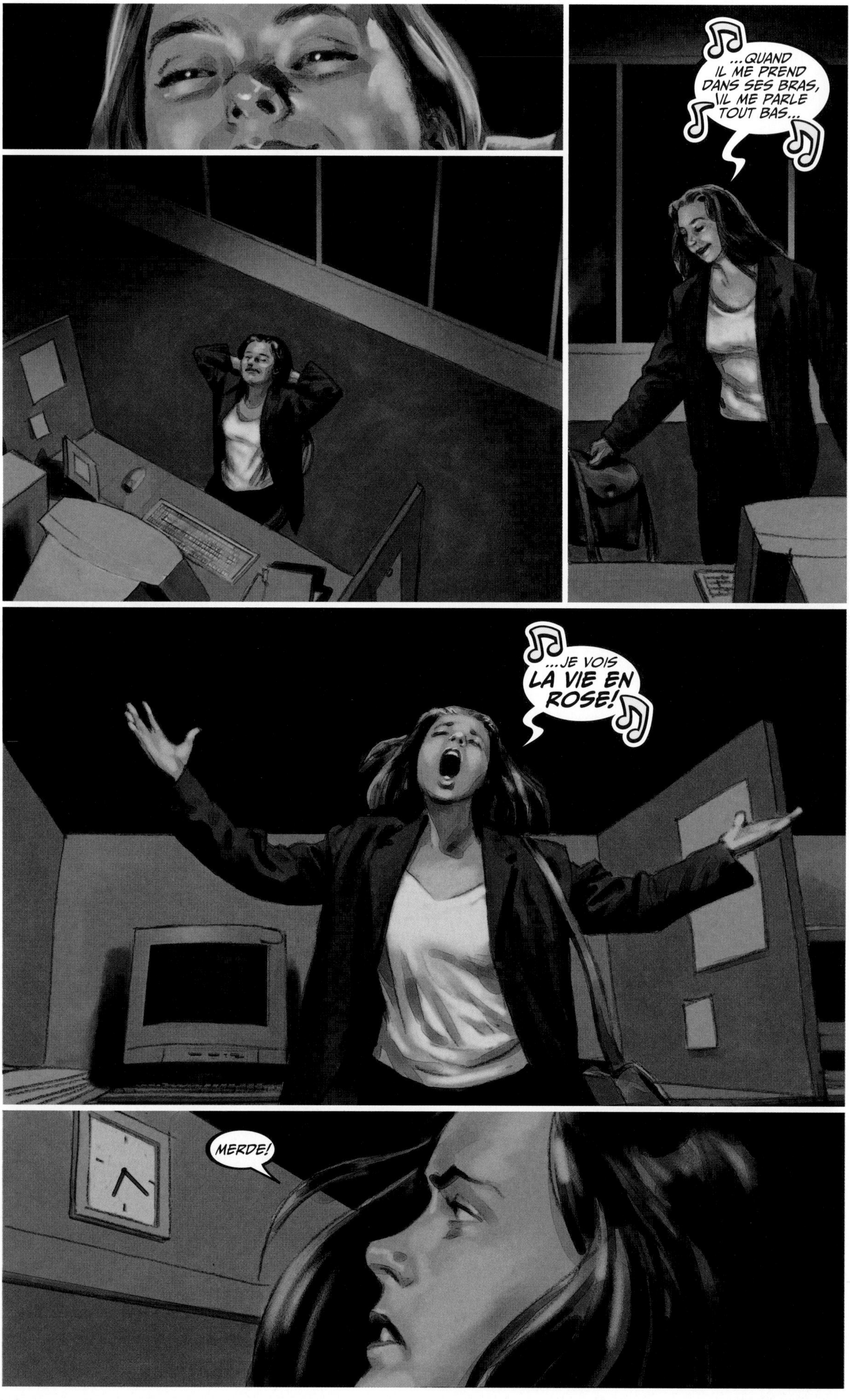
...QUAND IL ME PREND DANS SES BRAS, IL ME PARLE TOUT BAS...
...JE VOIS LA VIE EN ROSE!
MERDE!

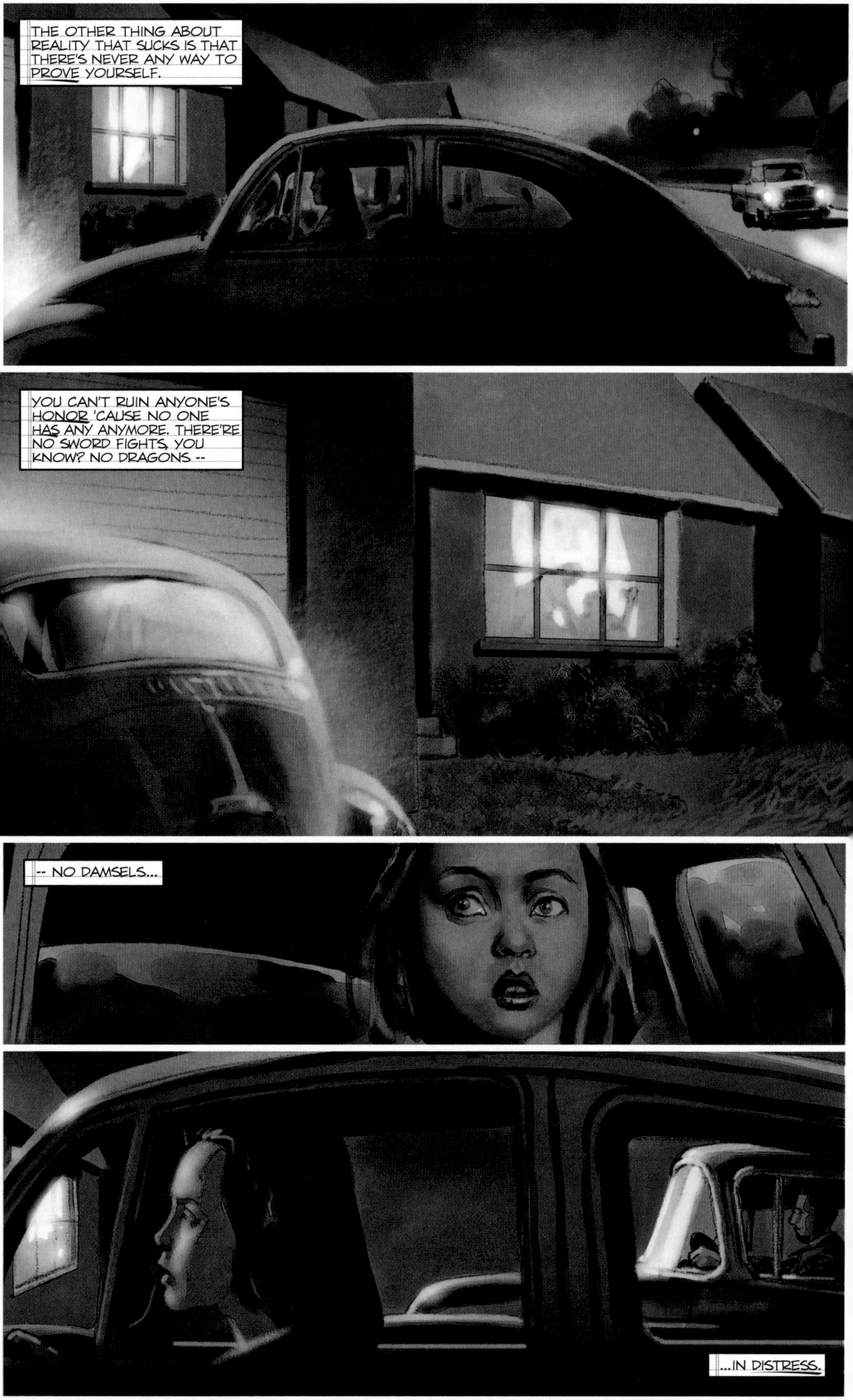
THE OTHER THING ABOUT REALITY THAT SUCKS IS THAT THERE'S NEVER ANY WAY TO PROVE YOURSELF.
YOU CAN'T RUIN ANYONE'S HONOR 'CAUSE NO ONE HAS ANY ANYMORE. THERE'RE NO SWORD FIGHTS, YOU KNOW? NO DRAGONS --
-- NO DAMSELS...
...IN DISTRESS.

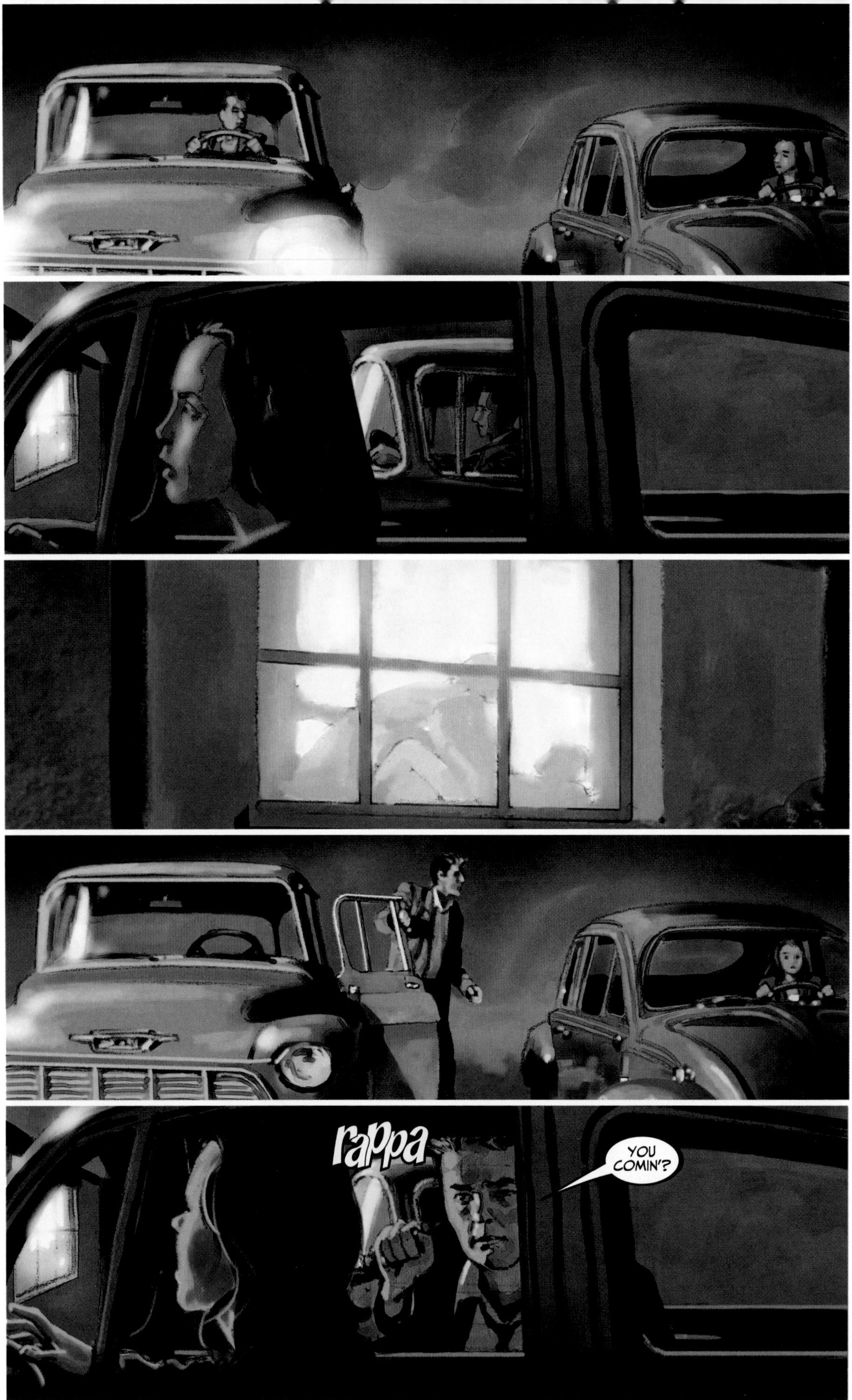
rappa
YOU COMIN'?

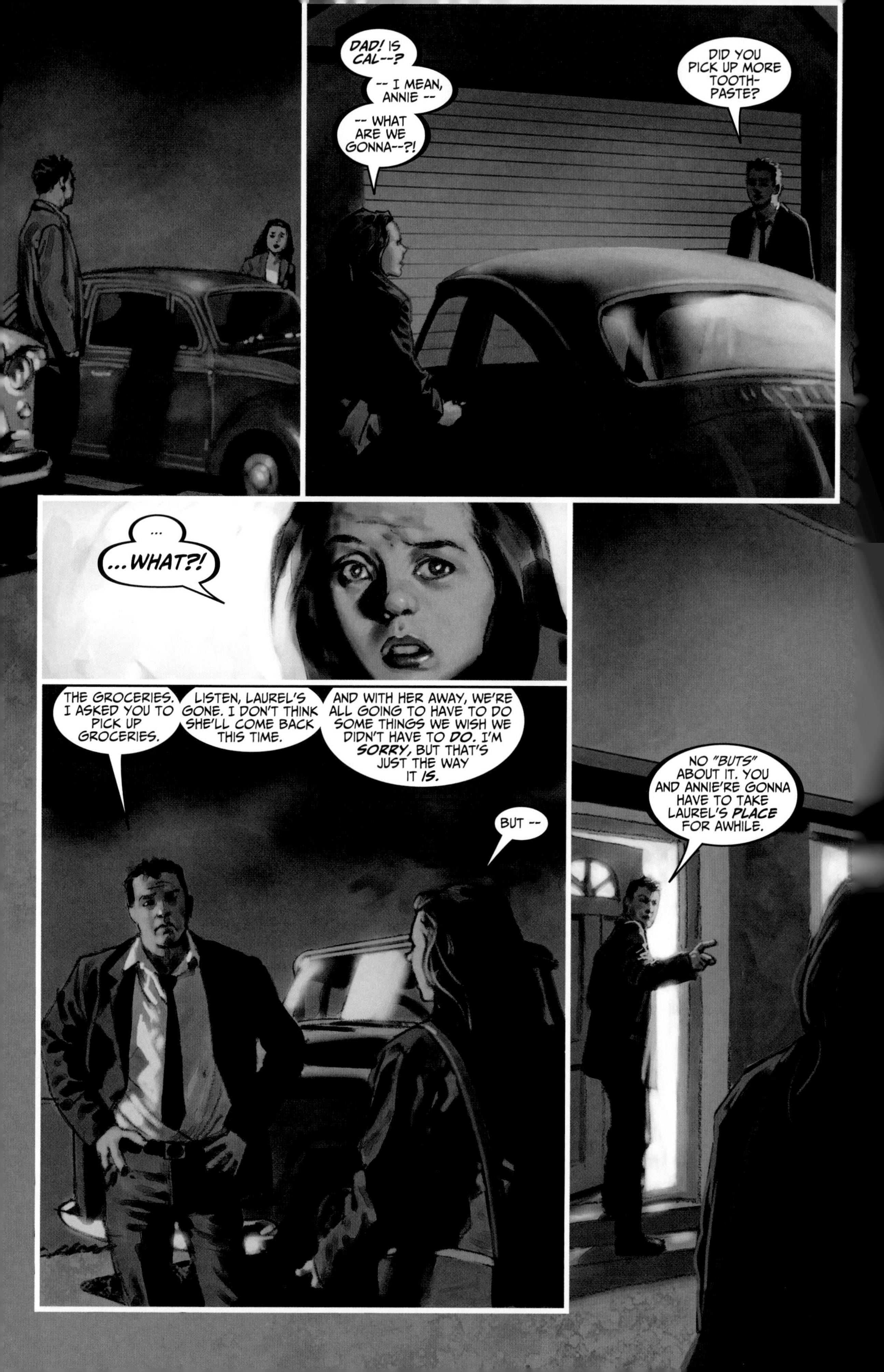
DAD! IS CAL--?
-- I MEAN, ANNIE --
-- WHAT ARE WE GONNA--?!
DID YOU PICK UP MORE TOOTH-PASTE?
...
...WHAT?!
THE GROCERIES. I ASKED YOU TO PICK UP GROCERIES.
LISTEN, LAUREL'S GONE. I DON'T THINK SHE'LL COME BACK THIS TIME.
AND WITH HER AWAY, WE'RE ALL GOING TO HAVE TO DO SOME THINGS WE WISH WE DIDN'T HAVE TO DO. I'M SORRY, BUT THAT'S JUST THE WAY IT IS.
BUT --
NO "BUTS" ABOUT IT. YOU AND ANNIE'RE GONNA HAVE TO TAKE LAUREL'S PLACE FOR AWHILE.

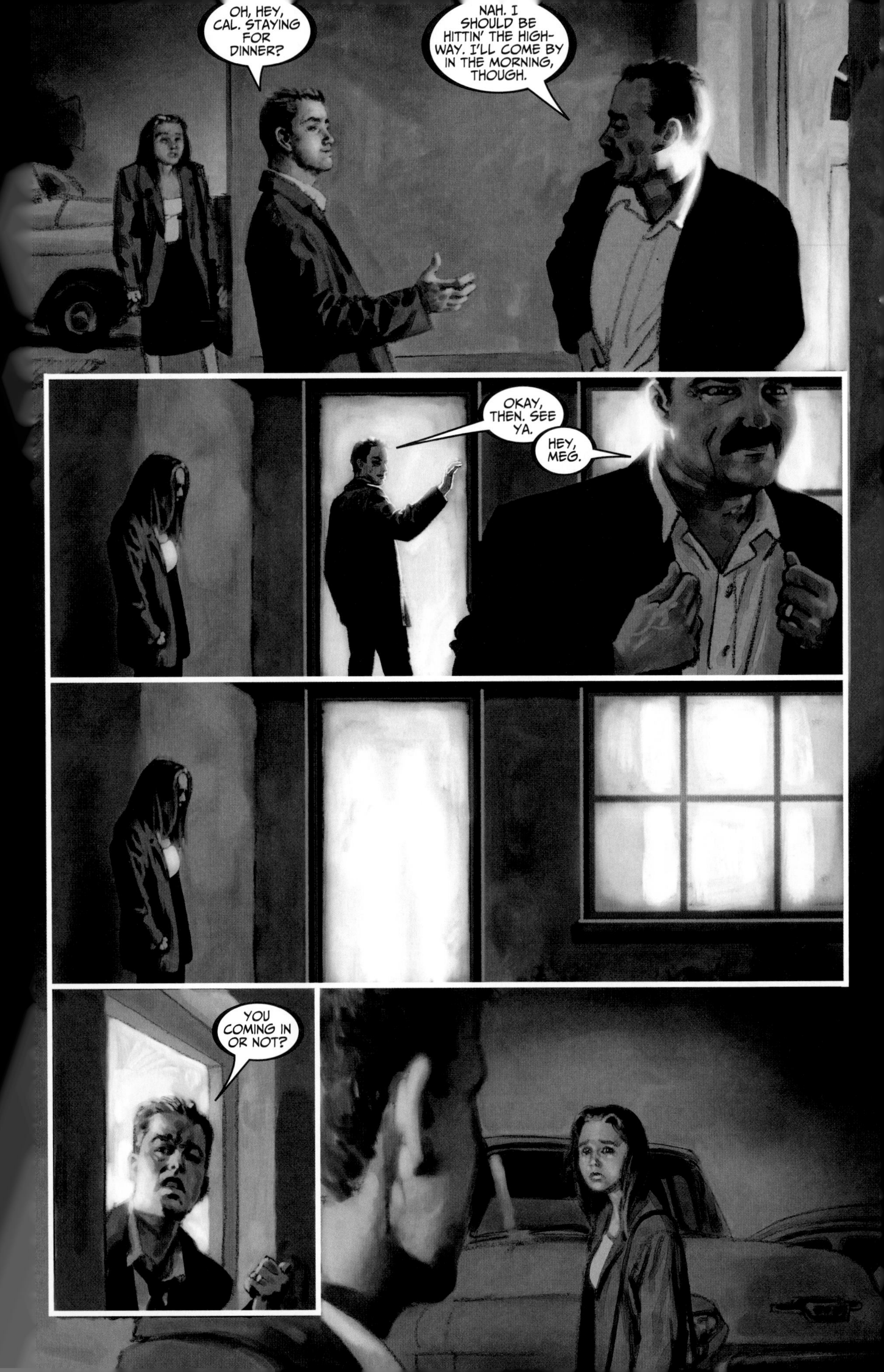
OH, HEY, CAL. STAYING FOR DINNER?
NAH. I SHOULD BE HITTIN' THE HIGH-WAY. I'LL COME BY IN THE MORNING, THOUGH.
OKAY, THEN. SEE YA.
HEY, MEG.
YOU COMING IN OR NOT?

Annie's Room
ANNIE?
knok knok knok
MEG?
ANNIE, WHAT HAPPENED TO YOUR WRIST?

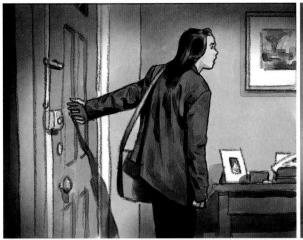

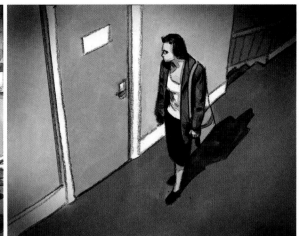

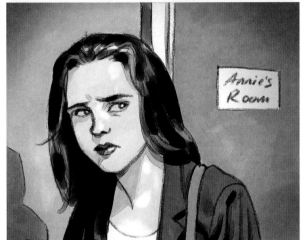

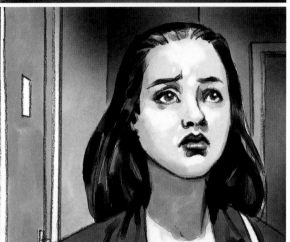

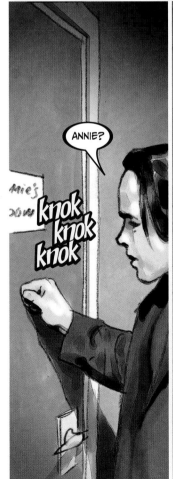

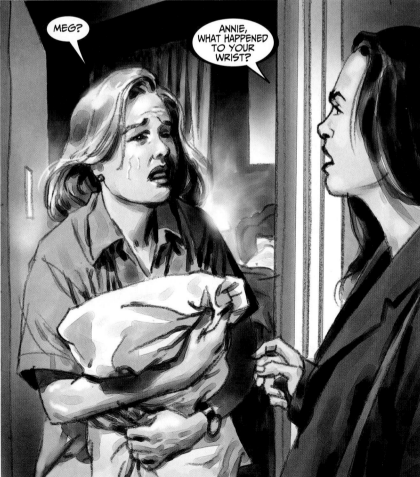

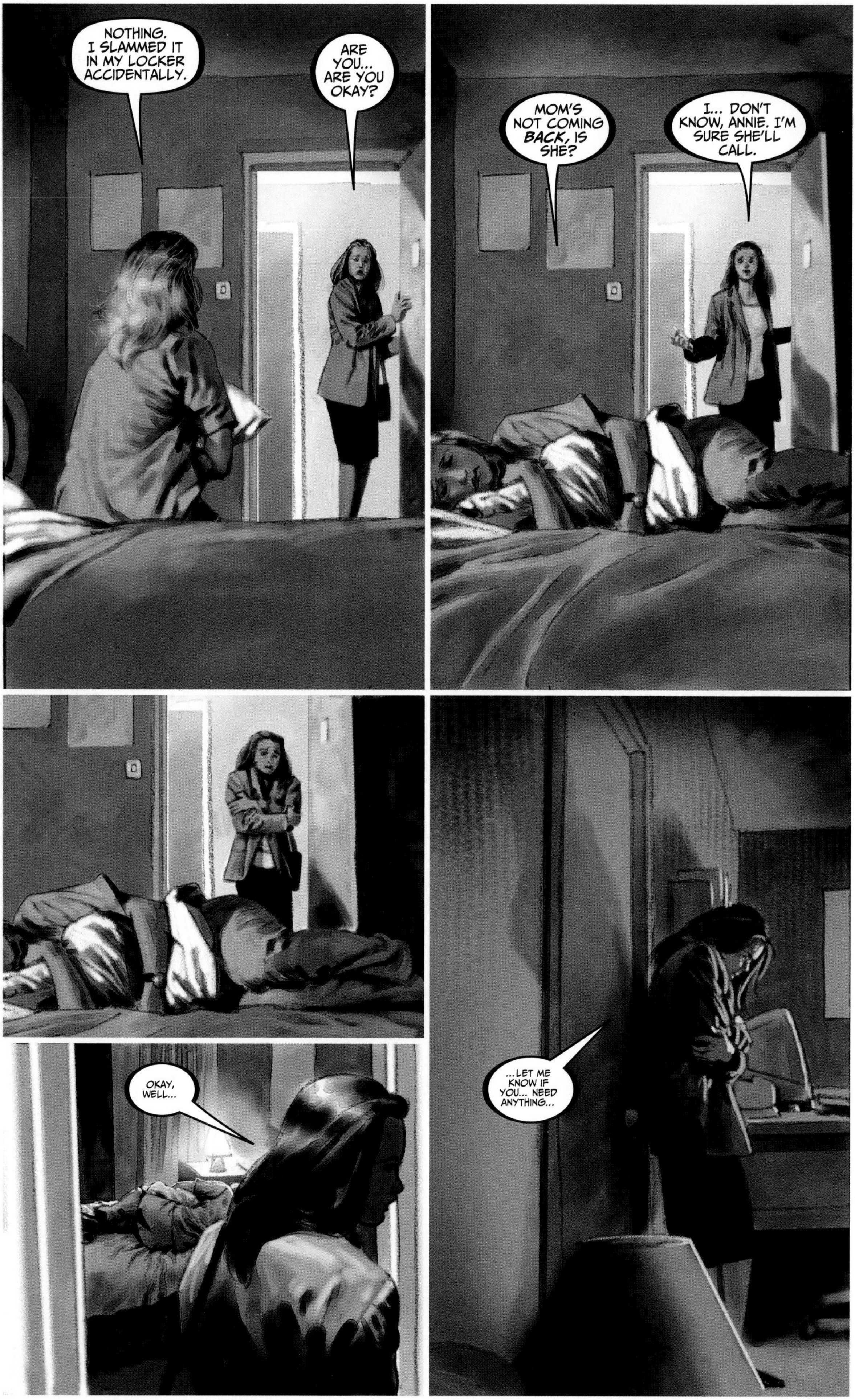
NOTHING. I SLAMMED IT IN MY LOCKER ACCIDENTALLY.
ARE YOU... ARE YOU OKAY?
MOM'S NOT COMING *BACK*, IS SHE?
I... DON'T KNOW, ANNIE. I'M SURE SHE'LL CALL.
OKAY, WELL...
...LET ME KNOW IF YOU... NEED ANYTHING...

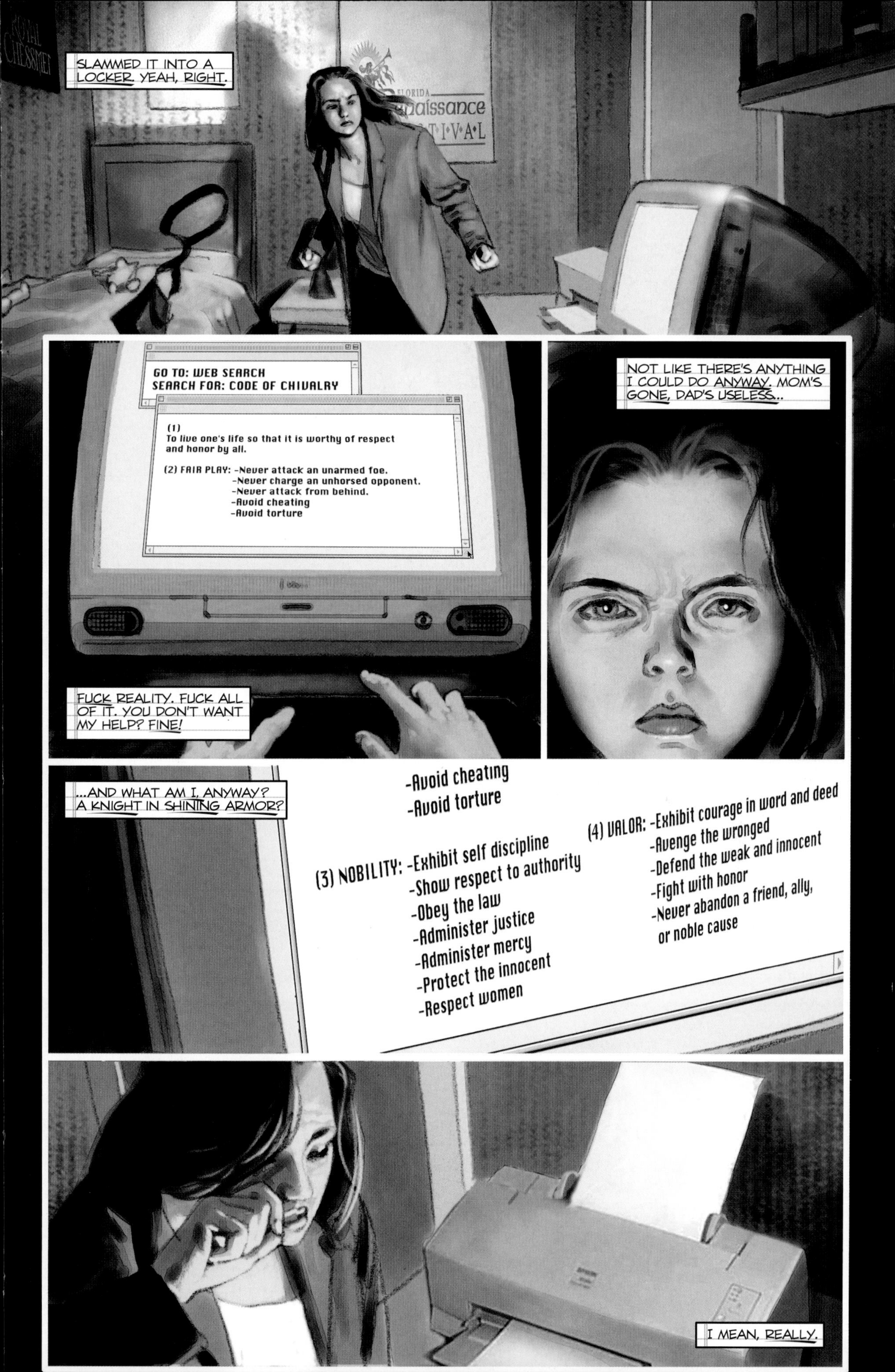

ROYAL CHESSMEN
SLAMMED IT INTO A LOCKER. YEAH, RIGHT.
FLORIDA Renaissance FESTIVAL
GO TO: WEB SEARCH
SEARCH FOR: CODE OF CHIVALRY
(1)
To live one's life so that it is worthy of respect and honor by all.
(2) FAIR PLAY: -Never attack an unarmed foe.
-Never charge an unhorsed opponent.
-Never attack from behind.
-Avoid cheating
-Avoid torture
FUCK REALITY. FUCK ALL OF IT. YOU DON'T WANT MY HELP? FINE!
NOT LIKE THERE'S ANYTHING I COULD DO ANYWAY. MOM'S GONE, DAD'S USELESS...
...AND WHAT AM I, ANYWAY? A KNIGHT IN SHINING ARMOR?
-Avoid cheating
-Avoid torture
(3) NOBILITY: -Exhibit self discipline
-Show respect to authority
-Obey the law
-Administer justice
-Administer mercy
-Protect the innocent
-Respect women
(4) VALOR: -Exhibit courage in word and deed
-Avenge the wronged
-Defend the weak and innocent
-Fight with honor
-Never abandon a friend, ally, or noble cause
I MEAN, REALLY.

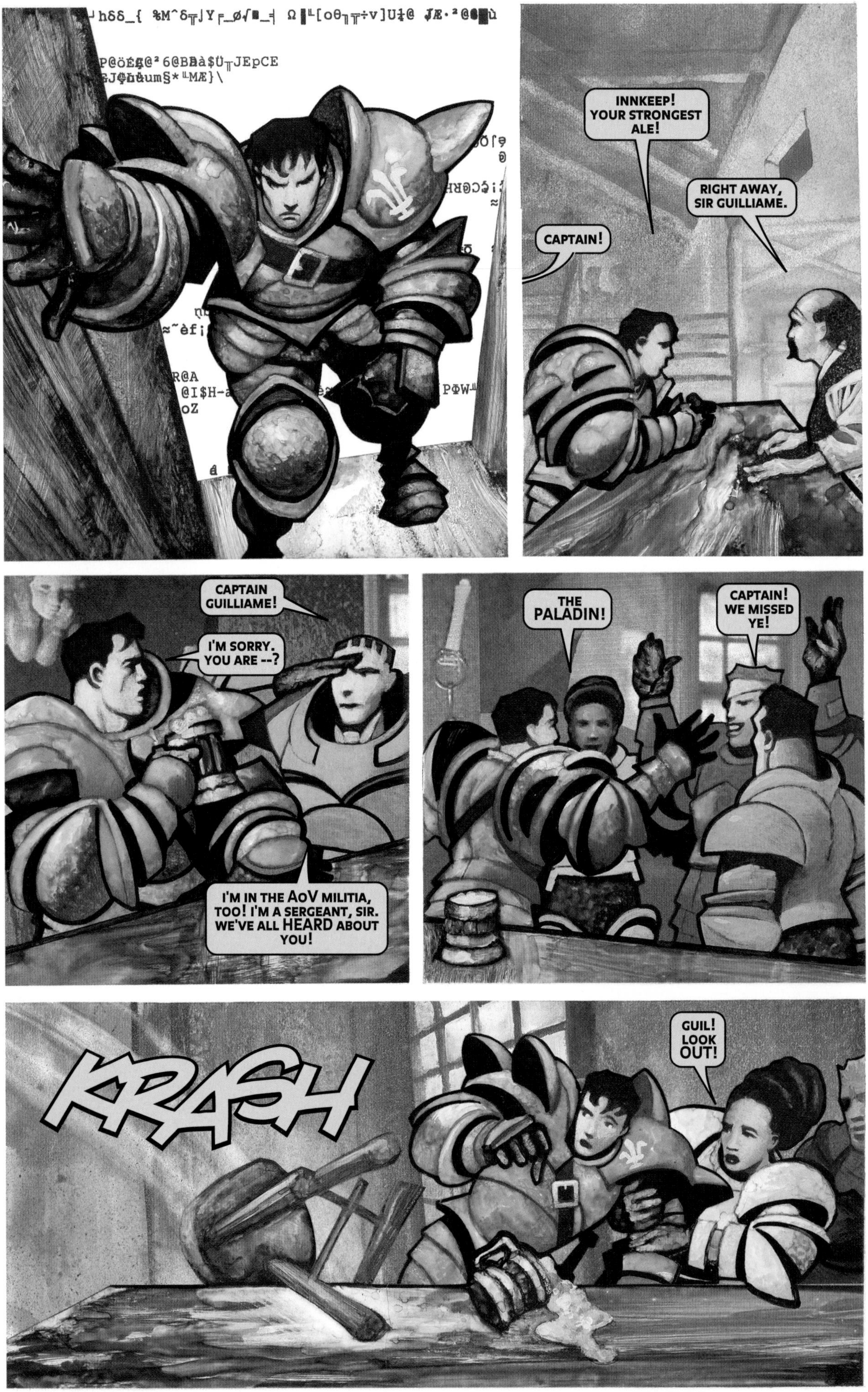
INNKEEP! YOUR STRONGEST ALE!
RIGHT AWAY, SIR GUILLIAME.
CAPTAIN!
CAPTAIN GUILLIAME!
I'M SORRY. YOU ARE --?
I'M IN THE AoV MILITIA, TOO! I'M A SERGEANT, SIR. WE'VE ALL HEARD ABOUT YOU!
THE PALADIN!
CAPTAIN! WE MISSED YE!
KRASH
GUIL! LOOK OUT!

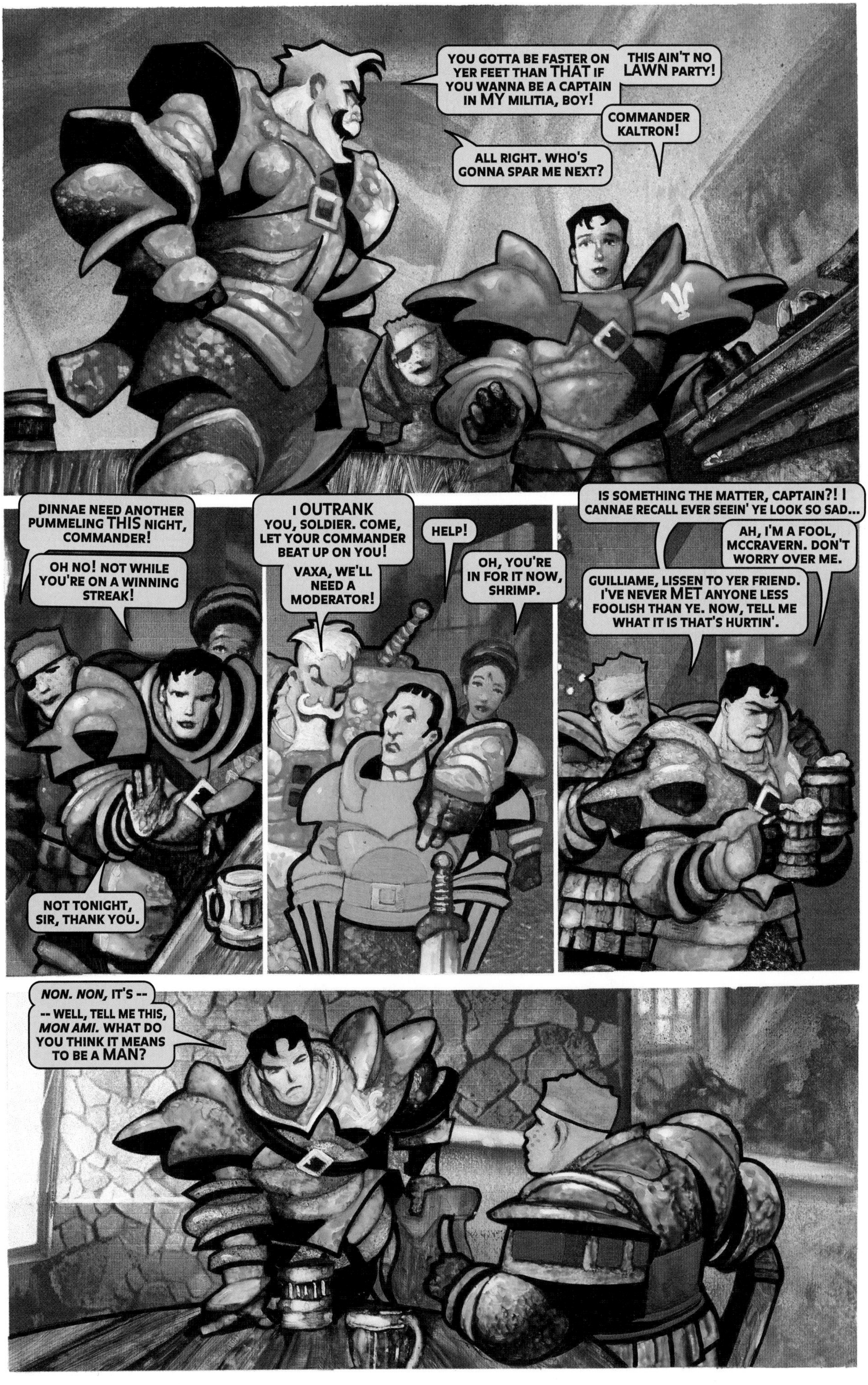
YOU GOTTA BE FASTER ON YER FEET THAN THAT IF YOU WANNA BE A CAPTAIN IN MY MILITIA, BOY!
THIS AIN'T NO LAWN PARTY!
COMMANDER KALTRON!
ALL RIGHT. WHO'S GONNA SPAR ME NEXT?
DINNAE NEED ANOTHER PUMMELING THIS NIGHT, COMMANDER!
OH NO! NOT WHILE YOU'RE ON A WINNING STREAK!
NOT TONIGHT, SIR, THANK YOU.
I OUTRANK YOU, SOLDIER. COME, LET YOUR COMMANDER BEAT UP ON YOU!
VAXA, WE'LL NEED A MODERATOR!
HELP!
OH, YOU'RE IN FOR IT NOW, SHRIMP.
IS SOMETHING THE MATTER, CAPTAIN?! I CANNAE RECALL EVER SEEIN' YE LOOK SO SAD...
AH, I'M A FOOL, MCCRAVERN. DON'T WORRY OVER ME.
GUILLIAME, LISSEN TO YER FRIEND. I'VE NEVER MET ANYONE LESS FOOLISH THAN YE. NOW, TELL ME WHAT IT IS THAT'S HURTIN'.
NON. NON, IT'S --
-- WELL, TELL ME THIS, MON AMI. WHAT DO YOU THINK IT MEANS TO BE A MAN?

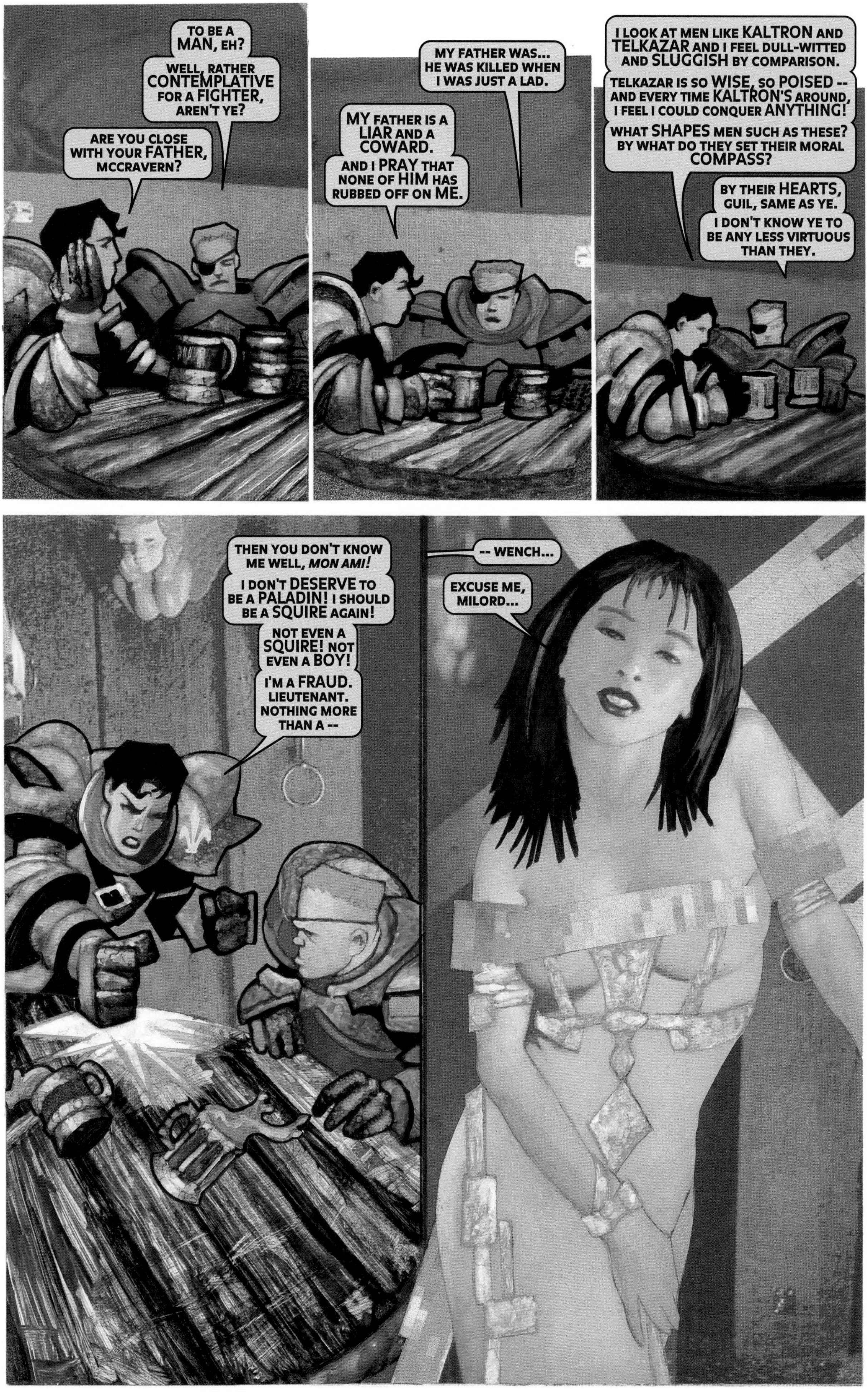
TO BE A MAN, EH?
WELL, RATHER CONTEMPLATIVE FOR A FIGHTER, AREN'T YE?
ARE YOU CLOSE WITH YOUR FATHER, MCCRAVERN?
MY FATHER WAS... HE WAS KILLED WHEN I WAS JUST A LAD.
MY FATHER IS A LIAR AND A COWARD.
AND I PRAY THAT NONE OF HIM HAS RUBBED OFF ON ME.
I LOOK AT MEN LIKE KALTRON AND TELKAZAR AND I FEEL DULL-WITTED AND SLUGGISH BY COMPARISON.
TELKAZAR IS SO WISE, SO POISED -- AND EVERY TIME KALTRON'S AROUND, I FEEL I COULD CONQUER ANYTHING!
WHAT SHAPES MEN SUCH AS THESE? BY WHAT DO THEY SET THEIR MORAL COMPASS?
BY THEIR HEARTS, GUIL, SAME AS YE.
I DON'T KNOW YE TO BE ANY LESS VIRTUOUS THAN THEY.
THEN YOU DON'T KNOW ME WELL, *MON AMI!*
I DON'T DESERVE TO BE A PALADIN! I SHOULD BE A SQUIRE AGAIN!
NOT EVEN A SQUIRE! NOT EVEN A BOY!
I'M A FRAUD. LIEUTENANT. NOTHING MORE THAN A --
-- WENCH...
EXCUSE ME, MILORD...

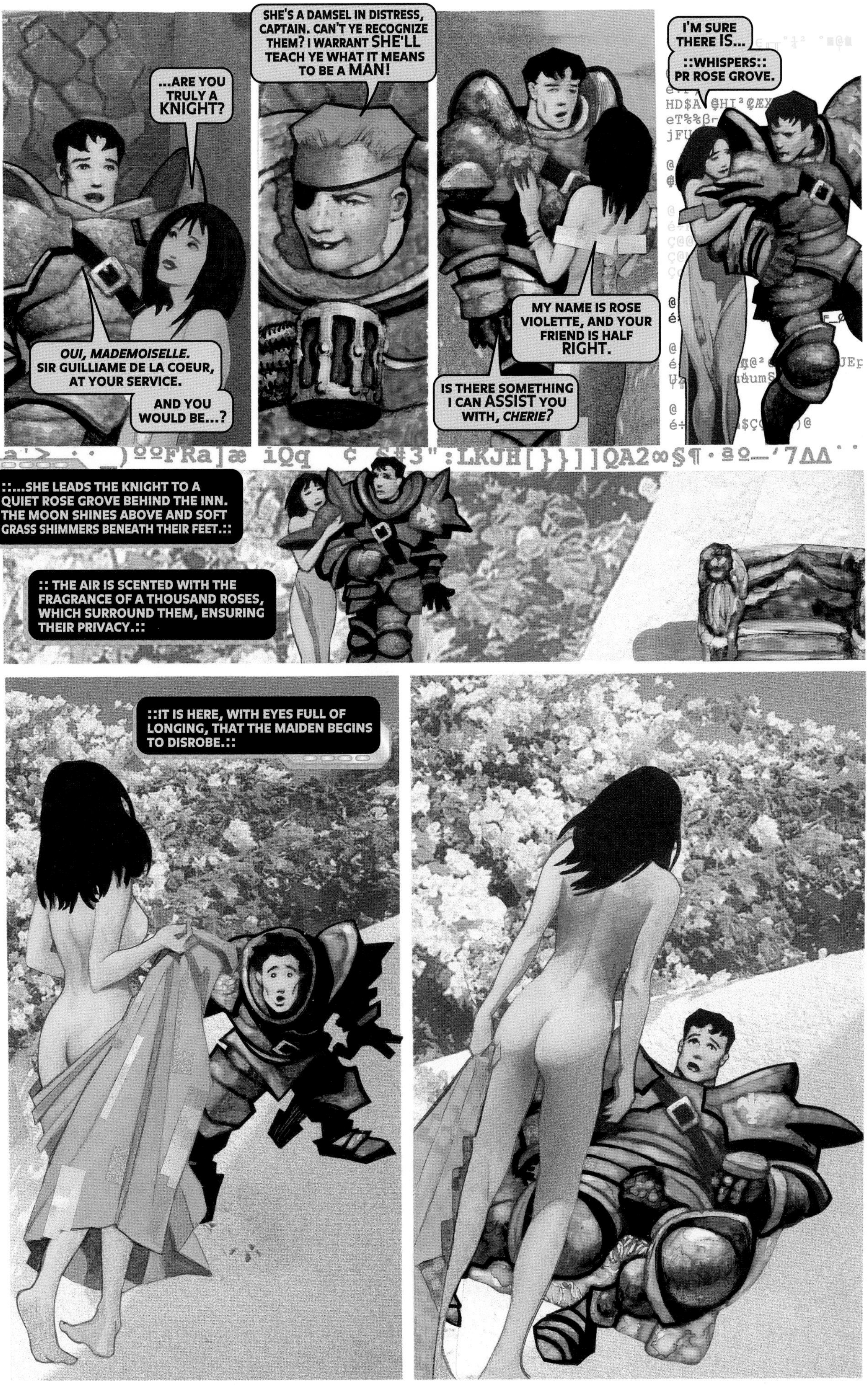
...ARE YOU TRULY A KNIGHT?
OUI, MADEMOISELLE. SIR GUILLIAME DE LA COEUR, AT YOUR SERVICE.
AND YOU WOULD BE...?
SHE'S A DAMSEL IN DISTRESS, CAPTAIN. CAN'T YE RECOGNIZE THEM? I WARRANT SHE'LL TEACH YE WHAT IT MEANS TO BE A MAN!
MY NAME IS ROSE VIOLETTE, AND YOUR FRIEND IS HALF RIGHT.
IS THERE SOMETHING I CAN ASSIST YOU WITH, *CHERIE?*
I'M SURE THERE IS...
::WHISPERS:: PR ROSE GROVE.
::...SHE LEADS THE KNIGHT TO A QUIET ROSE GROVE BEHIND THE INN. THE MOON SHINES ABOVE AND SOFT GRASS SHIMMERS BENEATH THEIR FEET.::
:: THE AIR IS SCENTED WITH THE FRAGRANCE OF A THOUSAND ROSES, WHICH SURROUND THEM, ENSURING THEIR PRIVACY.::
::IT IS HERE, WITH EYES FULL OF LONGING, THAT THE MAIDEN BEGINS TO DISROBE.::

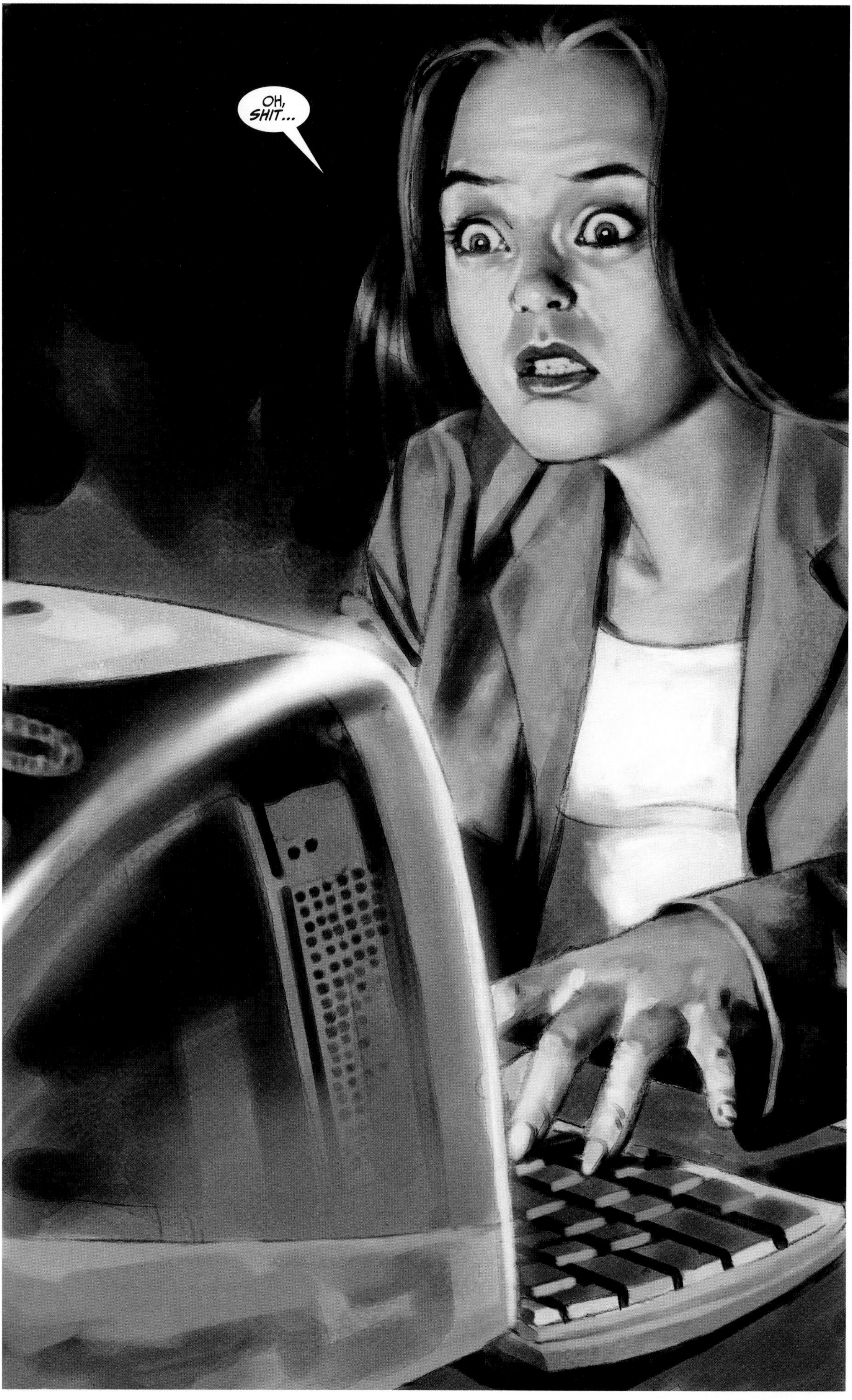
OH, SHIT...

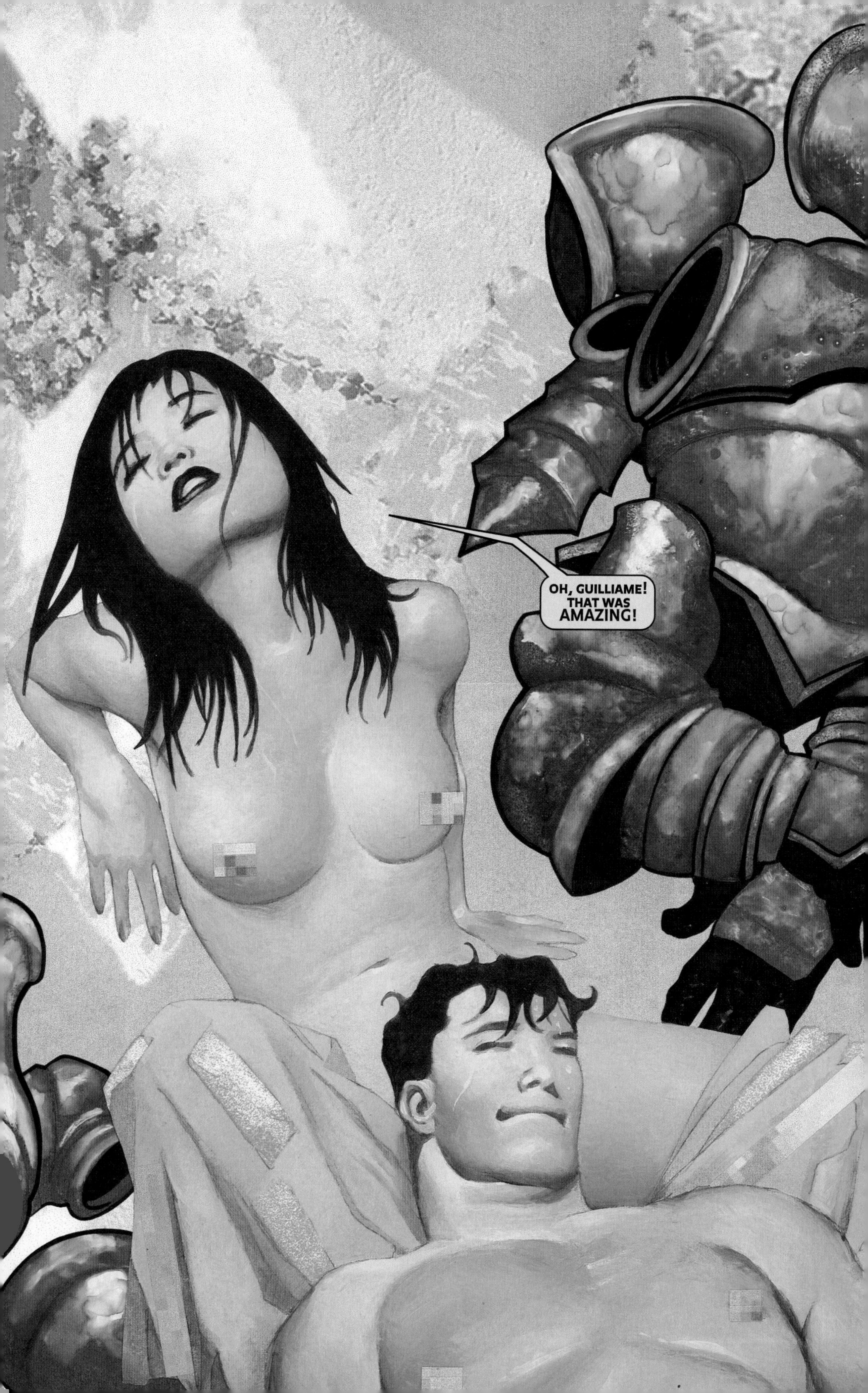
OH, GUILLIAME! THAT WAS AMAZING!

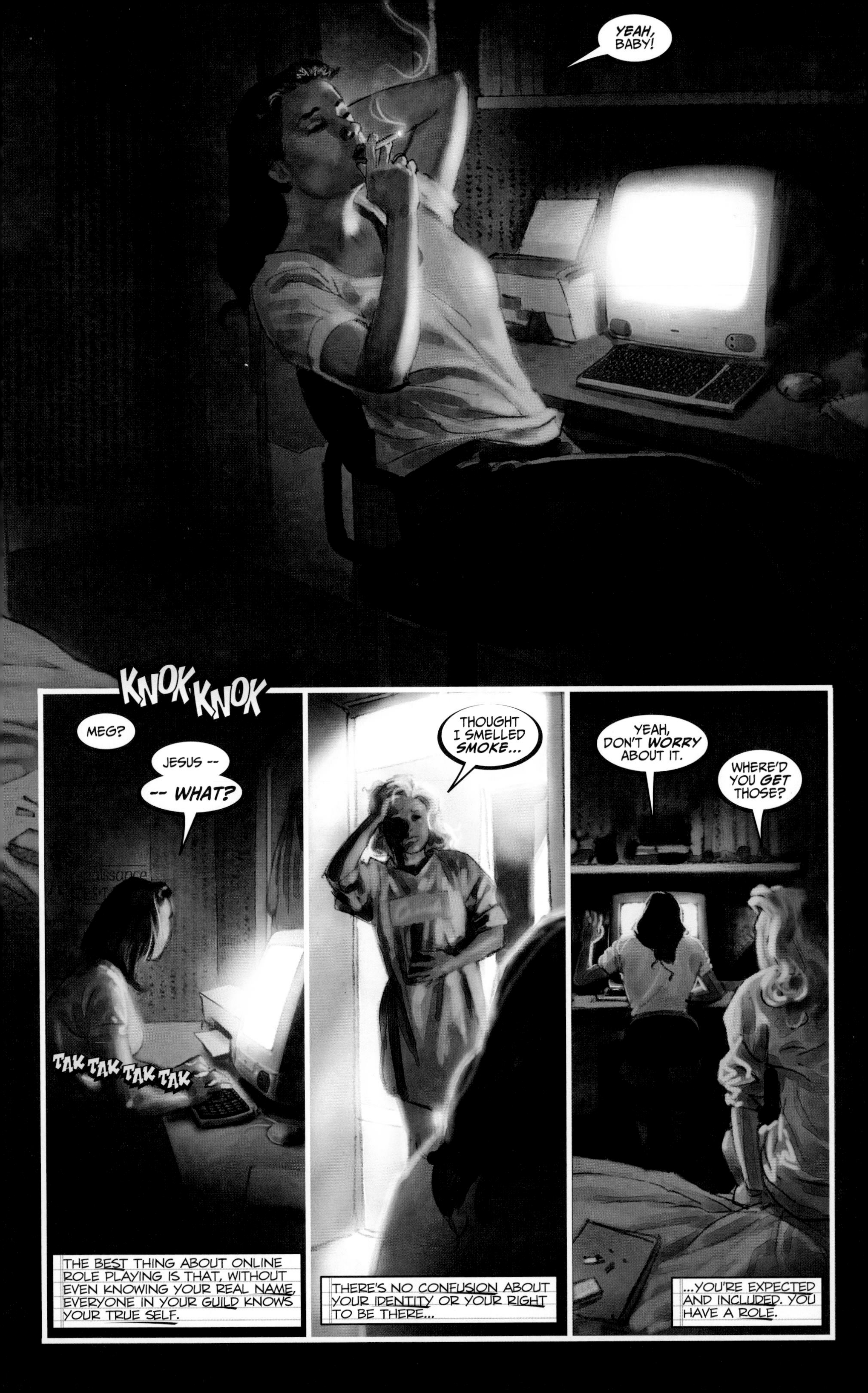
YEAH, BABY!
KNOK KNOK
MEG?
JESUS --
-- WHAT?
TAK TAK TAK TAK
THE BEST THING ABOUT ONLINE ROLE PLAYING IS THAT, WITHOUT EVEN KNOWING YOUR REAL NAME, EVERYONE IN YOUR GUILD KNOWS YOUR TRUE SELF.
THOUGHT I SMELLED SMOKE...
THERE'S NO CONFUSION ABOUT YOUR IDENTITY OR YOUR RIGHT TO BE THERE...
YEAH, DON'T WORRY ABOUT IT.
WHERE'D YOU GET THOSE?
...YOU'RE EXPECTED AND INCLUDED. YOU HAVE A ROLE.

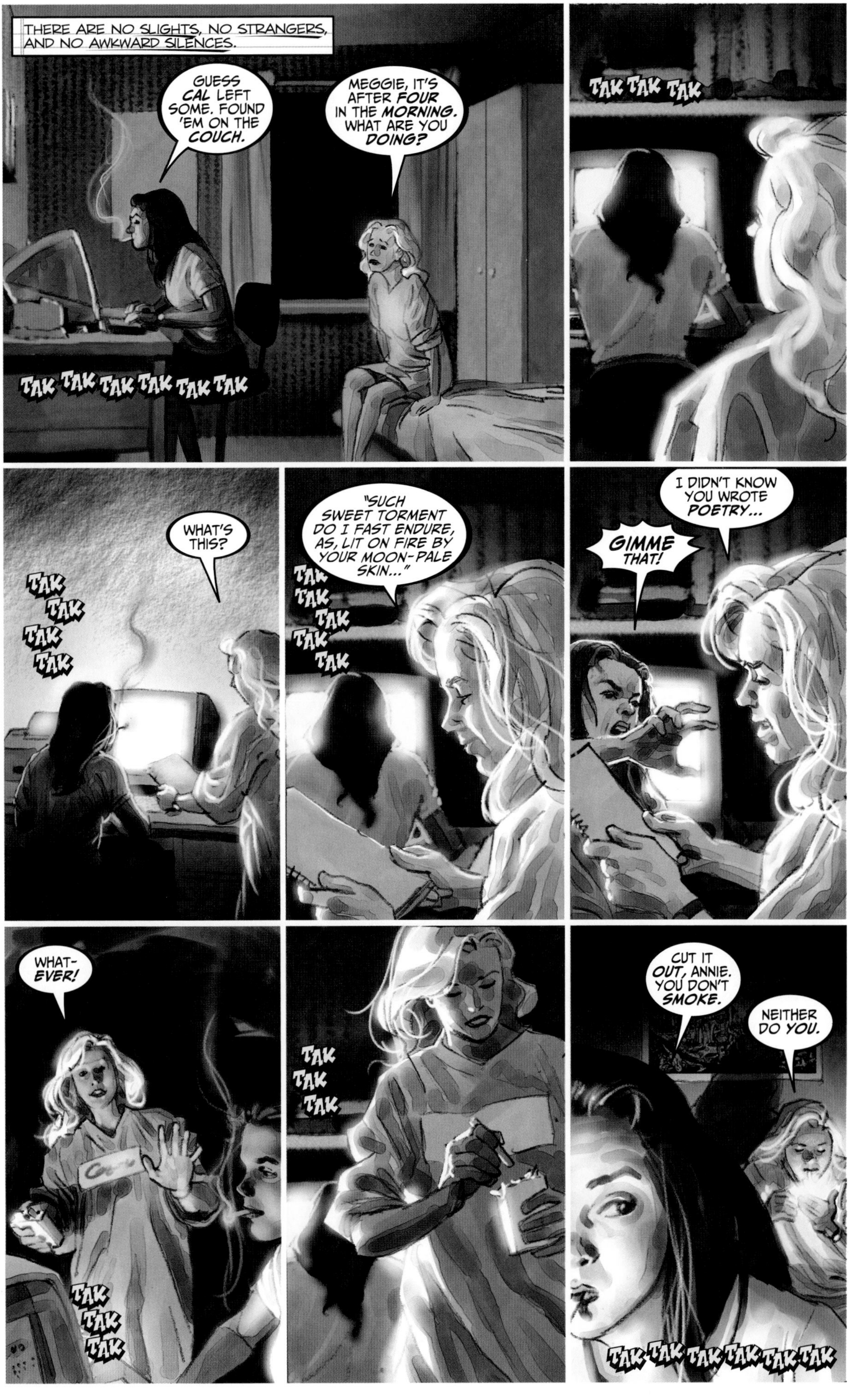
THERE ARE NO SLIGHTS, NO STRANGERS, AND NO AWKWARD SILENCES.
GUESS CAL LEFT SOME. FOUND 'EM ON THE COUCH.
MEGGIE, IT'S AFTER FOUR IN THE MORNING. WHAT ARE YOU DOING?
TAK TAK TAK TAK TAK TAK
TAK TAK TAK
WHAT'S THIS?
TAK TAK TAK TAK
"SUCH SWEET TORMENT DO I FAST ENDURE, AS, LIT ON FIRE BY YOUR MOON-PALE SKIN..."
TAK TAK TAK TAK TAK
I DIDN'T KNOW YOU WROTE POETRY...
GIMME THAT!
WHAT-EVER!
TAK TAK TAK
TAK TAK TAK
CUT IT OUT, ANNIE. YOU DON'T SMOKE.
NEITHER DO YOU.
TAK TAK TAK TAK TAK TAK

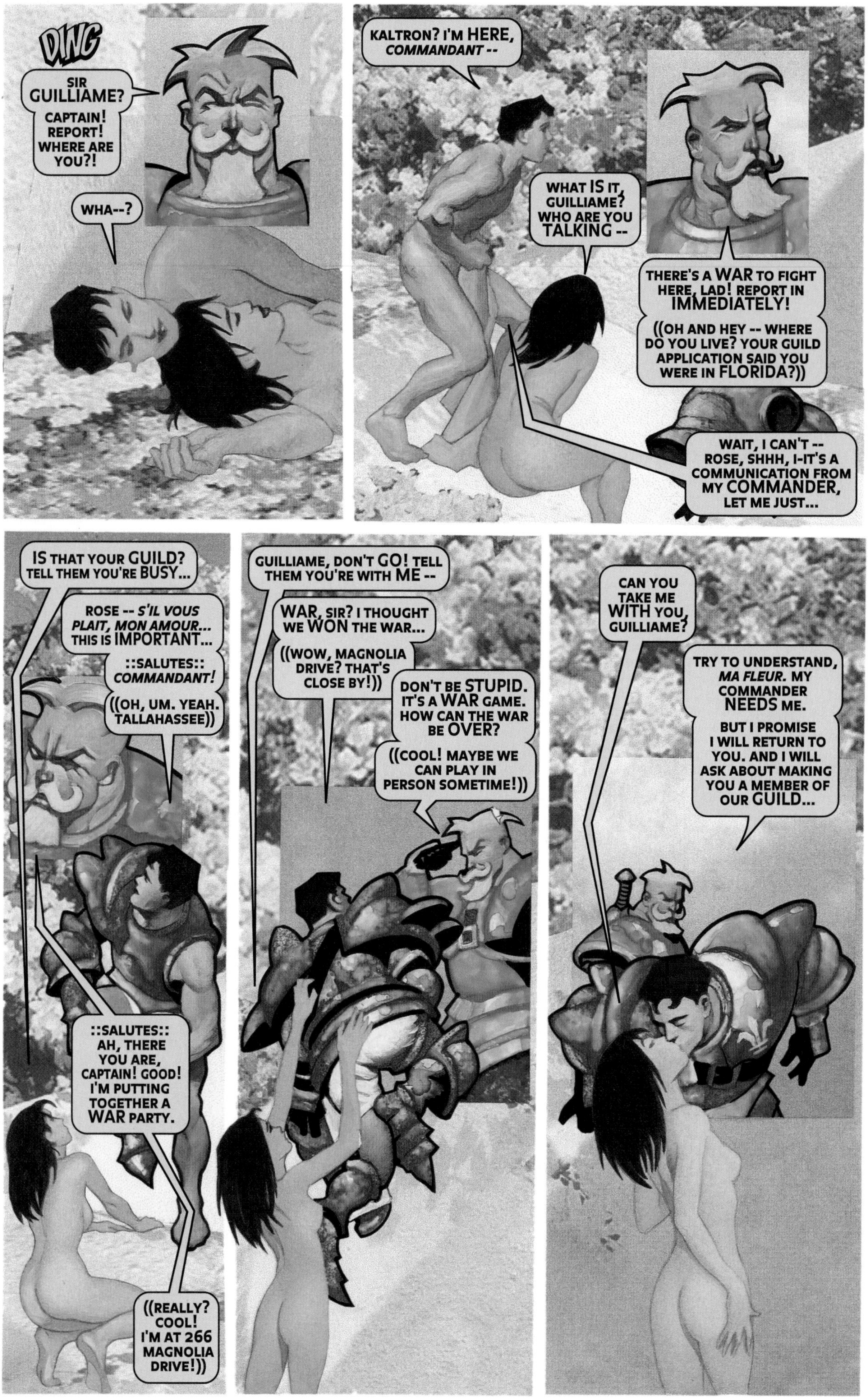
DING
SIR GUILLIAME? CAPTAIN! REPORT! WHERE ARE YOU?!
WHA--?
KALTRON? I'M HERE, COMMANDANT --
WHAT IS IT, GUILLIAME? WHO ARE YOU TALKING --
THERE'S A WAR TO FIGHT HERE, LAD! REPORT IN IMMEDIATELY!
((OH AND HEY -- WHERE DO YOU LIVE? YOUR GUILD APPLICATION SAID YOU WERE IN FLORIDA?))
WAIT, I CAN'T -- ROSE, SHHH, I-IT'S A COMMUNICATION FROM MY COMMANDER, LET ME JUST...
IS THAT YOUR GUILD? TELL THEM YOU'RE BUSY...
ROSE -- S'IL VOUS PLAIT, MON AMOUR... THIS IS IMPORTANT...
::SALUTES:: COMMANDANT!
((OH, UM. YEAH. TALLAHASSEE))
::SALUTES:: AH, THERE YOU ARE, CAPTAIN! GOOD! I'M PUTTING TOGETHER A WAR PARTY.
((REALLY? COOL! I'M AT 266 MAGNOLIA DRIVE!))
GUILLIAME, DON'T GO! TELL THEM YOU'RE WITH ME --
WAR, SIR? I THOUGHT WE WON THE WAR...
((WOW, MAGNOLIA DRIVE? THAT'S CLOSE BY!))
DON'T BE STUPID. IT'S A WAR GAME. HOW CAN THE WAR BE OVER?
((COOL! MAYBE WE CAN PLAY IN PERSON SOMETIME!))
CAN YOU TAKE ME WITH YOU, GUILLIAME?
TRY TO UNDERSTAND, MA FLEUR. MY COMMANDER NEEDS ME.
BUT I PROMISE I WILL RETURN TO YOU. AND I WILL ASK ABOUT MAKING YOU A MEMBER OF OUR GUILD...

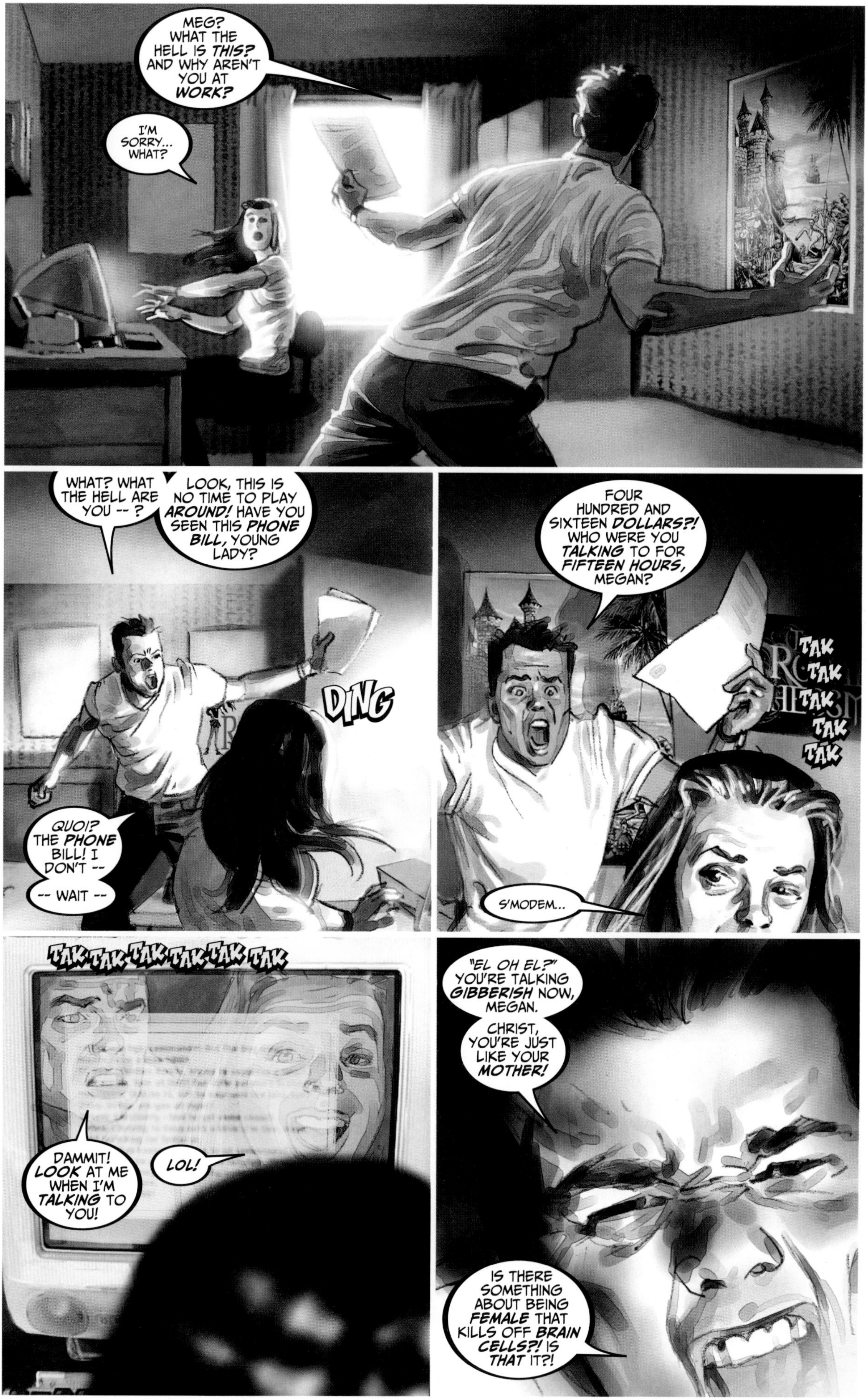
MEG? WHAT THE HELL IS THIS? AND WHY AREN'T YOU AT WORK?
I'M SORRY... WHAT?
WHAT? WHAT THE HELL ARE YOU -- ?
LOOK, THIS IS NO TIME TO PLAY AROUND! HAVE YOU SEEN THIS PHONE BILL, YOUNG LADY?
DING
QUOI? THE PHONE BILL! I DON'T --
-- WAIT --
FOUR HUNDRED AND SIXTEEN DOLLARS?! WHO WERE YOU TALKING TO FOR FIFTEEN HOURS, MEGAN?
TAK TAK TAK TAK TAK
S'MODEM...
TAK TAK TAK TAK TAK TAK
DAMMIT! LOOK AT ME WHEN I'M TALKING TO YOU!
LOL!
"EL OH EL?" YOU'RE TALKING GIBBERISH NOW, MEGAN.
CHRIST, YOU'RE JUST LIKE YOUR MOTHER!
IS THERE SOMETHING ABOUT BEING FEMALE THAT KILLS OFF BRAIN CELLS?! IS THAT IT?!

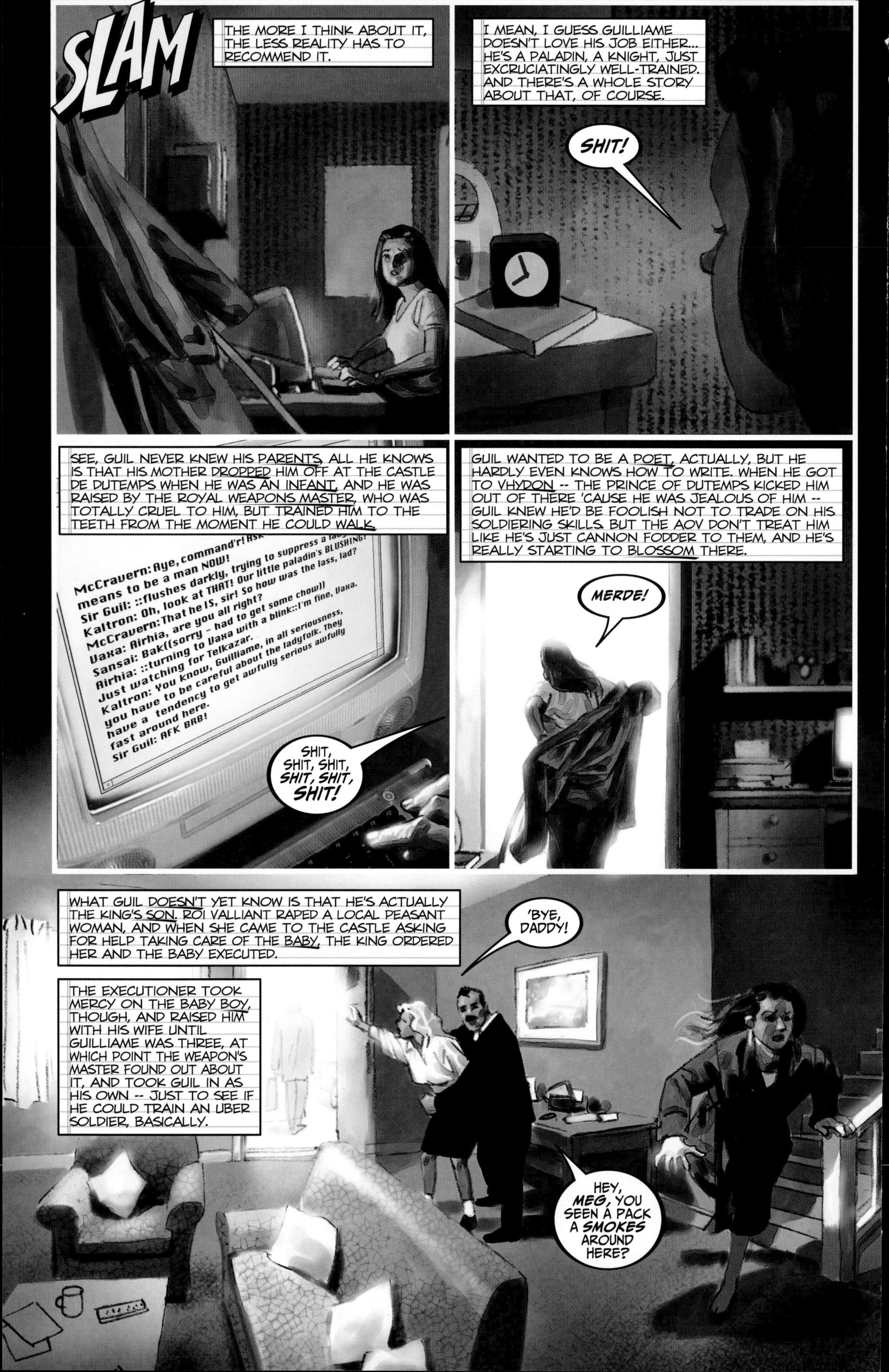
SLAM
THE MORE I THINK ABOUT IT, THE LESS REALITY HAS TO RECOMMEND IT.
I MEAN, I GUESS GUILLIAME DOESN'T LOVE HIS JOB EITHER... HE'S A PALADIN, A KNIGHT, JUST EXCRUCIATINGLY WELL-TRAINED. AND THERE'S A WHOLE STORY ABOUT THAT, OF COURSE.
SHIT!
SEE, GUIL NEVER KNEW HIS PARENTS, ALL HE KNOWS IS THAT HIS MOTHER DROPPED HIM OFF AT THE CASTLE DE DUTEMPS WHEN HE WAS AN INFANT, AND HE WAS RAISED BY THE ROYAL WEAPONS MASTER, WHO WAS TOTALLY CRUEL TO HIM, BUT TRAINED HIM TO THE TEETH FROM THE MOMENT HE COULD WALK.
McCravern: Aye, command'r!
means to be a man NOW!
Sir Guil: ::flushes darkly, trying to suppress a
Kaltron: Oh, look at THAT! Our little paladin's BLUSHING!
McCravern: That he IS, sir! So how was the lass, lad?
Vaxa: Airhia, are you all right?
Sansai: Bak((sorry - had to get some chow))
Airhia: ::turning to Vaxa with a blink:: I'm fine, Vaxa.
Just watching for Telkazar.
Kaltron: You know, Guilliame, in all seriousness, you have to be careful about the ladyfolk. They have a tendency to get awfully serious awfully fast around here.
Sir Guil: AFK BRB!
SHIT, SHIT, SHIT, SHIT, SHIT, SHIT!
GUIL WANTED TO BE A POET, ACTUALLY, BUT HE HARDLY EVEN KNOWS HOW TO WRITE. WHEN HE GOT TO VHYDON -- THE PRINCE OF DUTEMPS KICKED HIM OUT OF THERE 'CAUSE HE WAS JEALOUS OF HIM -- GUIL KNEW HE'D BE FOOLISH NOT TO TRADE ON HIS SOLDIERING SKILLS. BUT THE AOV DON'T TREAT HIM LIKE HE'S JUST CANNON FODDER TO THEM, AND HE'S REALLY STARTING TO BLOSSOM THERE.
MERDE!
WHAT GUIL DOESN'T YET KNOW IS THAT HE'S ACTUALLY THE KING'S SON. ROI VALLIANT RAPED A LOCAL PEASANT WOMAN, AND WHEN SHE CAME TO THE CASTLE ASKING FOR HELP TAKING CARE OF THE BABY, THE KING ORDERED HER AND THE BABY EXECUTED.
'BYE, DADDY!
THE EXECUTIONER TOOK MERCY ON THE BABY BOY, THOUGH, AND RAISED HIM WITH HIS WIFE UNTIL GUILLIAME WAS THREE, AT WHICH POINT THE WEAPON'S MASTER FOUND OUT ABOUT IT, AND TOOK GUIL IN AS HIS OWN -- JUST TO SEE IF HE COULD TRAIN AN UBER SOLDIER, BASICALLY.
HEY, MEG, YOU SEEN A PACK A SMOKES AROUND HERE?

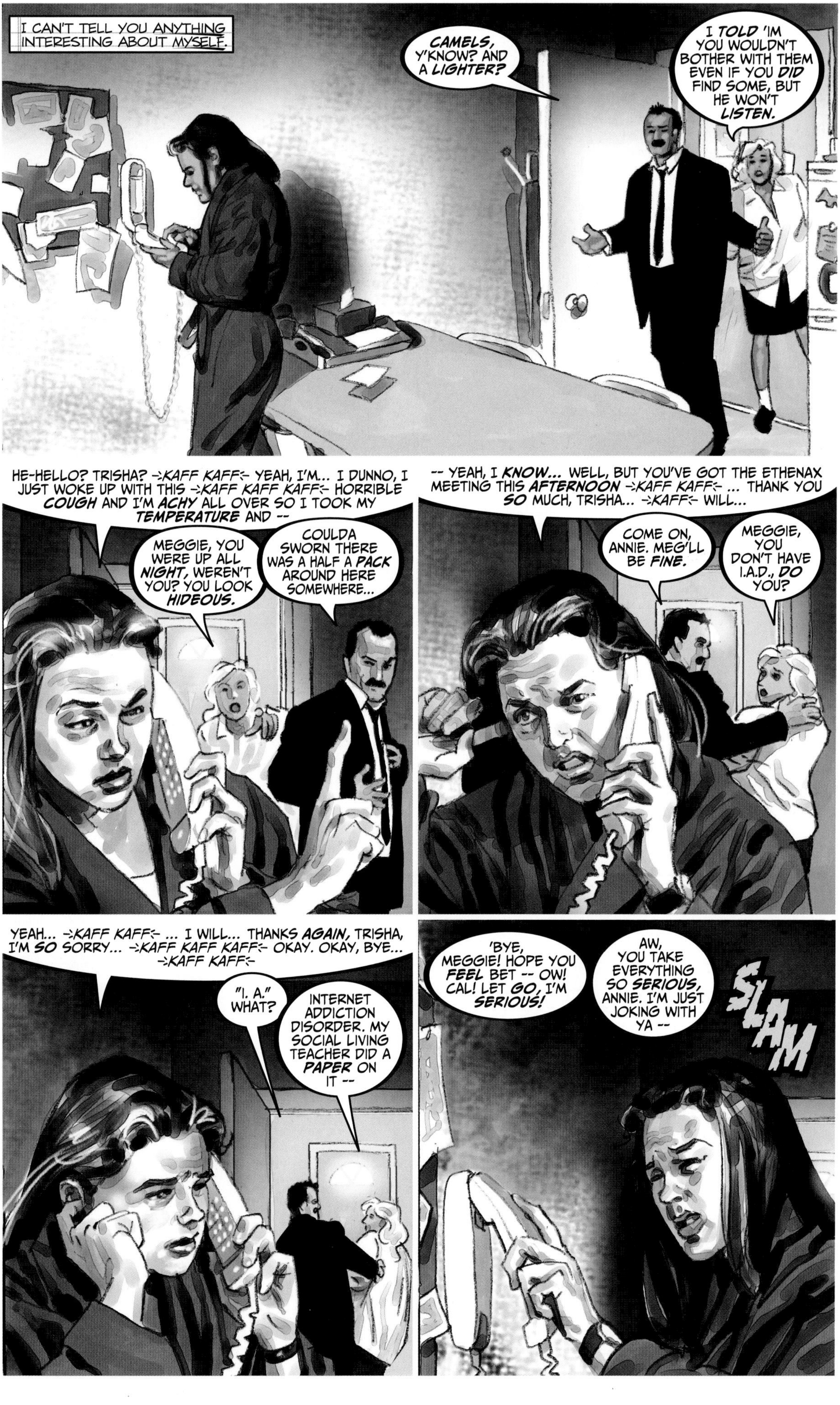
I CAN'T TELL YOU ANYTHING INTERESTING ABOUT MYSELF.
CAMELS, Y'KNOW? AND A LIGHTER?
I TOLD 'IM YOU WOULDN'T BOTHER WITH THEM EVEN IF YOU DID FIND SOME, BUT HE WON'T LISTEN.
HE-HELLO? TRISHA? -›KAFF KAFF‹- YEAH, I'M... I DUNNO, I JUST WOKE UP WITH THIS -›KAFF KAFF KAFF‹- HORRIBLE COUGH AND I'M ACHY ALL OVER SO I TOOK MY TEMPERATURE AND --
MEGGIE, YOU WERE UP ALL NIGHT, WEREN'T YOU? YOU LOOK HIDEOUS.
COULDA SWORN THERE WAS A HALF A PACK AROUND HERE SOMEWHERE...
-- YEAH, I KNOW... WELL, BUT YOU'VE GOT THE ETHENAX MEETING THIS AFTERNOON -›KAFF KAFF‹- ... THANK YOU SO MUCH, TRISHA... -›KAFF‹- WILL...
COME ON, ANNIE. MEG'LL BE FINE.
MEGGIE, YOU DON'T HAVE I.A.D., DO YOU?
YEAH... -›KAFF KAFF‹- ... I WILL... THANKS AGAIN, TRISHA, I'M SO SORRY... -›KAFF KAFF KAFF‹- OKAY. OKAY, BYE... -›KAFF KAFF‹-
"I. A." WHAT?
INTERNET ADDICTION DISORDER. MY SOCIAL LIVING TEACHER DID A PAPER ON IT --
'BYE, MEGGIE! HOPE YOU FEEL BET -- OW! CAL! LET GO, I'M SERIOUS!
AW, YOU TAKE EVERYTHING SO SERIOUS, ANNIE. I'M JUST JOKING WITH YA --
SLAM

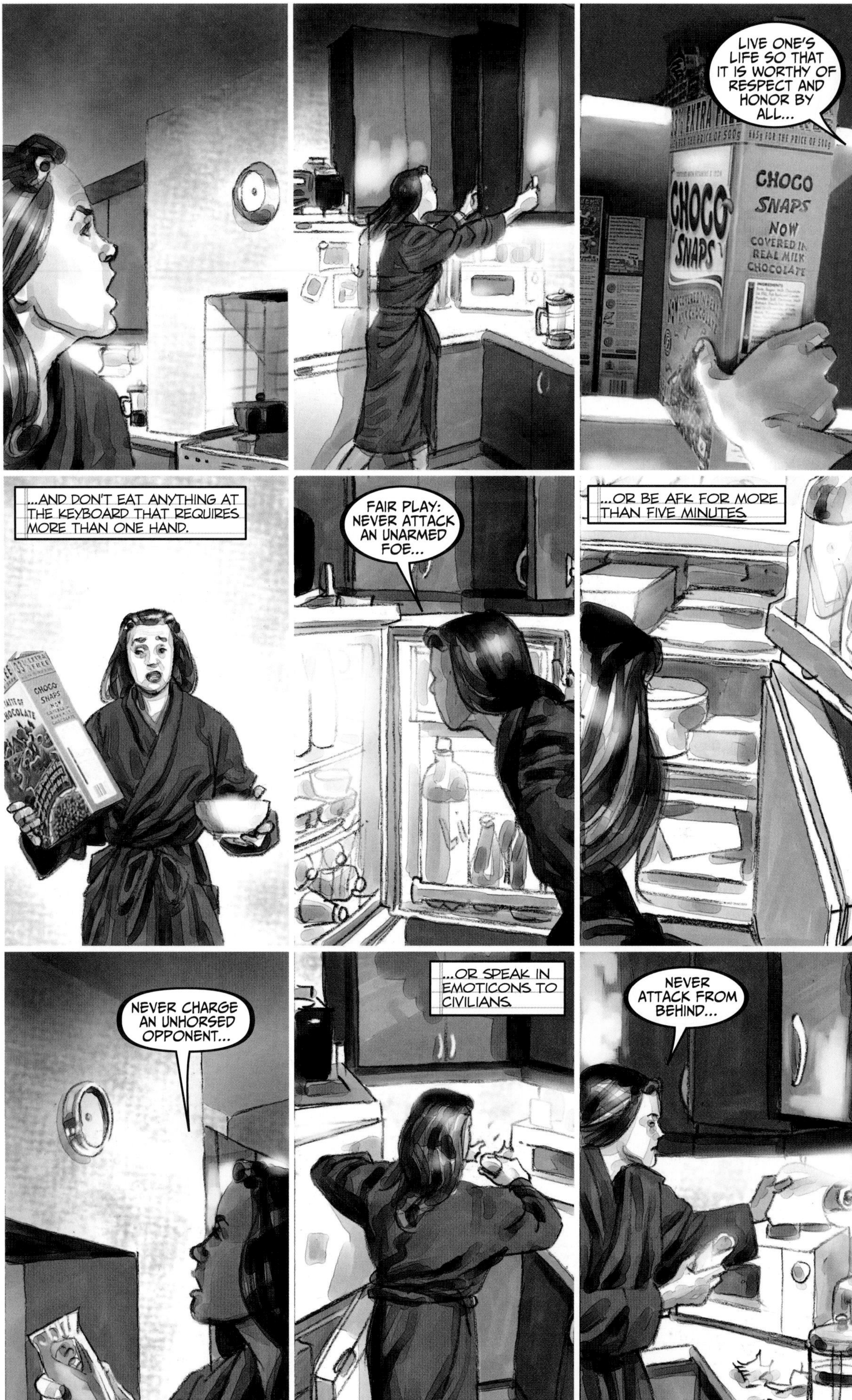
LIVE ONE'S LIFE SO THAT IT IS WORTHY OF RESPECT AND HONOR BY ALL...
CHOCO SNAPS
NOW COVERED IN REAL MILK CHOCOLATE
...AND DON'T EAT ANYTHING AT THE KEYBOARD THAT REQUIRES MORE THAN ONE HAND.
FAIR PLAY: NEVER ATTACK AN UNARMED FOE...
...OR BE AFK FOR MORE THAN FIVE MINUTES.
NEVER CHARGE AN UNHORSED OPPONENT...
...OR SPEAK IN EMOTICONS TO CIVILIANS.
NEVER ATTACK FROM BEHIND...

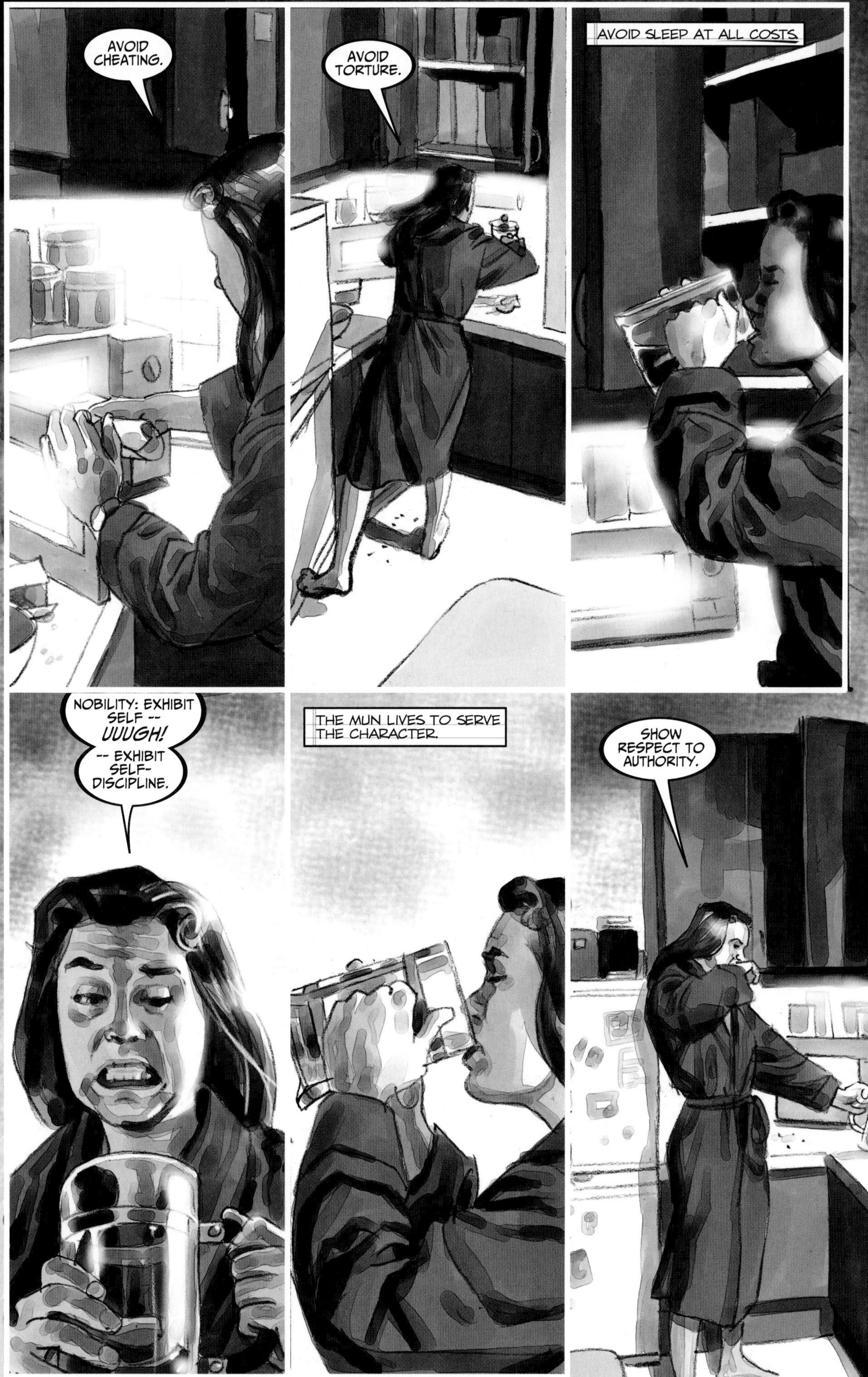
AVOID CHEATING.
AVOID TORTURE.
AVOID SLEEP AT ALL COSTS.
NOBILITY: EXHIBIT SELF -- UUUGH! -- EXHIBIT SELF-DISCIPLINE.
THE MUN LIVES TO SERVE THE CHARACTER.
SHOW RESPECT TO AUTHORITY.

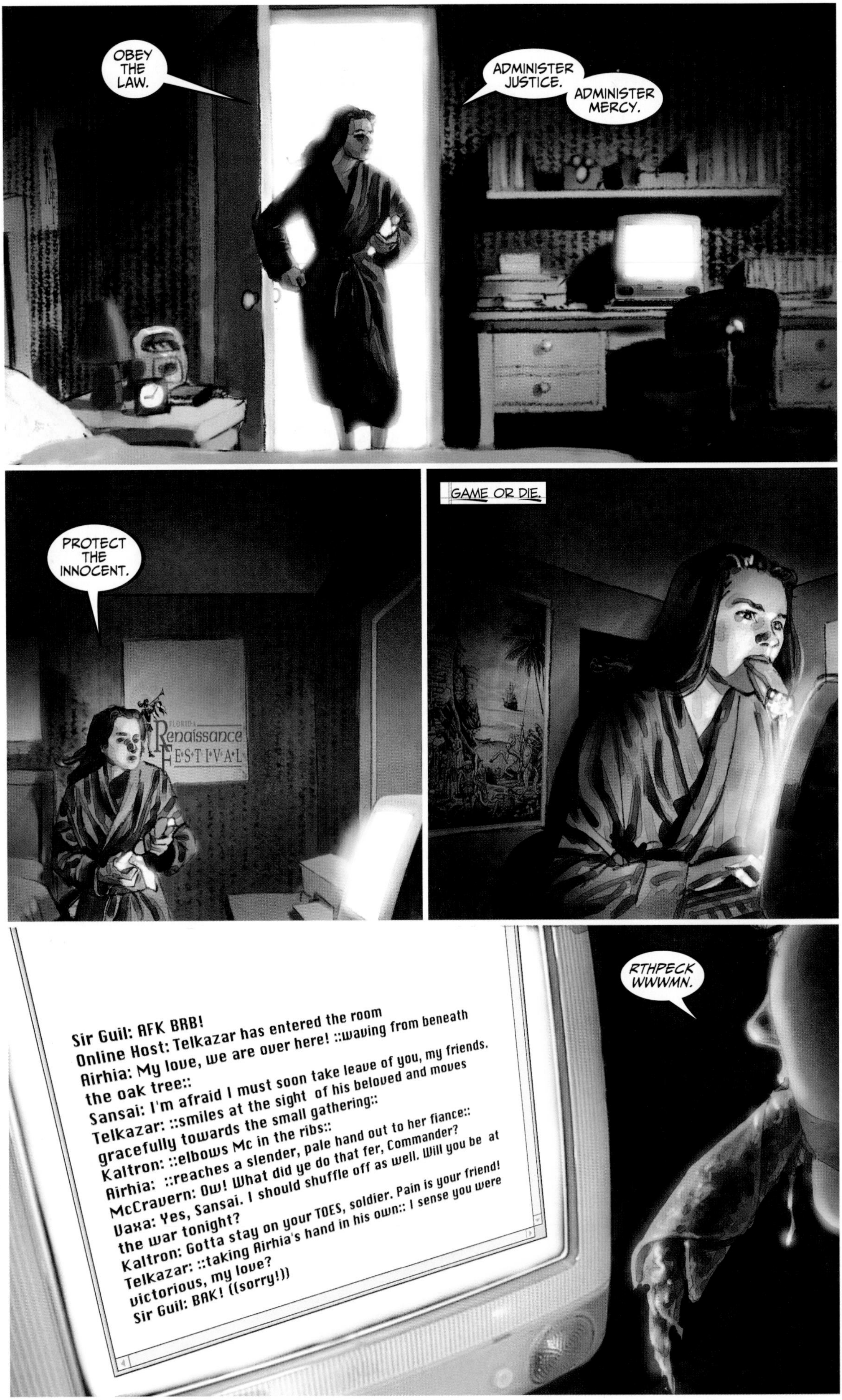
OBEY THE LAW.
ADMINISTER JUSTICE.
ADMINISTER MERCY.
PROTECT THE INNOCENT.
FLORIDA Renaissance FESTIVAL
GAME OR DIE.
Sir Guil: AFK BRB!
Online Host: Telkazar has entered the room
Airhia: My love, we are over here! ::waving from beneath the oak tree::
Sansai: I'm afraid I must soon take leave of you, my friends.
Telkazar: ::smiles at the sight of his beloved and moves gracefully towards the small gathering::
Kaltron: ::elbows Mc in the ribs::
Airhia: ::reaches a slender, pale hand out to her fiance::
McCravern: Ow! What did ye do that fer, Commander?
Vaxa: Yes, Sansai. I should shuffle off as well. Will you be at the war tonight?
Kaltron: Gotta stay on your TOES, soldier. Pain is your friend!
Telkazar: ::taking Airhia's hand in his own:: I sense you were victorious, my love?
Sir Guil: BAK! ((sorry!))
RTHPECK WWWMN.

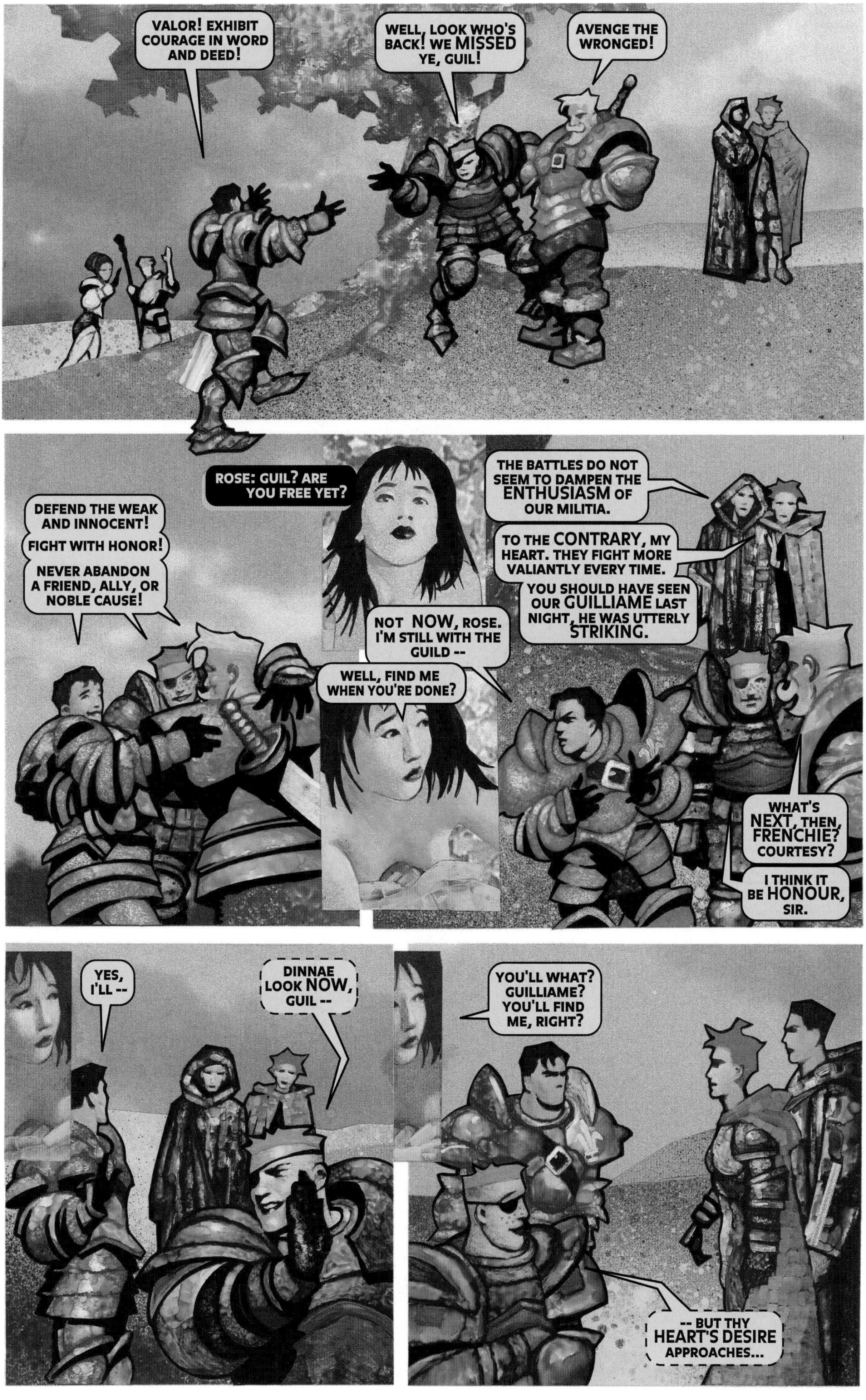
VALOR! EXHIBIT COURAGE IN WORD AND DEED!
WELL, LOOK WHO'S BACK! WE MISSED YE, GUIL!
AVENGE THE WRONGED!
DEFEND THE WEAK AND INNOCENT!
FIGHT WITH HONOR!
NEVER ABANDON A FRIEND, ALLY, OR NOBLE CAUSE!
ROSE: GUIL? ARE YOU FREE YET?
NOT NOW, ROSE. I'M STILL WITH THE GUILD --
WELL, FIND ME WHEN YOU'RE DONE?
THE BATTLES DO NOT SEEM TO DAMPEN THE ENTHUSIASM OF OUR MILITIA.
TO THE CONTRARY, MY HEART. THEY FIGHT MORE VALIANTLY EVERY TIME.
YOU SHOULD HAVE SEEN OUR GUILLIAME LAST NIGHT, HE WAS UTTERLY STRIKING.
WHAT'S NEXT, THEN, FRENCHIE? COURTESY?
I THINK IT BE HONOUR, SIR.
YES, I'LL --
DINNAE LOOK NOW, GUIL --
YOU'LL WHAT? GUILLIAME? YOU'LL FIND ME, RIGHT?
-- BUT THY HEART'S DESIRE APPROACHES...

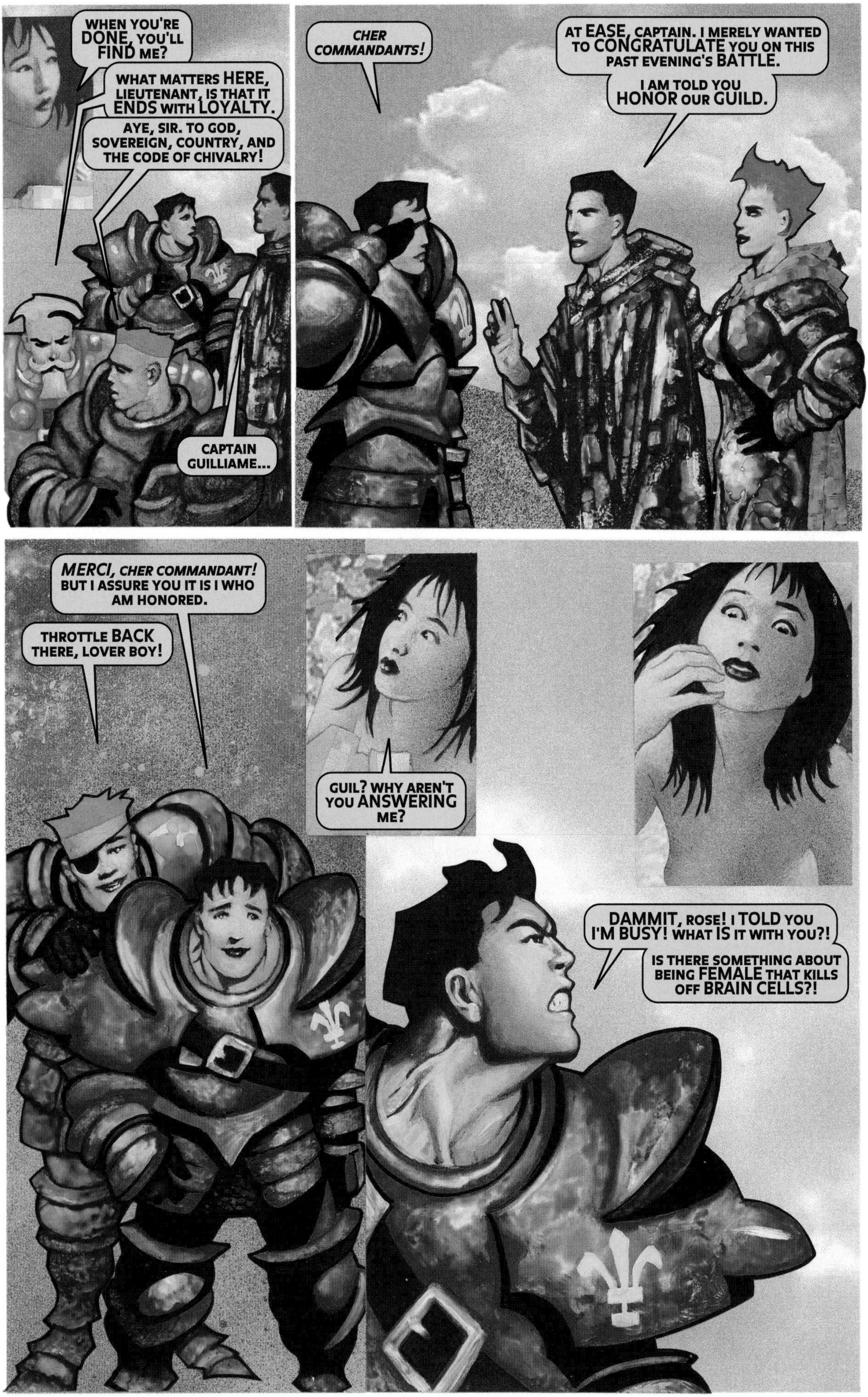
WHEN YOU'RE DONE, YOU'LL FIND ME?
WHAT MATTERS HERE, LIEUTENANT, IS THAT IT ENDS WITH LOYALTY.
AYE, SIR. TO GOD, SOVEREIGN, COUNTRY, AND THE CODE OF CHIVALRY!
CAPTAIN GUILLIAME...
CHER COMMANDANTS!
AT EASE, CAPTAIN. I MERELY WANTED TO CONGRATULATE YOU ON THIS PAST EVENING'S BATTLE.
I AM TOLD YOU HONOR OUR GUILD.
MERCI, CHER COMMANDANT! BUT I ASSURE YOU IT IS I WHO AM HONORED.
THROTTLE BACK THERE, LOVER BOY!
GUIL? WHY AREN'T YOU ANSWERING ME?
DAMMIT, ROSE! I TOLD YOU I'M BUSY! WHAT IS IT WITH YOU?!
IS THERE SOMETHING ABOUT BEING FEMALE THAT KILLS OFF BRAIN CELLS?!

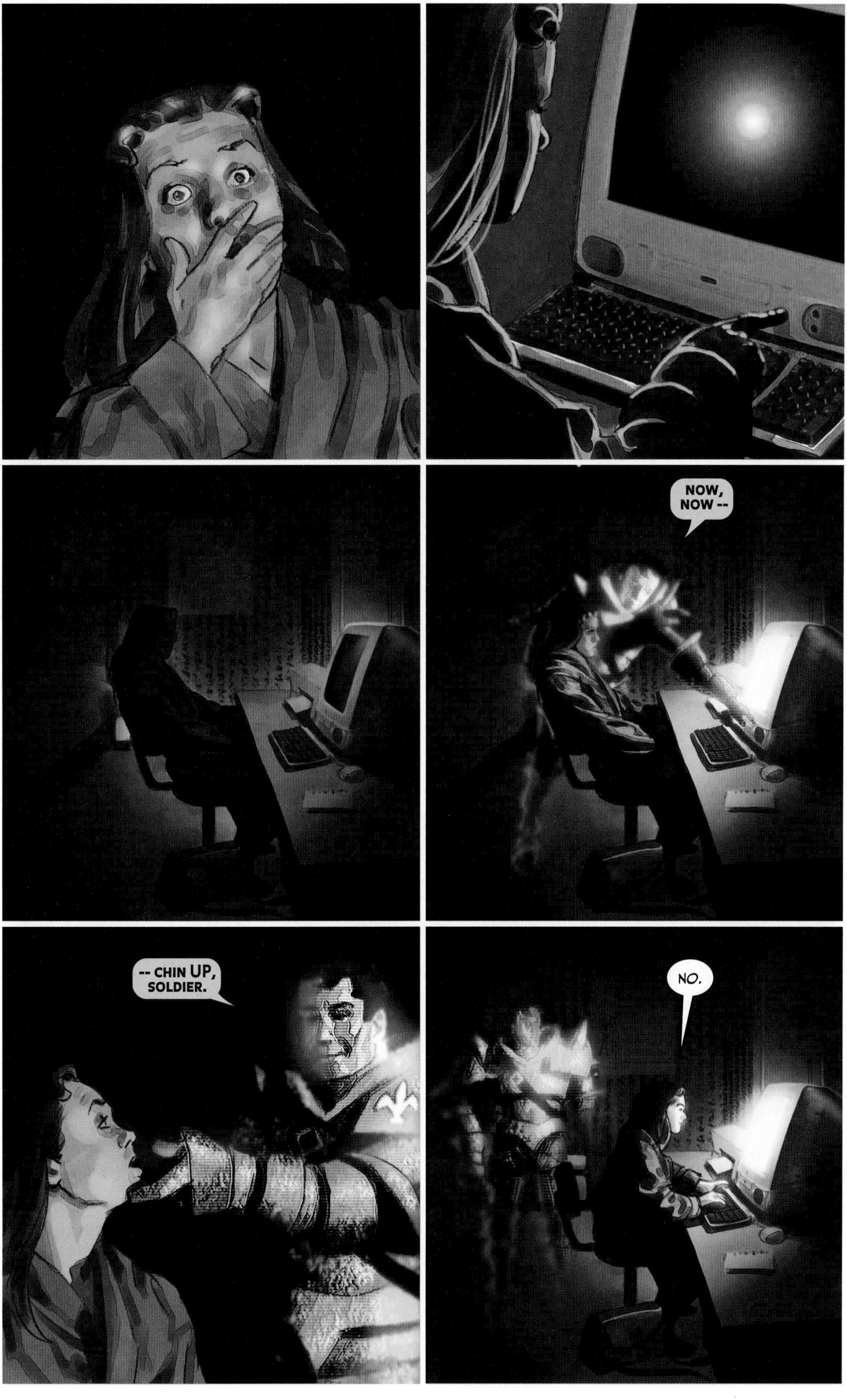
NOW, NOW --
-- CHIN UP, SOLDIER.
NO.

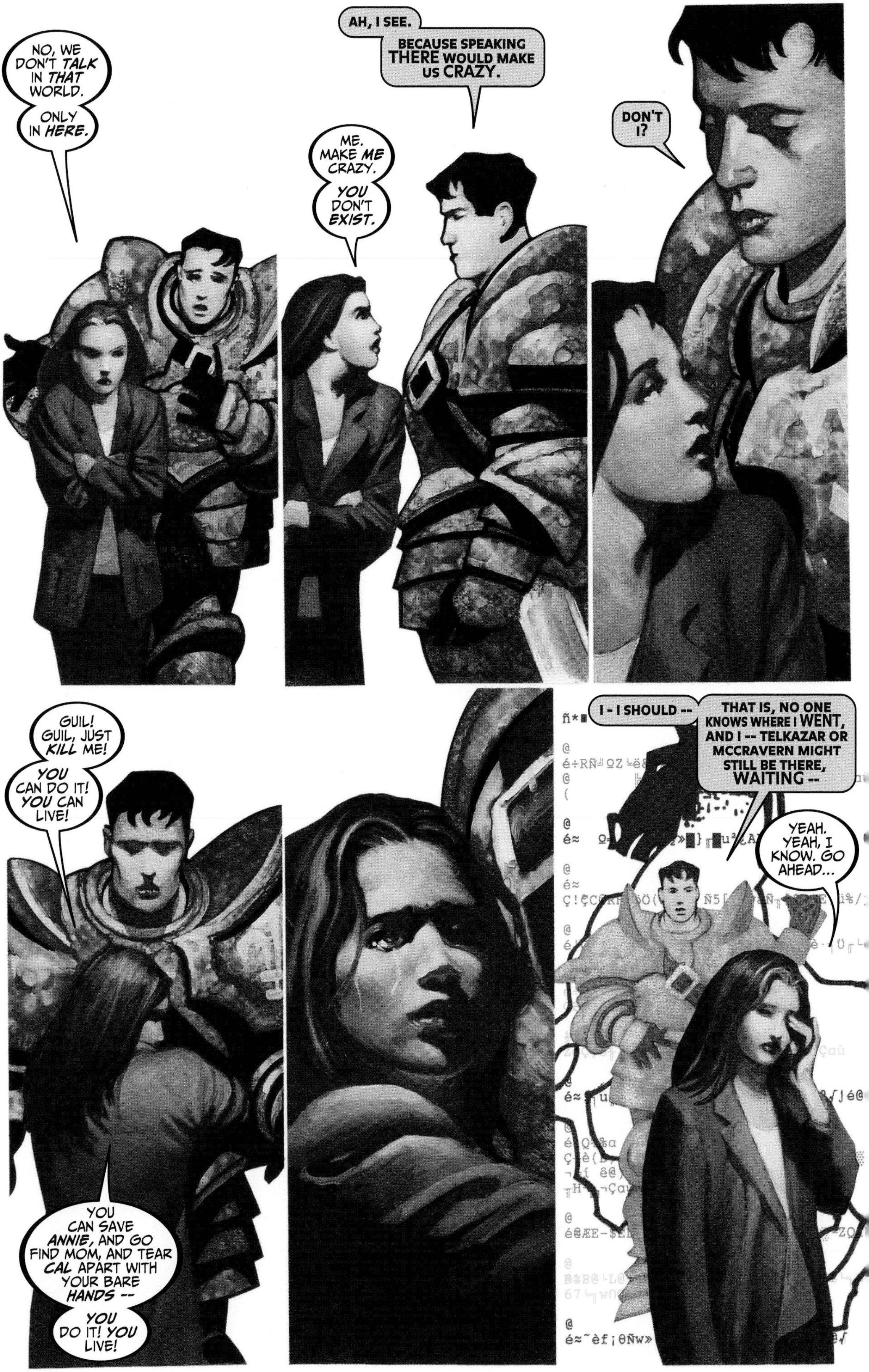
NO, WE DON'T TALK IN THAT WORLD.
ONLY IN HERE.
AH, I SEE.
BECAUSE SPEAKING THERE WOULD MAKE US CRAZY.
ME. MAKE ME CRAZY.
YOU DON'T EXIST.
DON'T I?
GUIL! GUIL, JUST KILL ME!
YOU CAN DO IT! YOU CAN LIVE!
YOU CAN SAVE ANNIE, AND GO FIND MOM, AND TEAR CAL APART WITH YOUR BARE HANDS --
YOU DO IT! YOU LIVE!
I - I SHOULD --
THAT IS, NO ONE KNOWS WHERE I WENT, AND I -- TELKAZAR OR MCCRAVERN MIGHT STILL BE THERE, WAITING --
YEAH. YEAH, I KNOW. GO AHEAD...

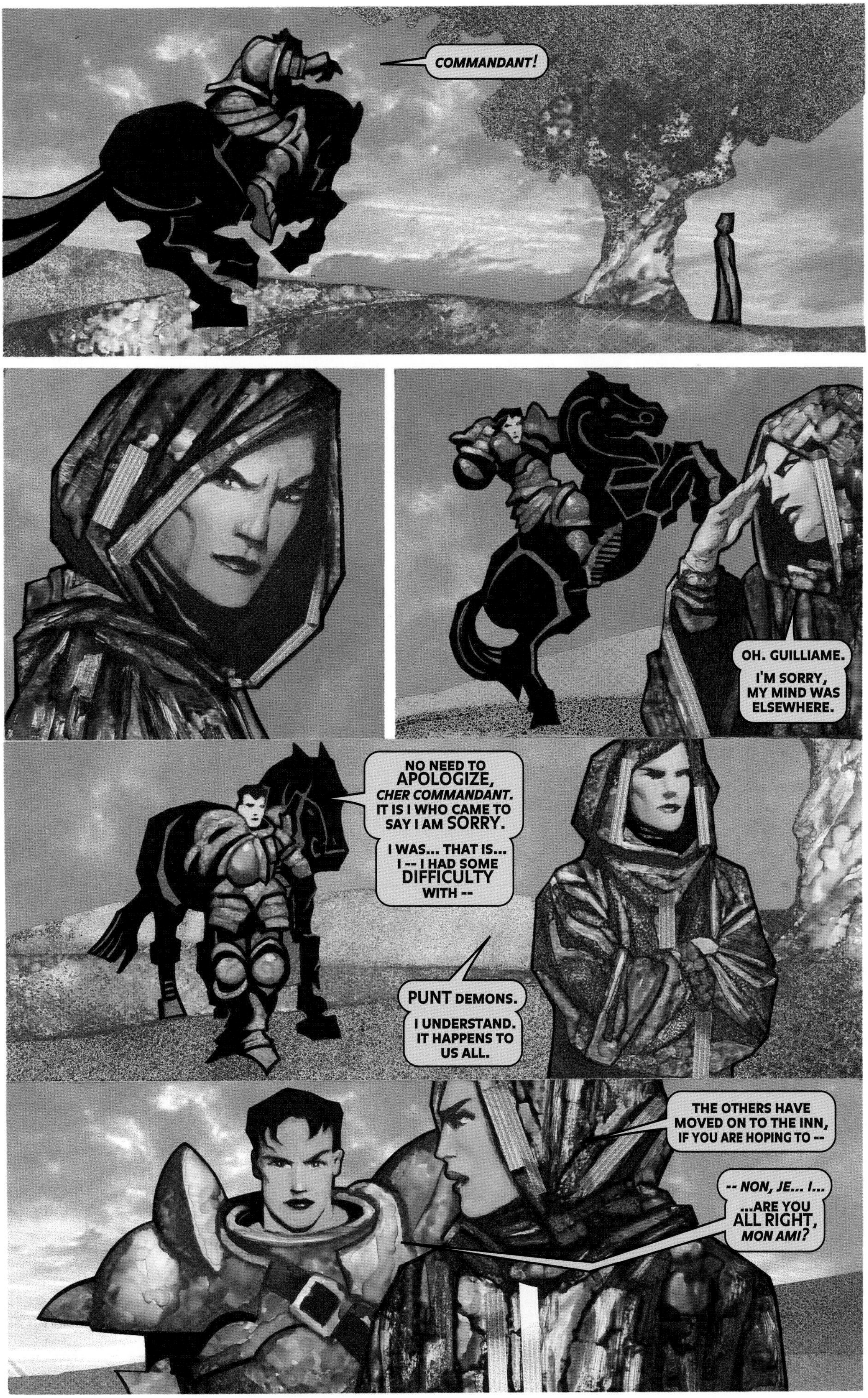
COMMANDANT!
OH. GUILLIAME.
I'M SORRY, MY MIND WAS ELSEWHERE.
NO NEED TO APOLOGIZE, CHER COMMANDANT. IT IS I WHO CAME TO SAY I AM SORRY.
I WAS... THAT IS... I -- I HAD SOME DIFFICULTY WITH --
PUNT DEMONS.
I UNDERSTAND. IT HAPPENS TO US ALL.
THE OTHERS HAVE MOVED ON TO THE INN, IF YOU ARE HOPING TO --
-- NON, JE... I...
...ARE YOU ALL RIGHT, MON AMI?

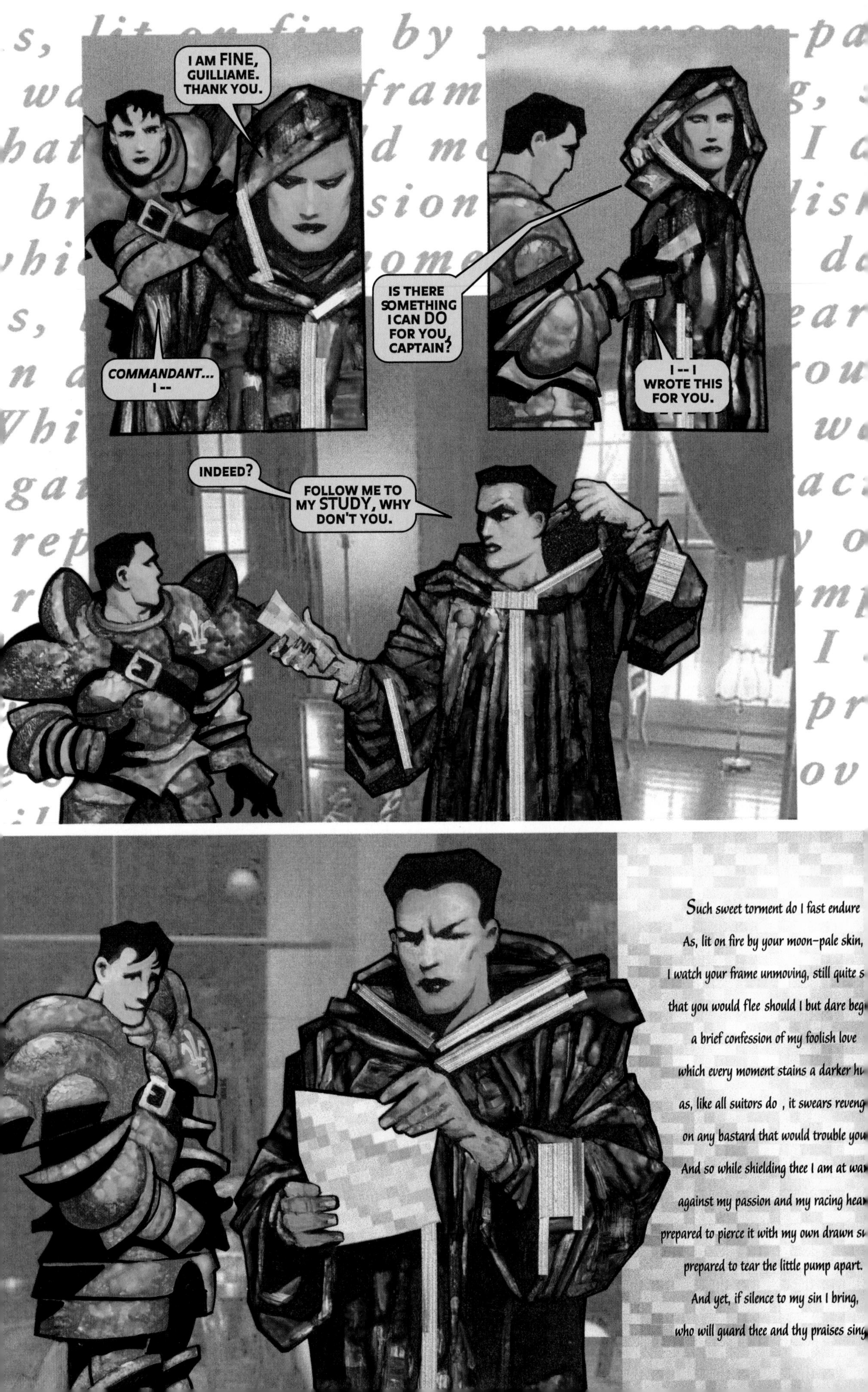
I AM FINE, GUILLIAME. THANK YOU.
COMMANDANT... I --
IS THERE SOMETHING I CAN DO FOR YOU, CAPTAIN?
I -- I WROTE THIS FOR YOU.
INDEED?
FOLLOW ME TO MY STUDY, WHY DON'T YOU.
Such sweet torment do I fast endure
As, lit on fire by your moon-pale skin,
I watch your frame unmoving, still quite s
that you would flee should I but dare beg
a brief confession of my foolish love
which every moment stains a darker h
as, like all suitors do , it swears reveng
on any bastard that would trouble you
And so while shielding thee I am at wa
against my passion and my racing hea
prepared to pierce it with my own drawn s
prepared to tear the little pump apart.
And yet, if silence to my sin I bring,
who will guard thee and thy praises sing

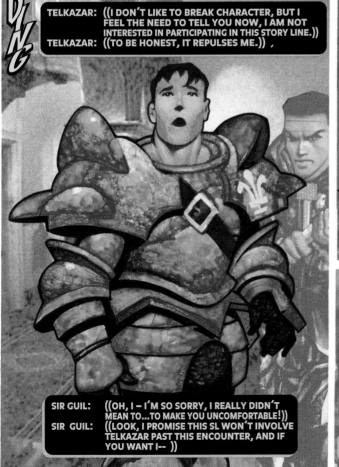

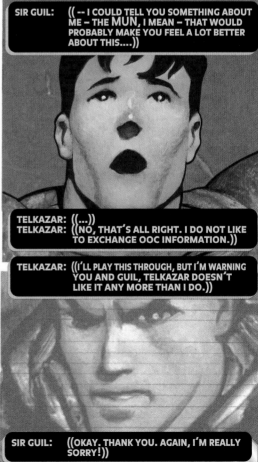

TELKAZAR: ((I DON'T LIKE TO BREAK CHARACTER, BUT I FEEL THE NEED TO TELL YOU NOW, I AM NOT INTERESTED IN PARTICIPATING IN THIS STORY LINE.))
TELKAZAR: ((TO BE HONEST, IT REPULSES ME.))

SIR GUIL: ((-- I COULD TELL YOU SOMETHING ABOUT ME – THE MUN, I MEAN – THAT WOULD PROBABLY MAKE YOU FEEL A LOT BETTER ABOUT THIS....))

TELKAZAR: ((...))
TELKAZAR: ((NO, THAT'S ALL RIGHT. I DO NOT LIKE TO EXCHANGE OOC INFORMATION.))

TELKAZAR: ((I'LL PLAY THIS THROUGH, BUT I'M WARNING YOU AND GUIL, TELKAZAR DOESN'T LIKE IT ANY MORE THAN I DO.))

SIR GUIL: ((OH, I – I'M SO SORRY, I REALLY DIDN'T MEAN TO...TO MAKE YOU UNCOMFORTABLE!))
SIR GUIL: ((LOOK, I PROMISE THIS SL WON'T INVOLVE TELKAZAR PAST THIS ENCOUNTER, AND IF YOU WANT I--))

SIR GUIL: ((OKAY. THANK YOU. AGAIN, I'M REALLY SORRY!))

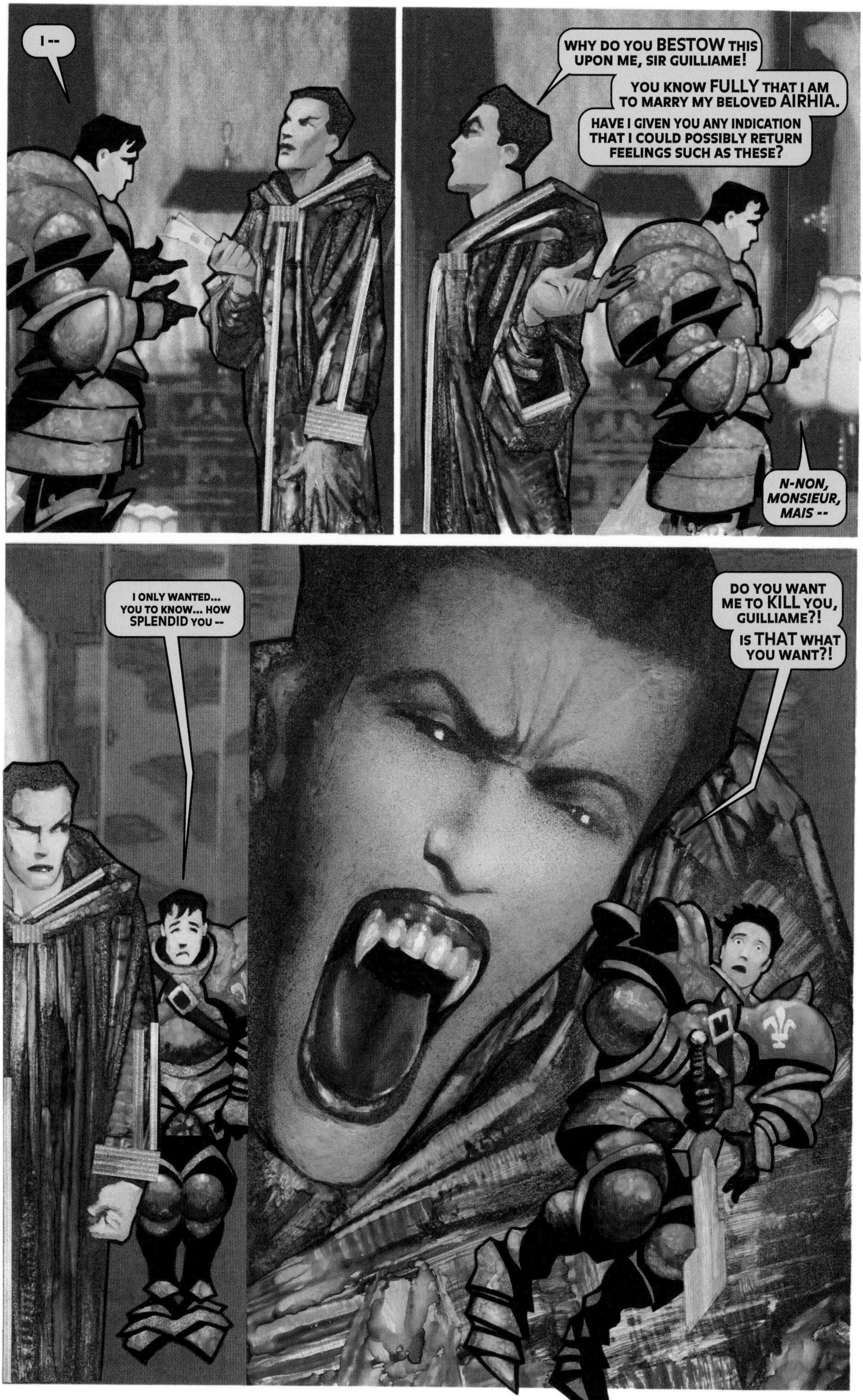
I --
WHY DO YOU BESTOW THIS UPON ME, SIR GUILLIAME!
YOU KNOW FULLY THAT I AM TO MARRY MY BELOVED AIRHIA.
HAVE I GIVEN YOU ANY INDICATION THAT I COULD POSSIBLY RETURN FEELINGS SUCH AS THESE?
N-NON, MONSIEUR, MAIS --
I ONLY WANTED... YOU TO KNOW... HOW SPLENDID YOU --
DO YOU WANT ME TO KILL YOU, GUILLIAME?!
IS THAT WHAT YOU WANT?!

KLANK

OUI, OUI -- JUST --

NON. NO, I DO NOT WISH FOR YOU TO KILL ME, *COMMANDANT.*

GOOD.

YOU'RE A VALUABLE MEMBER OF OUR MILITIA, GUILLIAME.

AND YOU ARE ALSO, I THINK, QUITE YOUNG, ARE YOU NOT?

OUI, COMMAN -- ER, YES, SIR. I AM NINETEEN.

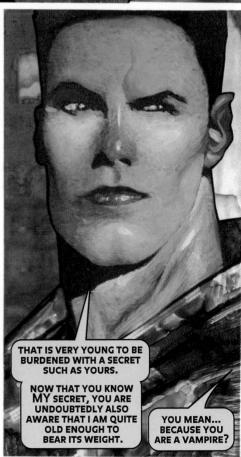

THAT IS VERY YOUNG TO BE BURDENED WITH A SECRET SUCH AS YOURS.

NOW THAT YOU KNOW MY SECRET, YOU ARE UNDOUBTEDLY ALSO AWARE THAT I AM QUITE OLD ENOUGH TO BEAR ITS WEIGHT.

YOU MEAN... BECAUSE YOU ARE A VAMPIRE?

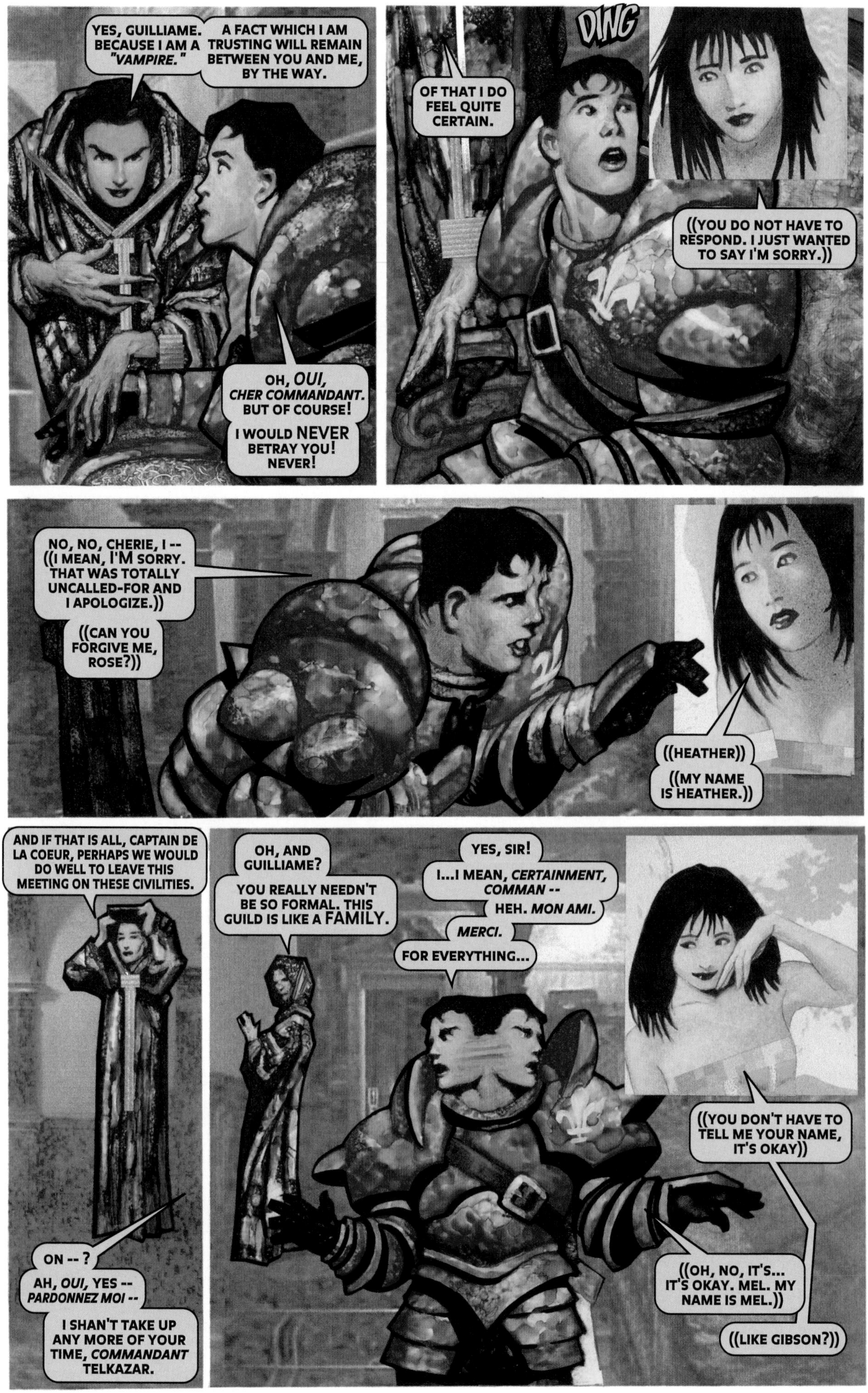
YES, GUILLIAME. BECAUSE I AM A "VAMPIRE."
A FACT WHICH I AM TRUSTING WILL REMAIN BETWEEN YOU AND ME, BY THE WAY.
OH, OUI, CHER COMMANDANT. BUT OF COURSE!
I WOULD NEVER BETRAY YOU! NEVER!
OF THAT I DO FEEL QUITE CERTAIN.
DING
((YOU DO NOT HAVE TO RESPOND. I JUST WANTED TO SAY I'M SORRY.))
NO, NO, CHERIE, I -- ((I MEAN, I'M SORRY. THAT WAS TOTALLY UNCALLED-FOR AND I APOLOGIZE.))
((CAN YOU FORGIVE ME, ROSE?))
((HEATHER))
((MY NAME IS HEATHER.))
AND IF THAT IS ALL, CAPTAIN DE LA COEUR, PERHAPS WE WOULD DO WELL TO LEAVE THIS MEETING ON THESE CIVILITIES.
ON -- ?
AH, OUI, YES -- PARDONNEZ MOI --
I SHAN'T TAKE UP ANY MORE OF YOUR TIME, COMMANDANT TELKAZAR.
OH, AND GUILLIAME?
YOU REALLY NEEDN'T BE SO FORMAL. THIS GUILD IS LIKE A FAMILY.
YES, SIR!
I...I MEAN, CERTAINMENT, COMMAN --
HEH. MON AMI.
MERCI.
FOR EVERYTHING...
((YOU DON'T HAVE TO TELL ME YOUR NAME, IT'S OKAY))
((OH, NO, IT'S... IT'S OKAY. MEL. MY NAME IS MEL.))
((LIKE GIBSON?))

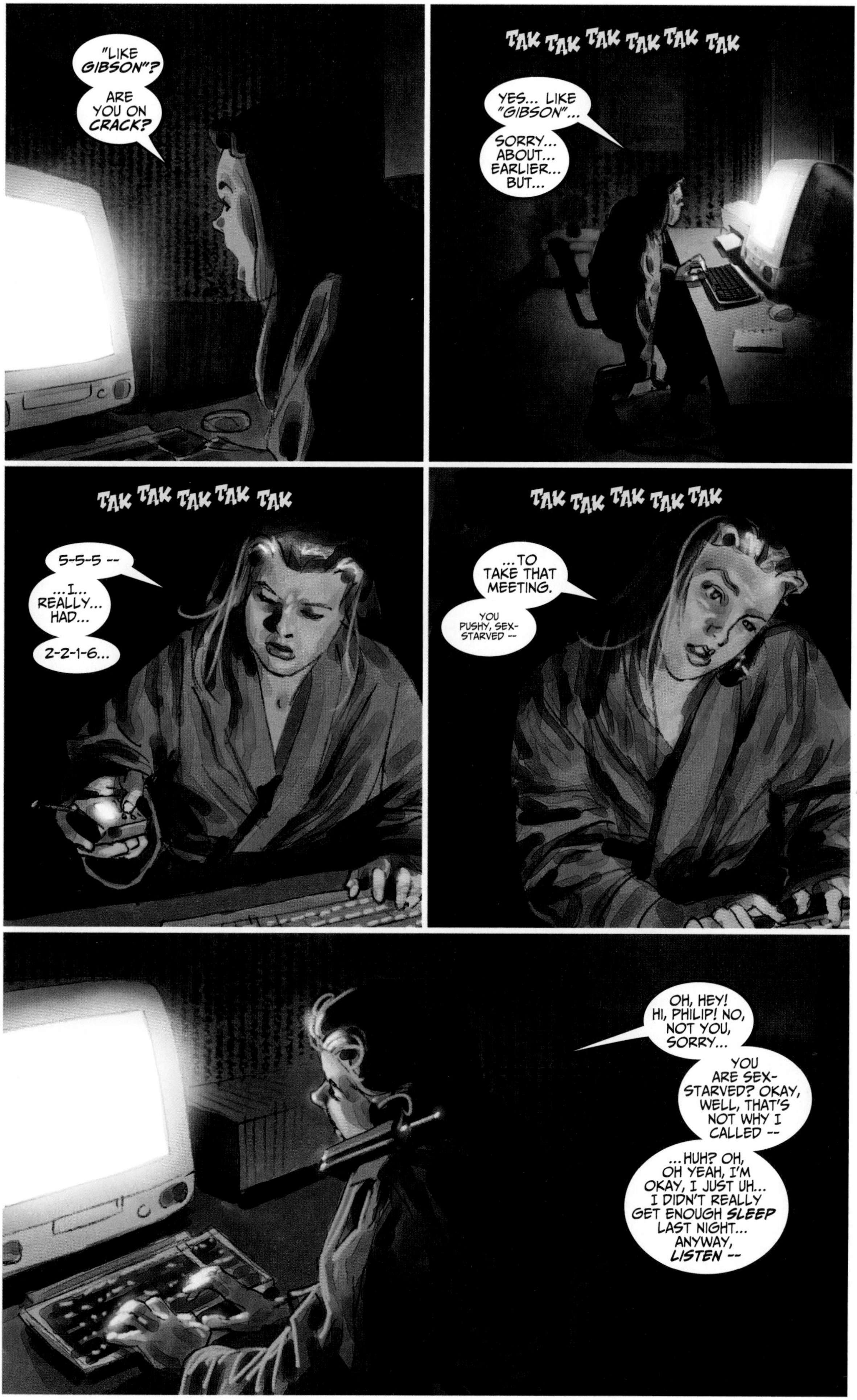
"LIKE GIBSON"?
ARE YOU ON CRACK?
TAK TAK TAK TAK TAK TAK
YES... LIKE "GIBSON"...
SORRY... ABOUT... EARLIER... BUT...
TAK TAK TAK TAK TAK
5-5-5 --
...I... REALLY... HAD...
2-2-1-6...
TAK TAK TAK TAK TAK
...TO TAKE THAT MEETING.
YOU PUSHY, SEX-STARVED --
OH, HEY! HI, PHILIP! NO, NOT YOU, SORRY...
YOU ARE SEX-STARVED? OKAY, WELL, THAT'S NOT WHY I CALLED --
...HUH? OH, OH YEAH, I'M OKAY, I JUST UH... I DIDN'T REALLY GET ENOUGH SLEEP LAST NIGHT... ANYWAY, LISTEN --

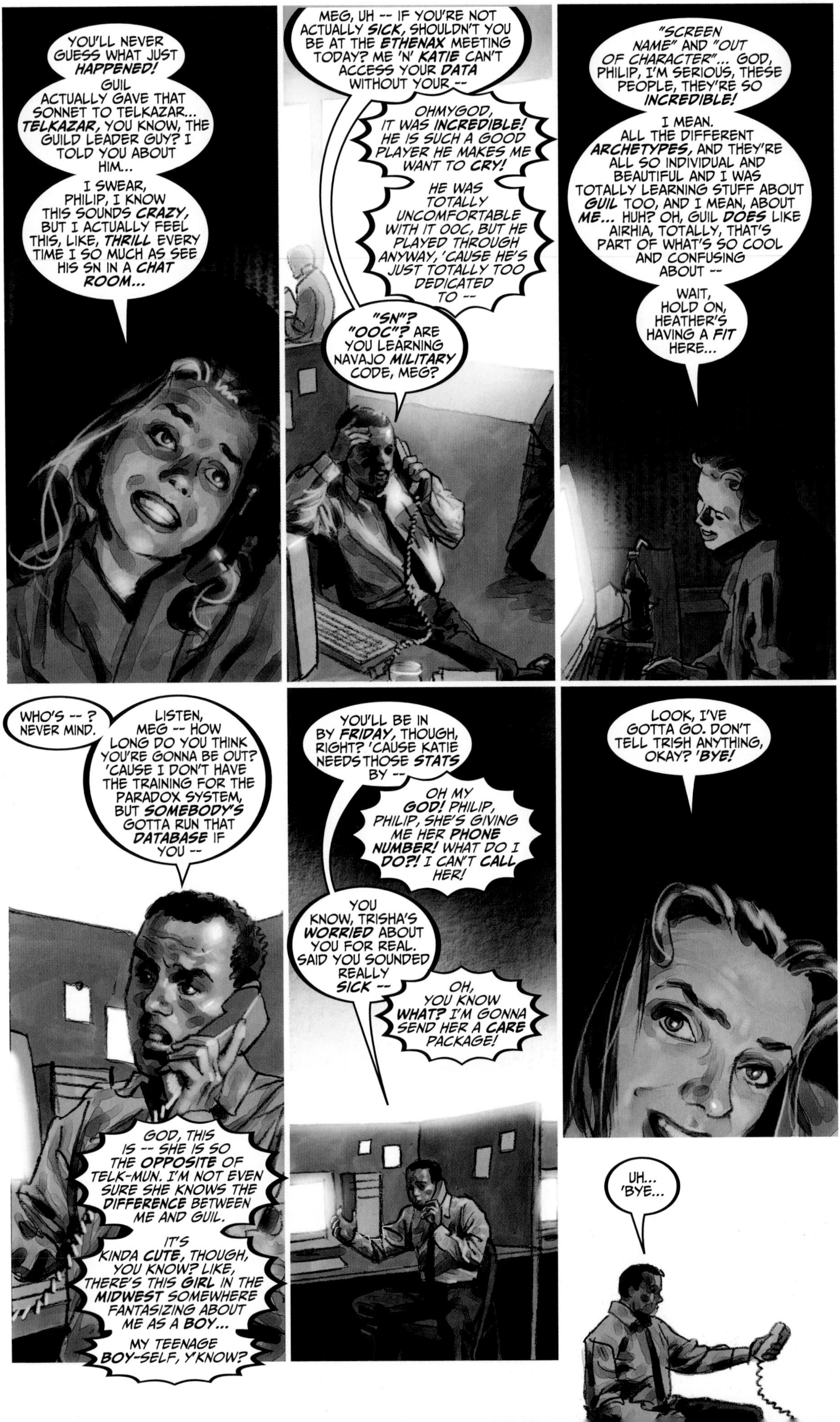
YOU'LL NEVER GUESS WHAT JUST HAPPENED!
GUIL ACTUALLY GAVE THAT SONNET TO TELKAZAR... TELKAZAR, YOU KNOW, THE GUILD LEADER GUY? I TOLD YOU ABOUT HIM...
I SWEAR, PHILIP, I KNOW THIS SOUNDS CRAZY, BUT I ACTUALLY FEEL THIS, LIKE, THRILL EVERY TIME I SO MUCH AS SEE HIS SN IN A CHAT ROOM...
MEG, UH -- IF YOU'RE NOT ACTUALLY SICK, SHOULDN'T YOU BE AT THE ETHENAX MEETING TODAY? ME 'N' KATIE CAN'T ACCESS YOUR DATA WITHOUT YOUR --
OHMYGOD, IT WAS INCREDIBLE! HE IS SUCH A GOOD PLAYER HE MAKES ME WANT TO CRY!
HE WAS TOTALLY UNCOMFORTABLE WITH IT OOC, BUT HE PLAYED THROUGH ANYWAY, 'CAUSE HE'S JUST TOTALLY TOO DEDICATED TO --
"SN"? "OOC"? ARE YOU LEARNING NAVAJO MILITARY CODE, MEG?
"SCREEN NAME" AND "OUT OF CHARACTER"... GOD, PHILIP, I'M SERIOUS, THESE PEOPLE, THEY'RE SO INCREDIBLE!
I MEAN. ALL THE DIFFERENT ARCHETYPES, AND THEY'RE ALL SO INDIVIDUAL AND BEAUTIFUL AND I WAS TOTALLY LEARNING STUFF ABOUT GUIL TOO, AND I MEAN, ABOUT ME... HUH? OH, GUIL DOES LIKE AIRHIA, TOTALLY, THAT'S PART OF WHAT'S SO COOL AND CONFUSING ABOUT --
WAIT, HOLD ON, HEATHER'S HAVING A FIT HERE...
WHO'S -- ? NEVER MIND.
LISTEN, MEG -- HOW LONG DO YOU THINK YOU'RE GONNA BE OUT? 'CAUSE I DON'T HAVE THE TRAINING FOR THE PARADOX SYSTEM, BUT SOMEBODY'S GOTTA RUN THAT DATABASE IF YOU --
GOD, THIS IS -- SHE IS SO THE OPPOSITE OF TELK-MUN. I'M NOT EVEN SURE SHE KNOWS THE DIFFERENCE BETWEEN ME AND GUIL.
IT'S KINDA CUTE, THOUGH, YOU KNOW? LIKE, THERE'S THIS GIRL IN THE MIDWEST SOMEWHERE FANTASIZING ABOUT ME AS A BOY...
MY TEENAGE BOY-SELF, Y'KNOW?
YOU'LL BE IN BY FRIDAY, THOUGH, RIGHT? 'CAUSE KATIE NEEDS THOSE STATS BY --
OH MY GOD! PHILIP, PHILIP, SHE'S GIVING ME HER PHONE NUMBER! WHAT DO I DO?! I CAN'T CALL HER!
YOU KNOW, TRISHA'S WORRIED ABOUT YOU FOR REAL. SAID YOU SOUNDED REALLY SICK --
OH, YOU KNOW WHAT? I'M GONNA SEND HER A CARE PACKAGE!
LOOK, I'VE GOTTA GO. DON'T TELL TRISH ANYTHING, OKAY? 'BYE!
UH... 'BYE...

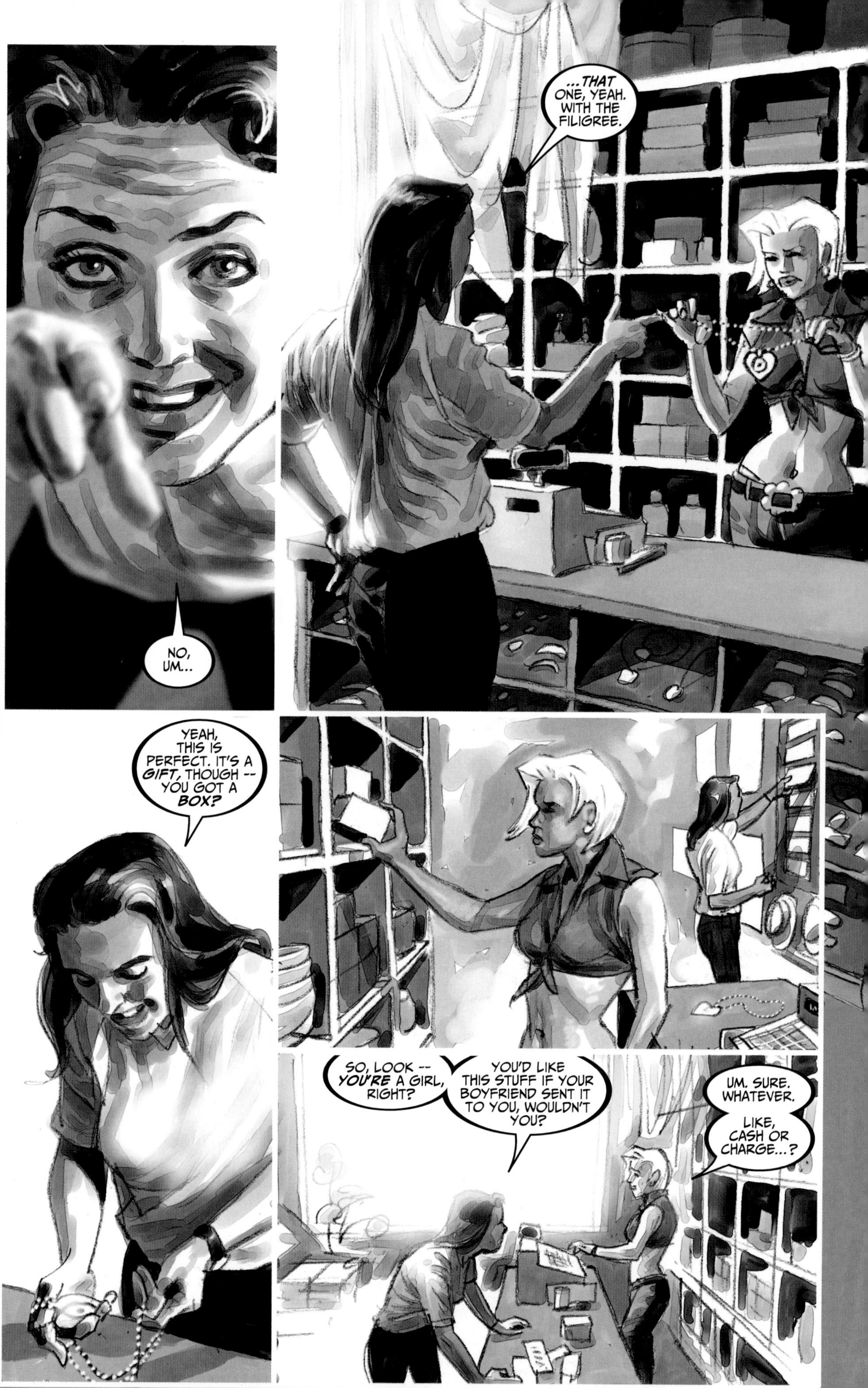
NO, UM...
...THAT ONE, YEAH. WITH THE FILIGREE.
YEAH, THIS IS PERFECT. IT'S A GIFT, THOUGH -- YOU GOT A BOX?
SO, LOOK -- YOU'RE A GIRL, RIGHT?
YOU'D LIKE THIS STUFF IF YOUR BOYFRIEND SENT IT TO YOU, WOULDN'T YOU?
UM. SURE. WHATEVER.
LIKE, CASH OR CHARGE...?

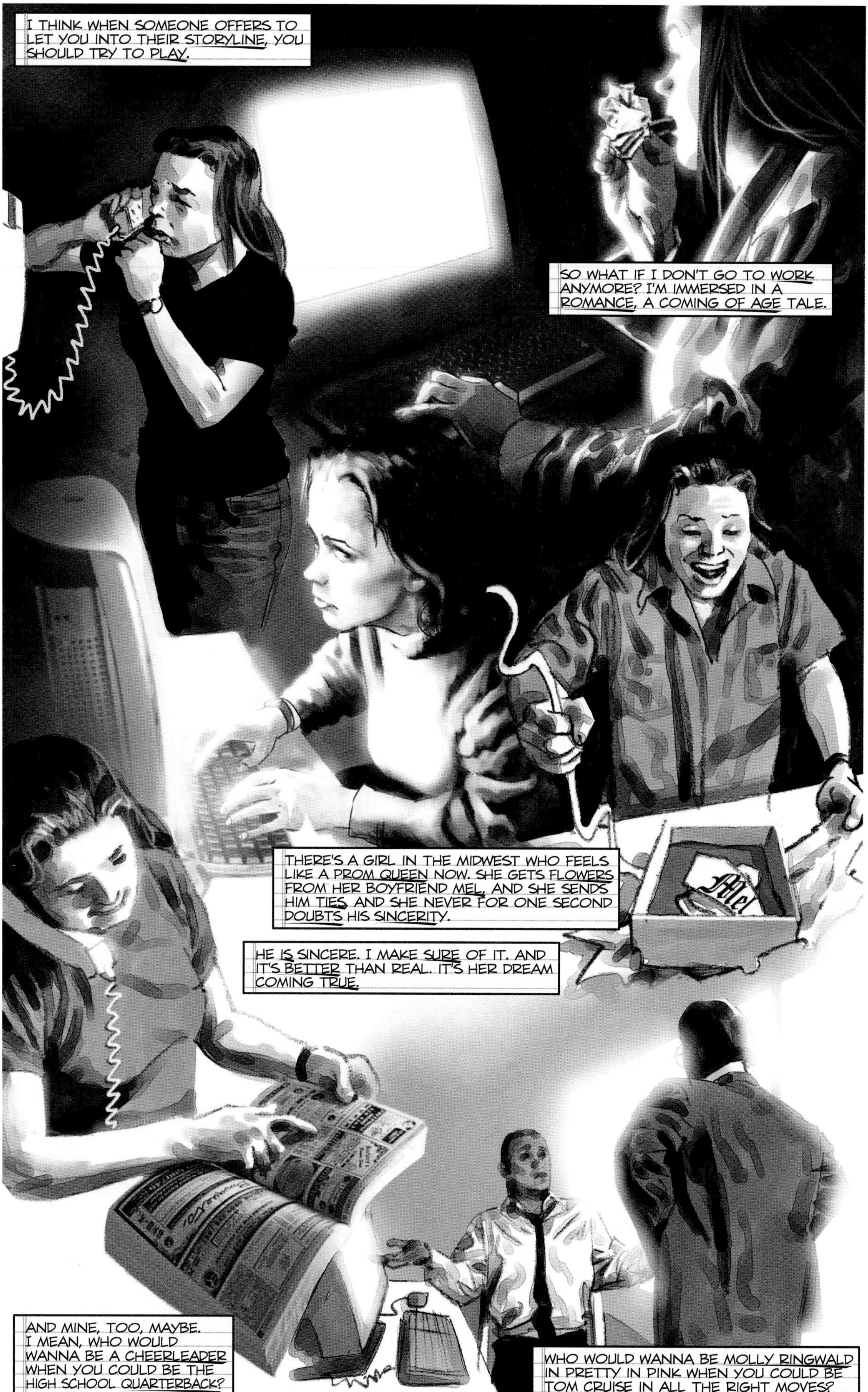
I THINK WHEN SOMEONE OFFERS TO LET YOU INTO THEIR STORYLINE, YOU SHOULD TRY TO PLAY.
SO WHAT IF I DON'T GO TO WORK ANYMORE? I'M IMMERSED IN A ROMANCE, A COMING OF AGE TALE.
THERE'S A GIRL IN THE MIDWEST WHO FEELS LIKE A PROM QUEEN NOW. SHE GETS FLOWERS FROM HER BOYFRIEND MEL, AND SHE SENDS HIM TIES AND SHE NEVER FOR ONE SECOND DOUBTS HIS SINCERITY.
Mel
HE IS SINCERE. I MAKE SURE OF IT. AND IT'S BETTER THAN REAL. IT'S HER DREAM COMING TRUE.
AND MINE, TOO, MAYBE. I MEAN, WHO WOULD WANNA BE A CHEERLEADER WHEN YOU COULD BE THE HIGH SCHOOL QUARTERBACK?
WHO WOULD WANNA BE MOLLY RINGWALD IN PRETTY IN PINK WHEN YOU COULD BE TOM CRUISE IN ALL THE RIGHT MOVES?

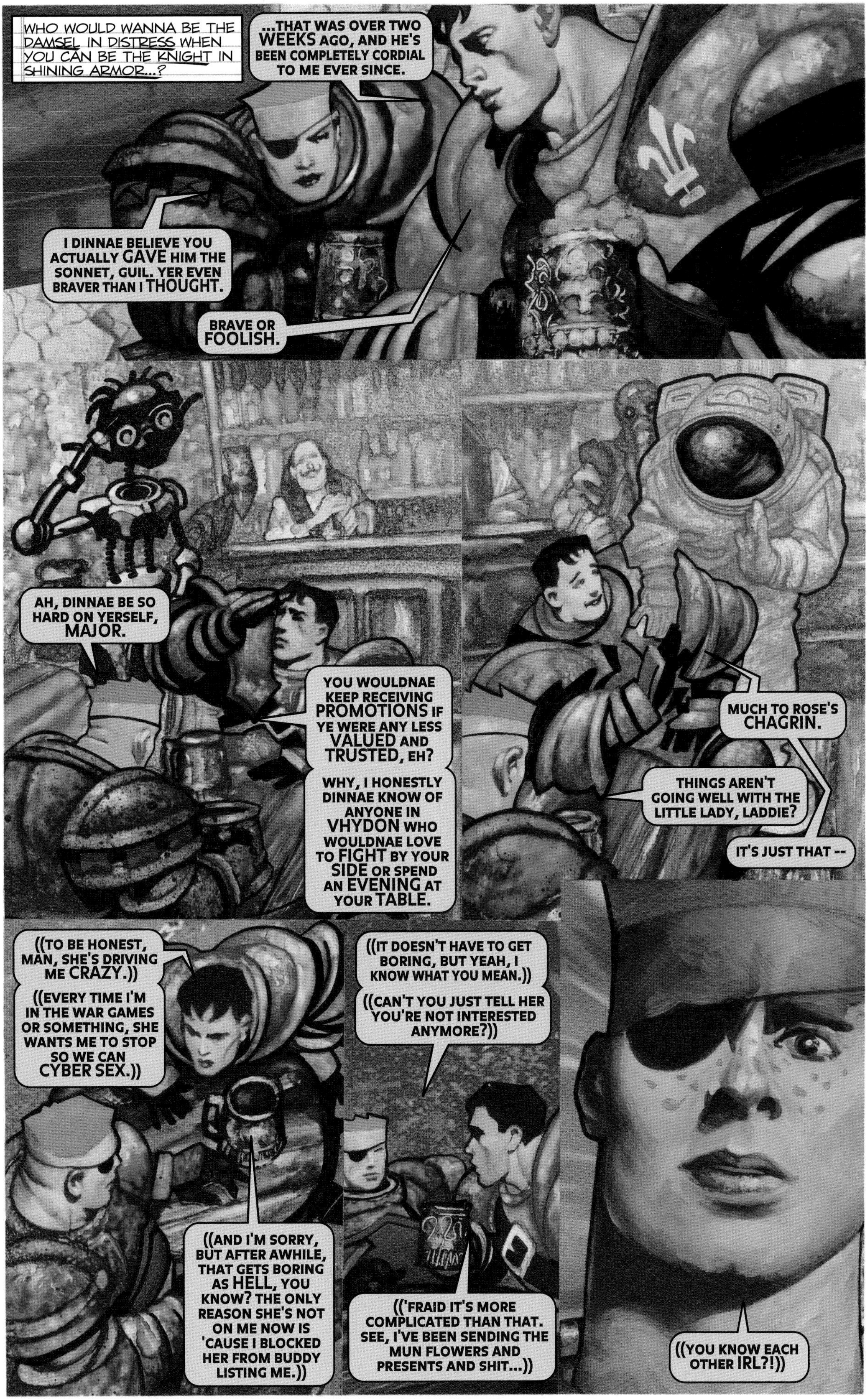
WHO WOULD WANNA BE THE DAMSEL IN DISTRESS WHEN YOU CAN BE THE KNIGHT IN SHINING ARMOR...?
...THAT WAS OVER TWO WEEKS AGO, AND HE'S BEEN COMPLETELY CORDIAL TO ME EVER SINCE.
I DINNAE BELIEVE YOU ACTUALLY GAVE HIM THE SONNET, GUIL. YER EVEN BRAVER THAN I THOUGHT.
BRAVE OR FOOLISH.
AH, DINNAE BE SO HARD ON YERSELF, MAJOR.
YOU WOULDNAE KEEP RECEIVING PROMOTIONS IF YE WERE ANY LESS VALUED AND TRUSTED, EH?
WHY, I HONESTLY DINNAE KNOW OF ANYONE IN VHYDON WHO WOULDNAE LOVE TO FIGHT BY YOUR SIDE OR SPEND AN EVENING AT YOUR TABLE.
MUCH TO ROSE'S CHAGRIN.
THINGS AREN'T GOING WELL WITH THE LITTLE LADY, LADDIE?
IT'S JUST THAT --
((TO BE HONEST, MAN, SHE'S DRIVING ME CRAZY.))
((EVERY TIME I'M IN THE WAR GAMES OR SOMETHING, SHE WANTS ME TO STOP SO WE CAN CYBER SEX.))
((AND I'M SORRY, BUT AFTER AWHILE, THAT GETS BORING AS HELL, YOU KNOW? THE ONLY REASON SHE'S NOT ON ME NOW IS 'CAUSE I BLOCKED HER FROM BUDDY LISTING ME.))
((IT DOESN'T HAVE TO GET BORING, BUT YEAH, I KNOW WHAT YOU MEAN.))
((CAN'T YOU JUST TELL HER YOU'RE NOT INTERESTED ANYMORE?))
(('FRAID IT'S MORE COMPLICATED THAN THAT. SEE, I'VE BEEN SENDING THE MUN FLOWERS AND PRESENTS AND SHIT...))
((YOU KNOW EACH OTHER IRL?!))

PR - private room
IC = in character
OOC = out of character
SL - story line
RP = Role Playing
SN - screen name
MUN is the "mundane" of the SN - the player
brb - be right back
afk = away from keyboard
;-) :-O :-P ;-D :-(
bak - back at keyboard
(( )) for OOC (or hugs??)
<< >> psychic bonded communication
IRL = "in real life"
LOL - laughing out loud
ROFL - rolling on floor laughing
(LMAO - my ass off)
IRL... IRL...
NO... BUT WE... EXCHANGED... ADDRESSES...!
FESTIVAL
HORROR STORIES? WAIT, HOLD ON, THIS SOUNDS GOOD, I NEED COFFEE, BRB...
To: McCraven
Chicago
McCraven : ((Oh, you know each other IRL?))
Sir Guil : ((No, but we exchanged addresses))
McCraven : ((Dude, you've gotta be careful with that. Not all muns are sane. There are some real horror stories out there....))
Send

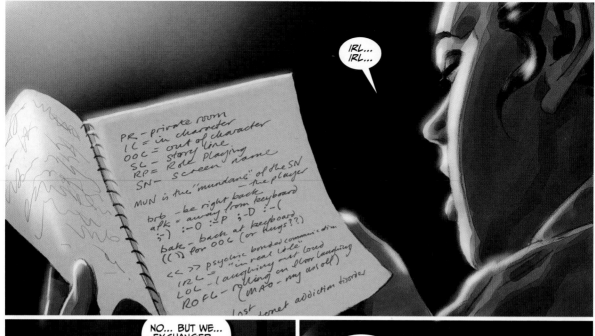

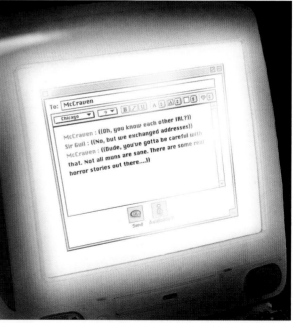

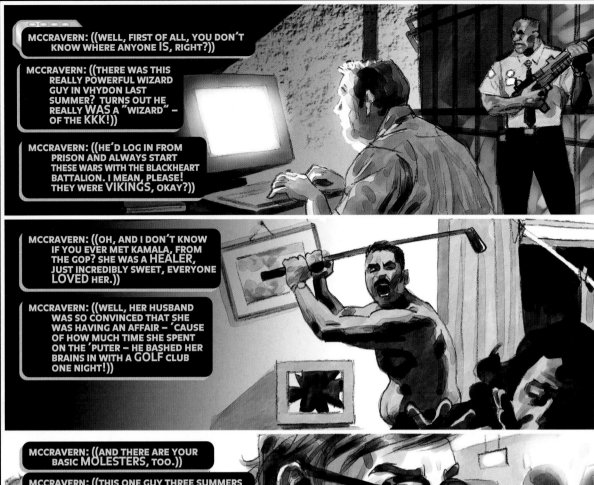

MCCRAVERN: ((WELL, FIRST OF ALL, YOU DON'T KNOW WHERE ANYONE IS, RIGHT?))

MCCRAVERN: ((THERE WAS THIS REALLY POWERFUL WIZARD GUY IN VHYDON LAST SUMMER? TURNS OUT HE REALLY WAS A "WIZARD" – OF THE KKK!))

MCCRAVERN: ((HE'D LOG IN FROM PRISON AND ALWAYS START THESE WARS WITH THE BLACKHEART BATTALION. I MEAN, PLEASE! THEY WERE VIKINGS, OKAY?))

MCCRAVERN: ((OH, AND I DON'T KNOW IF YOU EVER MET KAMALA, FROM THE GOP? SHE WAS A HEALER, JUST INCREDIBLY SWEET, EVERYONE LOVED HER.))

MCCRAVERN: ((WELL, HER HUSBAND WAS SO CONVINCED THAT SHE WAS HAVING AN AFFAIR – 'CAUSE OF HOW MUCH TIME SHE SPENT ON THE 'PUTER – HE BASHED HER BRAINS IN WITH A GOLF CLUB ONE NIGHT!))

MCCRAVERN: ((AND THERE ARE YOUR BASIC MOLESTERS, TOO.))

MCCRAVERN: ((THIS ONE GUY THREE SUMMERS AGO SET UP THIS WHOLE GUILD OF, LIKE, SUPERPOWERED HEALER NINJA BABES, JUST TO ATTRACT A BUNCH OF YOUNG GIRLS.))

MCCRAVERN: ((HE'D GIVE THEM HIS ADDRESS AND TALK THEM INTO LARPING – LIVE ACTION ROLE PLAYING, YOU KNOW?))

MCCRAVERN: ((I HEARD HE GOT ARRESTED LAST YEAR, FINALLY.))

MCCRAVERN: ((EVEN PEOPLE WE KNOW. LIKE VAXA...?))

MCCRAVERN: ((SHE'S GOT THREE KIDS, AND SHE'S SO ADDICTED TO THE COMPUTER STUFF THAT SHE NEVER DEALS WITH THEM. NO DAD AROUND, AND THE YOUNGEST ONE ALREADY KNOWS TO REACH FOR THE MOUSE WHEN HE NEEDS HIS MOM'S ATTENTION, 'CAUSE THAT'S THE ONLY THING SHE'LL NOTICE.))

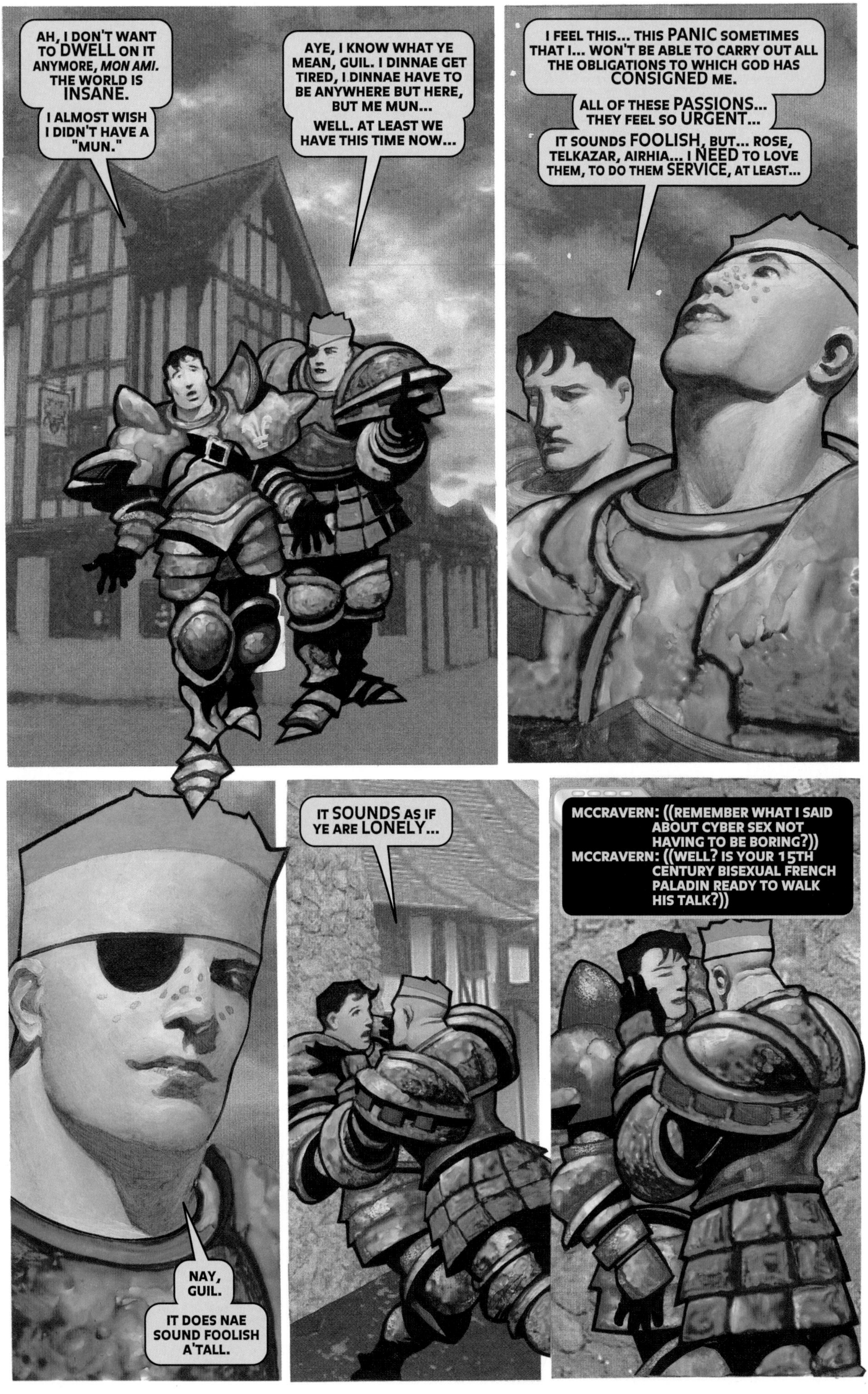
AH, I DON'T WANT TO DWELL ON IT ANYMORE, MON AMI. THE WORLD IS INSANE.
I ALMOST WISH I DIDN'T HAVE A "MUN."
AYE, I KNOW WHAT YE MEAN, GUIL. I DINNAE GET TIRED, I DINNAE HAVE TO BE ANYWHERE BUT HERE, BUT ME MUN...
WELL. AT LEAST WE HAVE THIS TIME NOW...
I FEEL THIS... THIS PANIC SOMETIMES THAT I... WON'T BE ABLE TO CARRY OUT ALL THE OBLIGATIONS TO WHICH GOD HAS CONSIGNED ME.
ALL OF THESE PASSIONS... THEY FEEL SO URGENT...
IT SOUNDS FOOLISH, BUT... ROSE, TELKAZAR, AIRHIA... I NEED TO LOVE THEM, TO DO THEM SERVICE, AT LEAST...
NAY, GUIL.
IT DOES NAE SOUND FOOLISH A'TALL.
IT SOUNDS AS IF YE ARE LONELY...
MCCRAVERN: ((REMEMBER WHAT I SAID ABOUT CYBER SEX NOT HAVING TO BE BORING?))
MCCRAVERN: ((WELL? IS YOUR 15TH CENTURY BISEXUAL FRENCH PALADIN READY TO WALK HIS TALK?))

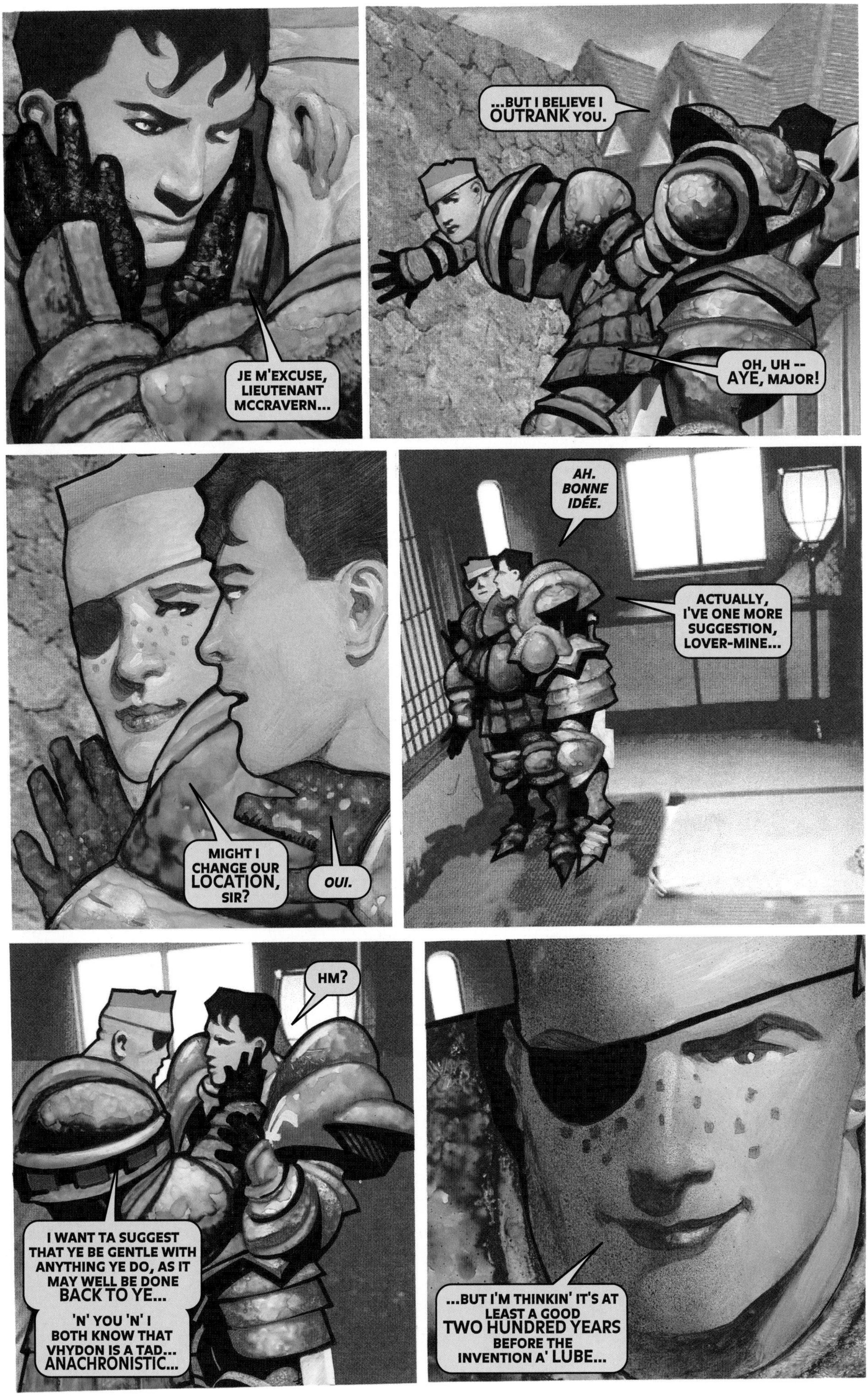
JE M'EXCUSE, LIEUTENANT MCCRAVERN...
...BUT I BELIEVE I OUTRANK YOU.
OH, UH -- AYE, MAJOR!
MIGHT I CHANGE OUR LOCATION, SIR?
OUI.
AH. BONNE IDÉE.
ACTUALLY, I'VE ONE MORE SUGGESTION, LOVER-MINE...
HM?
I WANT TA SUGGEST THAT YE BE GENTLE WITH ANYTHING YE DO, AS IT MAY WELL BE DONE BACK TO YE...
'N' YOU 'N' I BOTH KNOW THAT VHYDON IS A TAD... ANACHRONISTIC...
...BUT I'M THINKIN' IT'S AT LEAST A GOOD TWO HUNDRED YEARS BEFORE THE INVENTION A' LUBE...

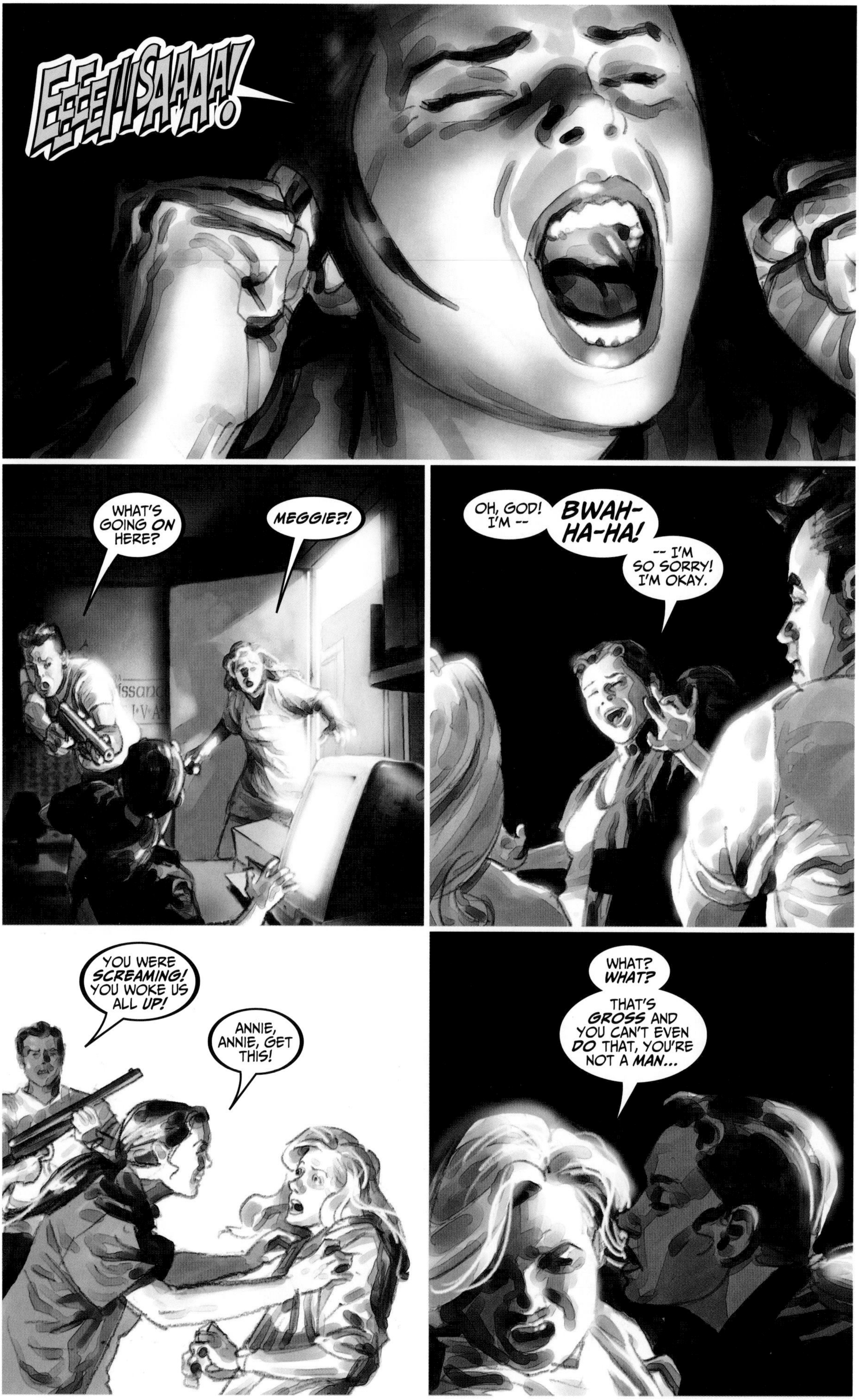
EEEEIISAAAA!
WHAT'S GOING ON HERE?
MEGGIE?!
OH, GOD! I'M --
BWAH-HA-HA!
-- I'M SO SORRY! I'M OKAY.
YOU WERE SCREAMING! YOU WOKE US ALL UP!
ANNIE, ANNIE, GET THIS!
WHAT? WHAT?
THAT'S GROSS AND YOU CAN'T EVEN DO THAT, YOU'RE NOT A MAN...

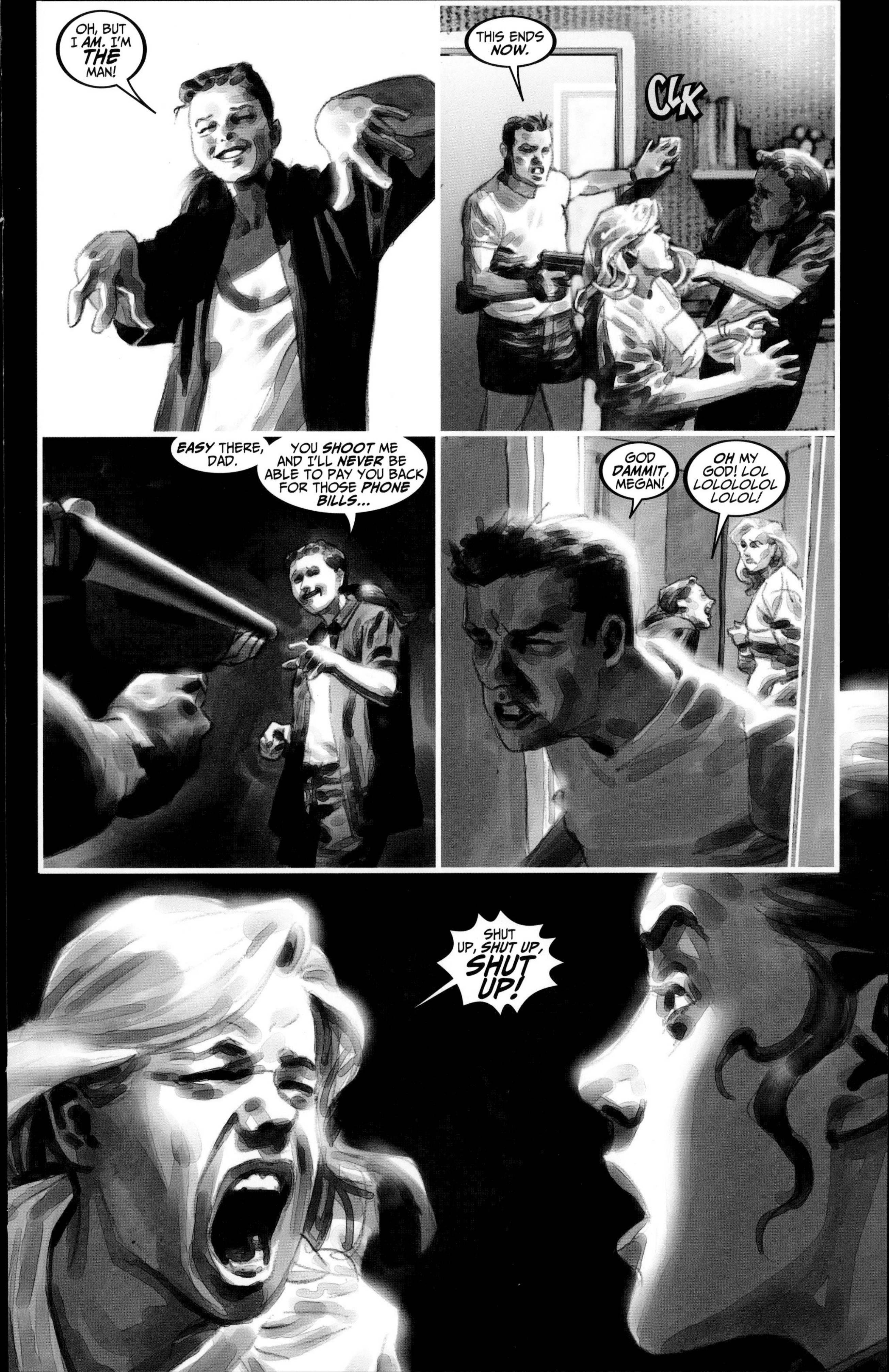
OH, BUT I AM. I'M THE MAN!
THIS ENDS NOW.
CLK
EASY THERE, DAD.
YOU SHOOT ME AND I'LL NEVER BE ABLE TO PAY YOU BACK FOR THOSE PHONE BILLS...
GOD DAMMIT, MEGAN!
OH MY GOD! LOL LOLOLOLOL LOLOL!
SHUT UP, SHUT UP, SHUT UP!

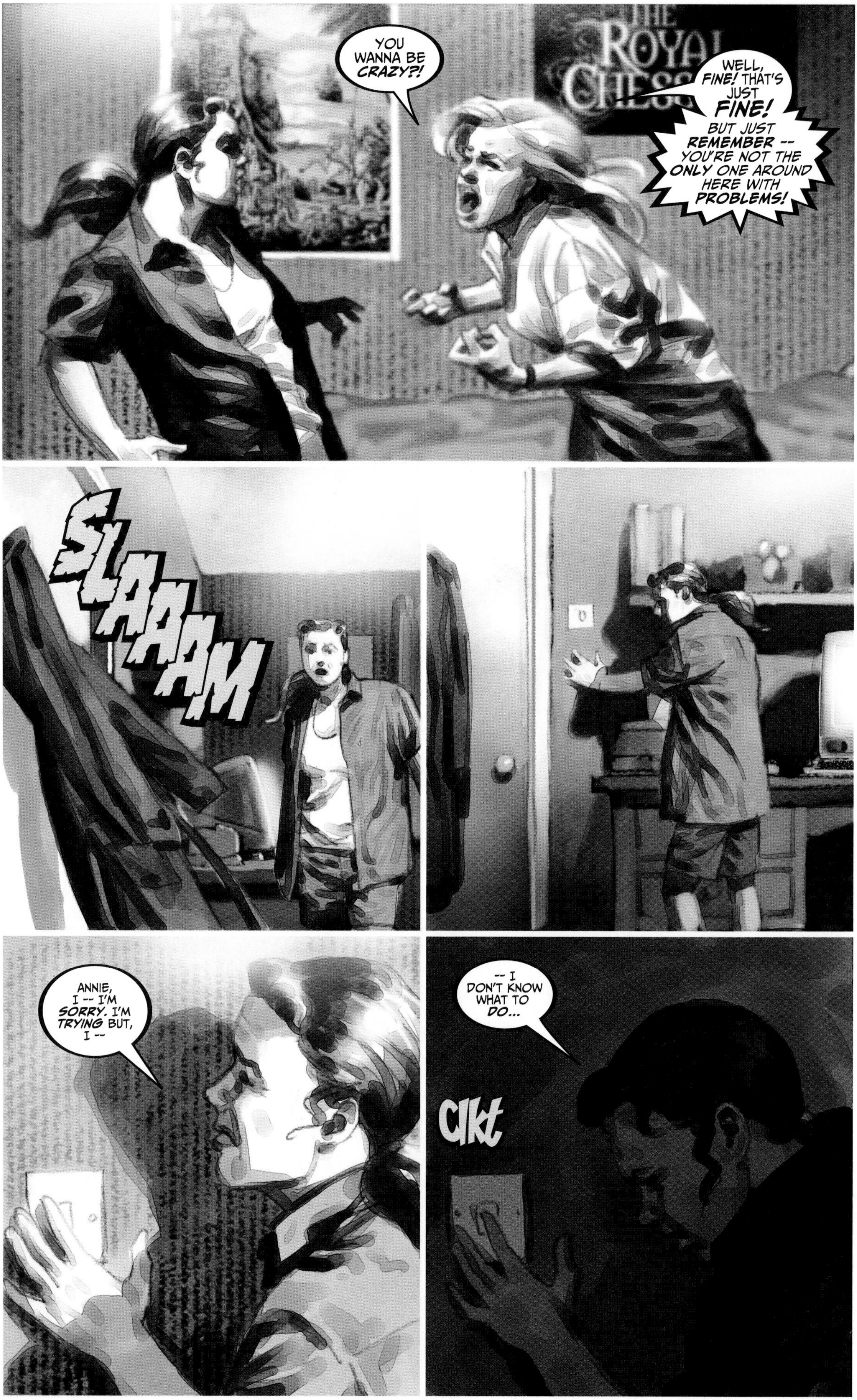

THE ROYAL CHESS
YOU WANNA BE CRAZY?!
WELL, FINE! THAT'S JUST FINE! BUT JUST REMEMBER -- YOU'RE NOT THE ONLY ONE AROUND HERE WITH PROBLEMS!
SLAAAAM
ANNIE, I -- I'M SORRY. I'M TRYING BUT, I --
-- I DON'T KNOW WHAT TO DO...
CLKT

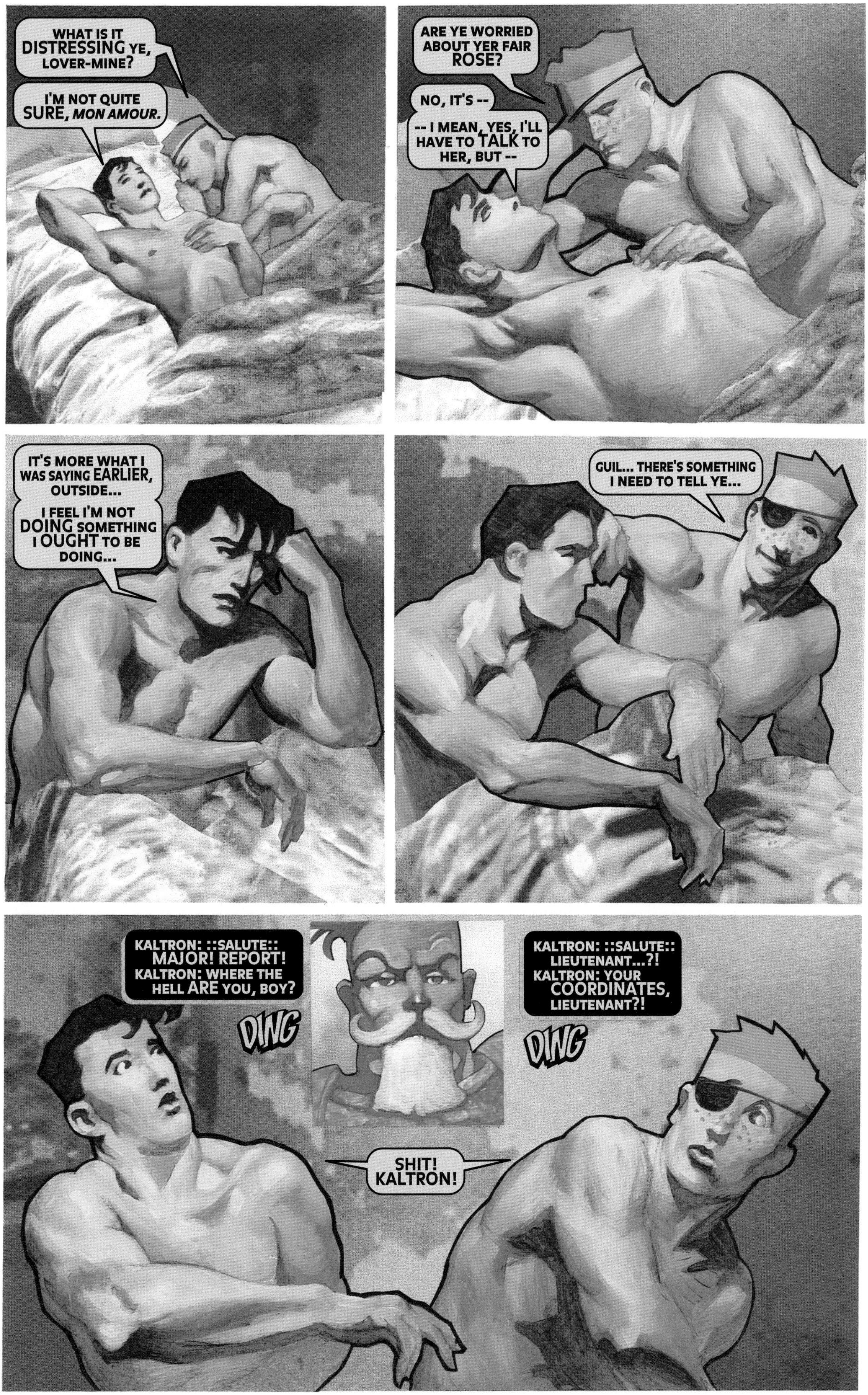
WHAT IS IT DISTRESSING YE, LOVER-MINE?
I'M NOT QUITE SURE, MON AMOUR.
ARE YE WORRIED ABOUT YER FAIR ROSE?
NO, IT'S --
-- I MEAN, YES, I'LL HAVE TO TALK TO HER, BUT --
IT'S MORE WHAT I WAS SAYING EARLIER, OUTSIDE...
I FEEL I'M NOT DOING SOMETHING I OUGHT TO BE DOING...
GUIL... THERE'S SOMETHING I NEED TO TELL YE...
KALTRON: ::SALUTE:: MAJOR! REPORT!
KALTRON: WHERE THE HELL ARE YOU, BOY?
DING
KALTRON: ::SALUTE:: LIEUTENANT...?!
KALTRON: YOUR COORDINATES, LIEUTENANT?!
DING
SHIT! KALTRON!

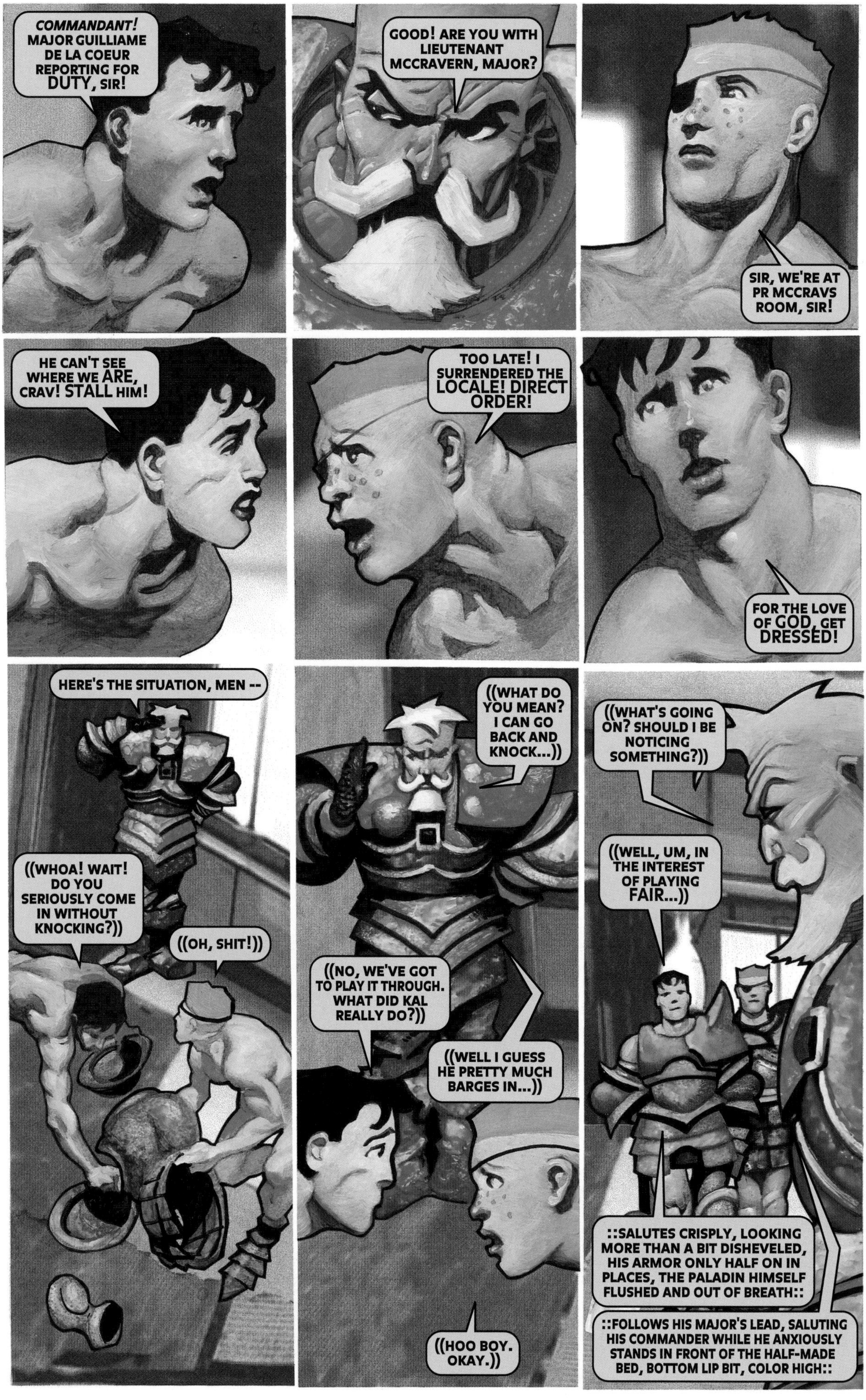
COMMANDANT! MAJOR GUILLIAME DE LA COEUR REPORTING FOR DUTY, SIR!
GOOD! ARE YOU WITH LIEUTENANT MCCRAVERN, MAJOR?
SIR, WE'RE AT PR MCCRAVS ROOM, SIR!
HE CAN'T SEE WHERE WE ARE, CRAV! STALL HIM!
TOO LATE! I SURRENDERED THE LOCALE! DIRECT ORDER!
FOR THE LOVE OF GOD, GET DRESSED!
HERE'S THE SITUATION, MEN --
((WHOA! WAIT! DO YOU SERIOUSLY COME IN WITHOUT KNOCKING?))
((OH, SHIT!))
((WHAT DO YOU MEAN? I CAN GO BACK AND KNOCK...))
((NO, WE'VE GOT TO PLAY IT THROUGH. WHAT DID KAL REALLY DO?))
((WELL I GUESS HE PRETTY MUCH BARGES IN...))
((HOO BOY. OKAY.))
((WHAT'S GOING ON? SHOULD I BE NOTICING SOMETHING?))
((WELL, UM, IN THE INTEREST OF PLAYING FAIR...))
::SALUTES CRISPLY, LOOKING MORE THAN A BIT DISHEVELED, HIS ARMOR ONLY HALF ON IN PLACES, THE PALADIN HIMSELF FLUSHED AND OUT OF BREATH::
::FOLLOWS HIS MAJOR'S LEAD, SALUTING HIS COMMANDER WHILE HE ANXIOUSLY STANDS IN FRONT OF THE HALF-MADE BED, BOTTOM LIP BIT, COLOR HIGH::

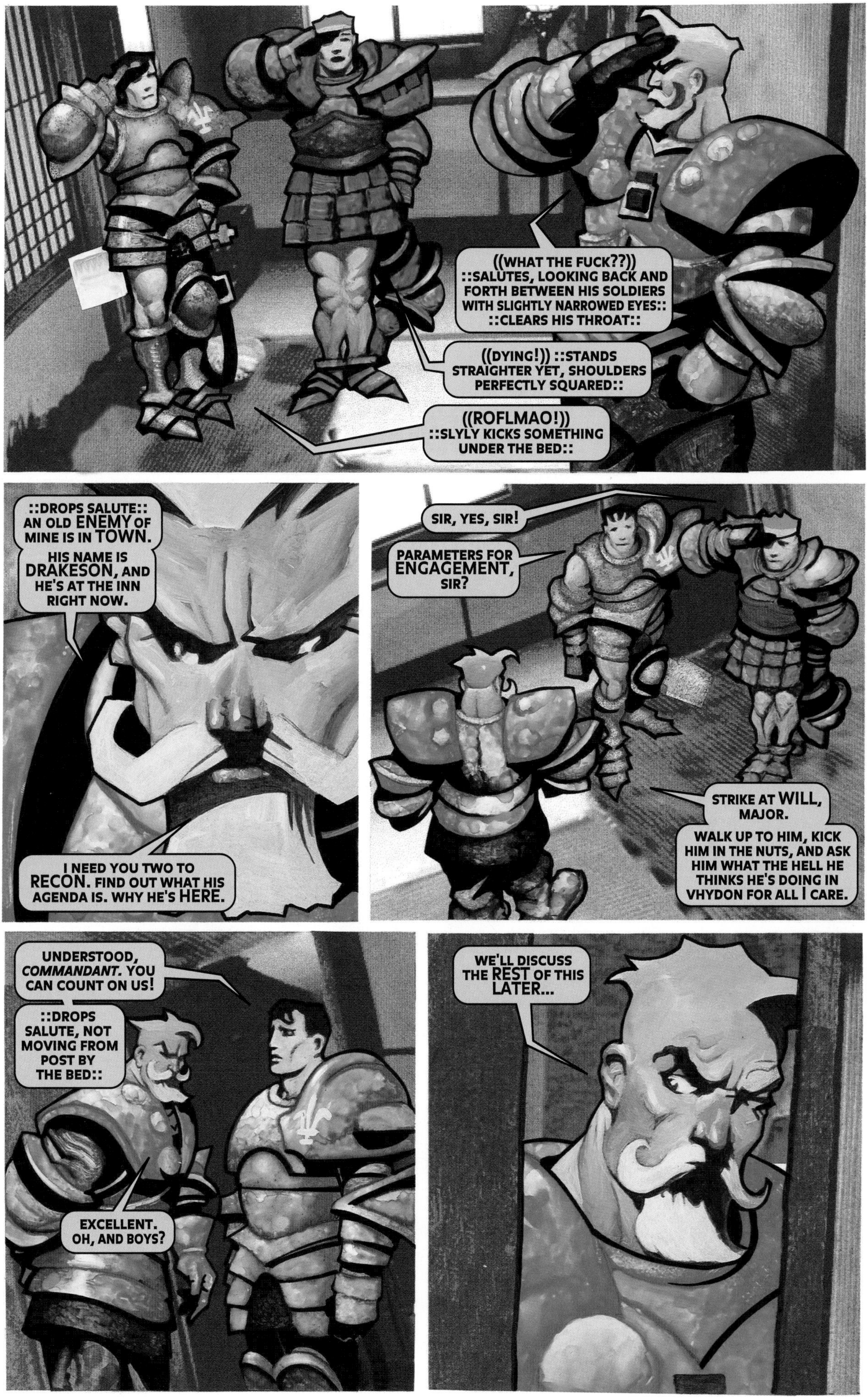
((WHAT THE FUCK??)) ::SALUTES, LOOKING BACK AND FORTH BETWEEN HIS SOLDIERS WITH SLIGHTLY NARROWED EYES:: ::CLEARS HIS THROAT::
((DYING!)) ::STANDS STRAIGHTER YET, SHOULDERS PERFECTLY SQUARED::
((ROFLMAO!)) ::SLYLY KICKS SOMETHING UNDER THE BED::
::DROPS SALUTE:: AN OLD ENEMY OF MINE IS IN TOWN.
HIS NAME IS DRAKESON, AND HE'S AT THE INN RIGHT NOW.
I NEED YOU TWO TO RECON. FIND OUT WHAT HIS AGENDA IS. WHY HE'S HERE.
SIR, YES, SIR!
PARAMETERS FOR ENGAGEMENT, SIR?
STRIKE AT WILL, MAJOR.
WALK UP TO HIM, KICK HIM IN THE NUTS, AND ASK HIM WHAT THE HELL HE THINKS HE'S DOING IN VHYDON FOR ALL I CARE.
UNDERSTOOD, *COMMANDANT.* YOU CAN COUNT ON US!
::DROPS SALUTE, NOT MOVING FROM POST BY THE BED::
EXCELLENT. OH, AND BOYS?
WE'LL DISCUSS THE REST OF THIS LATER...

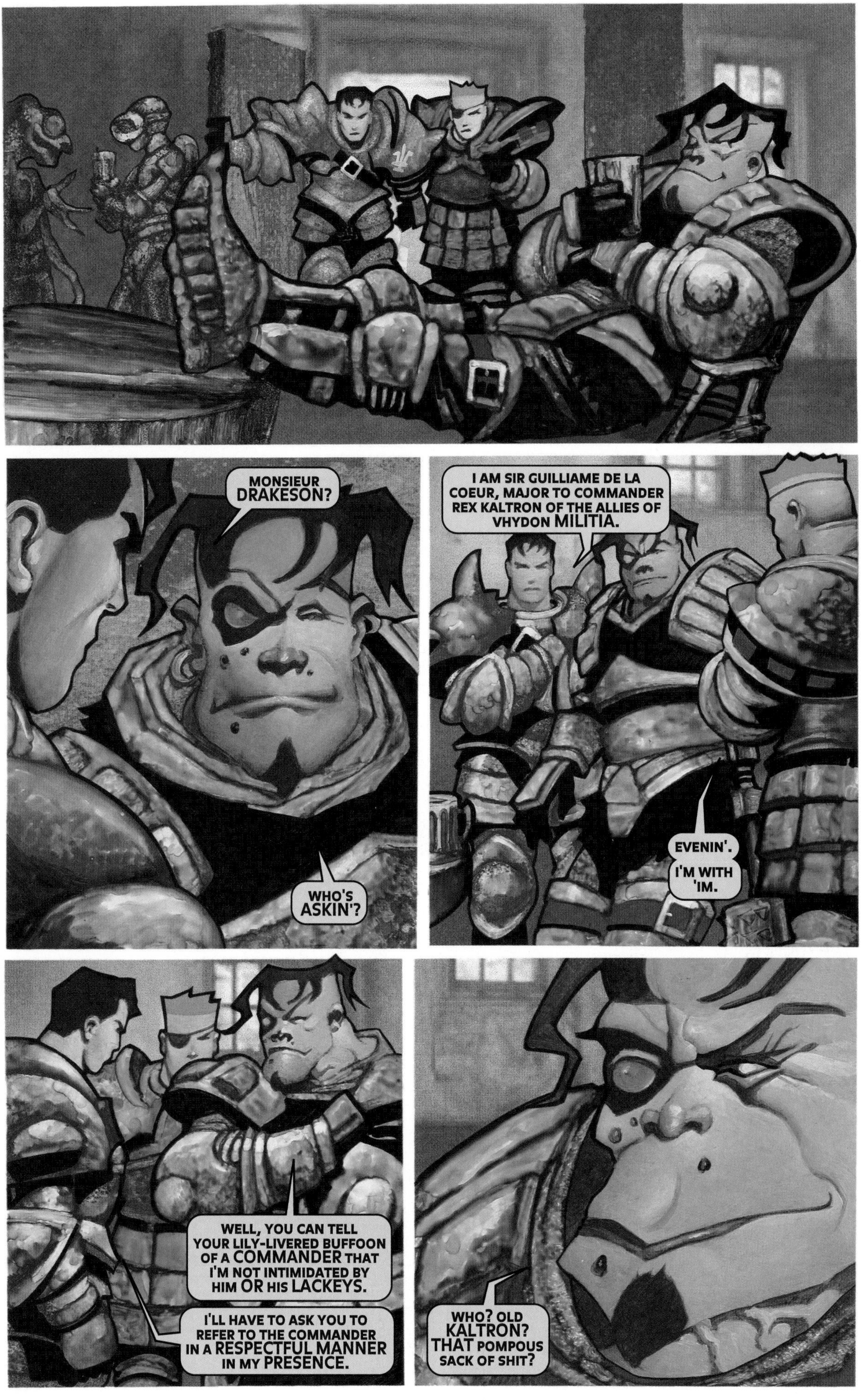
MONSIEUR DRAKESON?
WHO'S ASKIN'?
I AM SIR GUILLIAME DE LA COEUR, MAJOR TO COMMANDER REX KALTRON OF THE ALLIES OF VHYDON MILITIA.
EVENIN'. I'M WITH 'IM.
WELL, YOU CAN TELL YOUR LILY-LIVERED BUFFOON OF A COMMANDER THAT I'M NOT INTIMIDATED BY HIM OR HIS LACKEYS.
I'LL HAVE TO ASK YOU TO REFER TO THE COMMANDER IN A RESPECTFUL MANNER IN MY PRESENCE.
WHO? OLD KALTRON? THAT POMPOUS SACK OF SHIT?

I WARN YOU FOR THE LAST TIME --

YEAH? AND WHAT DO YOU THINK YOU'RE GOING TO DO TO ME?

YOU'RE A KNIGHT, AREN'T YOU, SON? HONOR-bound?

WELL, I'LL MAKE THIS EASY ON YOU, TIN CAN.

YOU WANT TO PROTECT KALTRON'S HONOR?

I CHALLENGE YOU TO A DM!

DING

SIR GUIL: <<DM?>>
MCCRAVERN: <<DEATH MATCH, GUIL! DINNAE DO IT!>>
SIR GUIL: <<I MUST! KALTRON'S HONOR IS AT STAKE!>>
MCCRAVERN: <<GUIL, I'M TRYIN' TO HAIL HIM, AND I CANNAE FIND HIM IN VHYDON. SOMETHING ISN'T RIGHT HERE -->>

WELL? WHAT DO YOU SAY, YOU OVERGROWN CHILD?

ARE YOU GOING TO LET ME WANDER THE INNS OF VHYDON, SMEARING YOUR COMMANDER'S GOOD NAME --

-- OR ARE YOU GOING TO ACCEPT MY CHALLENGE?

HAVE YOU HONOR? ARE YOU ENOUGH OF A MAN?

I ACCEPT!

MAJOR, NO!

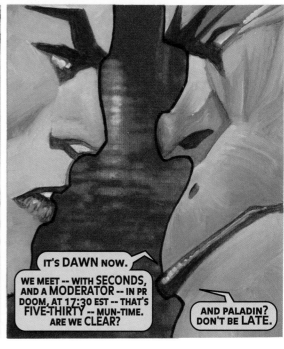

IT'S DAWN NOW.

WE MEET -- WITH SECONDS, AND A MODERATOR -- IN PR DOOM, AT 17:30 EST -- THAT'S FIVE-THIRTY -- MUN-TIME. ARE WE CLEAR?

AND PALADIN? DON'T BE LATE.

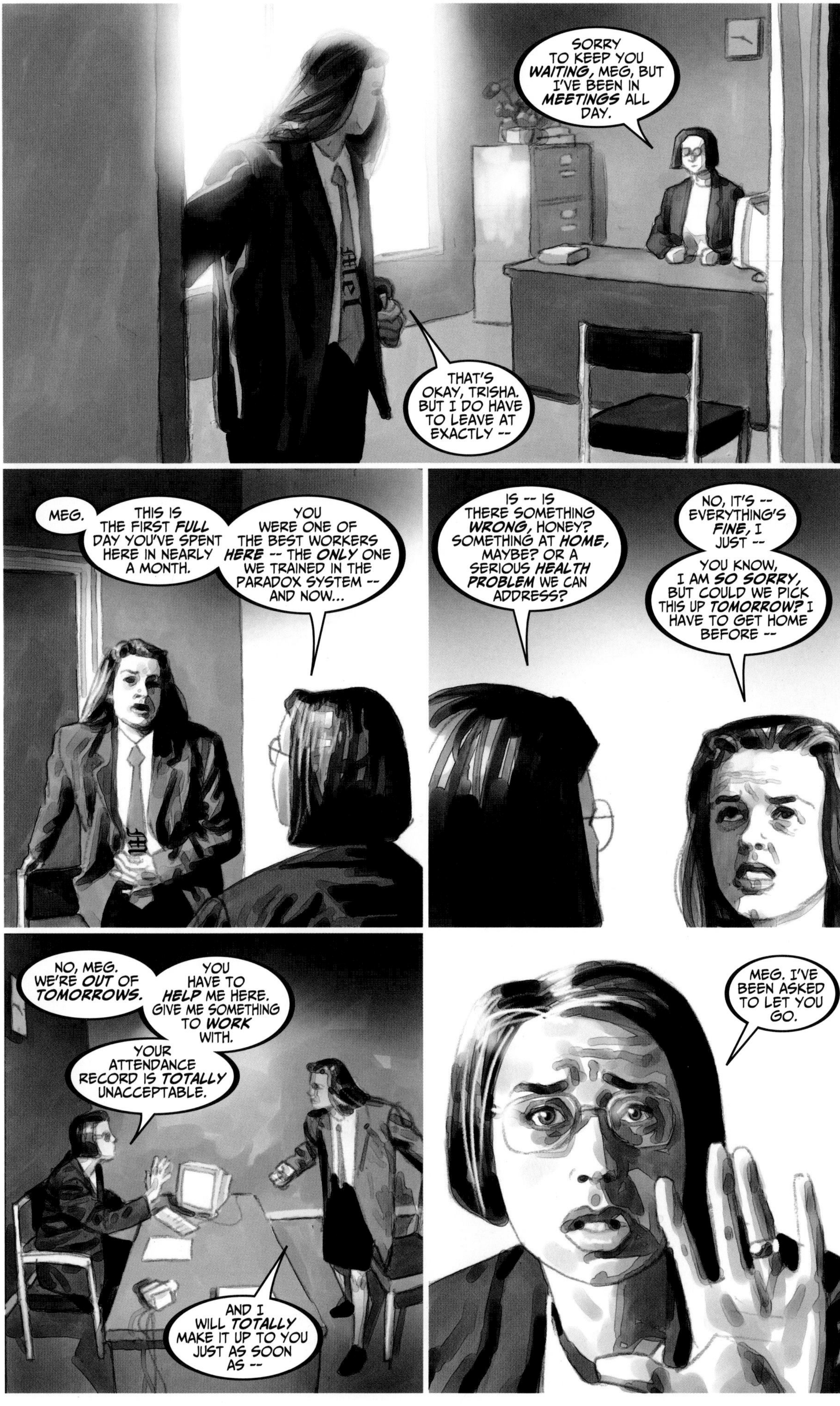
SORRY TO KEEP YOU WAITING, MEG, BUT I'VE BEEN IN MEETINGS ALL DAY.
THAT'S OKAY, TRISHA. BUT I DO HAVE TO LEAVE AT EXACTLY --
MEG.
THIS IS THE FIRST FULL DAY YOU'VE SPENT HERE IN NEARLY A MONTH.
YOU WERE ONE OF THE BEST WORKERS HERE -- THE ONLY ONE WE TRAINED IN THE PARADOX SYSTEM -- AND NOW...
IS -- IS THERE SOMETHING WRONG, HONEY? SOMETHING AT HOME, MAYBE? OR A SERIOUS HEALTH PROBLEM WE CAN ADDRESS?
NO, IT'S -- EVERYTHING'S FINE, I JUST --
YOU KNOW, I AM SO SORRY, BUT COULD WE PICK THIS UP TOMORROW? I HAVE TO GET HOME BEFORE --
NO, MEG. WE'RE OUT OF TOMORROWS.
YOU HAVE TO HELP ME HERE. GIVE ME SOMETHING TO WORK WITH.
YOUR ATTENDANCE RECORD IS TOTALLY UNACCEPTABLE.
AND I WILL TOTALLY MAKE IT UP TO YOU JUST AS SOON AS --
MEG. I'VE BEEN ASKED TO LET YOU GO.

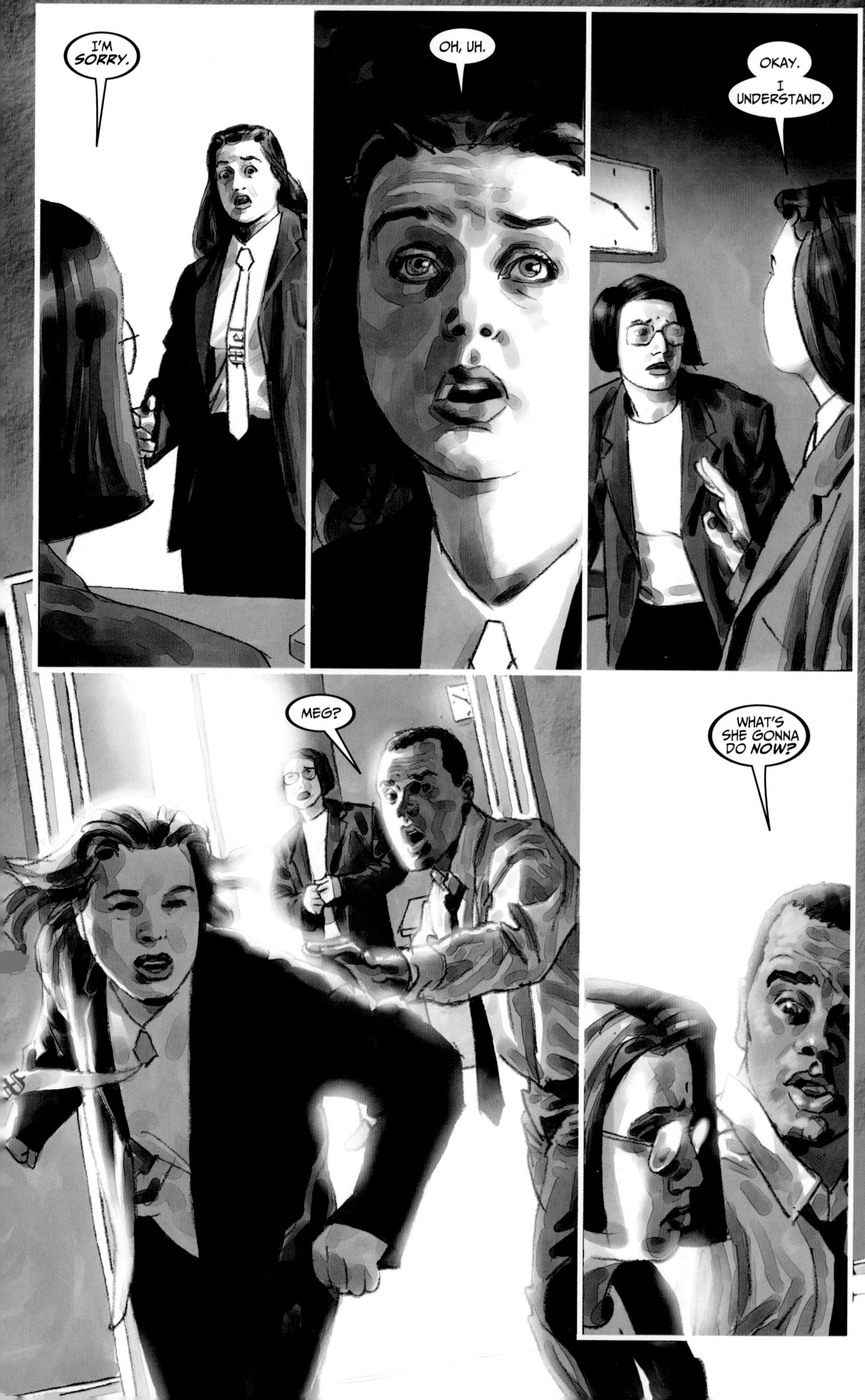
I'M SORRY.
OH, UH.
OKAY. I UNDERSTAND.
MEG?
WHAT'S SHE GONNA DO NOW?

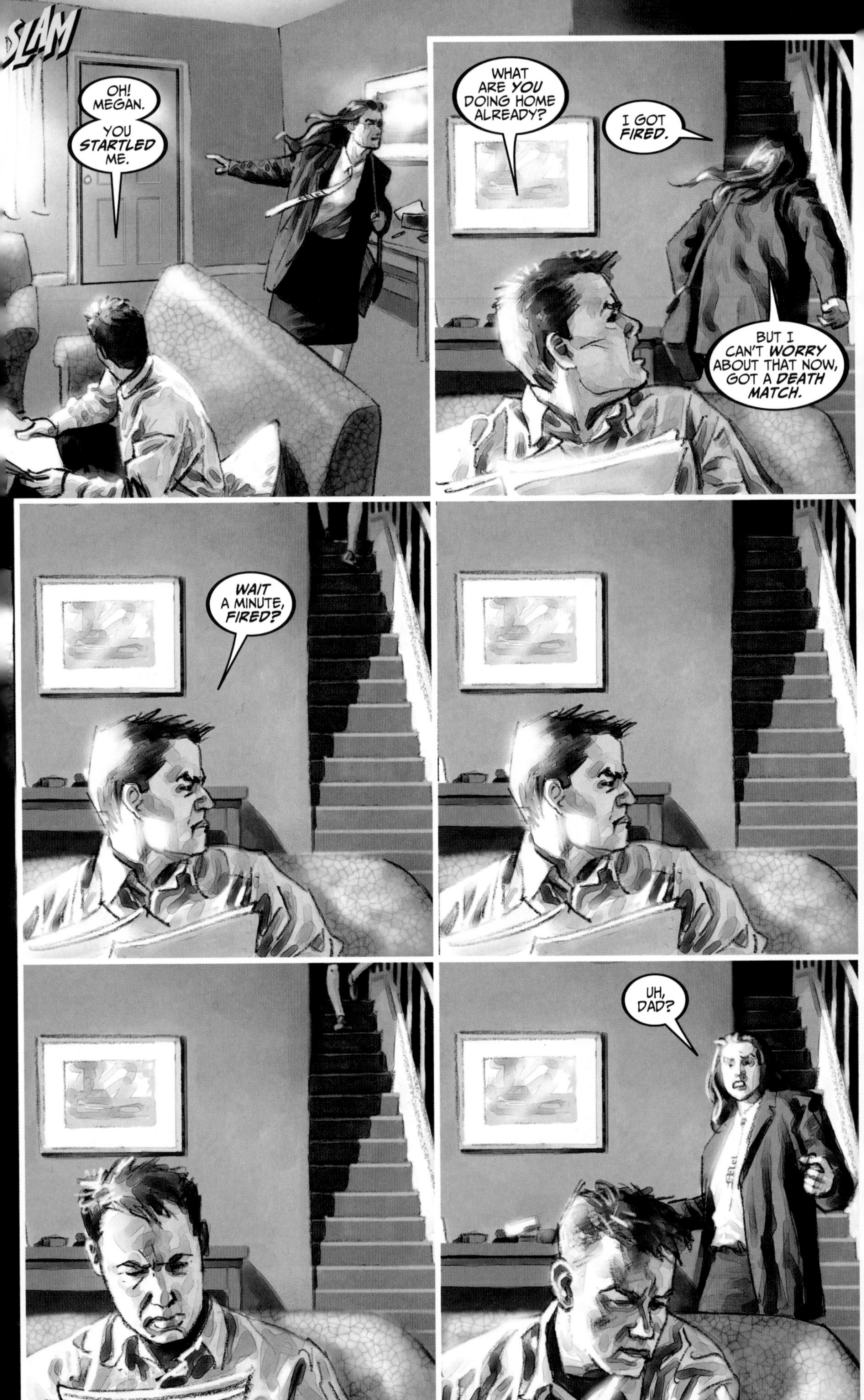
SLAM
OH! MEGAN.
YOU STARTLED ME.
WHAT ARE YOU DOING HOME ALREADY?
I GOT FIRED.
BUT I CAN'T WORRY ABOUT THAT NOW, GOT A DEATH MATCH.
WAIT A MINUTE, FIRED?
UH, DAD?

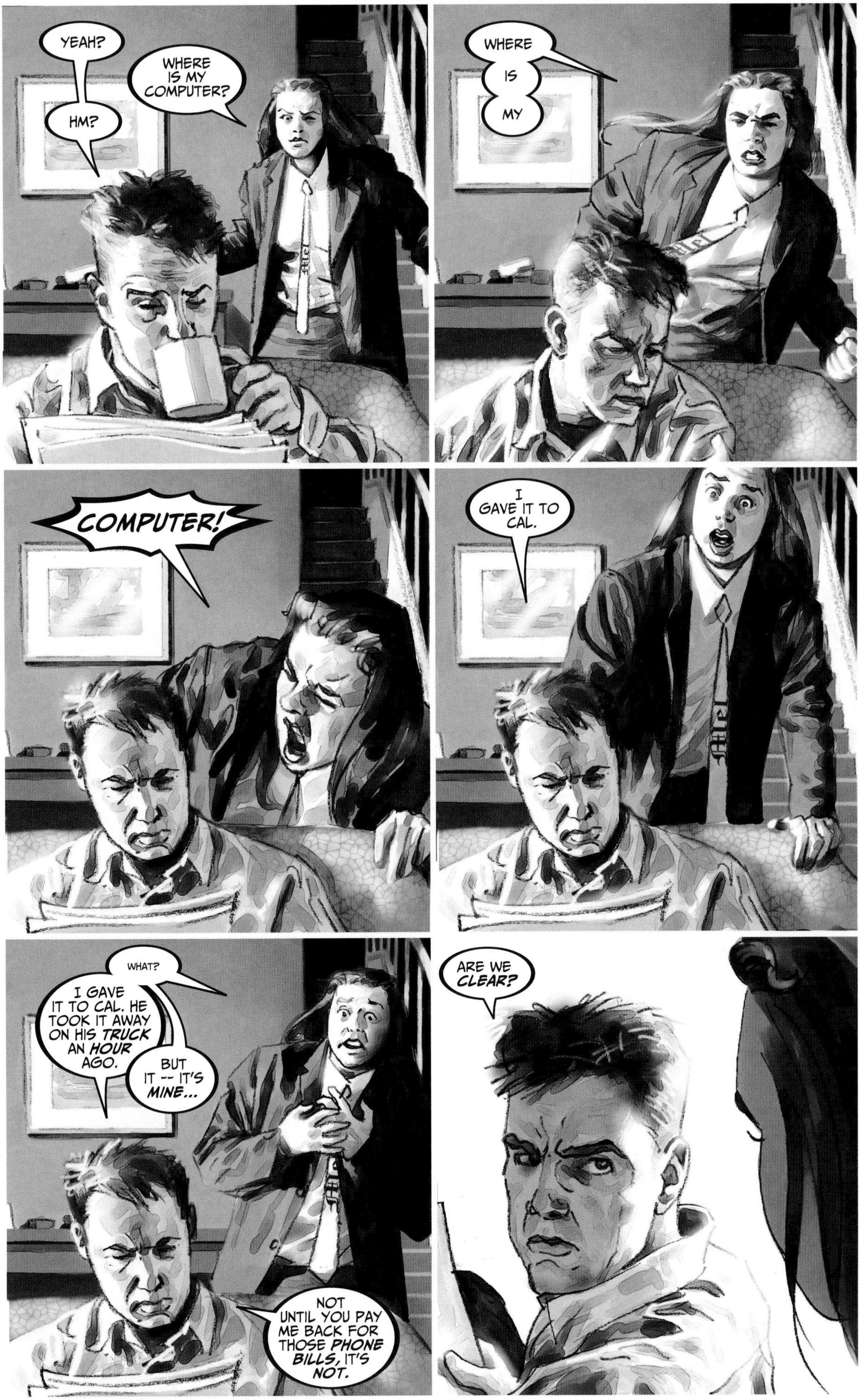
YEAH?
HM?
WHERE IS MY COMPUTER?
WHERE
IS
MY
COMPUTER!
I GAVE IT TO CAL.
WHAT?
I GAVE IT TO CAL. HE TOOK IT AWAY ON HIS TRUCK AN HOUR AGO.
BUT IT -- IT'S MINE...
NOT UNTIL YOU PAY ME BACK FOR THOSE PHONE BILLS, IT'S NOT.
ARE WE CLEAR?

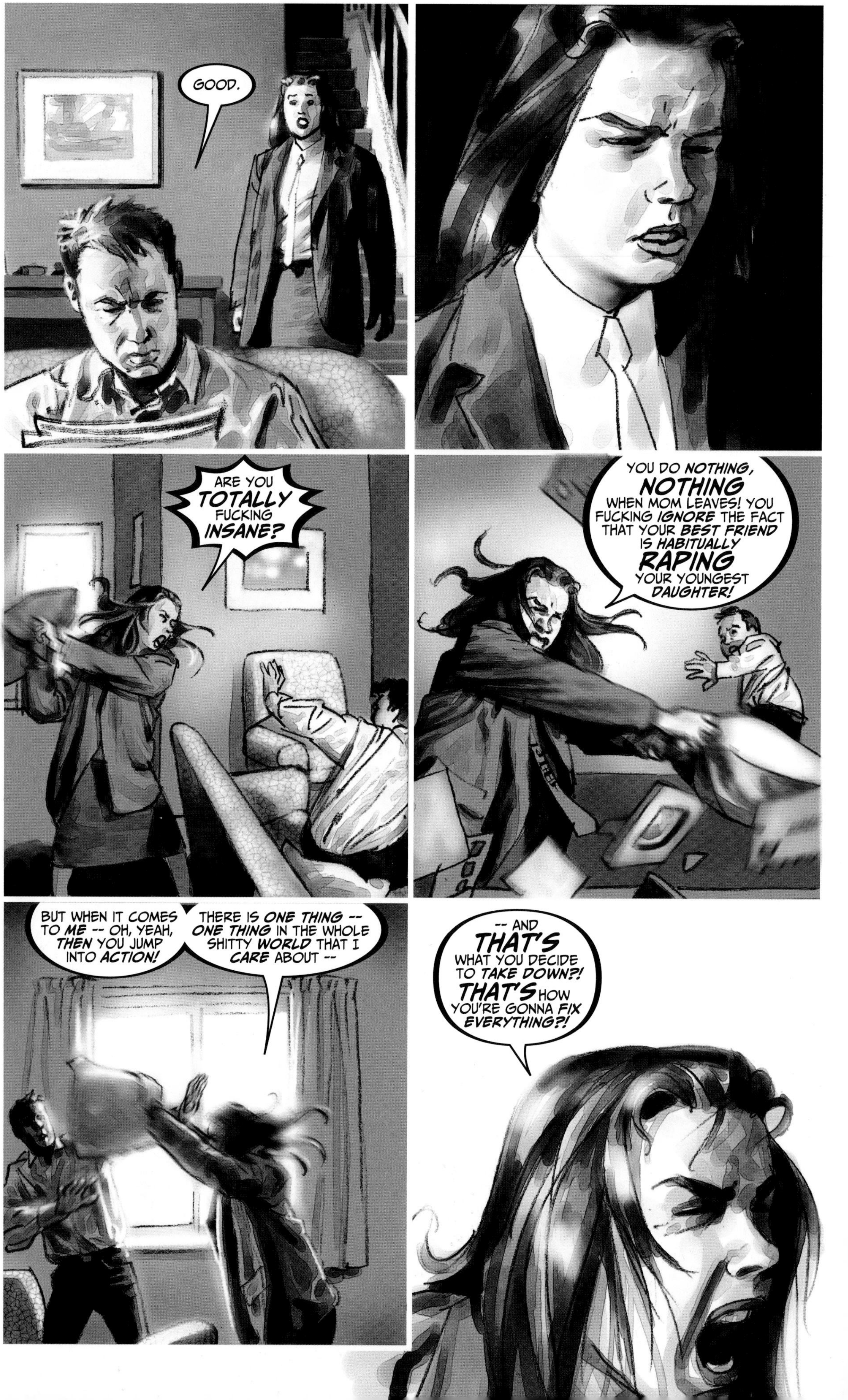
GOOD.
ARE YOU TOTALLY FUCKING INSANE?
YOU DO NOTHING, NOTHING WHEN MOM LEAVES! YOU FUCKING IGNORE THE FACT THAT YOUR BEST FRIEND IS HABITUALLY RAPING YOUR YOUNGEST DAUGHTER!
BUT WHEN IT COMES TO ME -- OH, YEAH, THEN YOU JUMP INTO ACTION!
THERE IS ONE THING -- ONE THING IN THE WHOLE SHITTY WORLD THAT I CARE ABOUT --
-- AND THAT'S WHAT YOU DECIDE TO TAKE DOWN?! THAT'S HOW YOU'RE GONNA FIX EVERYTHING?!

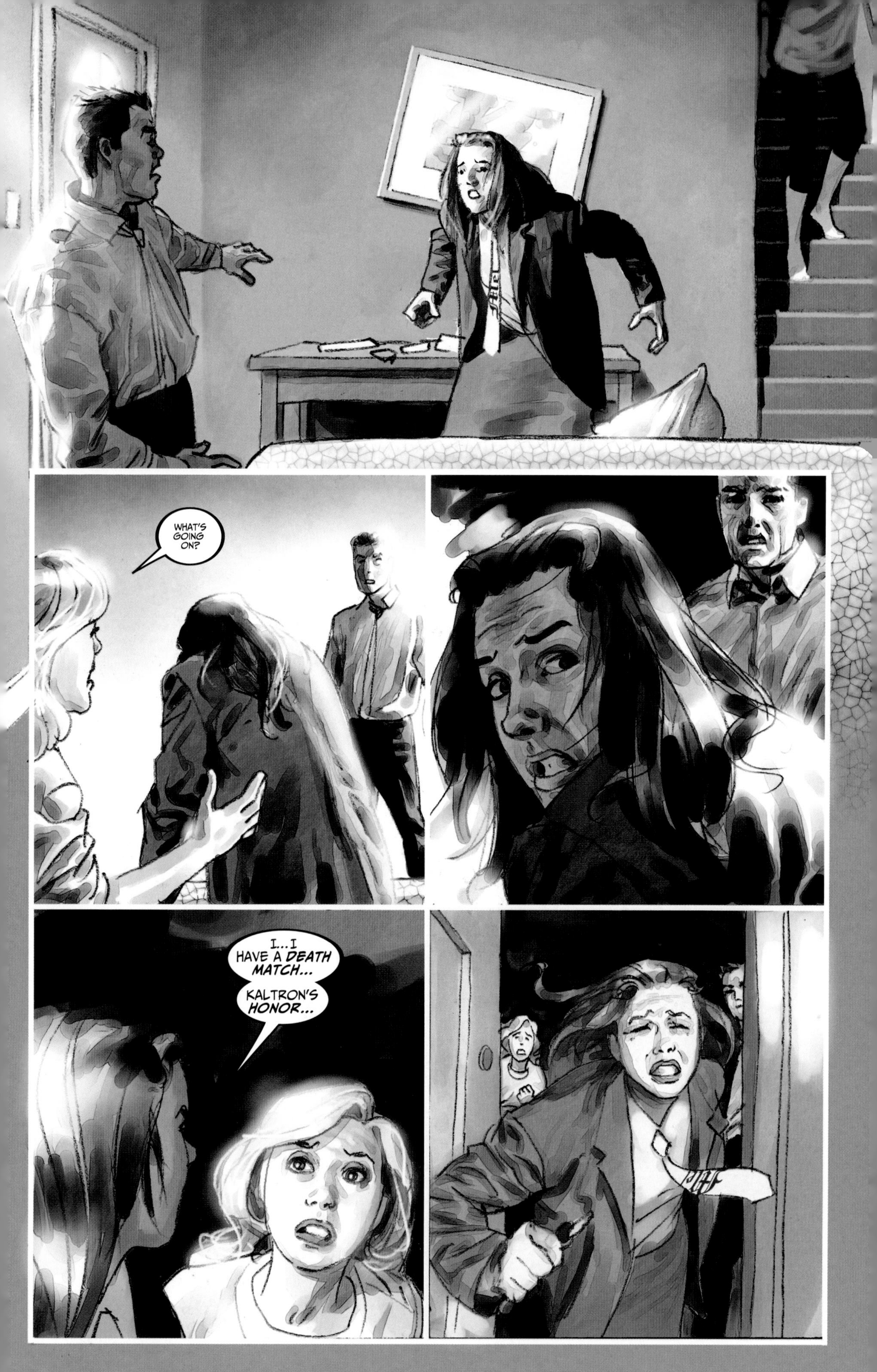
WHAT'S GOING ON?
I...I HAVE A *DEATH MATCH*...
KALTRON'S *HONOR*...

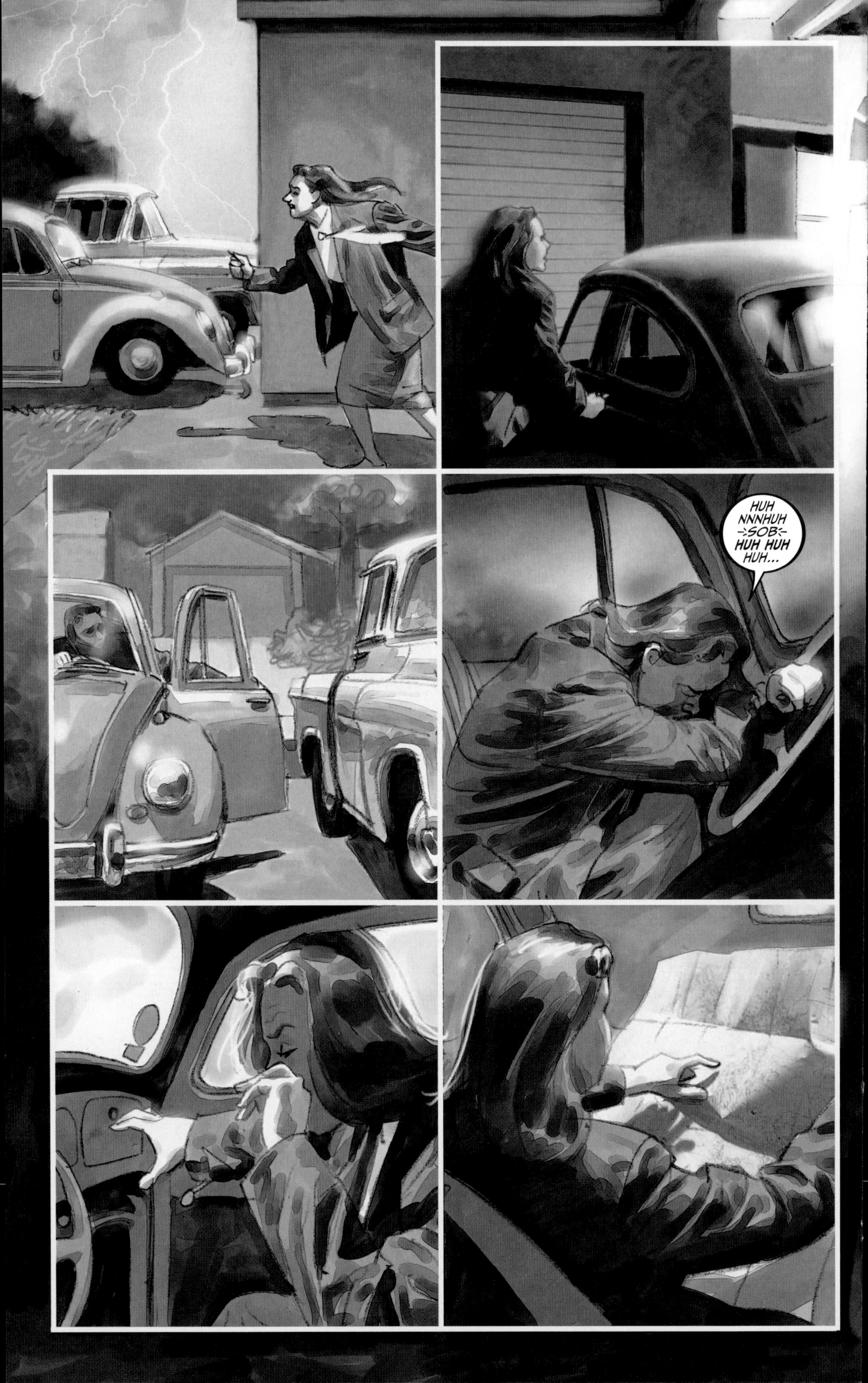
HUH NNNHUH -SOB- HUH HUH HUH...

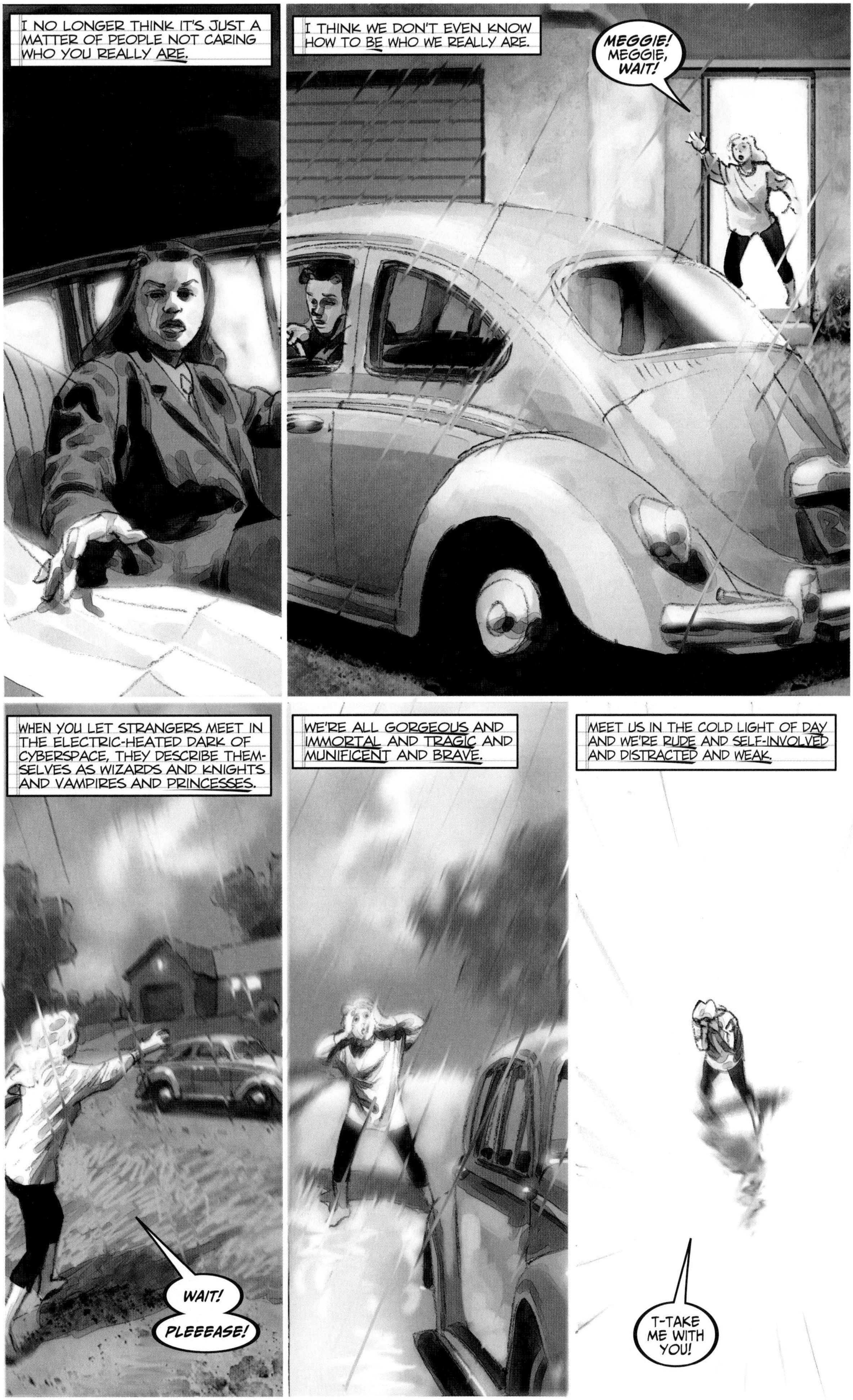
I NO LONGER THINK IT'S JUST A MATTER OF PEOPLE NOT CARING WHO YOU REALLY ARE.
I THINK WE DON'T EVEN KNOW HOW TO BE WHO WE REALLY ARE.
MEGGIE! MEGGIE, WAIT!
WHEN YOU LET STRANGERS MEET IN THE ELECTRIC-HEATED DARK OF CYBERSPACE, THEY DESCRIBE THEMSELVES AS WIZARDS AND KNIGHTS AND VAMPIRES AND PRINCESSES.
WAIT!
PLEEEASE!
WE'RE ALL GORGEOUS AND IMMORTAL AND TRAGIC AND MUNIFICENT AND BRAVE.
MEET US IN THE COLD LIGHT OF DAY AND WE'RE RUDE AND SELF-INVOLVED AND DISTRACTED AND WEAK.
T-TAKE ME WITH YOU!

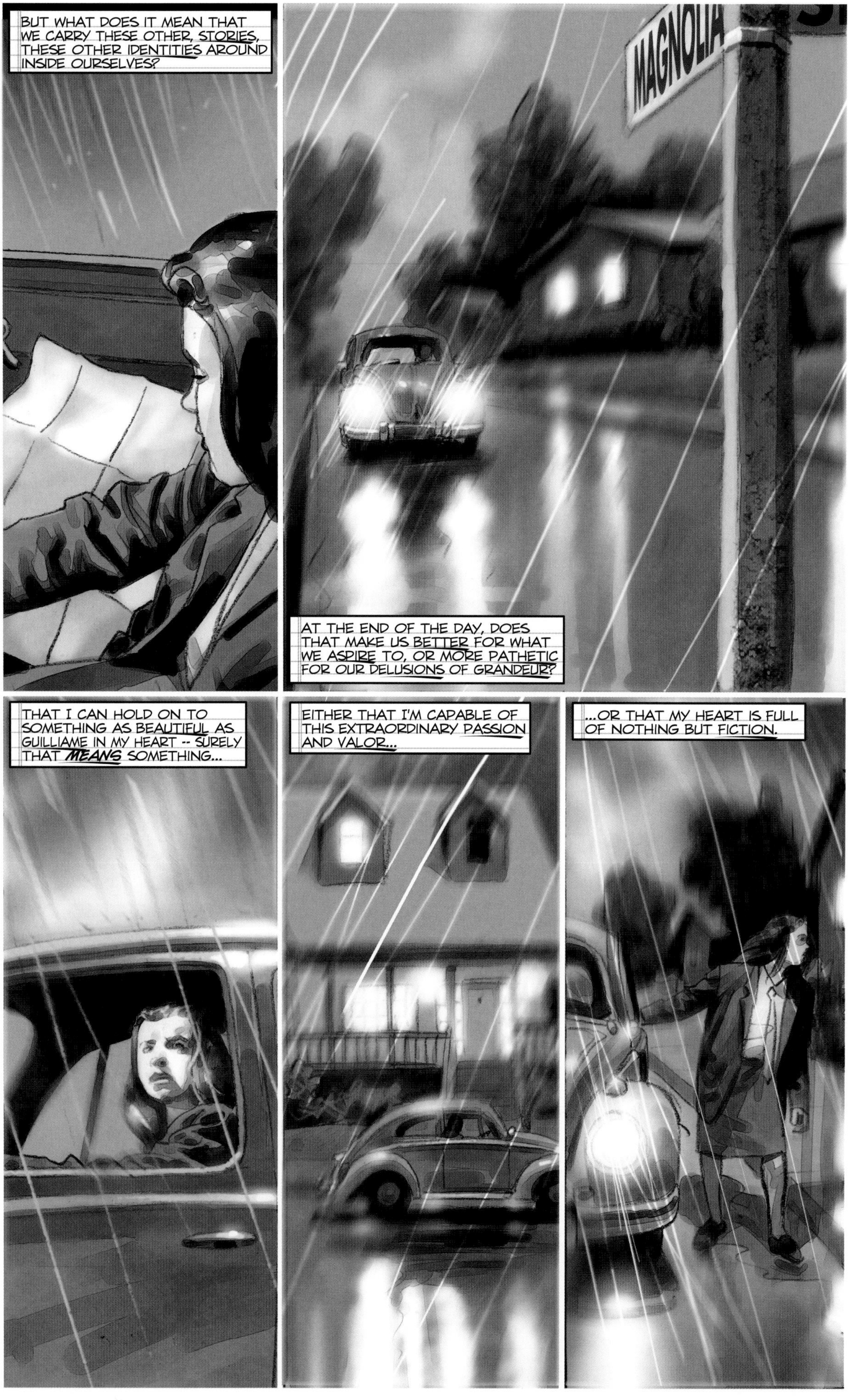
BUT WHAT DOES IT MEAN THAT WE CARRY THESE OTHER, STORIES, THESE OTHER IDENTITIES AROUND INSIDE OURSELVES?
MAGNOLIA
AT THE END OF THE DAY, DOES THAT MAKE US BETTER FOR WHAT WE ASPIRE TO, OR MORE PATHETIC FOR OUR DELUSIONS OF GRANDEUR?
THAT I CAN HOLD ON TO SOMETHING AS BEAUTIFUL AS GUILLIAME IN MY HEART -- SURELY THAT MEANS SOMETHING...
EITHER THAT I'M CAPABLE OF THIS EXTRAORDINARY PASSION AND VALOR...
...OR THAT MY HEART IS FULL OF NOTHING BUT FICTION.

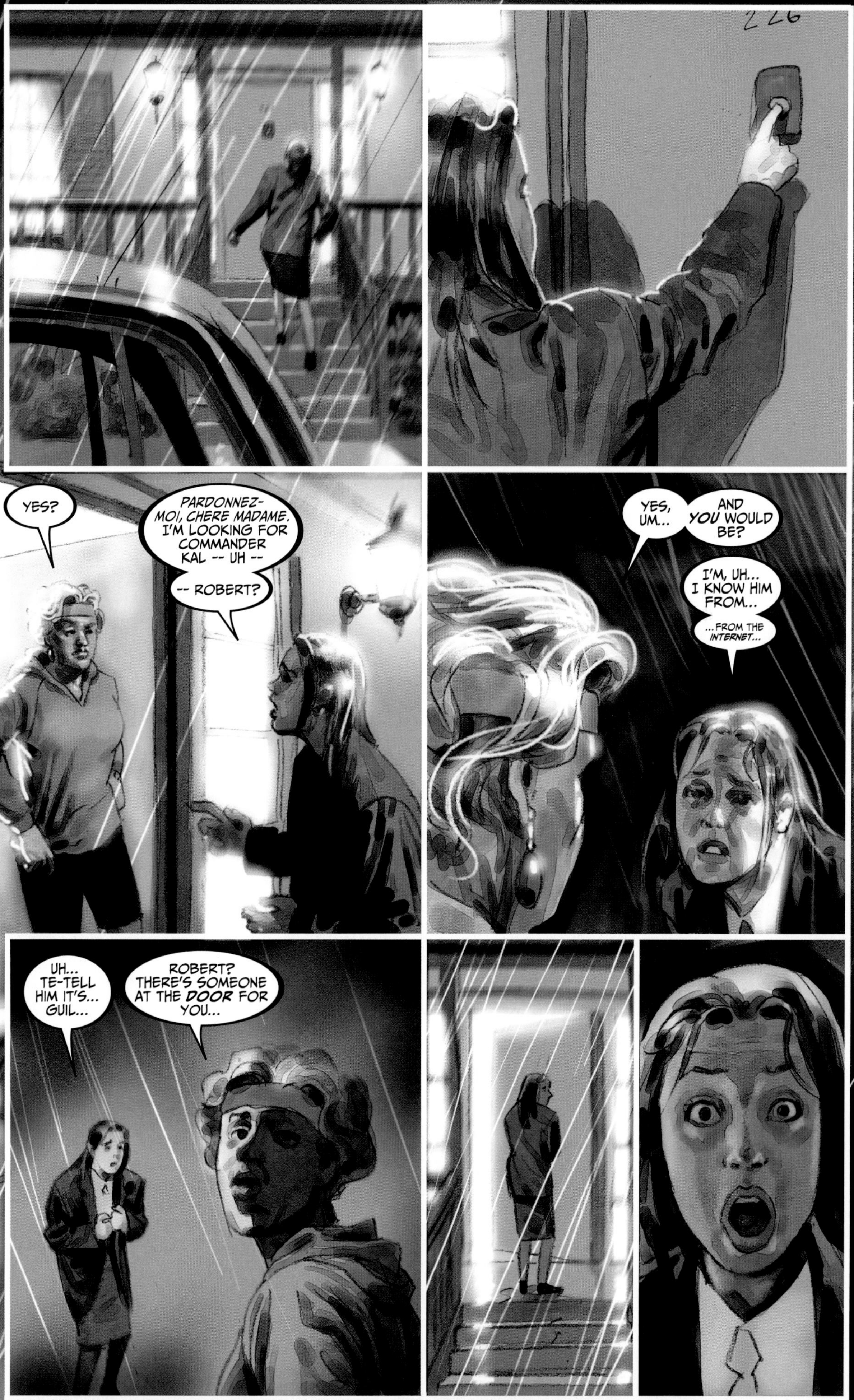
YES?
PARDONNEZ-MOI, CHERE MADAME. I'M LOOKING FOR COMMANDER KAL -- UH --
-- ROBERT?
YES, UM...
AND *YOU* WOULD BE?
I'M, UH... I KNOW HIM FROM...
...FROM THE *INTERNET*...
UH... TE-TELL HIM IT'S... GUIL...
ROBERT? THERE'S SOMEONE AT THE ***DOOR*** FOR YOU...

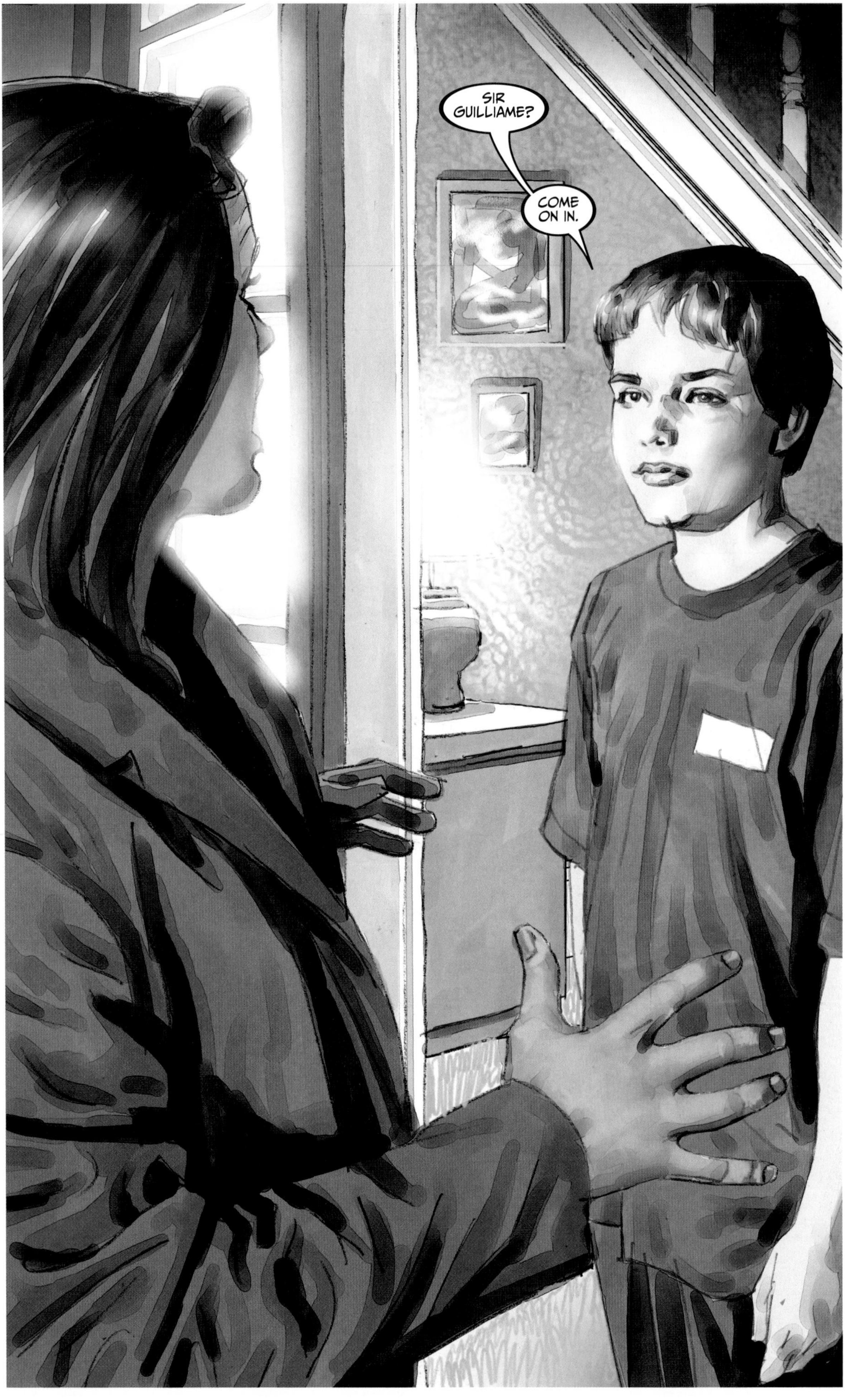
SIR GUILLIAME?
COME ON IN.

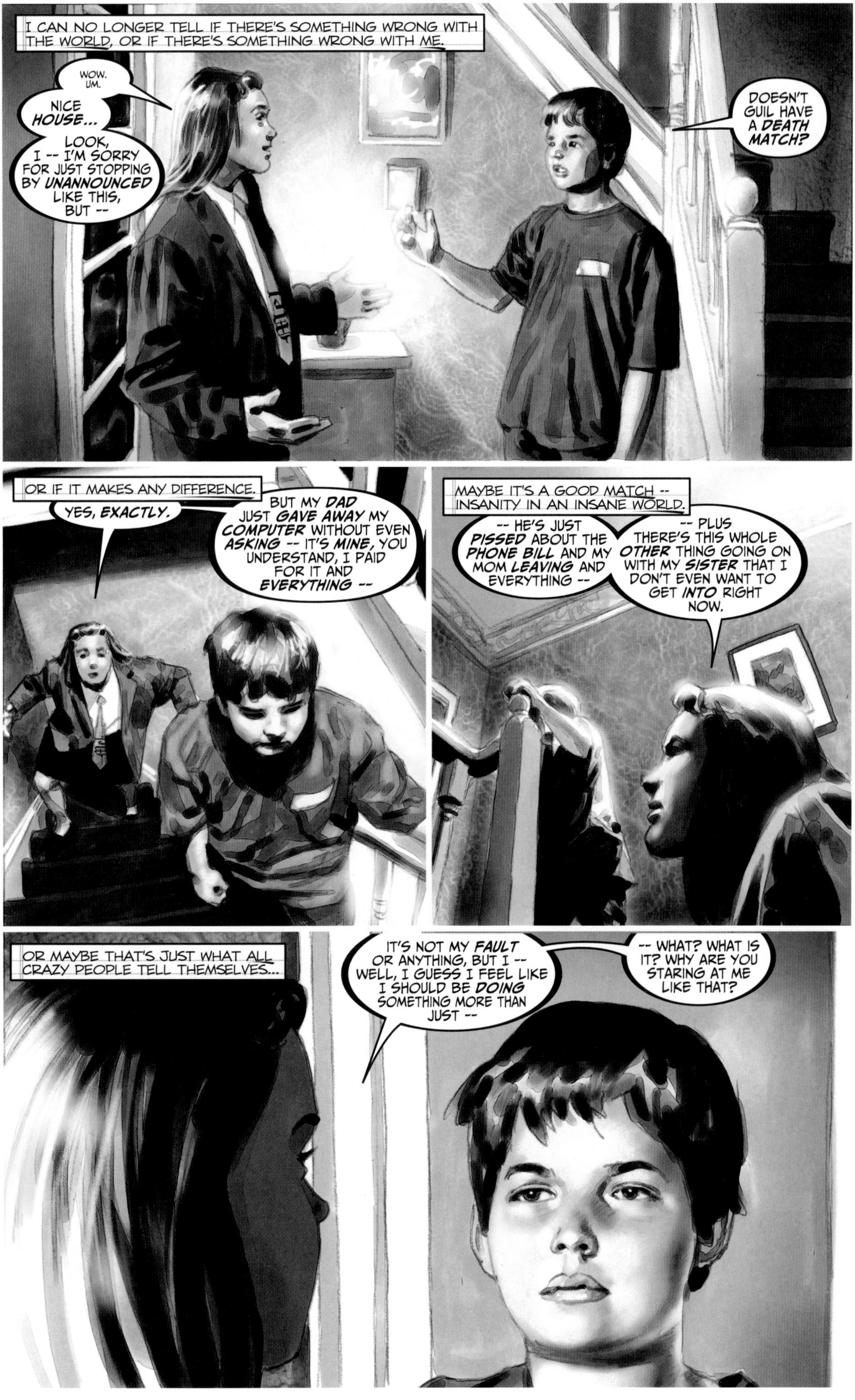
I CAN NO LONGER TELL IF THERE'S SOMETHING WRONG WITH THE WORLD, OR IF THERE'S SOMETHING WRONG WITH ME.
WOW. UM.
NICE HOUSE...
LOOK, I -- I'M SORRY FOR JUST STOPPING BY UNANNOUNCED LIKE THIS, BUT --
DOESN'T GUIL HAVE A DEATH MATCH?
OR IF IT MAKES ANY DIFFERENCE.
YES, EXACTLY.
BUT MY DAD JUST GAVE AWAY MY COMPUTER WITHOUT EVEN ASKING -- IT'S MINE, YOU UNDERSTAND, I PAID FOR IT AND EVERYTHING --
MAYBE IT'S A GOOD MATCH -- INSANITY IN AN INSANE WORLD.
-- HE'S JUST PISSED ABOUT THE PHONE BILL AND MY MOM LEAVING AND EVERYTHING --
-- PLUS THERE'S THIS WHOLE OTHER THING GOING ON WITH MY SISTER THAT I DON'T EVEN WANT TO GET INTO RIGHT NOW.
OR MAYBE THAT'S JUST WHAT ALL CRAZY PEOPLE TELL THEMSELVES...
IT'S NOT MY FAULT OR ANYTHING, BUT I -- WELL, I GUESS I FEEL LIKE I SHOULD BE DOING SOMETHING MORE THAN JUST --
-- WHAT? WHAT IS IT? WHY ARE YOU STARING AT ME LIKE THAT?

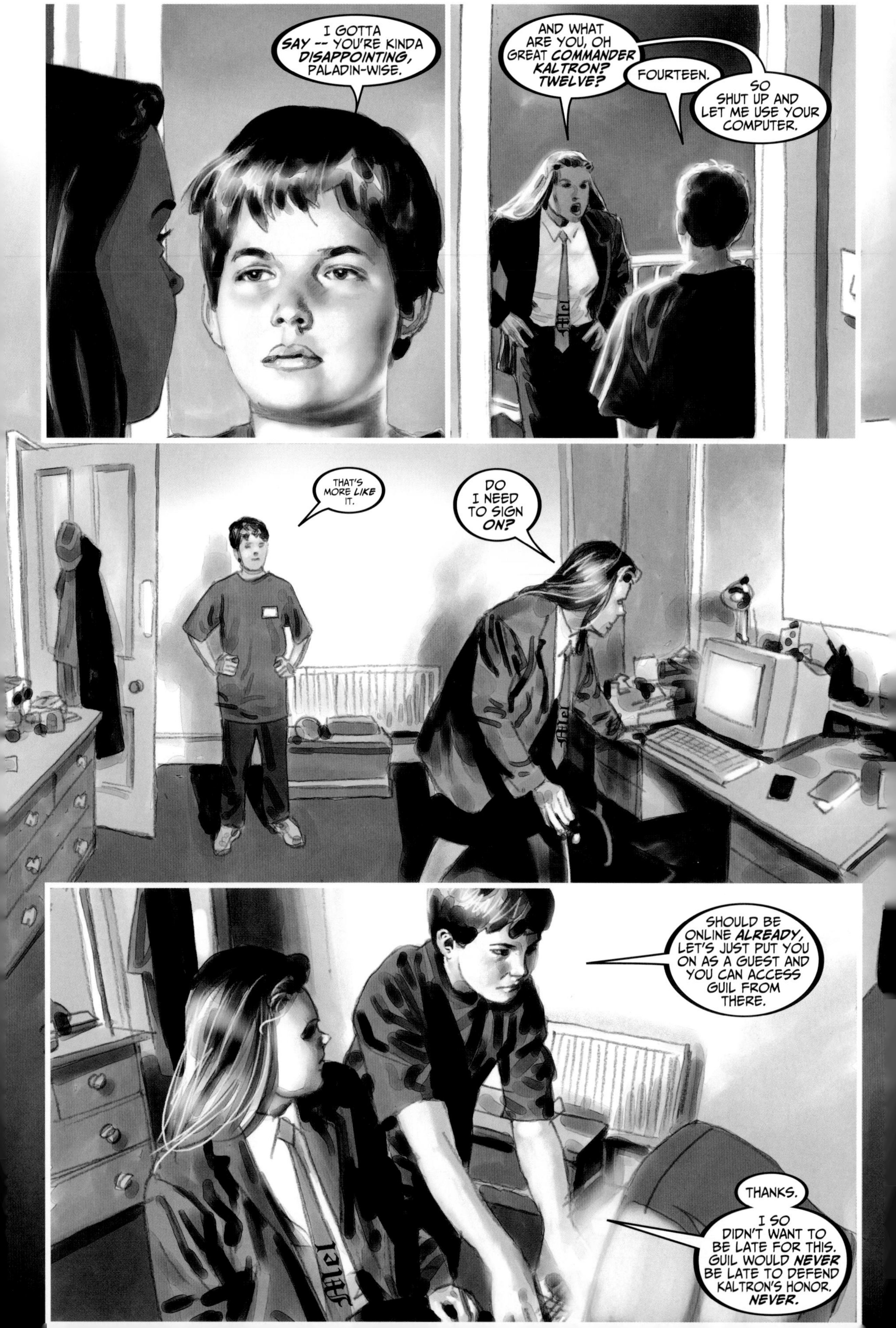
I GOTTA *SAY* -- YOU'RE KINDA *DISAPPOINTING,* PALADIN-WISE.
AND WHAT ARE YOU, OH GREAT *COMMANDER KALTRON? TWELVE?*
FOURTEEN.
SO SHUT UP AND LET ME USE YOUR COMPUTER.
THAT'S MORE *LIKE* IT.
DO I NEED TO SIGN *ON?*
SHOULD BE ONLINE *ALREADY,* LET'S JUST PUT YOU ON AS A GUEST AND YOU CAN ACCESS GUIL FROM THERE.
THANKS.
I SO DIDN'T WANT TO BE LATE FOR THIS. GUIL WOULD *NEVER* BE LATE TO DEFEND KALTRON'S HONOR. *NEVER.*

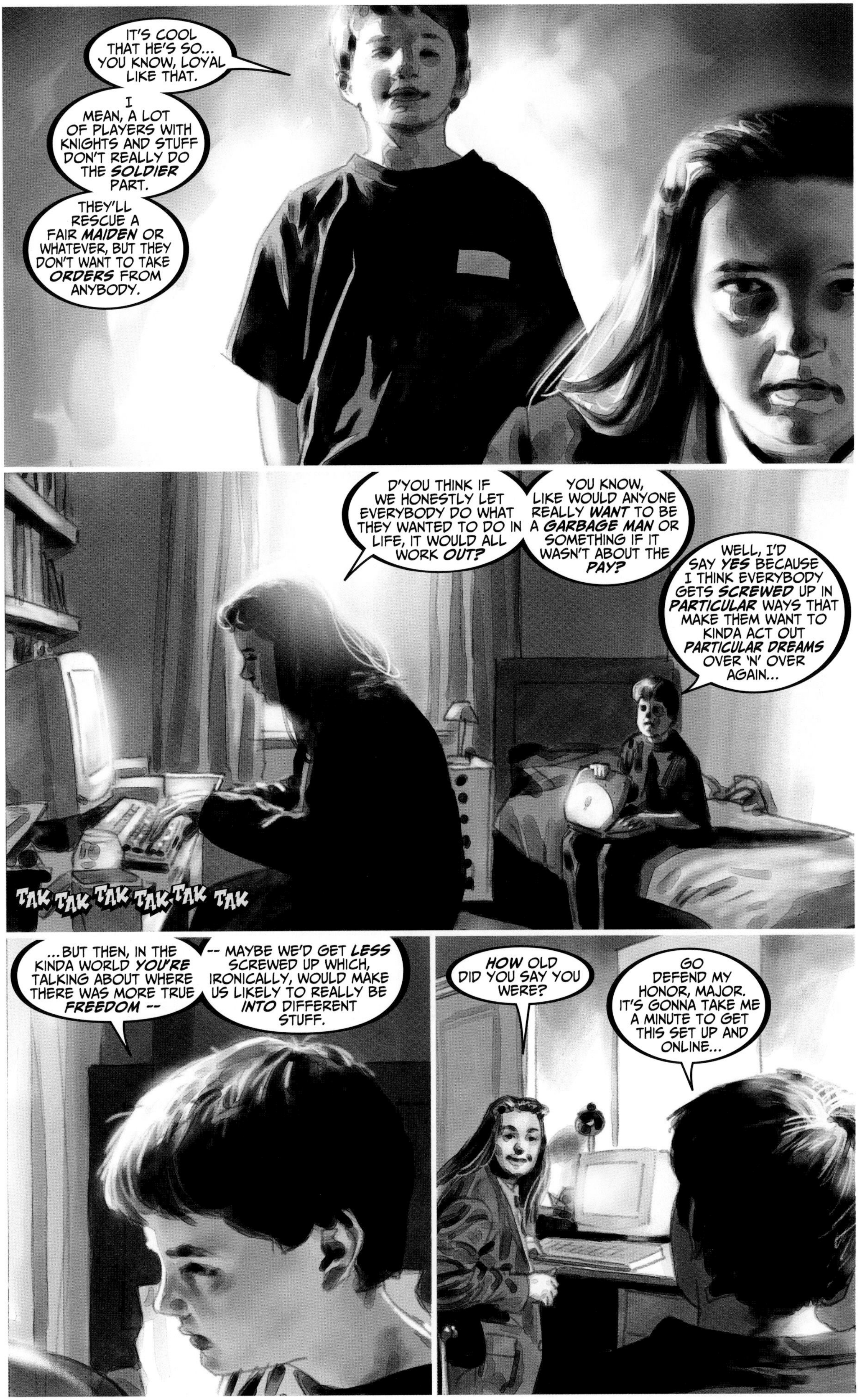
IT'S COOL THAT HE'S SO... YOU KNOW, LOYAL LIKE THAT.
I MEAN, A LOT OF PLAYERS WITH KNIGHTS AND STUFF DON'T REALLY DO THE SOLDIER PART.
THEY'LL RESCUE A FAIR MAIDEN OR WHATEVER, BUT THEY DON'T WANT TO TAKE ORDERS FROM ANYBODY.
D'YOU THINK IF WE HONESTLY LET EVERYBODY DO WHAT THEY WANTED TO DO IN LIFE, IT WOULD ALL WORK OUT?
YOU KNOW, LIKE WOULD ANYONE REALLY WANT TO BE A GARBAGE MAN OR SOMETHING IF IT WASN'T ABOUT THE PAY?
WELL, I'D SAY YES BECAUSE I THINK EVERYBODY GETS SCREWED UP IN PARTICULAR WAYS THAT MAKE THEM WANT TO KINDA ACT OUT PARTICULAR DREAMS OVER 'N' OVER AGAIN...
TAK TAK TAK TAK TAK TAK
...BUT THEN, IN THE KINDA WORLD YOU'RE TALKING ABOUT WHERE THERE WAS MORE TRUE FREEDOM --
-- MAYBE WE'D GET LESS SCREWED UP WHICH, IRONICALLY, WOULD MAKE US LIKELY TO REALLY BE INTO DIFFERENT STUFF.
HOW OLD DID YOU SAY YOU WERE?
GO DEFEND MY HONOR, MAJOR. IT'S GONNA TAKE ME A MINUTE TO GET THIS SET UP AND ONLINE...

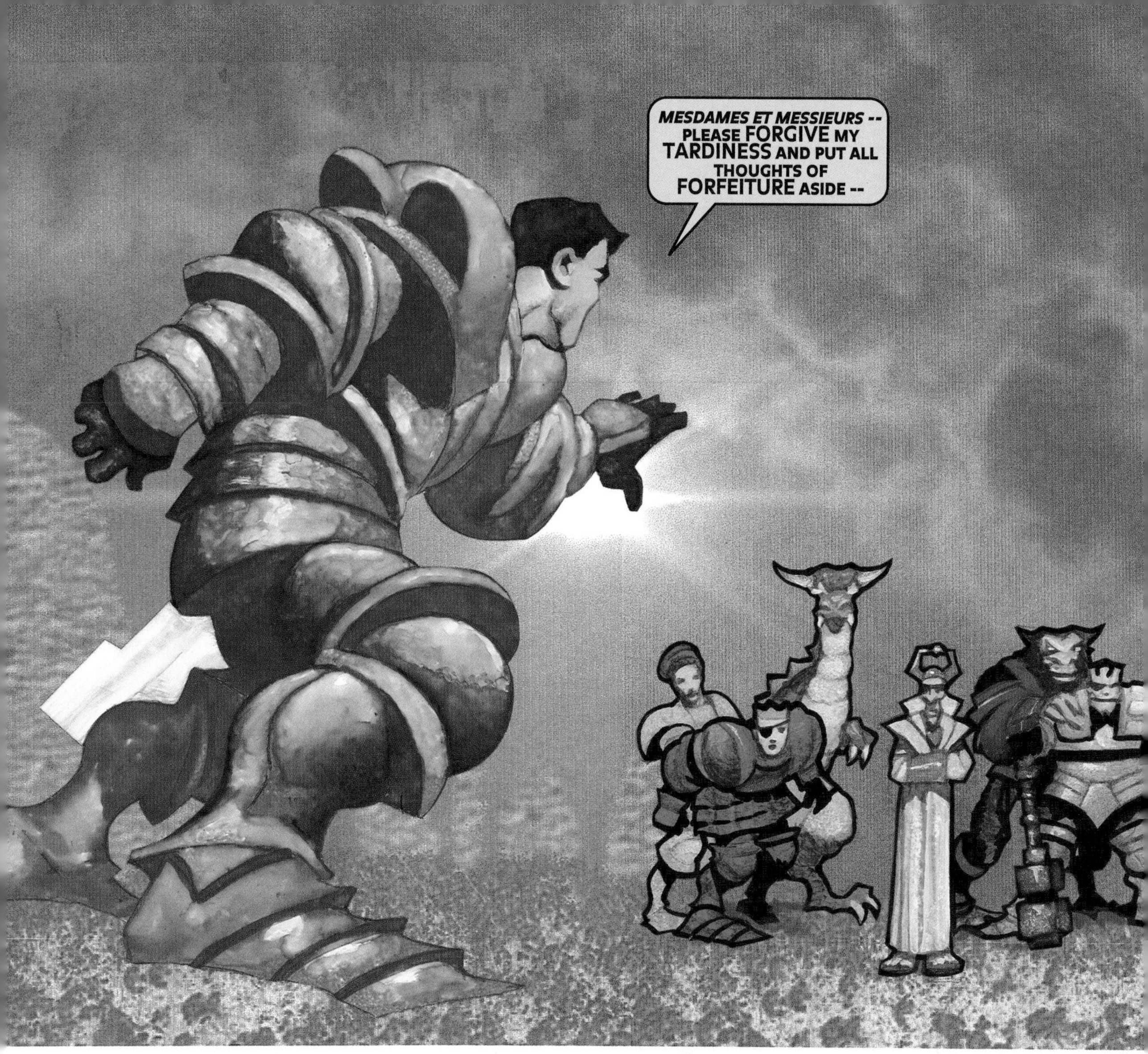
MESDAMES ET MESSIEURS -- PLEASE FORGIVE MY TARDINESS AND PUT ALL THOUGHTS OF FORFEITURE ASIDE --

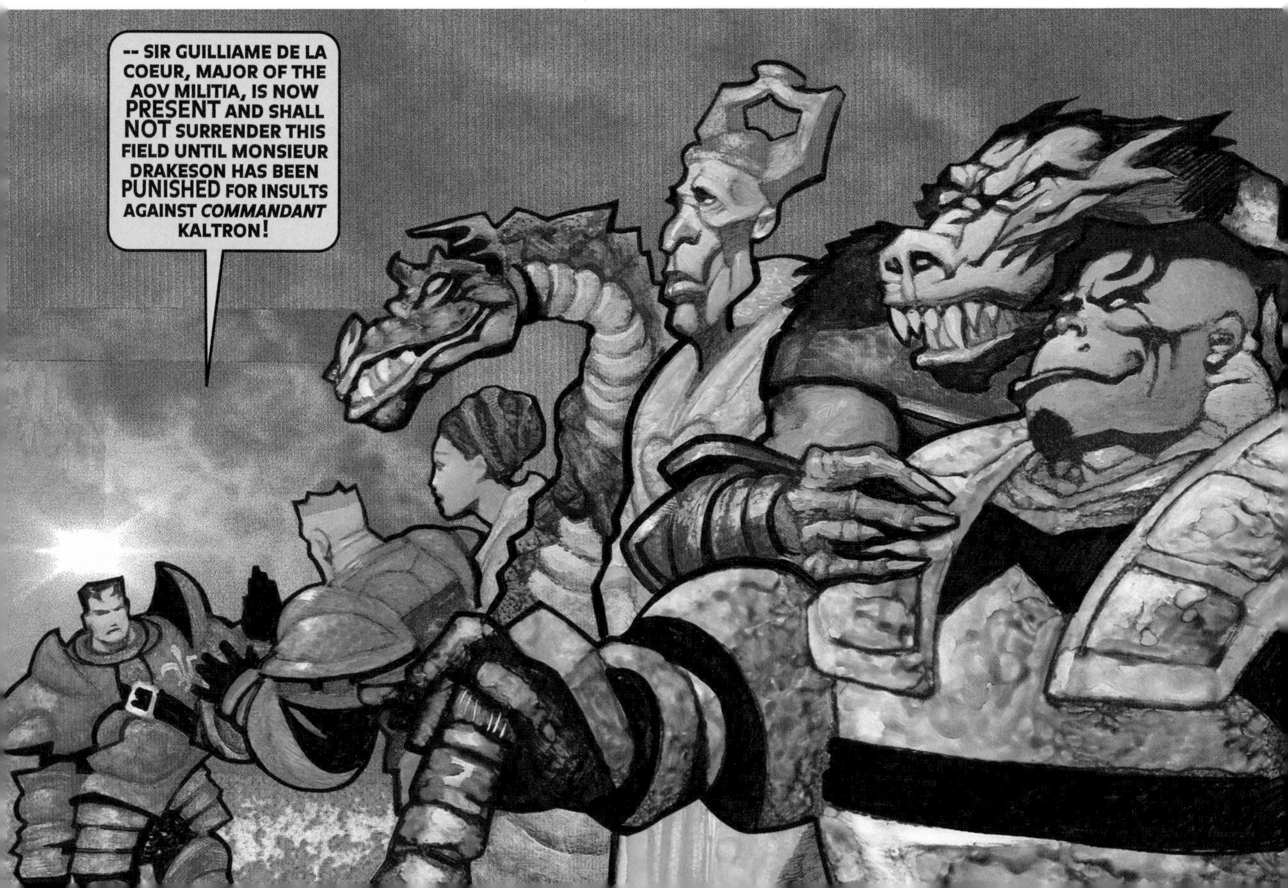
-- SIR GUILLIAME DE LA COEUR, MAJOR OF THE AOV MILITIA, IS NOW PRESENT AND SHALL NOT SURRENDER THIS FIELD UNTIL MONSIEUR DRAKESON HAS BEEN PUNISHED FOR INSULTS AGAINST COMMANDANT KALTRON!

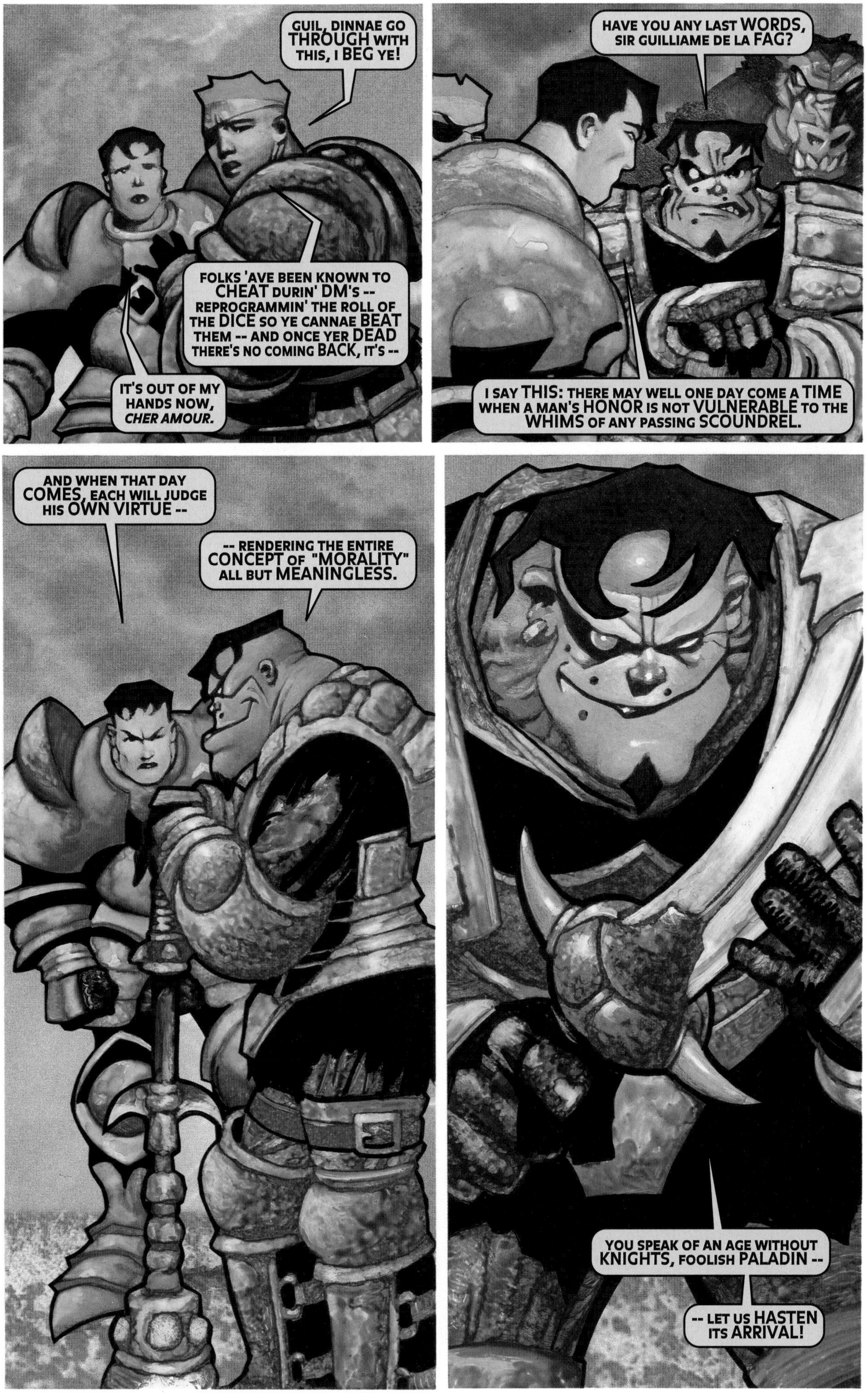
GUIL, DINNAE GO THROUGH WITH THIS, I BEG YE!
FOLKS 'AVE BEEN KNOWN TO CHEAT DURIN' DM's -- REPROGRAMMIN' THE ROLL OF THE DICE SO YE CANNAE BEAT THEM -- AND ONCE YER DEAD THERE'S NO COMING BACK, IT'S --
IT'S OUT OF MY HANDS NOW, CHER AMOUR.
HAVE YOU ANY LAST WORDS, SIR GUILLIAME DE LA FAG?
I SAY THIS: THERE MAY WELL ONE DAY COME A TIME WHEN A MAN'S HONOR IS NOT VULNERABLE TO THE WHIMS OF ANY PASSING SCOUNDREL.
AND WHEN THAT DAY COMES, EACH WILL JUDGE HIS OWN VIRTUE --
-- RENDERING THE ENTIRE CONCEPT OF "MORALITY" ALL BUT MEANINGLESS.
YOU SPEAK OF AN AGE WITHOUT KNIGHTS, FOOLISH PALADIN --
-- LET US HASTEN ITS ARRIVAL!

ROLLING 2D20, WITH COMBAT TO TWELVE POINTS.

ARE THE SECONDS PRESENT AND IN ACCORD?

YES.

... AYE.

COMBATANTS WILL NOW ROLL 1D6 FOR FIRST STRIKE PRIVILEGE.

//roll (1d6)
3

//roll (1d6)
5

MERCI, MODERATOR.

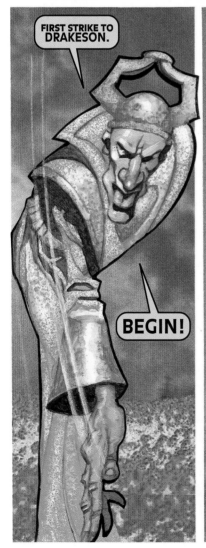

FIRST STRIKE TO DRAKESON.

BEGIN!

::THE OLD MAN MOVES WITH SURPRISING AGILITY, LUNGING TOWARDS THE SIMPERING PALADIN::

//roll (2d20)
Drakeson rolled
2 20-sided dice:
10 16

::THE KNIGHT ARCS HIS FAITHFUL BROADSWORD IN AN ATTEMPT TO PARRY::

//roll (2d20)
Sir Guil rolled
2 20-sided dice:
12 4

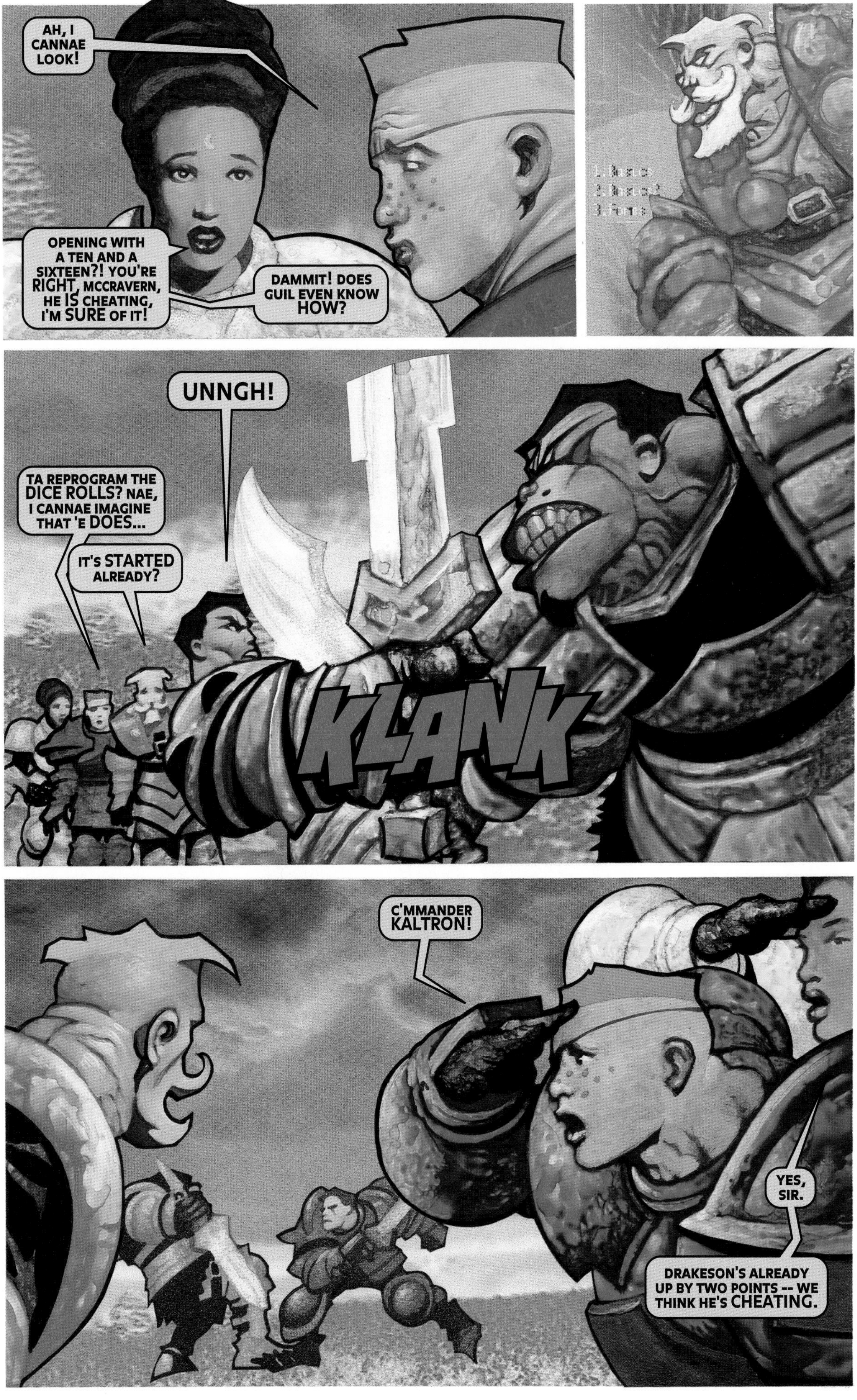

AH, I CANNAE LOOK!
OPENING WITH A TEN AND A SIXTEEN?! YOU'RE RIGHT, MCCRAVERN, HE IS CHEATING, I'M SURE OF IT!
DAMMIT! DOES GUIL EVEN KNOW HOW?
UNNGH!
TA REPROGRAM THE DICE ROLLS? NAE, I CANNAE IMAGINE THAT 'E DOES...
IT'S STARTED ALREADY?
KLANK
C'MMANDER KALTRON!
YES, SIR.
DRAKESON'S ALREADY UP BY TWO POINTS -- WE THINK HE'S CHEATING.

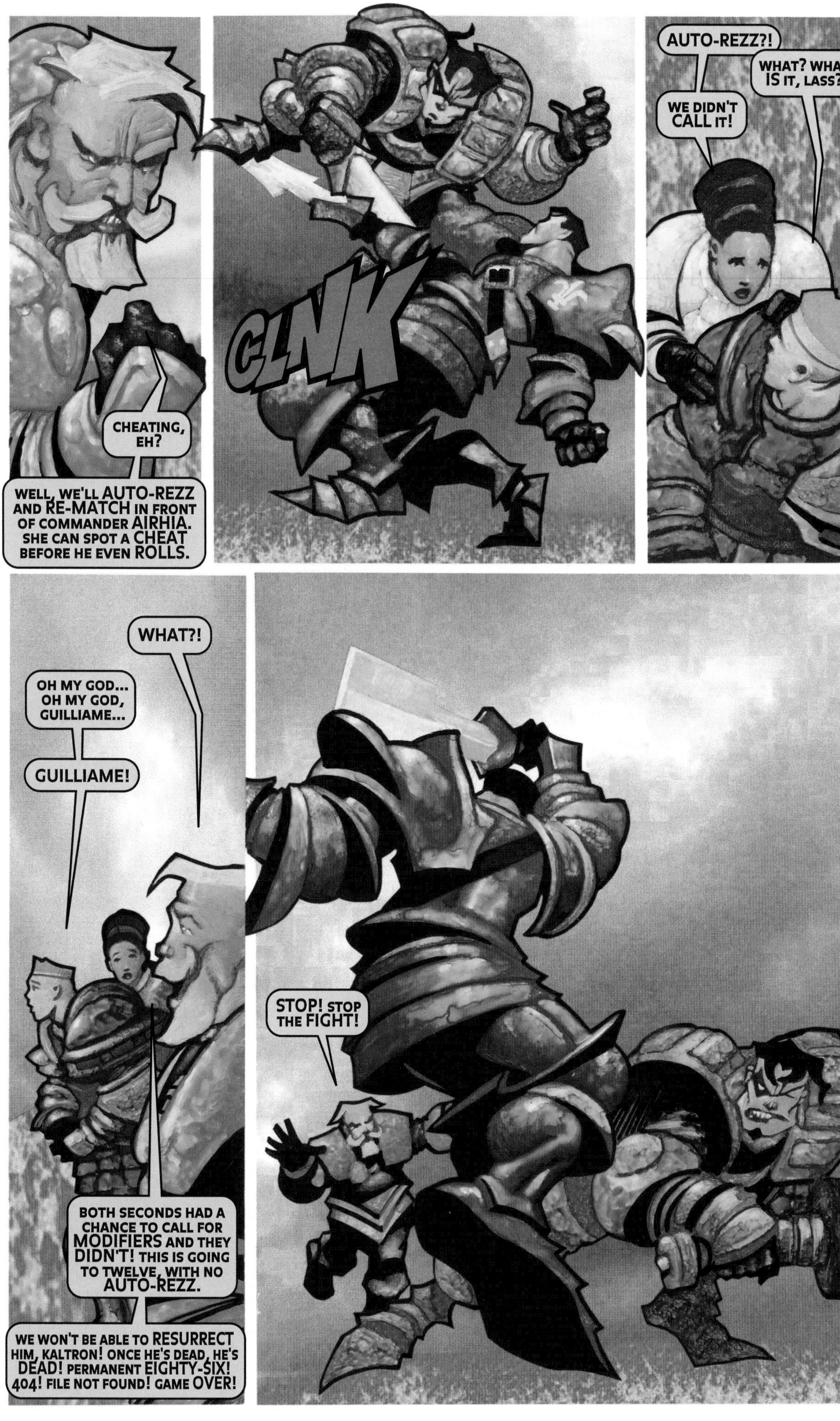
CHEATING, EH?
WELL, WE'LL AUTO-REZZ AND RE-MATCH IN FRONT OF COMMANDER AIRHIA. SHE CAN SPOT A CHEAT BEFORE HE EVEN ROLLS.
CLNK
AUTO-REZZ?!
WHAT? WHAT IS IT, LASS?
WE DIDN'T CALL IT!
WHAT?!
OH MY GOD... OH MY GOD, GUILLIAME...
GUILLIAME!
BOTH SECONDS HAD A CHANCE TO CALL FOR MODIFIERS AND THEY DIDN'T! THIS IS GOING TO TWELVE, WITH NO AUTO-REZZ.
WE WON'T BE ABLE TO RESURRECT HIM, KALTRON! ONCE HE'S DEAD, HE'S DEAD! PERMANENT EIGHTY-SIX! 404! FILE NOT FOUND! GAME OVER!
STOP! STOP THE FIGHT!

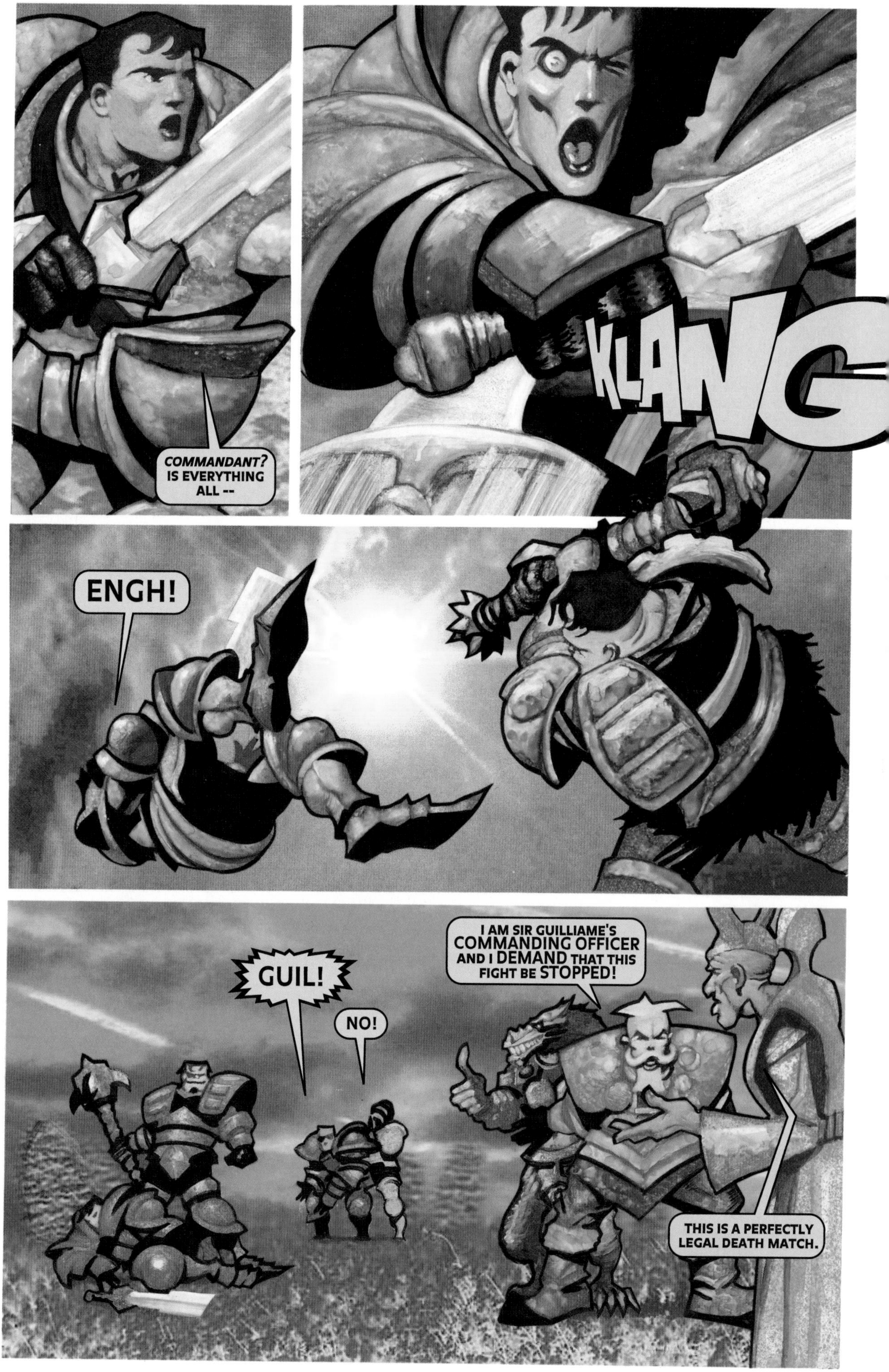
COMMANDANT? IS EVERYTHING ALL --
KLANG
ENGH!
GUIL!
NO!
I AM SIR GUILLIAME'S COMMANDING OFFICER AND I DEMAND THAT THIS FIGHT BE STOPPED!
THIS IS A PERFECTLY LEGAL DEATH MATCH.

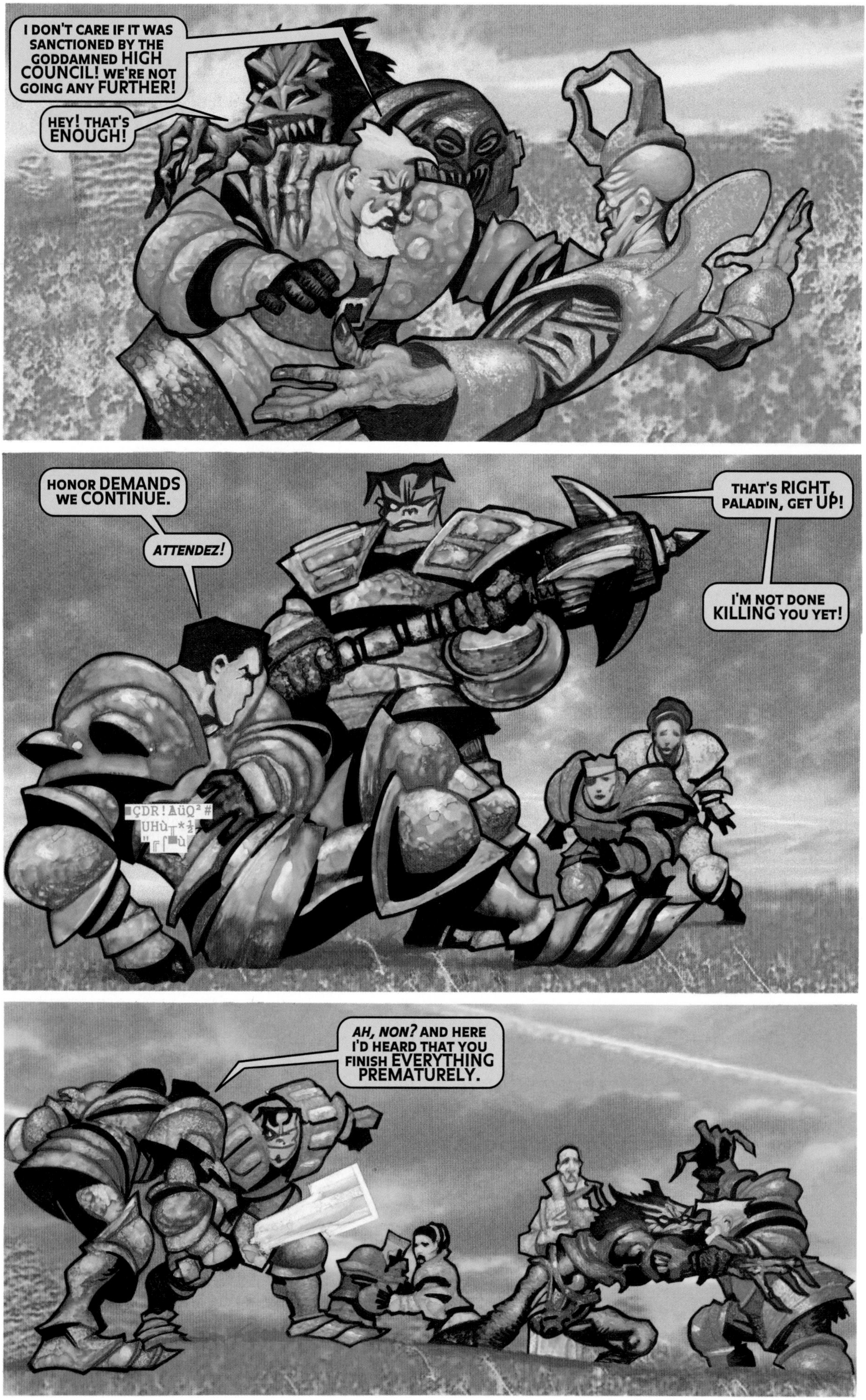
I DON'T CARE IF IT WAS SANCTIONED BY THE GODDAMNED HIGH COUNCIL! WE'RE NOT GOING ANY FURTHER!
HEY! THAT'S ENOUGH!
HONOR DEMANDS WE CONTINUE.
ATTENDEZ!
THAT'S RIGHT, PALADIN, GET UP!
I'M NOT DONE KILLING YOU YET!
AH, NON? AND HERE I'D HEARD THAT YOU FINISH EVERYTHING PREMATURELY.

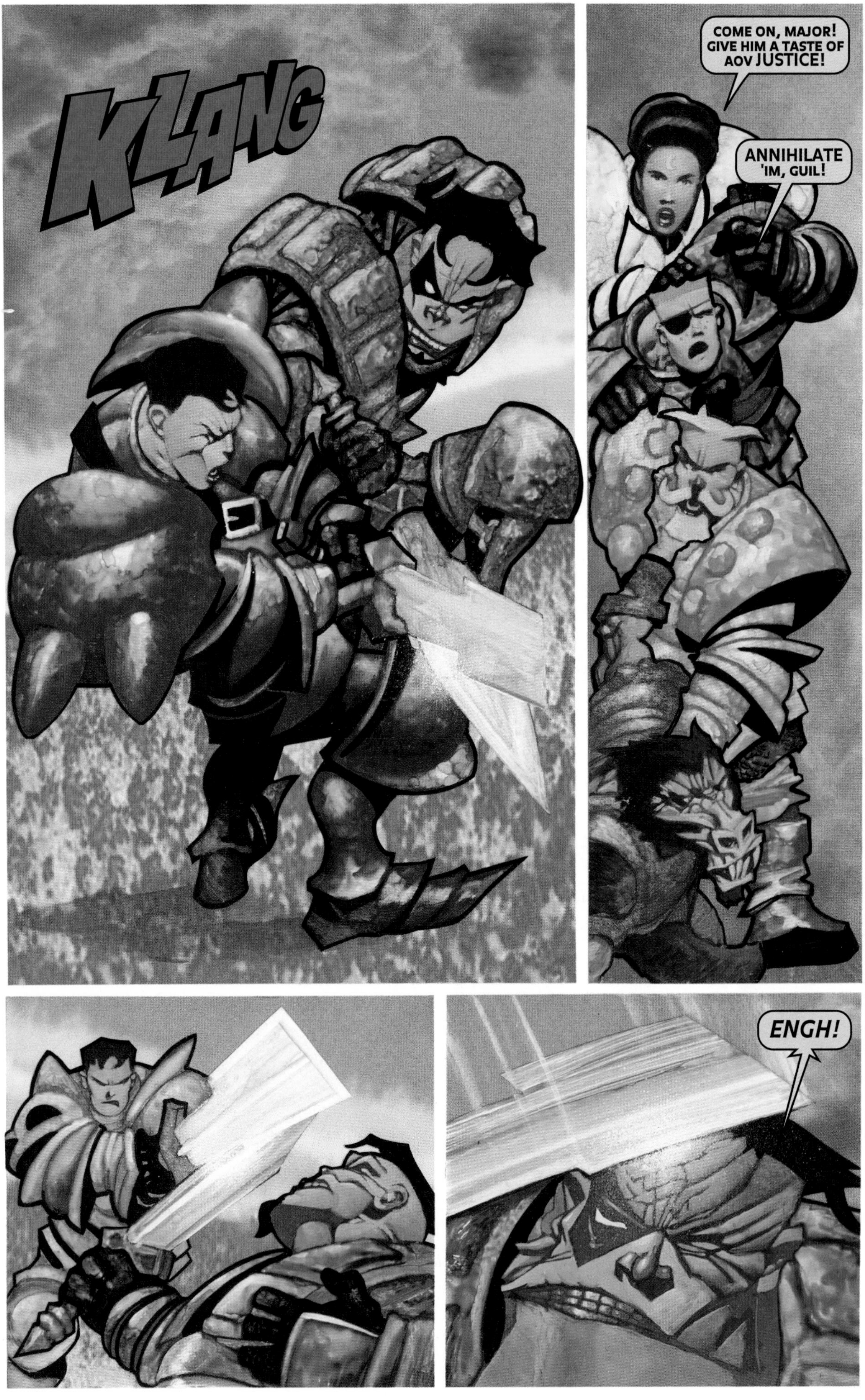
KLANG
COME ON, MAJOR! GIVE HIM A TASTE OF AOV JUSTICE!
ANNIHILATE 'IM, GUIL!
ENGH!

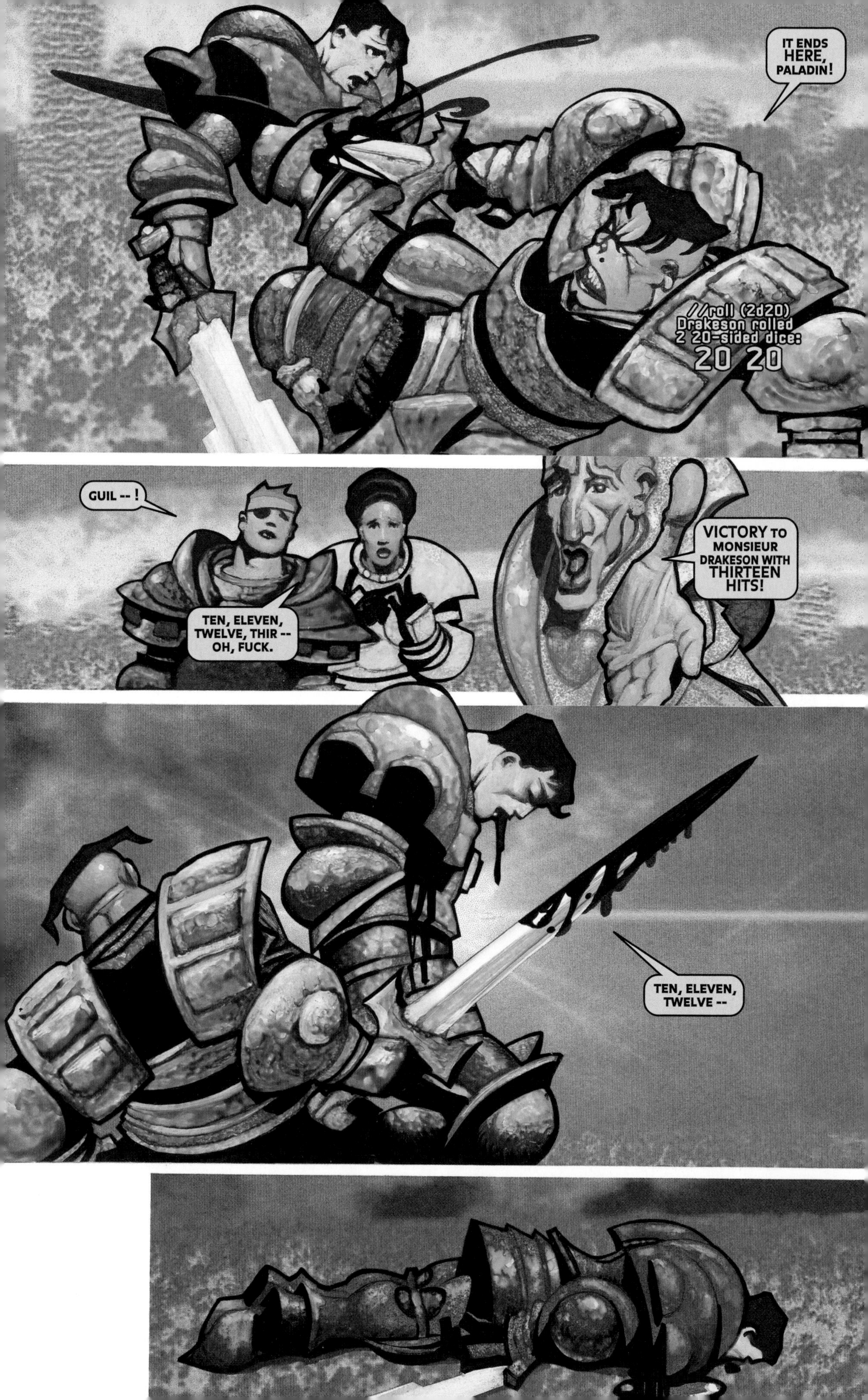

IT ENDS HERE, PALADIN!
//roll (2d20) Drakeson rolled 2 20-sided dice: 20 20
GUIL -- !
TEN, ELEVEN, TWELVE, THIR -- OH, FUCK.
VICTORY TO MONSIEUR DRAKESON WITH THIRTEEN HITS!
TEN, ELEVEN, TWELVE --

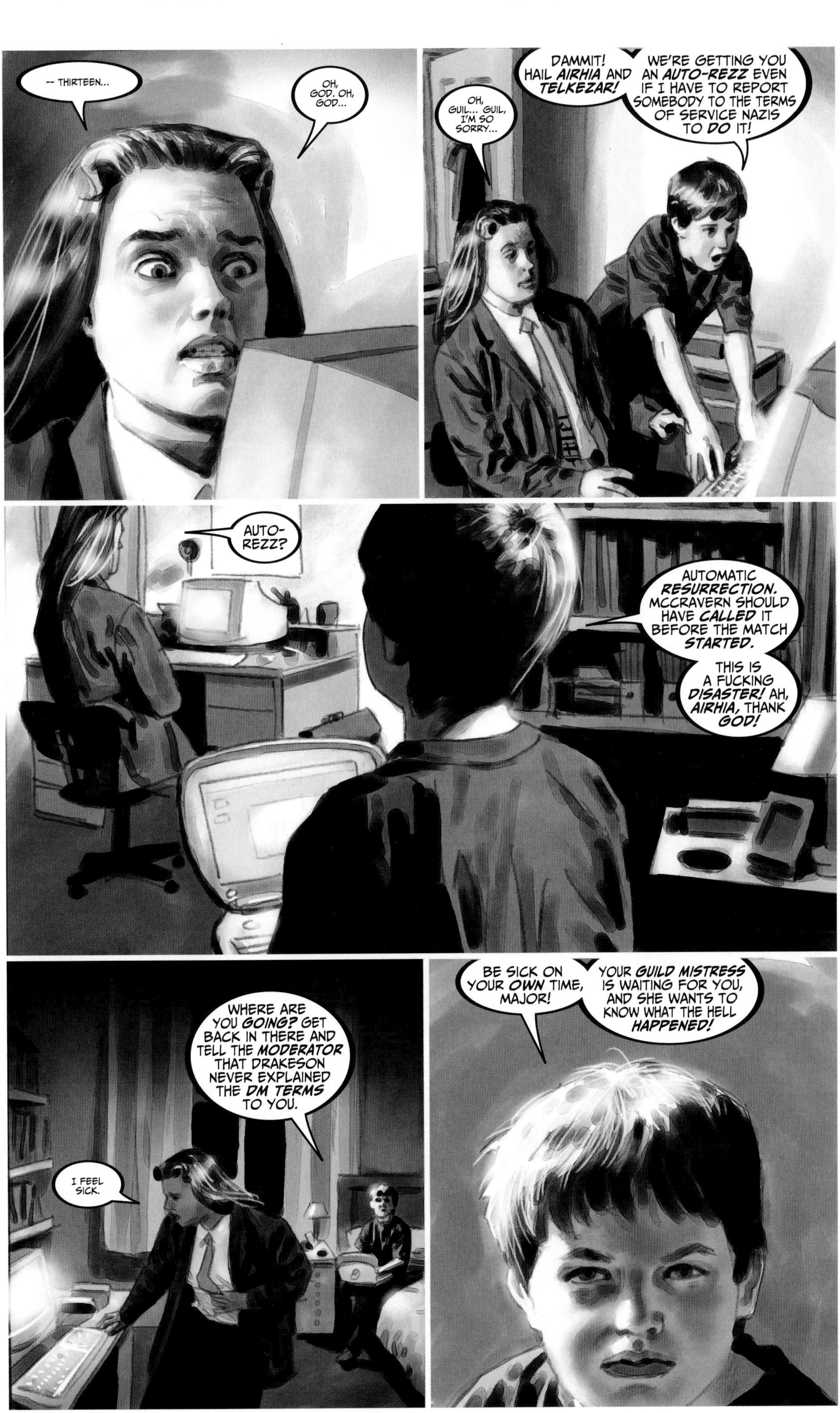
-- THIRTEEN...
OH, GOD. OH, GOD...
OH, GUIL... GUIL, I'M SO SORRY...
DAMMIT! HAIL AIRHIA AND TELKEZAR!
WE'RE GETTING YOU AN AUTO-REZZ EVEN IF I HAVE TO REPORT SOMEBODY TO THE TERMS OF SERVICE NAZIS TO DO IT!
AUTO-REZZ?
AUTOMATIC RESURRECTION. MCCRAVERN SHOULD HAVE CALLED IT BEFORE THE MATCH STARTED.
THIS IS A FUCKING DISASTER! AH, AIRHIA, THANK GOD!
WHERE ARE YOU GOING? GET BACK IN THERE AND TELL THE MODERATOR THAT DRAKESON NEVER EXPLAINED THE DM TERMS TO YOU.
I FEEL SICK.
BE SICK ON YOUR OWN TIME, MAJOR!
YOUR GUILD MISTRESS IS WAITING FOR YOU, AND SHE WANTS TO KNOW WHAT THE HELL HAPPENED!

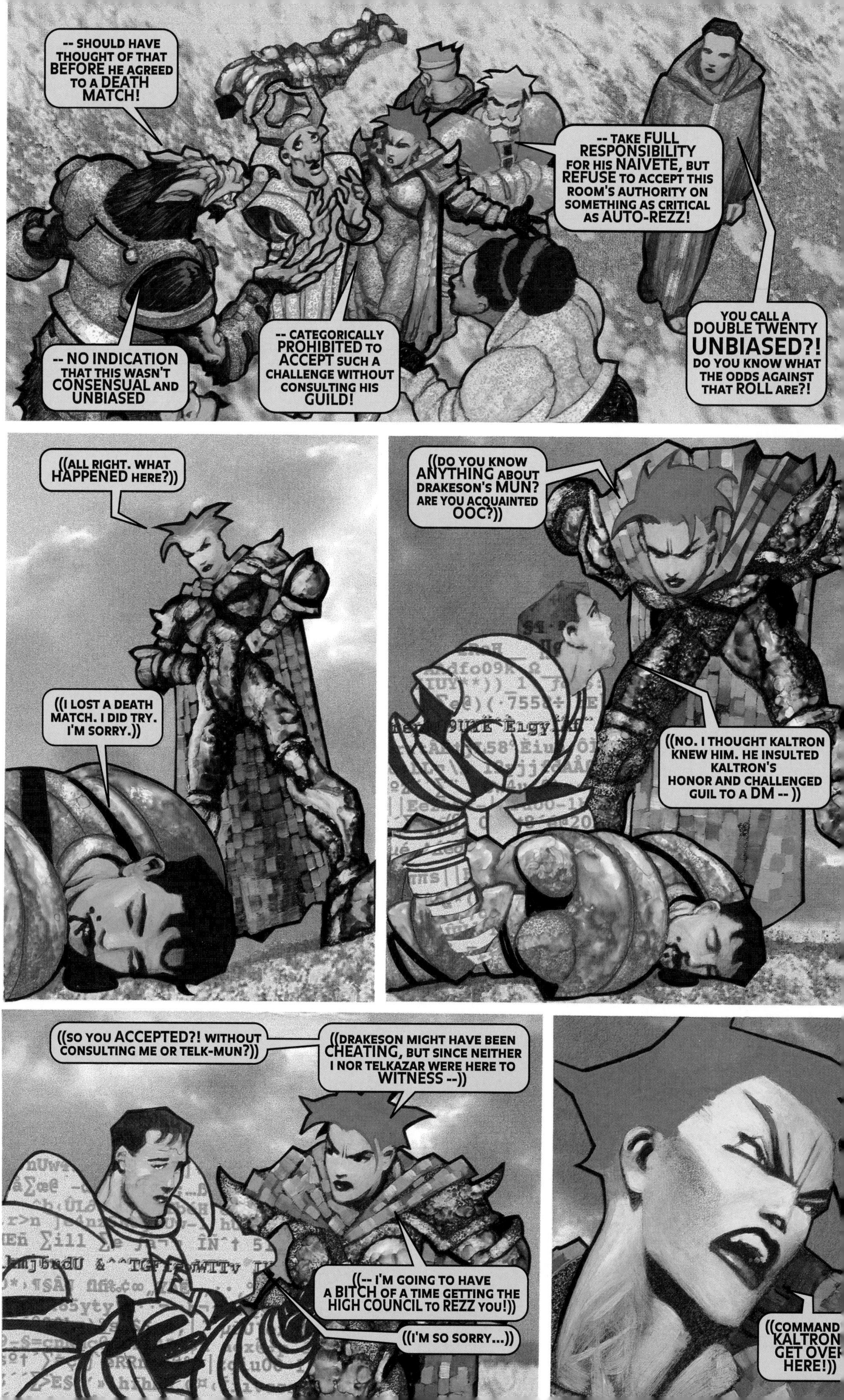
-- SHOULD HAVE THOUGHT OF THAT BEFORE HE AGREED TO A DEATH MATCH!
-- NO INDICATION THAT THIS WASN'T CONSENSUAL AND UNBIASED
-- CATEGORICALLY PROHIBITED TO ACCEPT SUCH A CHALLENGE WITHOUT CONSULTING HIS GUILD!
-- TAKE FULL RESPONSIBILITY FOR HIS NAIVETE, BUT REFUSE TO ACCEPT THIS ROOM'S AUTHORITY ON SOMETHING AS CRITICAL AS AUTO-REZZ!
YOU CALL A DOUBLE TWENTY UNBIASED?! DO YOU KNOW WHAT THE ODDS AGAINST THAT ROLL ARE?!
((ALL RIGHT. WHAT HAPPENED HERE?))
((I LOST A DEATH MATCH. I DID TRY. I'M SORRY.))
((DO YOU KNOW ANYTHING ABOUT DRAKESON'S MUN? ARE YOU ACQUAINTED OOC?))
((NO. I THOUGHT KALTRON KNEW HIM. HE INSULTED KALTRON'S HONOR AND CHALLENGED GUIL TO A DM --))
((SO YOU ACCEPTED?! WITHOUT CONSULTING ME OR TELK-MUN?))
((DRAKESON MIGHT HAVE BEEN CHEATING, BUT SINCE NEITHER I NOR TELKAZAR WERE HERE TO WITNESS --))
((-- I'M GOING TO HAVE A BITCH OF A TIME GETTING THE HIGH COUNCIL TO REZZ YOU!))
((I'M SO SORRY...))
((COMMAND KALTRON GET OVER HERE!))

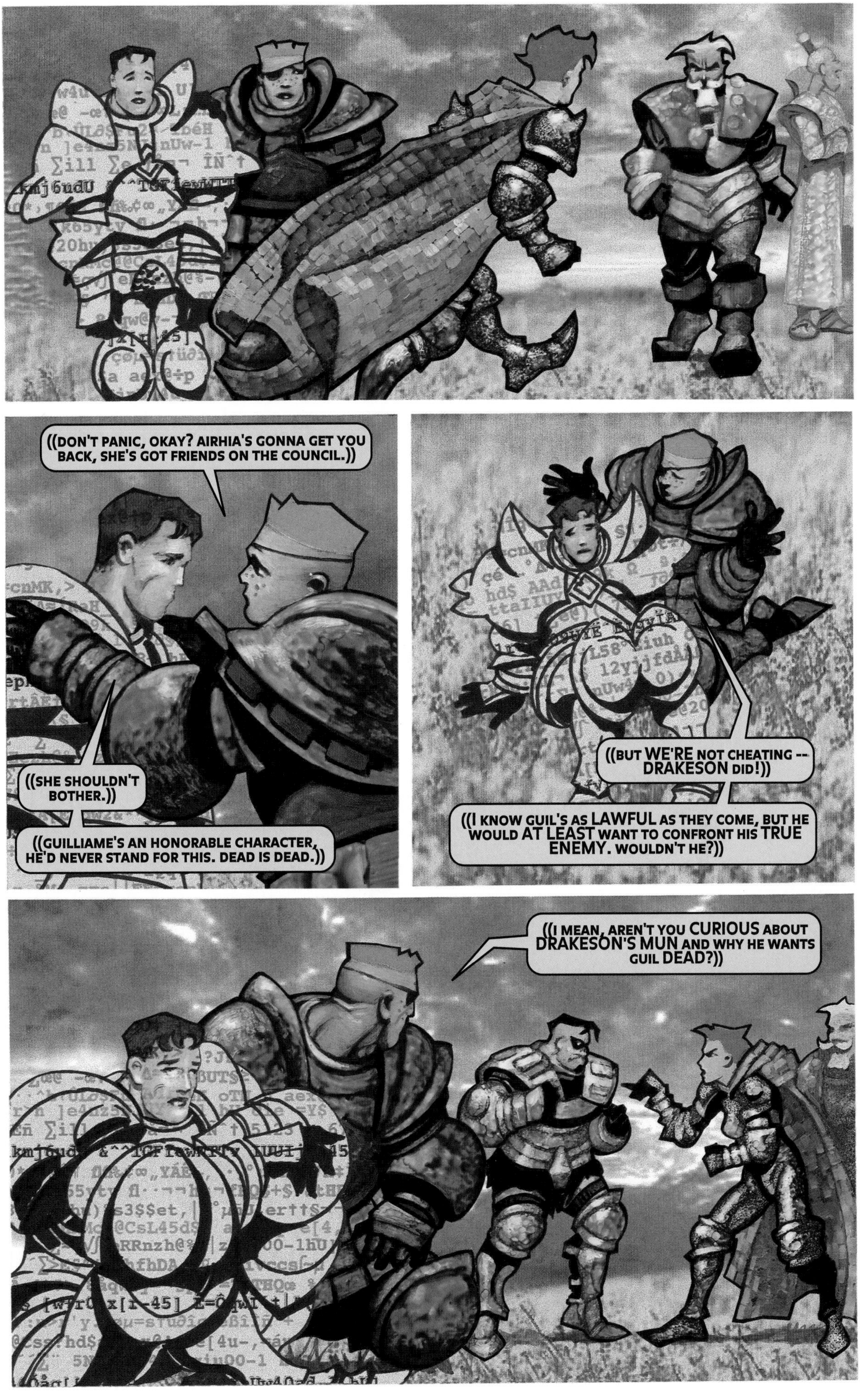
((DON'T PANIC, OKAY? AIRHIA'S GONNA GET YOU BACK, SHE'S GOT FRIENDS ON THE COUNCIL.))
((SHE SHOULDN'T BOTHER.))
((GUILLIAME'S AN HONORABLE CHARACTER, HE'D NEVER STAND FOR THIS. DEAD IS DEAD.))
((BUT WE'RE NOT CHEATING -- DRAKESON DID!))
((I KNOW GUIL'S AS LAWFUL AS THEY COME, BUT HE WOULD AT LEAST WANT TO CONFRONT HIS TRUE ENEMY. WOULDN'T HE?))
((I MEAN, AREN'T YOU CURIOUS ABOUT DRAKESON'S MUN AND WHY HE WANTS GUIL DEAD?))

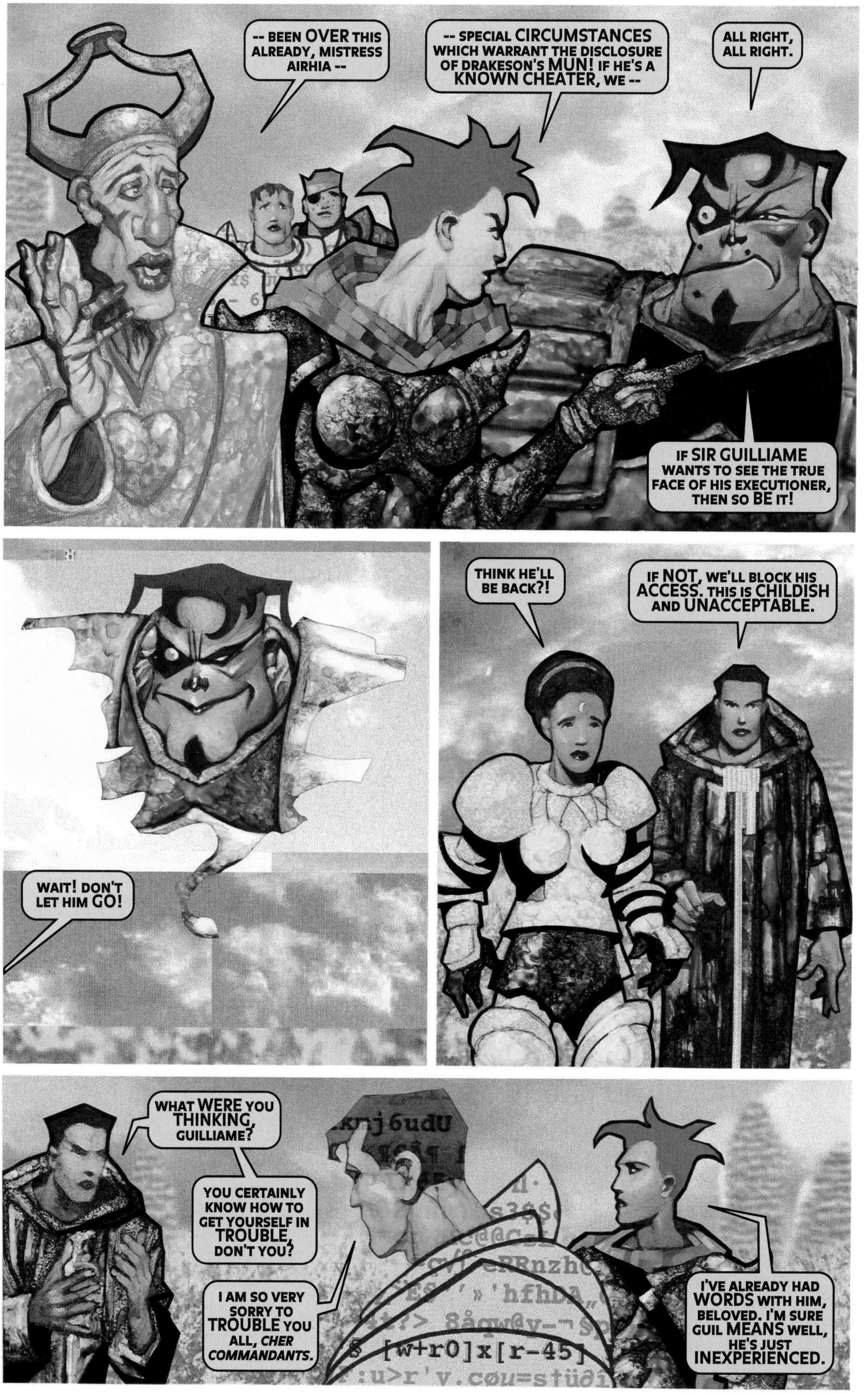
-- BEEN OVER THIS ALREADY, MISTRESS AIRHIA --
-- SPECIAL CIRCUMSTANCES WHICH WARRANT THE DISCLOSURE OF DRAKESON's MUN! IF HE'S A KNOWN CHEATER, WE --
ALL RIGHT, ALL RIGHT.
IF SIR GUILLIAME WANTS TO SEE THE TRUE FACE OF HIS EXECUTIONER, THEN SO BE IT!
WAIT! DON'T LET HIM GO!
THINK HE'LL BE BACK?!
IF NOT, WE'LL BLOCK HIS ACCESS. THIS IS CHILDISH AND UNACCEPTABLE.
WHAT WERE YOU THINKING, GUILLIAME?
YOU CERTAINLY KNOW HOW TO GET YOURSELF IN TROUBLE, DON'T YOU?
I AM SO VERY SORRY TO TROUBLE YOU ALL, *CHER COMMANDANTS*.
I'VE ALREADY HAD WORDS WITH HIM, BELOVED. I'M SURE GUIL MEANS WELL, HE'S JUST INEXPERIENCED.

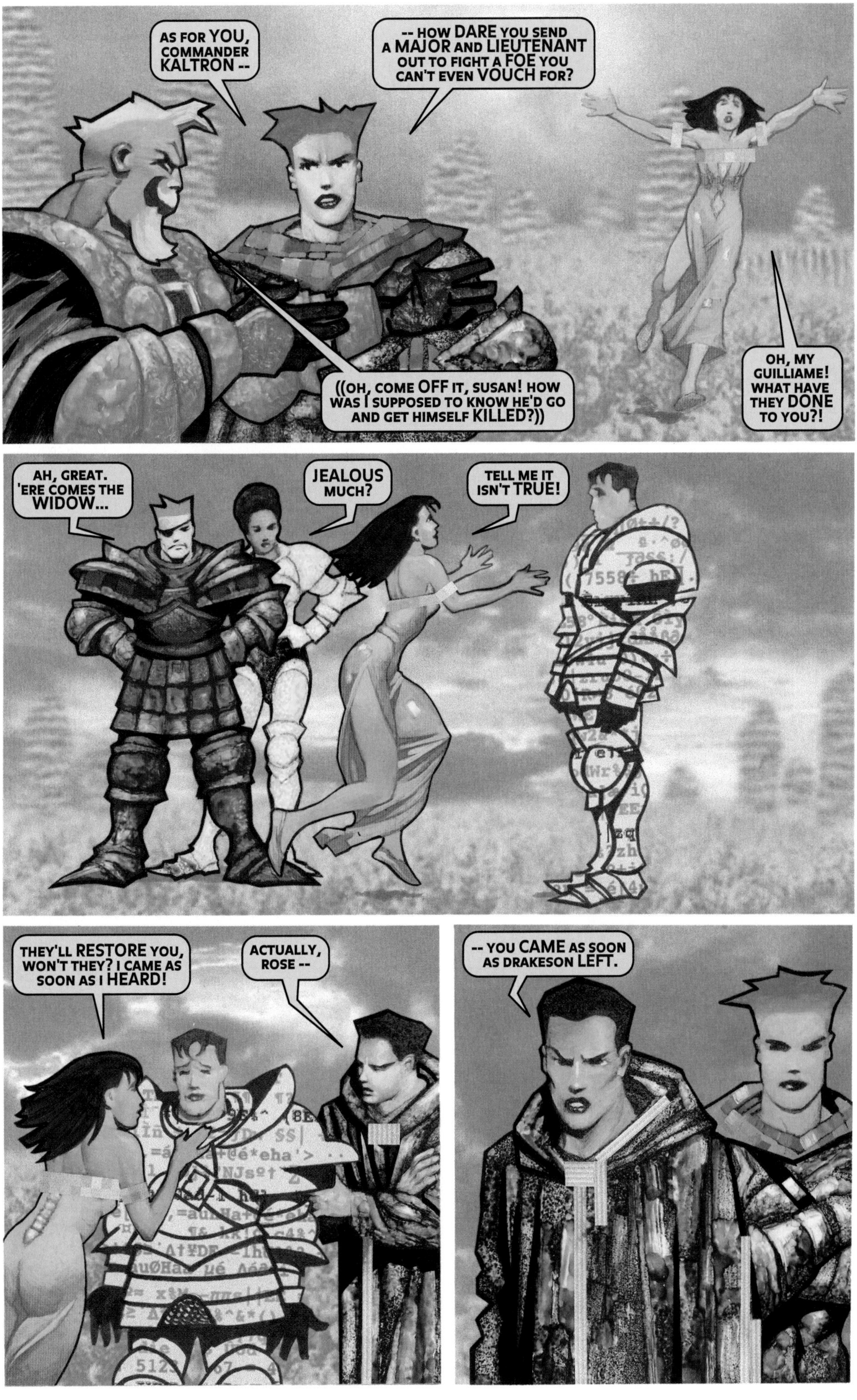
AS FOR YOU, COMMANDER KALTRON --
-- HOW DARE YOU SEND A MAJOR AND LIEUTENANT OUT TO FIGHT A FOE YOU CAN'T EVEN VOUCH FOR?
((OH, COME OFF IT, SUSAN! HOW WAS I SUPPOSED TO KNOW HE'D GO AND GET HIMSELF KILLED?))
OH, MY GUILLIAME! WHAT HAVE THEY DONE TO YOU?!
AH, GREAT. 'ERE COMES THE WIDOW...
JEALOUS MUCH?
TELL ME IT ISN'T TRUE!
THEY'LL RESTORE YOU, WON'T THEY? I CAME AS SOON AS I HEARD!
ACTUALLY, ROSE --
-- YOU CAME AS SOON AS DRAKESON LEFT.

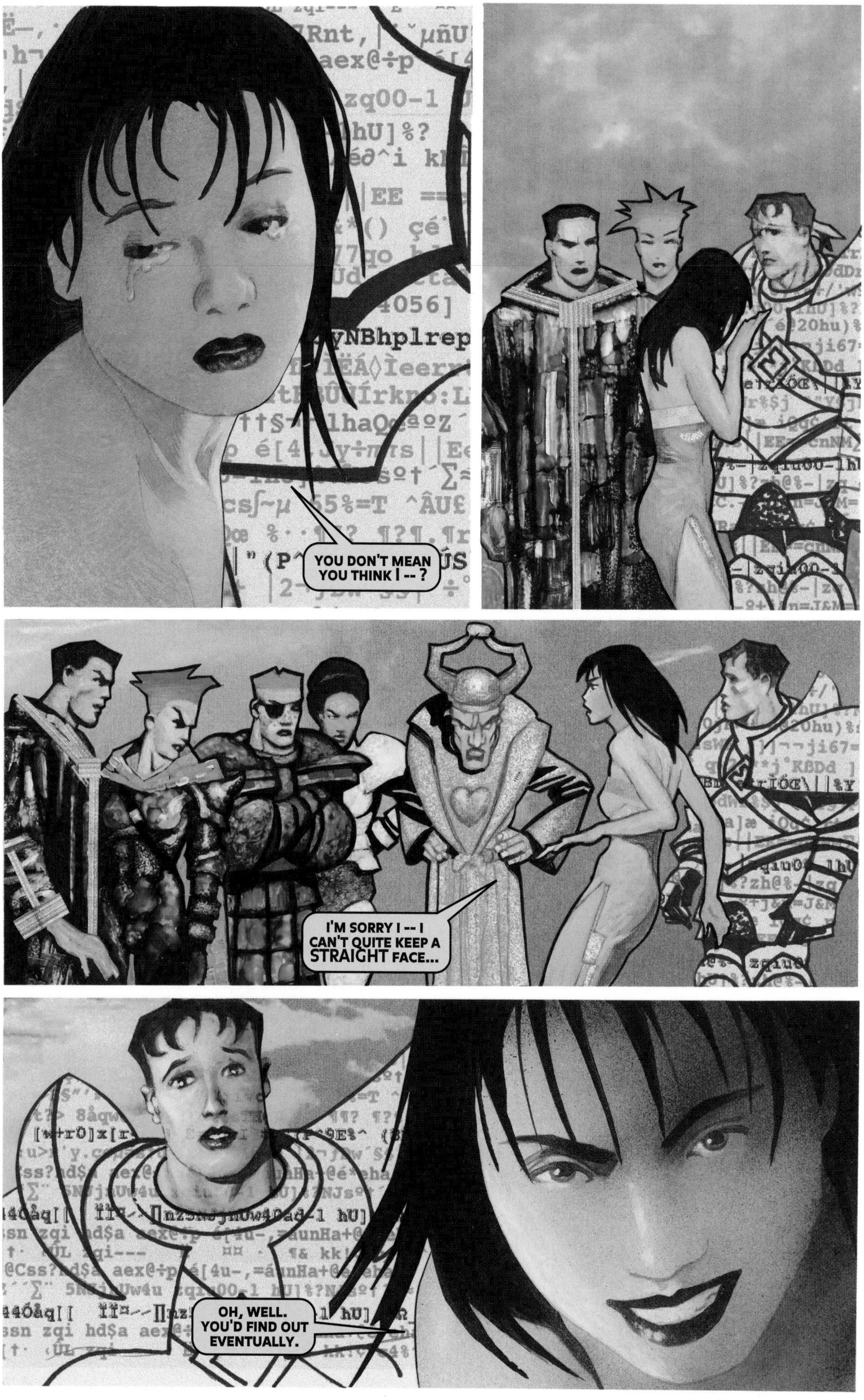
YOU DON'T MEAN YOU THINK I -- ?
I'M SORRY I -- I CAN'T QUITE KEEP A STRAIGHT FACE...
OH, WELL. YOU'D FIND OUT EVENTUALLY.

BUT -- BUT, ROSE --

-- WHY?!

WHY?! BECAUSE YOU NEVER SPEND ANY TIME WITH ME ANYMORE, MEL!

YOU ALWAYS WANT TO HANG OUT WITH YOUR STUPID GUILD, HAVING STUPID WARS OR STUPID MEETINGS WITH YOUR STUPID COMMANDERS!

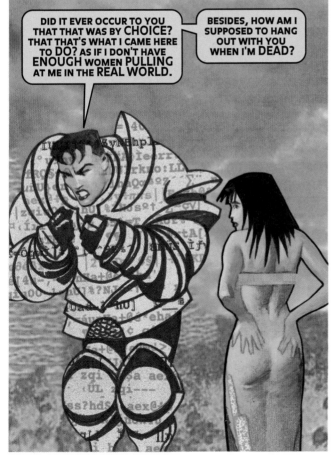

DID IT EVER OCCUR TO YOU THAT THAT WAS BY CHOICE? THAT THAT'S WHAT I CAME HERE TO DO? AS IF I DON'T HAVE ENOUGH WOMEN PULLING AT ME IN THE REAL WORLD.

BESIDES, HOW AM I SUPPOSED TO HANG OUT WITH YOU WHEN I'M DEAD?

DON'T YOU SEE? I DID IT FOR YOU, FOR US!

YOU CAN INVENT A NEW SCREEN NAME AND IT CAN BE LIKE IT WAS BEFORE...

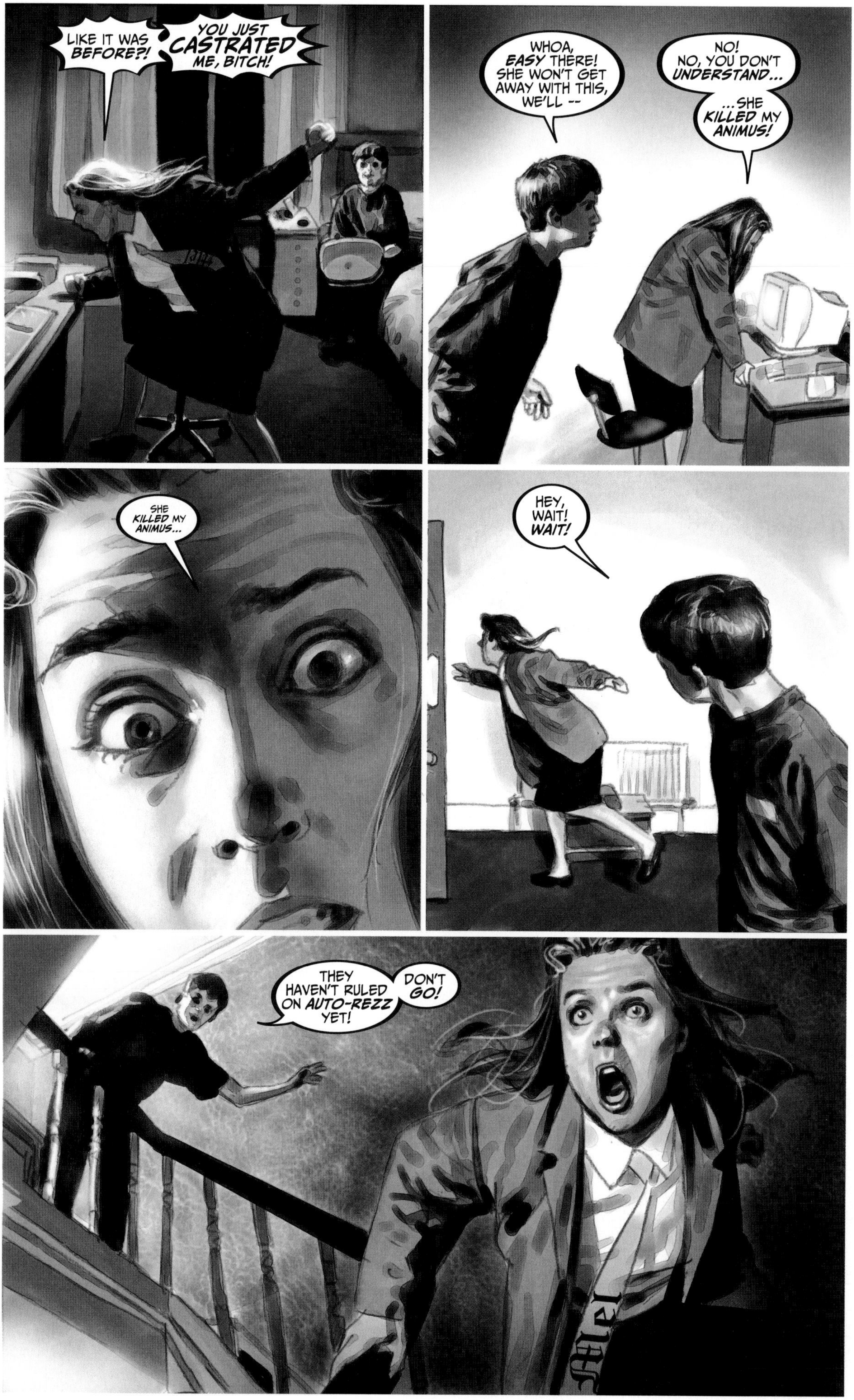
LIKE IT WAS BEFORE?!
YOU JUST CASTRATED ME, BITCH!
WHOA, EASY THERE! SHE WON'T GET AWAY WITH THIS, WE'LL --
NO! NO, YOU DON'T UNDERSTAND...
...SHE KILLED MY ANIMUS!
SHE KILLED MY ANIMUS...
HEY, WAIT! WAIT!
THEY HAVEN'T RULED ON AUTO-REZZ YET!
DON'T GO!

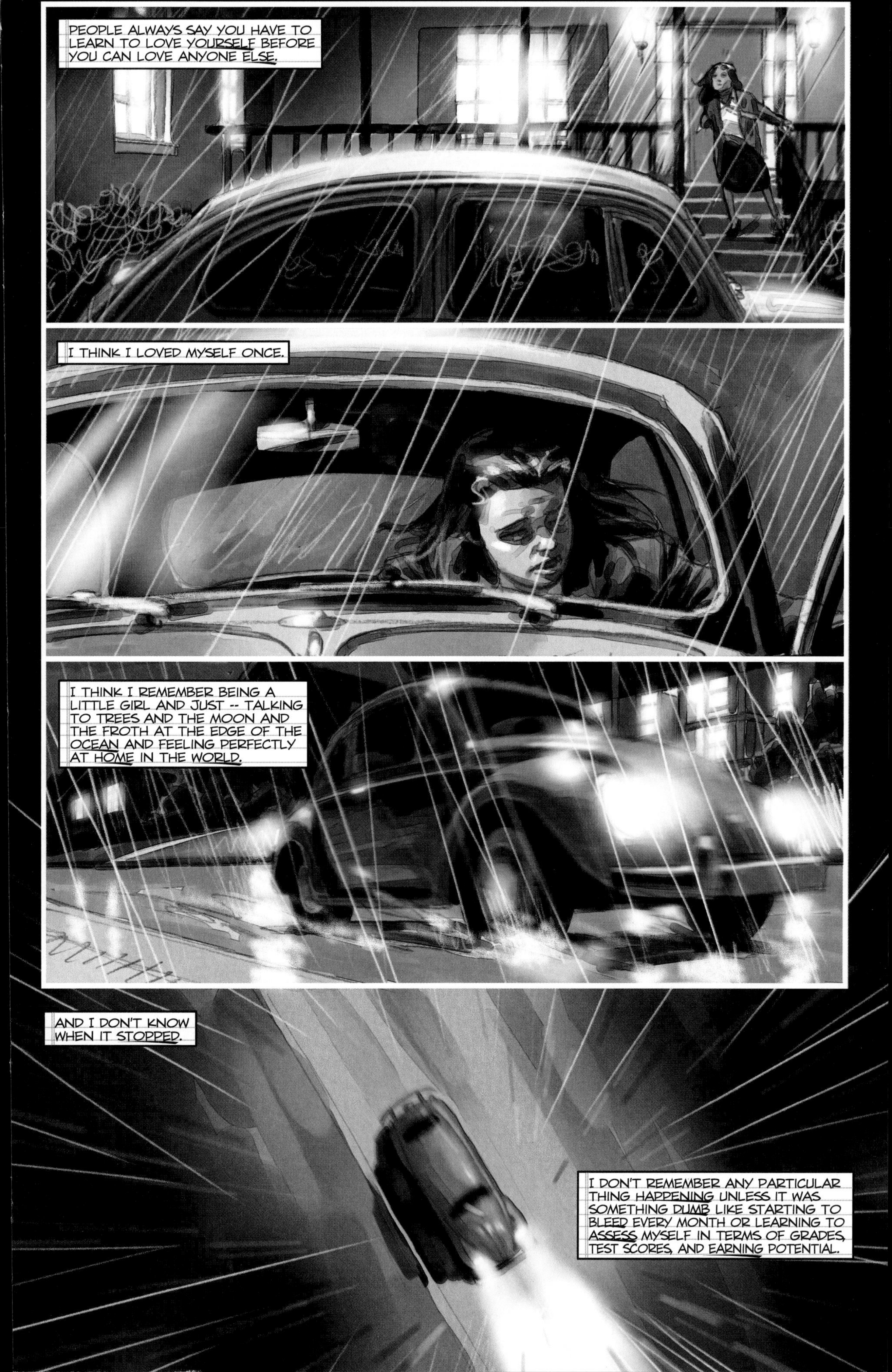

PEOPLE ALWAYS SAY YOU HAVE TO LEARN TO LOVE YOURSELF BEFORE YOU CAN LOVE ANYONE ELSE.
I THINK I LOVED MYSELF ONCE.
I THINK I REMEMBER BEING A LITTLE GIRL AND JUST -- TALKING TO TREES AND THE MOON AND THE FROTH AT THE EDGE OF THE OCEAN AND FEELING PERFECTLY AT HOME IN THE WORLD.
AND I DON'T KNOW WHEN IT STOPPED.
I DON'T REMEMBER ANY PARTICULAR THING HAPPENING UNLESS IT WAS SOMETHING DUMB LIKE STARTING TO BLEED EVERY MONTH OR LEARNING TO ASSESS MYSELF IN TERMS OF GRADES, TEST SCORES, AND EARNING POTENTIAL.

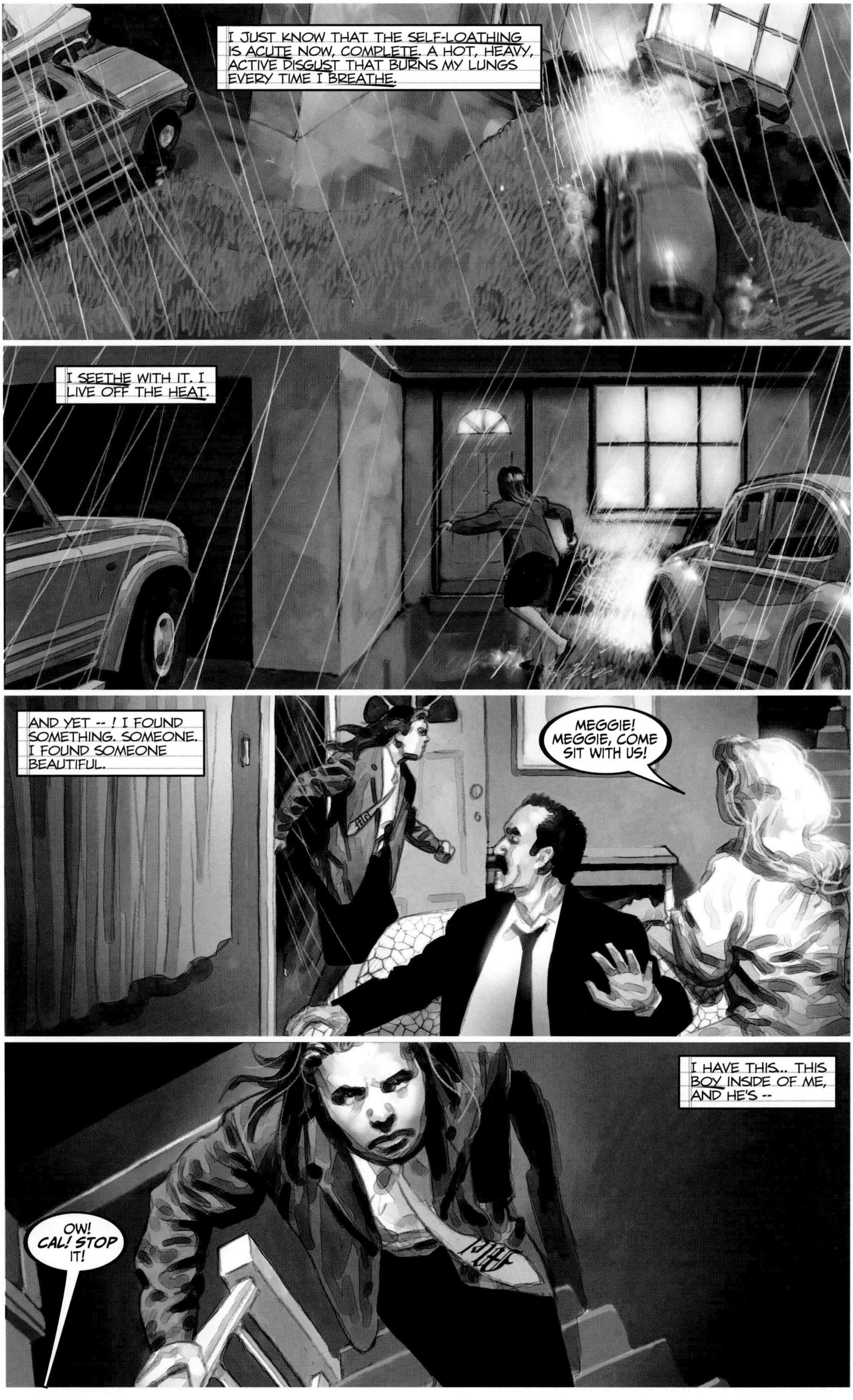
I JUST KNOW THAT THE SELF-LOATHING IS ACUTE NOW, COMPLETE. A HOT, HEAVY, ACTIVE DISGUST THAT BURNS MY LUNGS EVERY TIME I BREATHE.
I SEETHE WITH IT. I LIVE OFF THE HEAT.
AND YET -- ! I FOUND SOMETHING. SOMEONE. I FOUND SOMEONE BEAUTIFUL.
MEGGIE! MEGGIE, COME SIT WITH US!
I HAVE THIS... THIS BOY INSIDE OF ME, AND HE'S --
OW! CAL! STOP IT!

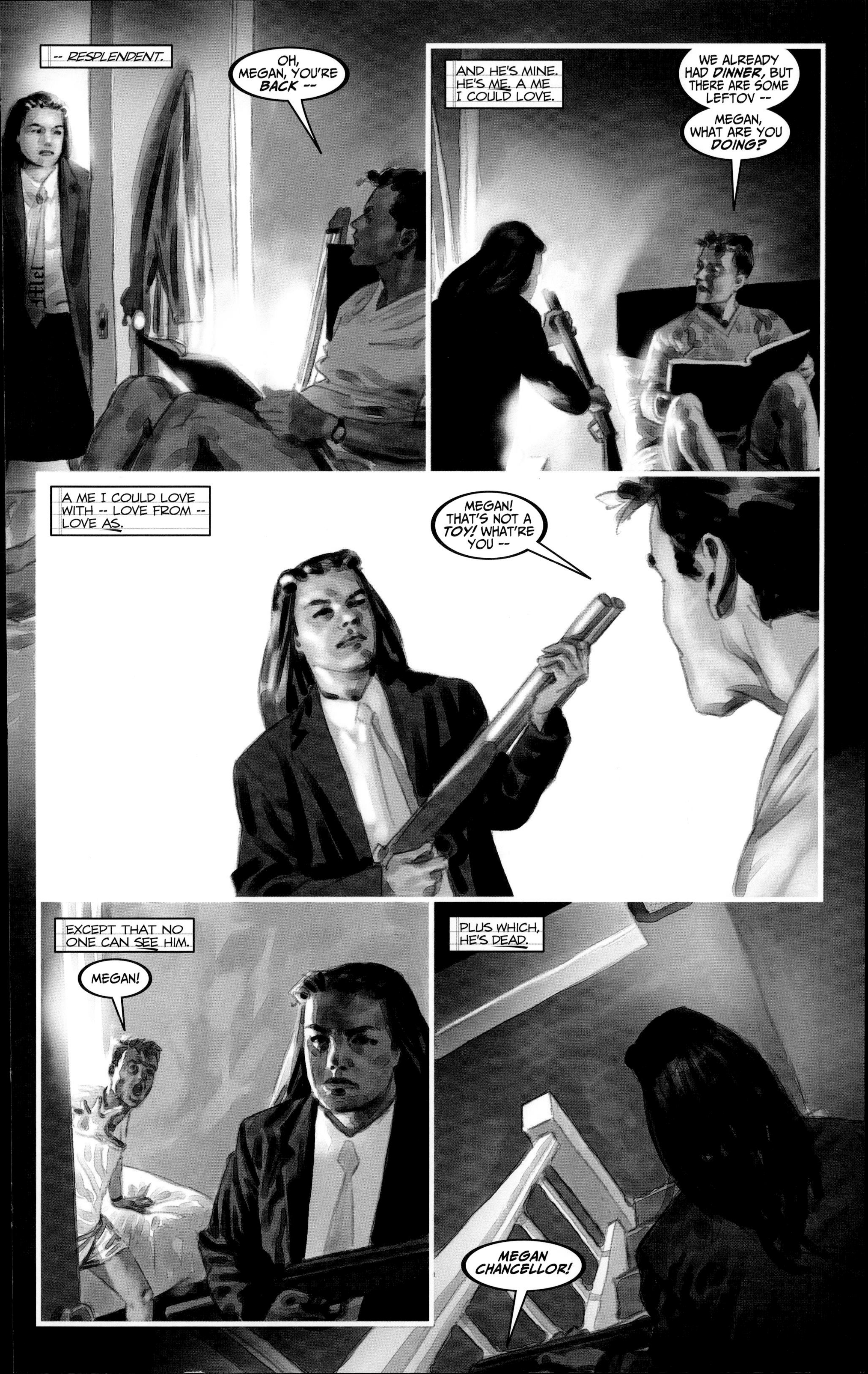
-- RESPLENDENT.
OH, MEGAN, YOU'RE BACK --
AND HE'S MINE. HE'S ME. A ME I COULD LOVE.
WE ALREADY HAD DINNER, BUT THERE ARE SOME LEFTOV --
MEGAN, WHAT ARE YOU DOING?
A ME I COULD LOVE WITH -- LOVE FROM -- LOVE AS.
MEGAN! THAT'S NOT A TOY! WHAT'RE YOU --
EXCEPT THAT NO ONE CAN SEE HIM.
MEGAN!
PLUS WHICH, HE'S DEAD.
MEGAN CHANCELLOR!

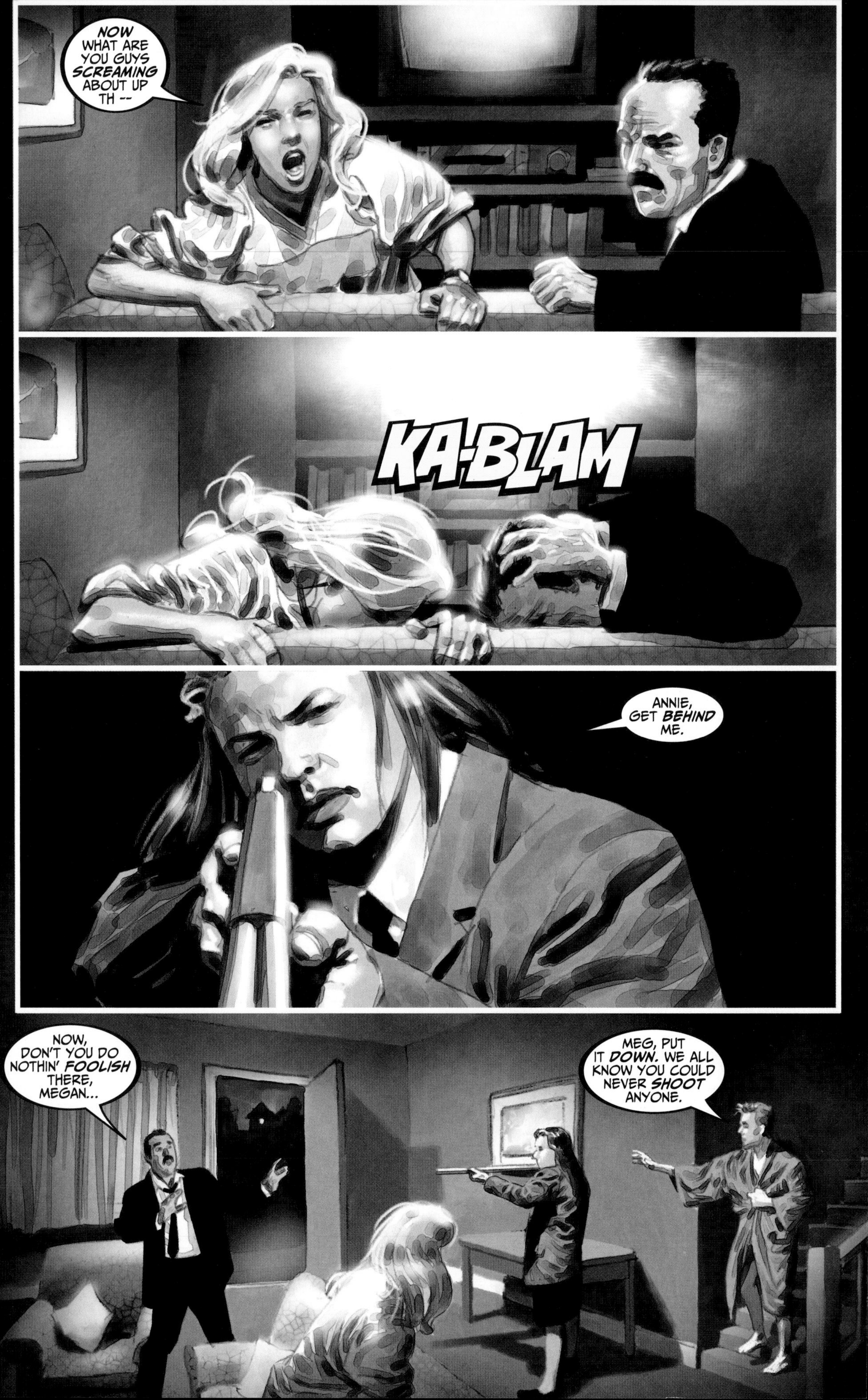
NOW WHAT ARE YOU GUYS SCREAMING ABOUT UP TH --
KA-BLAM
ANNIE, GET BEHIND ME.
NOW, DON'T YOU DO NOTHIN' FOOLISH THERE, MEGAN...
MEG, PUT IT DOWN. WE ALL KNOW YOU COULD NEVER SHOOT ANYONE.

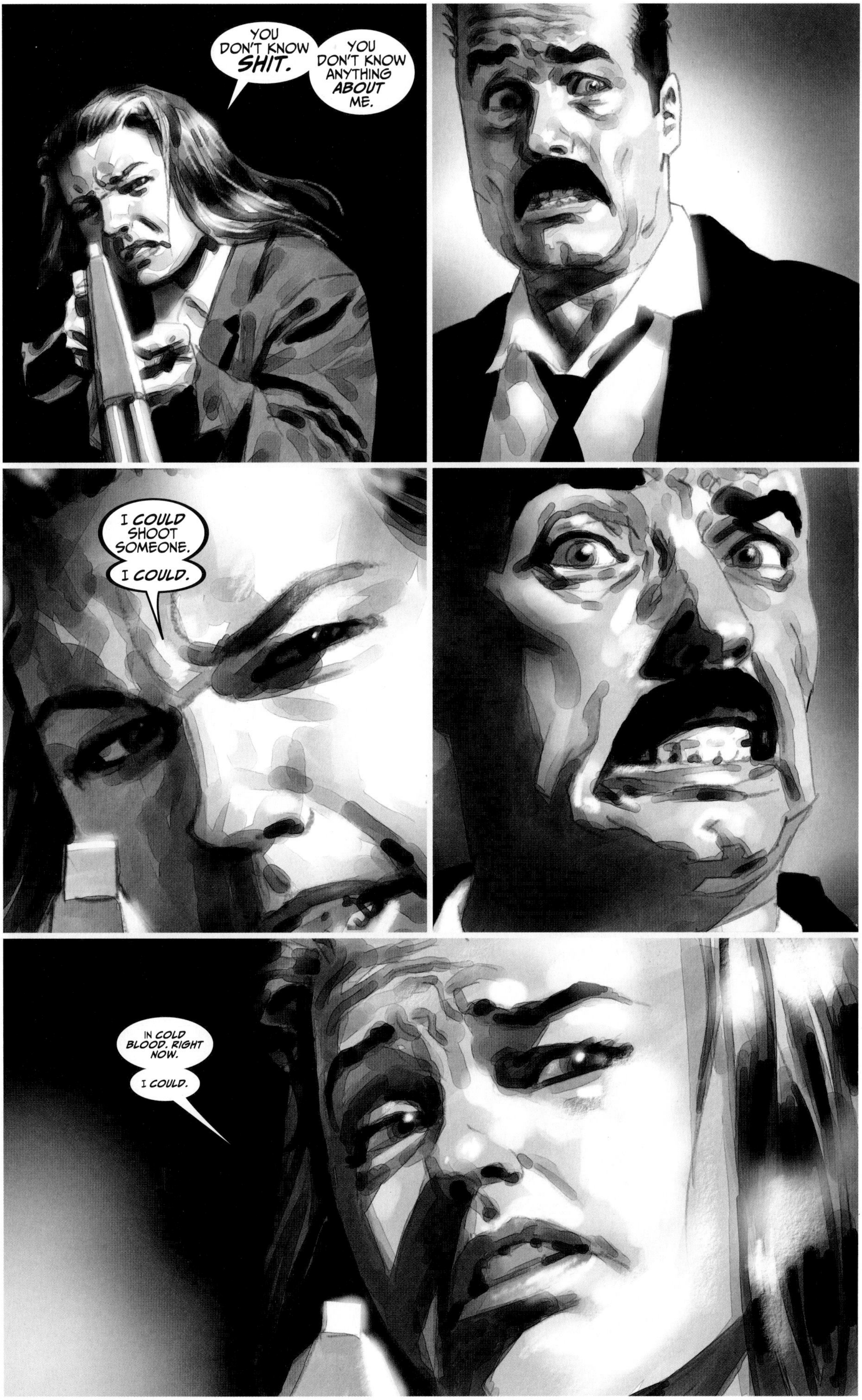
YOU DON'T KNOW SHIT.
YOU DON'T KNOW ANYTHING ABOUT ME.
I COULD SHOOT SOMEONE.
I COULD.
IN COLD BLOOD. RIGHT NOW.
I COULD.

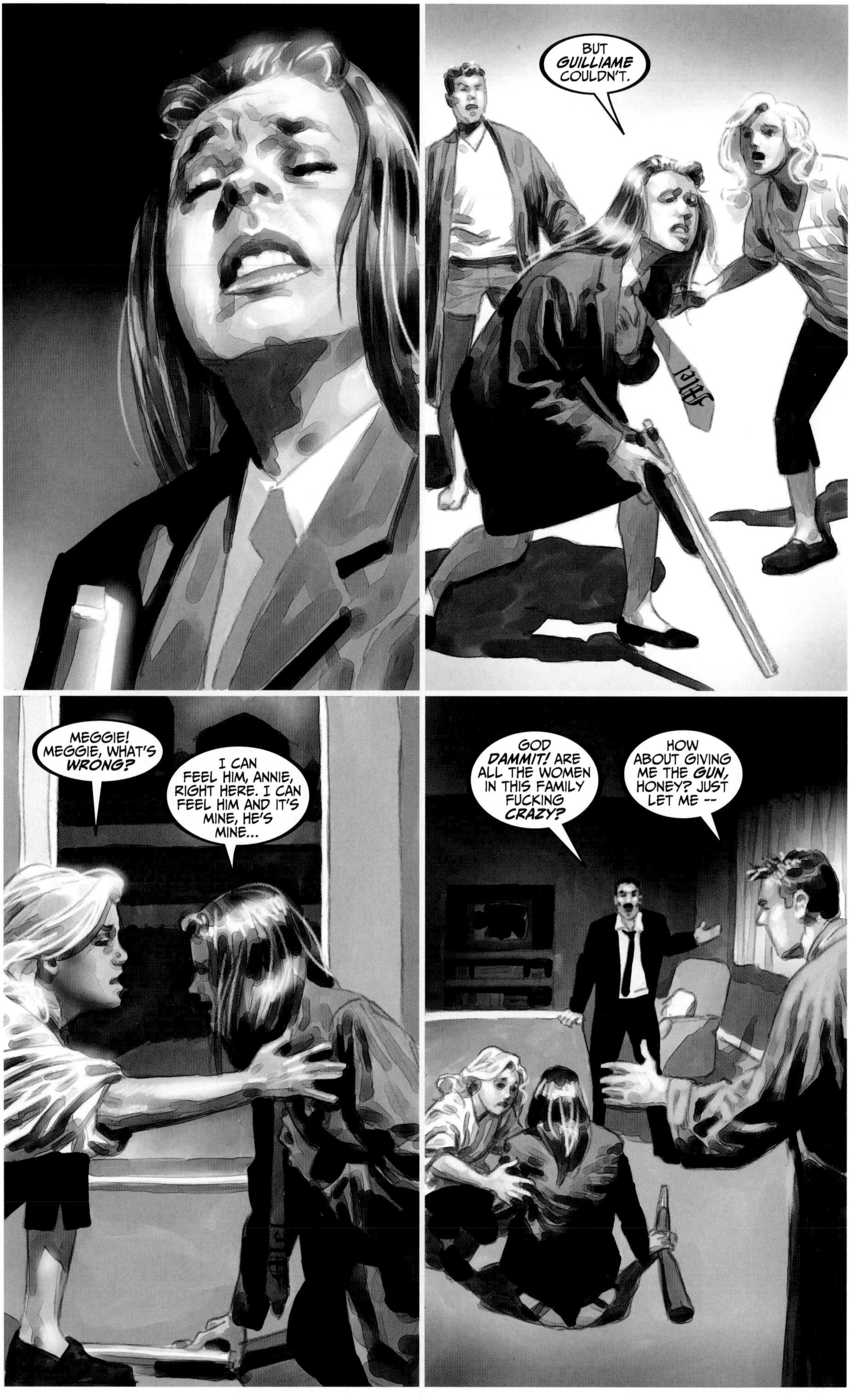
BUT GUILLIAME COULDN'T.
MEGGIE! MEGGIE, WHAT'S WRONG?
I CAN FEEL HIM, ANNIE, RIGHT HERE. I CAN FEEL HIM AND IT'S MINE, HE'S MINE...
GOD DAMMIT! ARE ALL THE WOMEN IN THIS FAMILY FUCKING CRAZY?
HOW ABOUT GIVING ME THE GUN, HONEY? JUST LET ME --

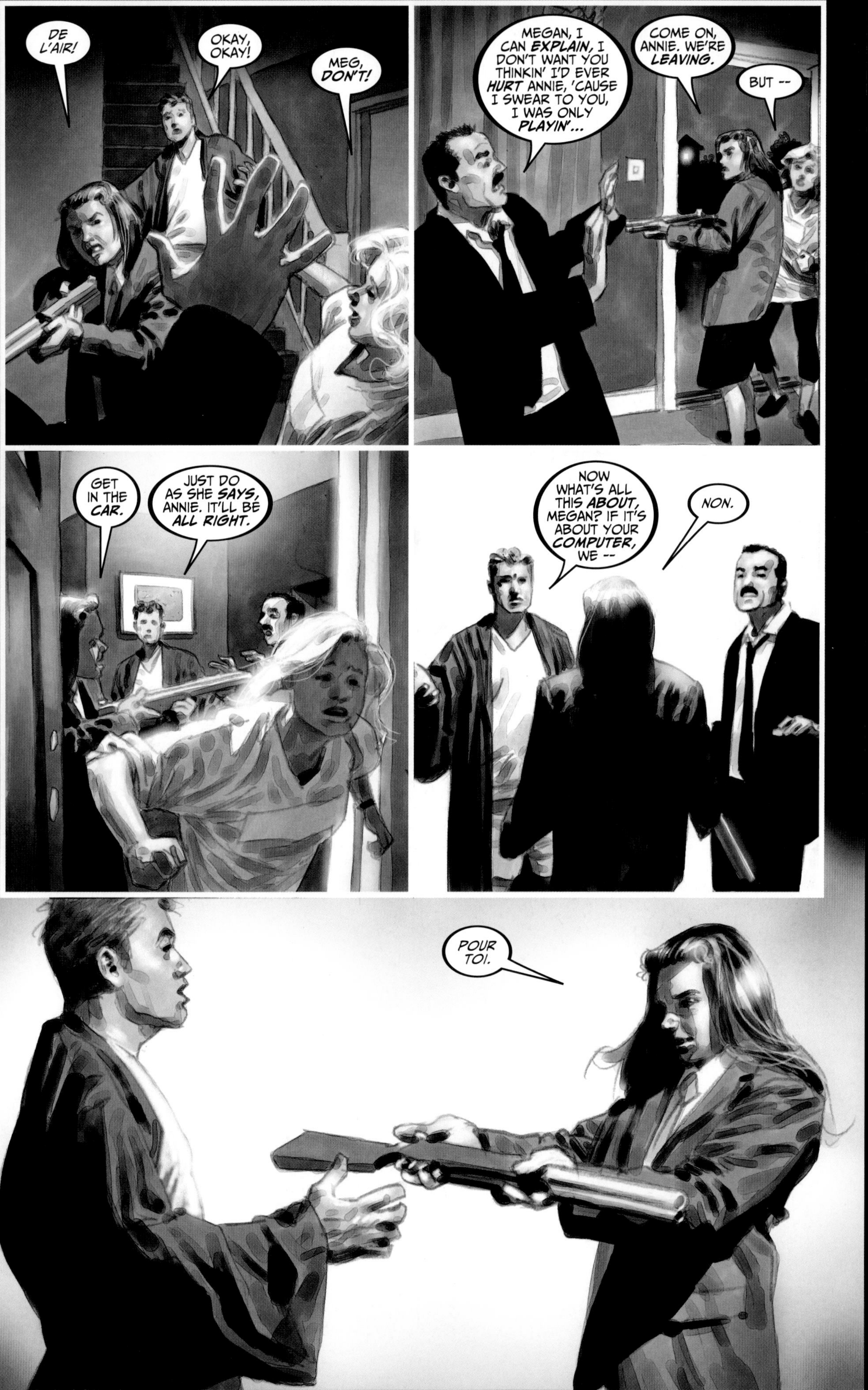

DE L'AIR!
OKAY, OKAY!
MEG, DON'T!
MEGAN, I CAN EXPLAIN, I DON'T WANT YOU THINKIN' I'D EVER HURT ANNIE, 'CAUSE I SWEAR TO YOU, I WAS ONLY PLAYIN'...
COME ON, ANNIE. WE'RE LEAVING.
BUT --
GET IN THE CAR.
JUST DO AS SHE SAYS, ANNIE. IT'LL BE ALL RIGHT.
NOW WHAT'S ALL THIS ABOUT, MEGAN? IF IT'S ABOUT YOUR COMPUTER, WE --
NON.
POUR TOI.

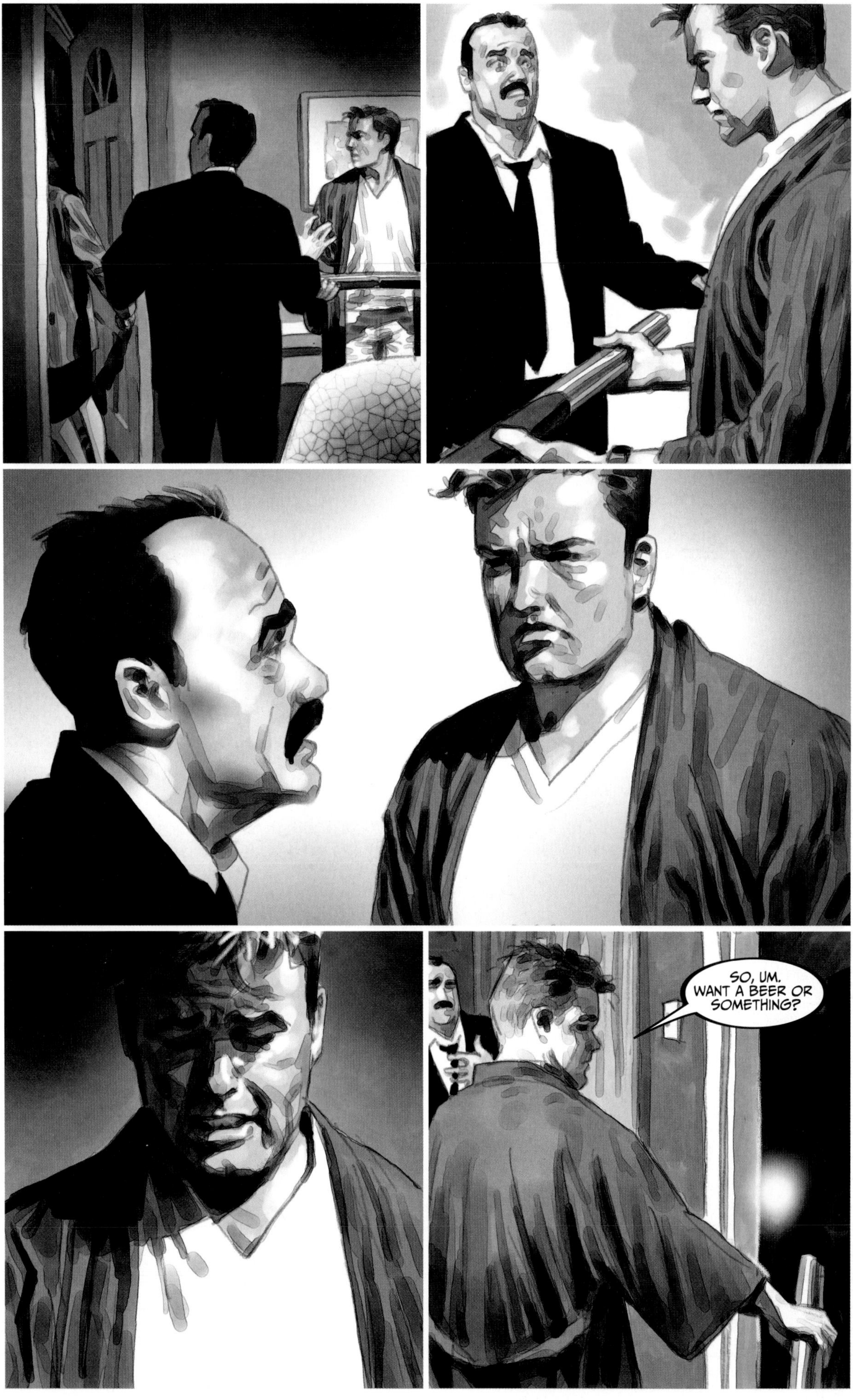
SO, UM.
WANT A BEER OR
SOMETHING?

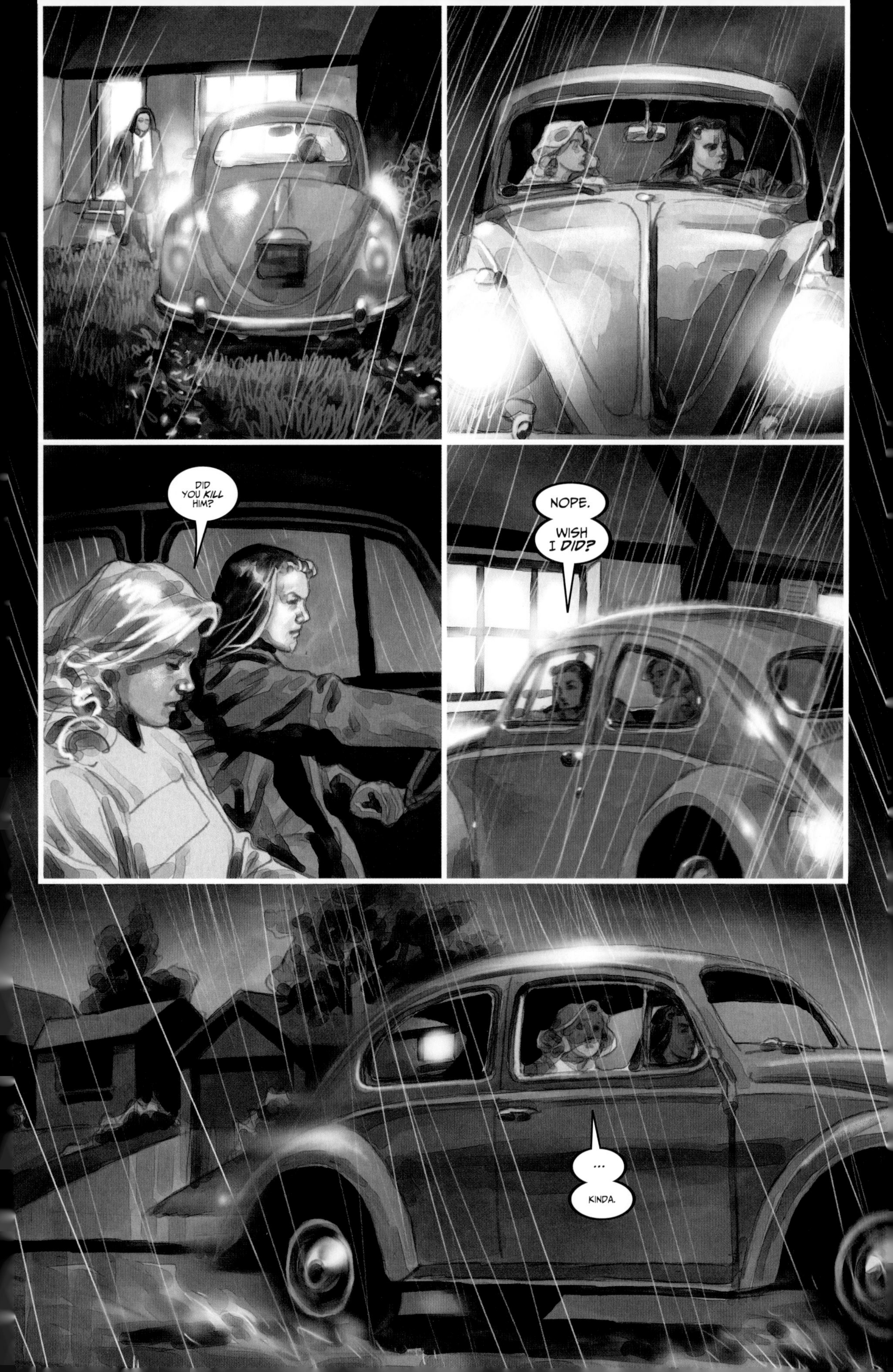
DID YOU KILL HIM?
NOPE.
WISH I DID?
...
KINDA.

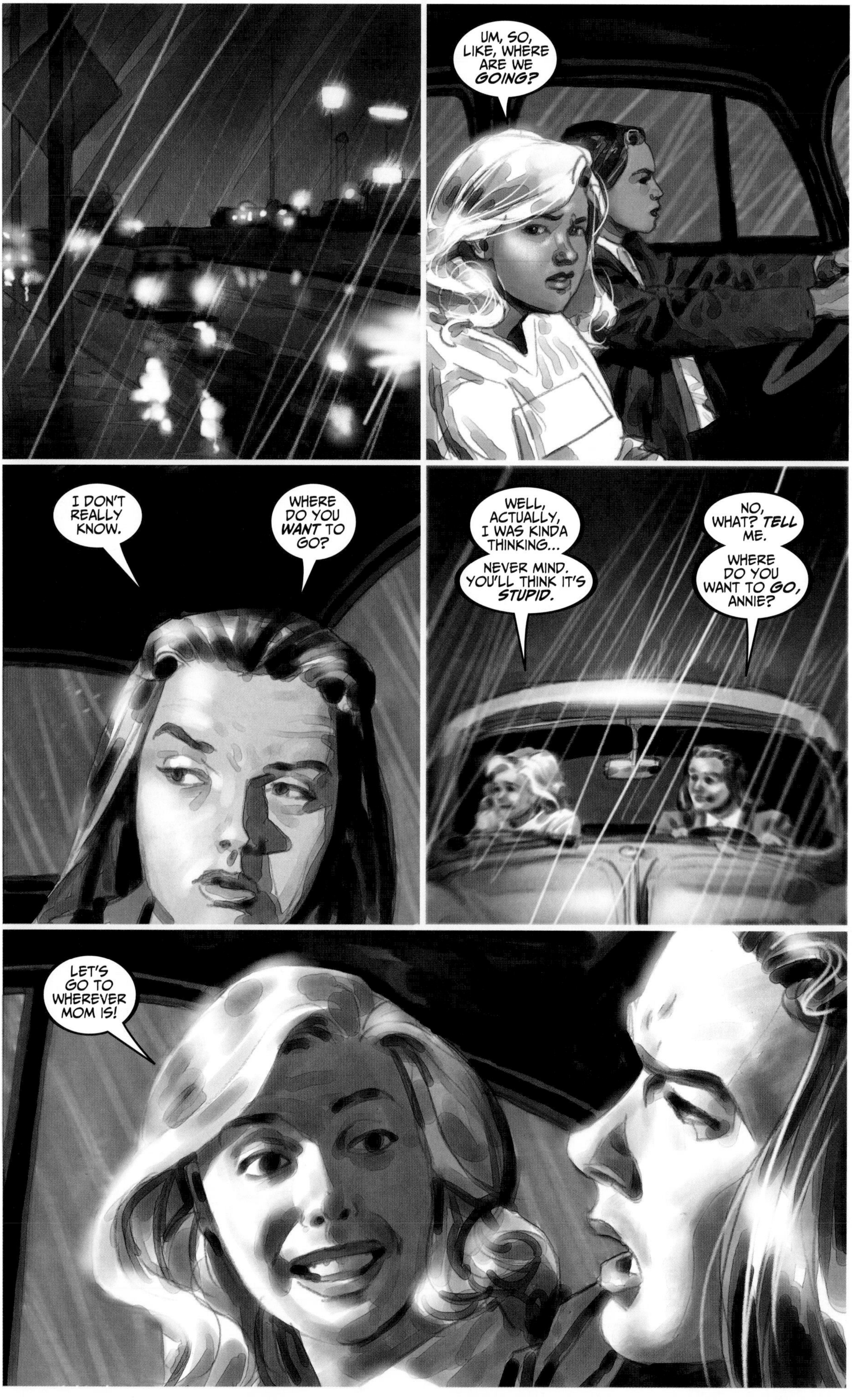
UM, SO, LIKE, WHERE ARE WE GOING?
I DON'T REALLY KNOW.
WHERE DO YOU WANT TO GO?
WELL, ACTUALLY, I WAS KINDA THINKING...
NEVER MIND. YOU'LL THINK IT'S STUPID.
NO, WHAT? TELL ME.
WHERE DO YOU WANT TO GO, ANNIE?
LET'S GO TO WHEREVER MOM IS!

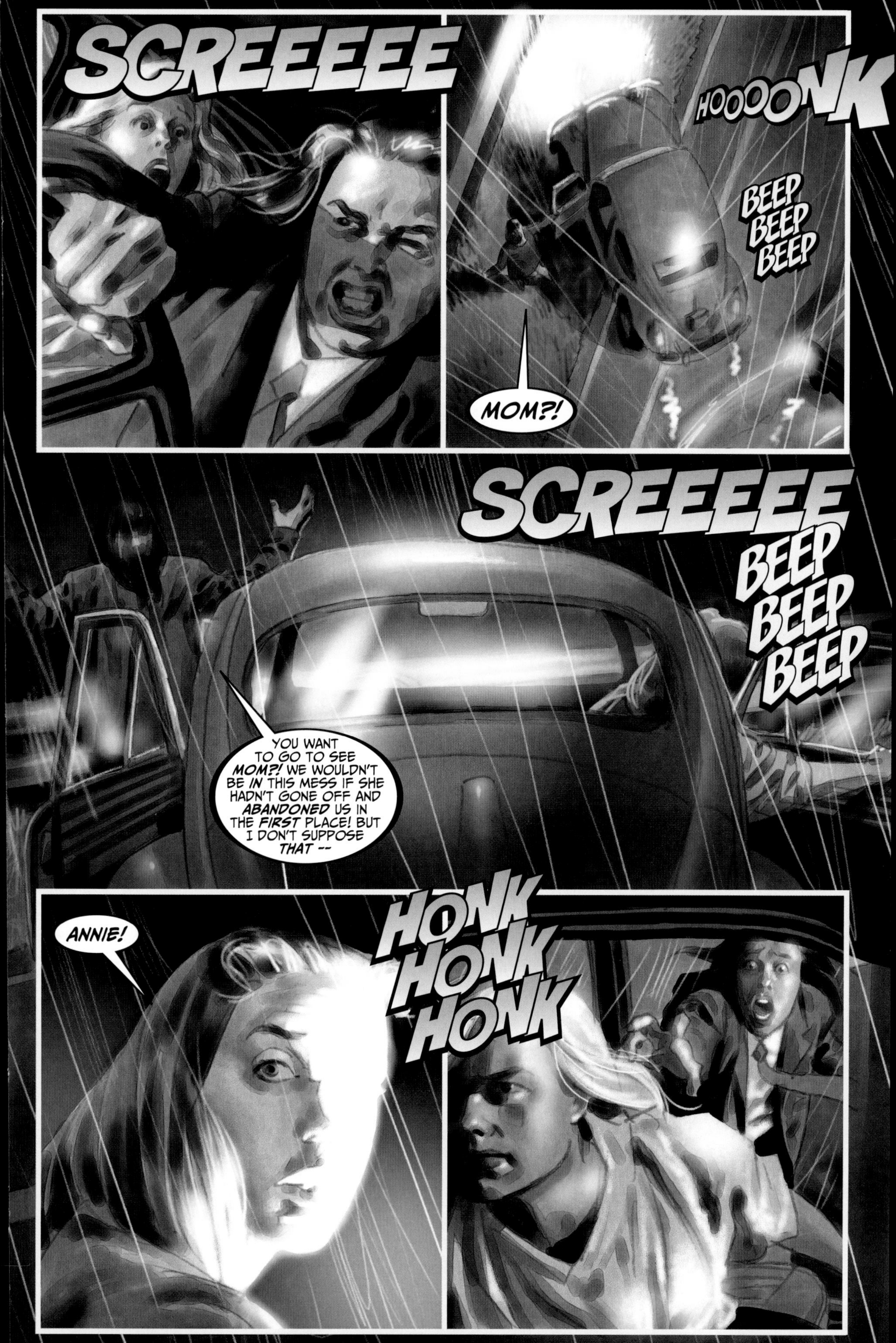
SCREEEEEE
HOOOONK
BEEP BEEP BEEP
MOM?!
SCREEEEEE
BEEP BEEP BEEP
YOU WANT TO GO TO SEE *MOM?!* WE WOULDN'T BE *IN* THIS MESS IF SHE HADN'T GONE OFF AND *ABANDONED* US IN THE *FIRST* PLACE! BUT I DON'T SUPPOSE *THAT* --
ANNIE!
HONK HONK HONK

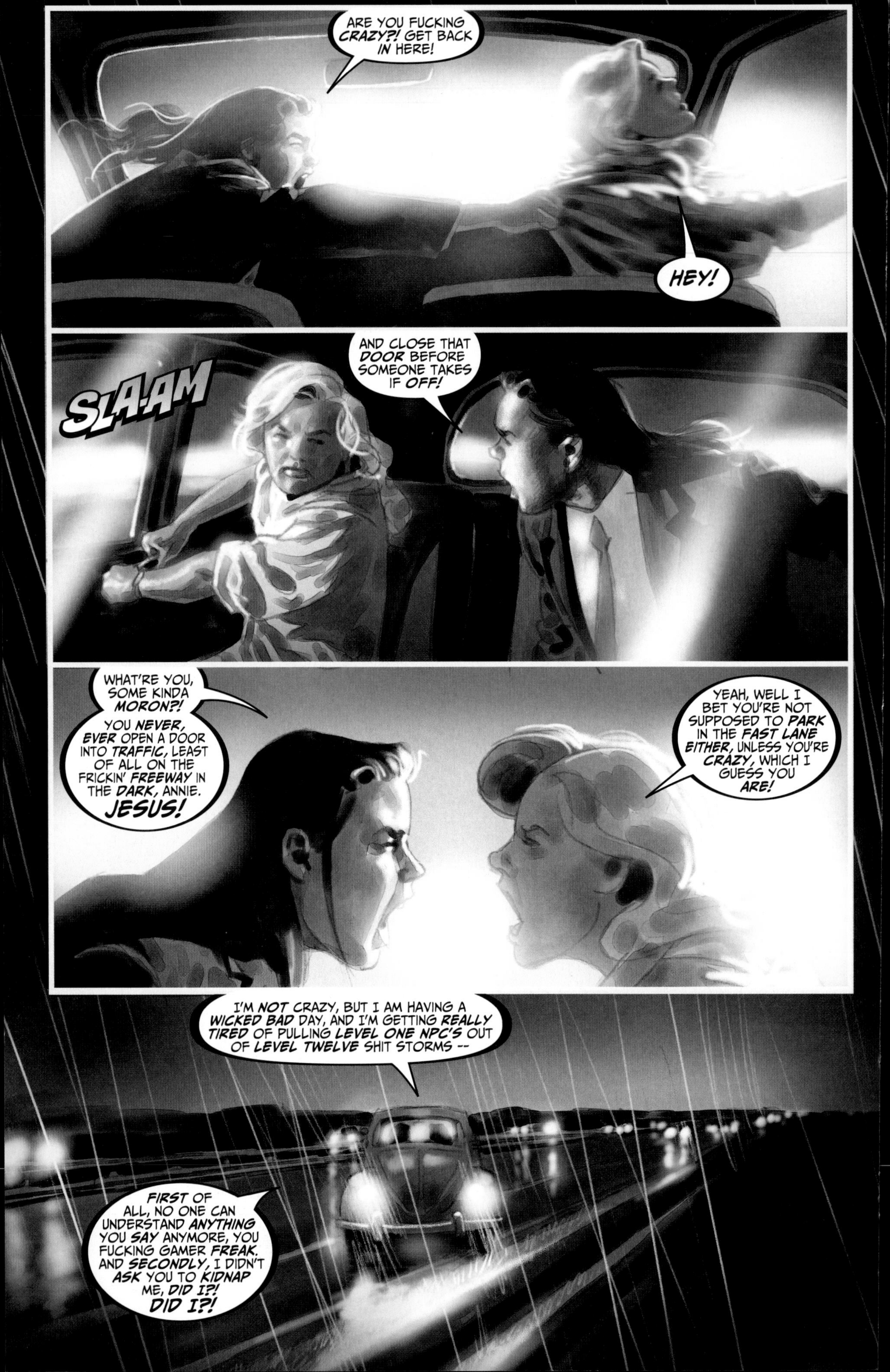

ARE YOU FUCKING CRAZY?! GET BACK IN HERE!
HEY!
SLA-AM
AND CLOSE THAT DOOR BEFORE SOMEONE TAKES IF OFF!
WHAT'RE YOU, SOME KINDA MORON?!
YOU NEVER, EVER OPEN A DOOR INTO TRAFFIC, LEAST OF ALL ON THE FRICKIN' FREEWAY IN THE DARK, ANNIE. JESUS!
YEAH, WELL I BET YOU'RE NOT SUPPOSED TO PARK IN THE FAST LANE EITHER, UNLESS YOU'RE CRAZY, WHICH I GUESS YOU ARE!
I'M NOT CRAZY, BUT I AM HAVING A WICKED BAD DAY, AND I'M GETTING REALLY TIRED OF PULLING LEVEL ONE NPC'S OUT OF LEVEL TWELVE SHIT STORMS --
FIRST OF ALL, NO ONE CAN UNDERSTAND ANYTHING YOU SAY ANYMORE, YOU FUCKING GAMER FREAK. AND SECONDLY, I DIDN'T ASK YOU TO KIDNAP ME, DID I?! DID I?!

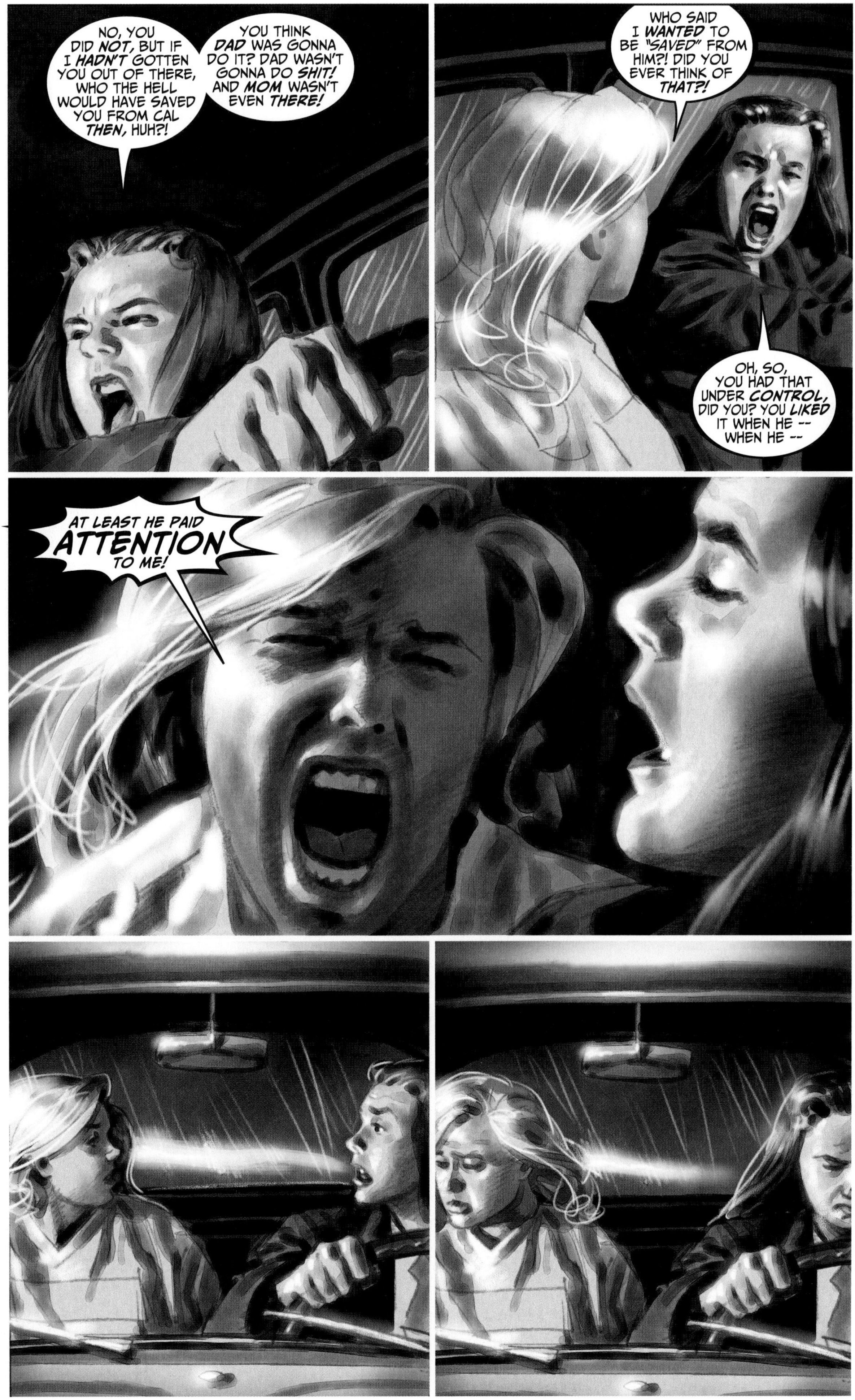
NO, YOU DID NOT, BUT IF I HADN'T GOTTEN YOU OUT OF THERE, WHO THE HELL WOULD HAVE SAVED YOU FROM CAL THEN, HUH?!
YOU THINK DAD WAS GONNA DO IT? DAD WASN'T GONNA DO SHIT! AND MOM WASN'T EVEN THERE!
WHO SAID I WANTED TO BE "SAVED" FROM HIM?! DID YOU EVER THINK OF THAT?!
OH, SO, YOU HAD THAT UNDER CONTROL, DID YOU? YOU LIKED IT WHEN HE -- WHEN HE --
AT LEAST HE PAID ATTENTION TO ME!

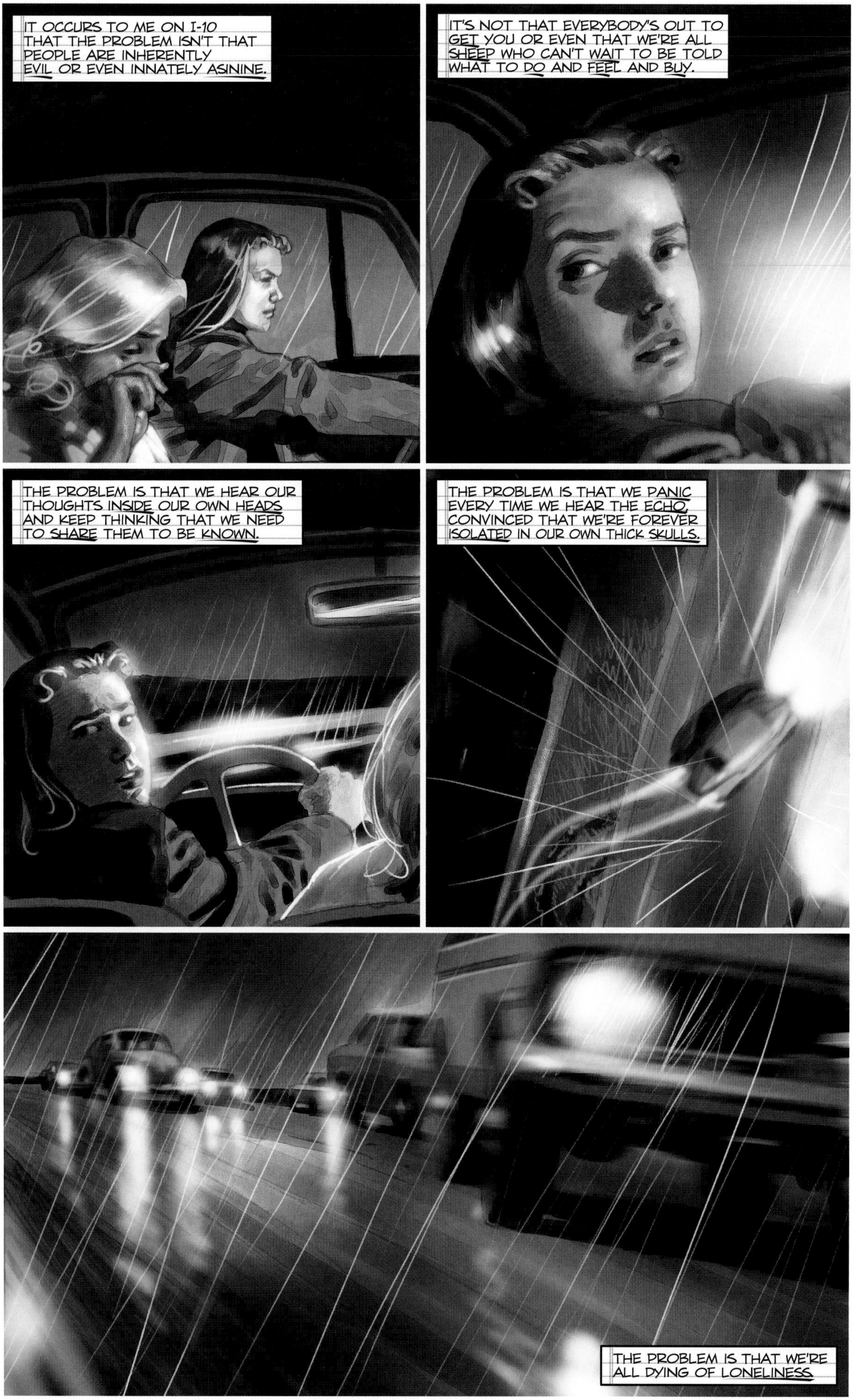
IT OCCURS TO ME ON I-10 THAT THE PROBLEM ISN'T THAT PEOPLE ARE INHERENTLY EVIL OR EVEN INNATELY ASININE.
IT'S NOT THAT EVERYBODY'S OUT TO GET YOU OR EVEN THAT WE'RE ALL SHEEP WHO CAN'T WAIT TO BE TOLD WHAT TO DO AND FEEL AND BUY.
THE PROBLEM IS THAT WE HEAR OUR THOUGHTS INSIDE OUR OWN HEADS AND KEEP THINKING THAT WE NEED TO SHARE THEM TO BE KNOWN.
THE PROBLEM IS THAT WE PANIC EVERY TIME WE HEAR THE ECHO, CONVINCED THAT WE'RE FOREVER ISOLATED IN OUR OWN THICK SKULLS.
THE PROBLEM IS THAT WE'RE ALL DYING OF LONELINESS.

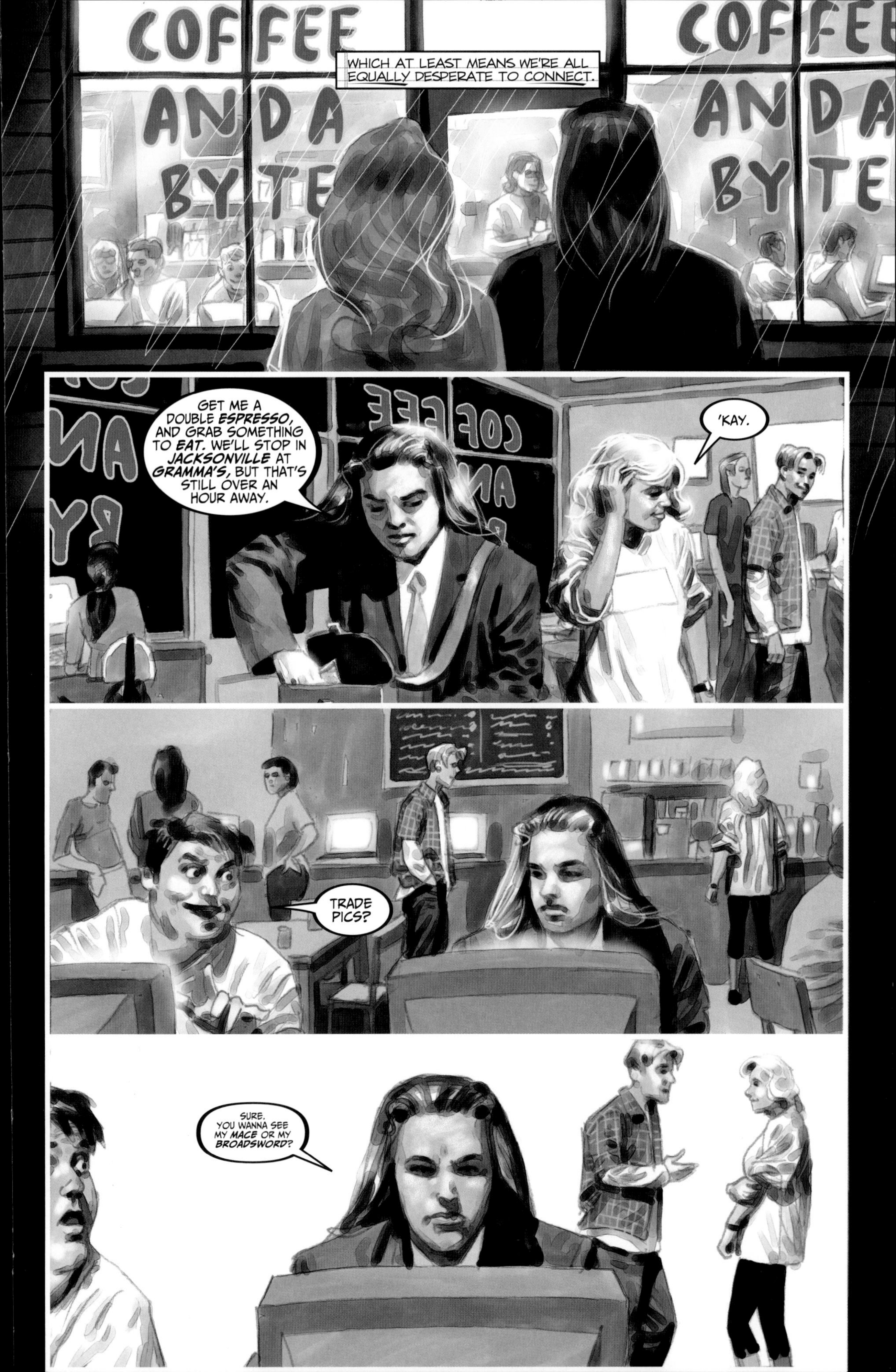
WHICH AT LEAST MEANS WE'RE ALL EQUALLY DESPERATE TO CONNECT.
COFFEE AND A BYTE
GET ME A DOUBLE ESPRESSO, AND GRAB SOMETHING TO EAT. WE'LL STOP IN JACKSONVILLE AT GRAMMA'S, BUT THAT'S STILL OVER AN HOUR AWAY.
'KAY.
TRADE PICS?
SURE. YOU WANNA SEE MY MACE OR MY BROADSWORD?

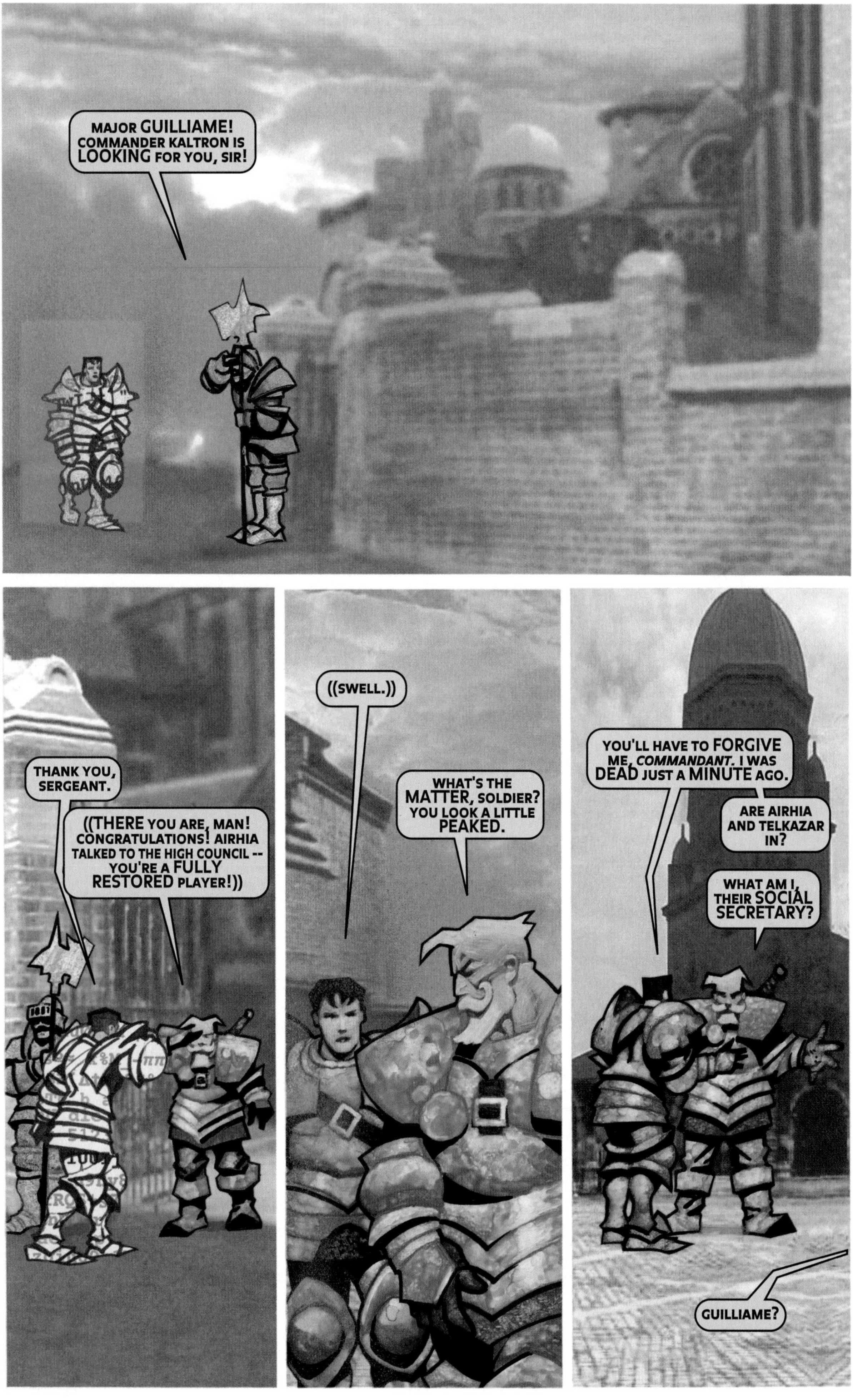
MAJOR GUILLIAME! COMMANDER KALTRON IS LOOKING FOR YOU, SIR!
THANK YOU, SERGEANT.
((THERE YOU ARE, MAN! CONGRATULATIONS! AIRHIA TALKED TO THE HIGH COUNCIL -- YOU'RE A FULLY RESTORED PLAYER!))
((SWELL.))
WHAT'S THE MATTER, SOLDIER? YOU LOOK A LITTLE PEAKED.
YOU'LL HAVE TO FORGIVE ME, *COMMANDANT.* I WAS DEAD JUST A MINUTE AGO.
ARE AIRHIA AND TELKAZAR IN?
WHAT AM I, THEIR SOCIAL SECRETARY?
GUILLIAME?

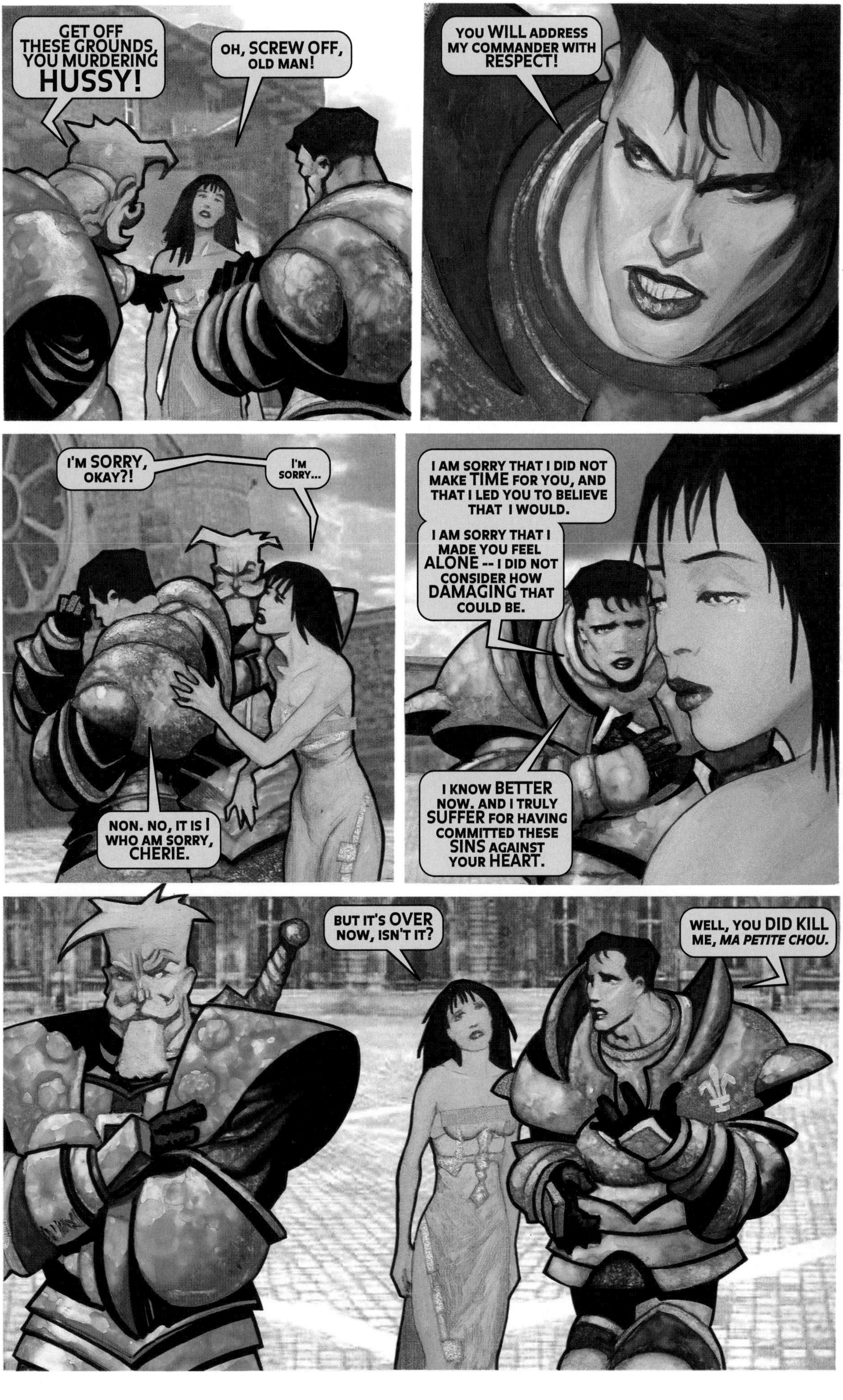
GET OFF THESE GROUNDS, YOU MURDERING HUSSY!
OH, SCREW OFF, OLD MAN!
YOU WILL ADDRESS MY COMMANDER WITH RESPECT!
I'M SORRY, OKAY?!
I'M SORRY...
NON. NO, IT IS I WHO AM SORRY, CHERIE.
I AM SORRY THAT I DID NOT MAKE TIME FOR YOU, AND THAT I LED YOU TO BELIEVE THAT I WOULD.
I AM SORRY THAT I MADE YOU FEEL ALONE -- I DID NOT CONSIDER HOW DAMAGING THAT COULD BE.
I KNOW BETTER NOW. AND I TRULY SUFFER FOR HAVING COMMITTED THESE SINS AGAINST YOUR HEART.
BUT IT'S OVER NOW, ISN'T IT?
WELL, YOU DID KILL ME, *MA PETITE CHOU.*

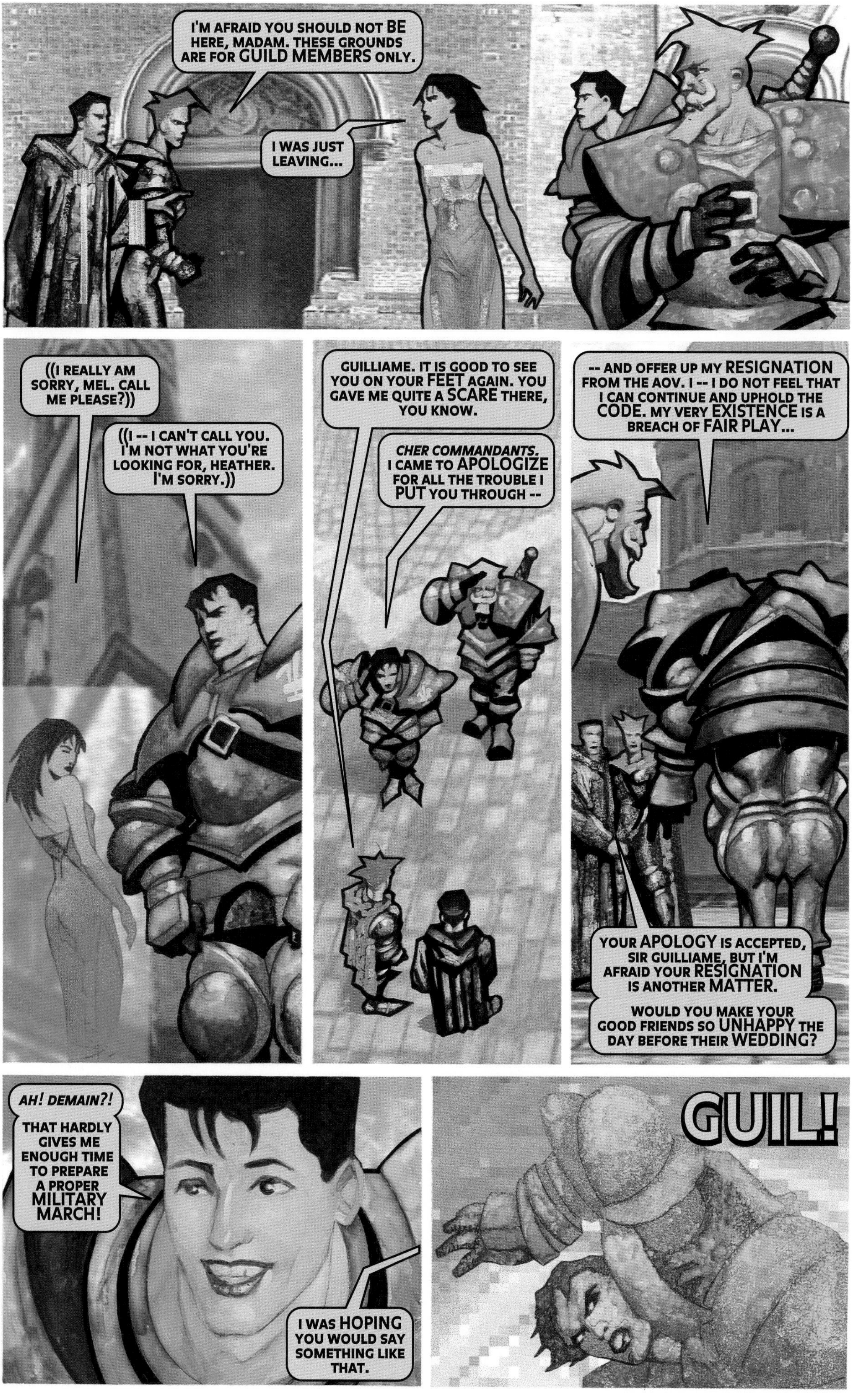
I'M AFRAID YOU SHOULD NOT BE HERE, MADAM. THESE GROUNDS ARE FOR GUILD MEMBERS ONLY.
I WAS JUST LEAVING...
((I REALLY AM SORRY, MEL. CALL ME PLEASE?))
((I -- I CAN'T CALL YOU. I'M NOT WHAT YOU'RE LOOKING FOR, HEATHER. I'M SORRY.))
GUILLIAME. IT IS GOOD TO SEE YOU ON YOUR FEET AGAIN. YOU GAVE ME QUITE A SCARE THERE, YOU KNOW.
CHER COMMANDANTS. I CAME TO APOLOGIZE FOR ALL THE TROUBLE I PUT YOU THROUGH --
-- AND OFFER UP MY RESIGNATION FROM THE AOV. I -- I DO NOT FEEL THAT I CAN CONTINUE AND UPHOLD THE CODE. MY VERY EXISTENCE IS A BREACH OF FAIR PLAY...
YOUR APOLOGY IS ACCEPTED, SIR GUILLIAME, BUT I'M AFRAID YOUR RESIGNATION IS ANOTHER MATTER.
WOULD YOU MAKE YOUR GOOD FRIENDS SO UNHAPPY THE DAY BEFORE THEIR WEDDING?
AH! DEMAIN?!
THAT HARDLY GIVES ME ENOUGH TIME TO PREPARE A PROPER MILITARY MARCH!
I WAS HOPING YOU WOULD SAY SOMETHING LIKE THAT.
GUIL!

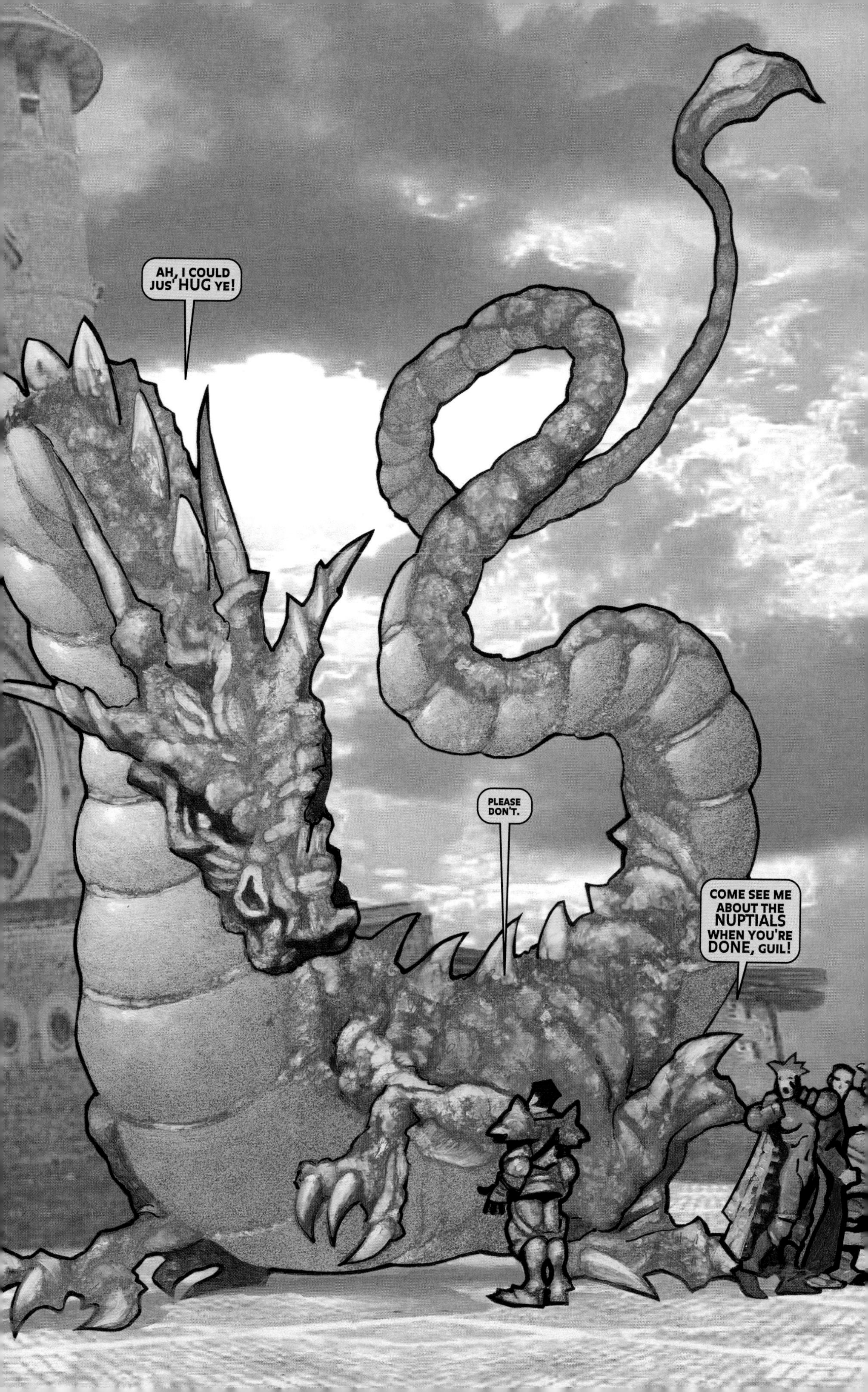
AH, I COULD JUS' HUG YE!
PLEASE DON'T.
COME SEE ME ABOUT THE NUPTIALS WHEN YOU'RE DONE, GUIL!

NOW, MAJOR, DINNAE TELL ME YOU DINNAE RECOGNIZE YER OWN TRUE LOVE?

M -- MCCRAVERN?!

AYE! WHO ELSE, LOVER-MINE?

I THOUGHT THE DRAGONS WERE SUPPOSED TO BECOME PRINCESSES OR HELPLESS THINGS THAT NEED OUR LOVE, NOT THE OTHER WAY AROUND.

ENH, WELL -- FIFTEENTH-CENTURY FRENCH PALADINS ARE NAE SUPPOSED TO HAVE READ RILKE, EITHER, BUT YE DINNAE HEAR ME COMPLAININ'.

LIEUTENANT! I HAD SEX WITH A DRAGON?

INDEED. HOW IMPRESSIVE ARE YOU?

I'M PRETTY FRICKIN' IMPRESSIVE!

THAT'S WHAT WE'VE BEEN TELLIN' YE!

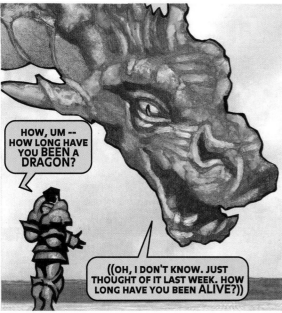

HOW, UM -- HOW LONG HAVE YOU BEEN A DRAGON?

((OH, I DON'T KNOW. JUST THOUGHT OF IT LAST WEEK. HOW LONG HAVE YOU BEEN ALIVE?))

((TOUCHÉ.))

((UM, SO LISTEN -- I KNOW YOU WERE PRETTY BUMMED ABOUT THE DEATH MATCH AND EVERYTHING.))

((LEMME ASK YOU SOMETHING OOC --))

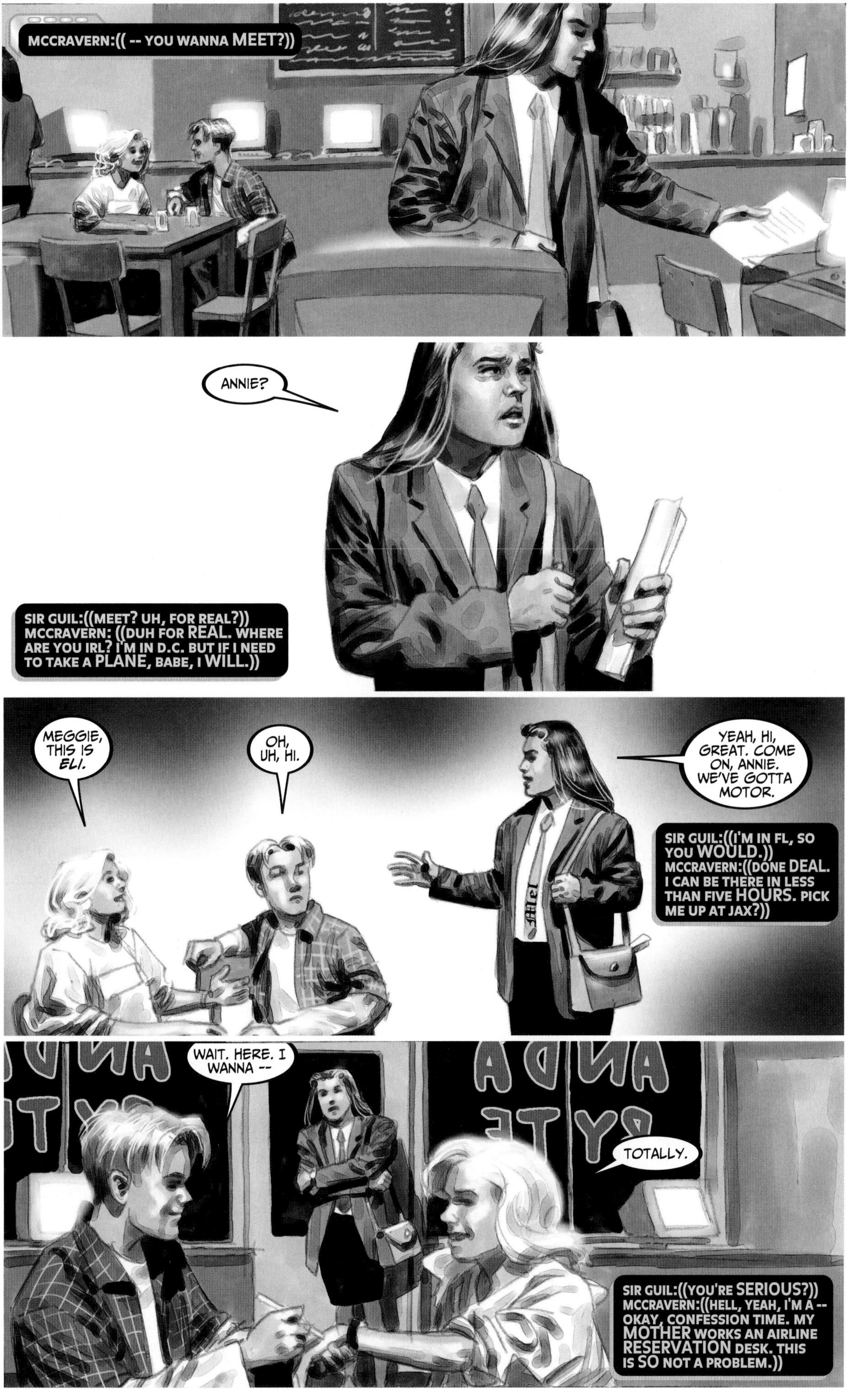
MCCRAVERN:((-- YOU WANNA MEET?))
ANNIE?
SIR GUIL:((MEET? UH, FOR REAL?))
MCCRAVERN: ((DUH FOR REAL. WHERE ARE YOU IRL? I'M IN D.C. BUT IF I NEED TO TAKE A PLANE, BABE, I WILL.))
MEGGIE, THIS IS ELI.
OH, UH, HI.
YEAH, HI, GREAT. COME ON, ANNIE. WE'VE GOTTA MOTOR.
SIR GUIL:((I'M IN FL, SO YOU WOULD.))
MCCRAVERN:((DONE DEAL. I CAN BE THERE IN LESS THAN FIVE HOURS. PICK ME UP AT JAX?))
WAIT. HERE. I WANNA --
TOTALLY.
SIR GUIL:((YOU'RE SERIOUS?))
MCCRAVERN:((HELL, YEAH, I'M A -- OKAY, CONFESSION TIME. MY MOTHER WORKS AN AIRLINE RESERVATION DESK. THIS IS SO NOT A PROBLEM.))

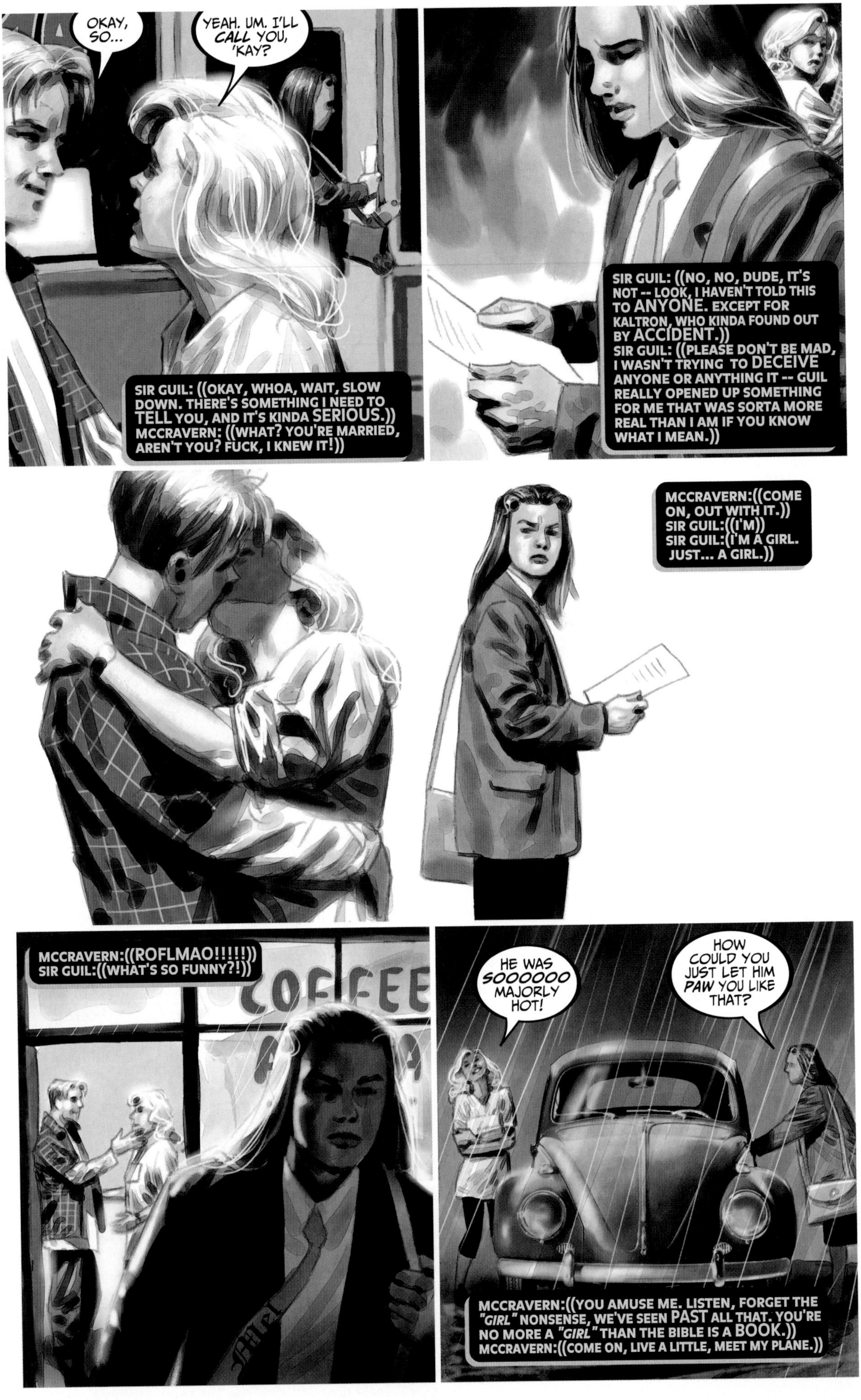
OKAY, SO...
YEAH. UM. I'LL CALL YOU, 'KAY?
SIR GUIL: ((OKAY, WHOA, WAIT, SLOW DOWN. THERE'S SOMETHING I NEED TO TELL YOU, AND IT'S KINDA SERIOUS.))
MCCRAVERN: ((WHAT? YOU'RE MARRIED, AREN'T YOU? FUCK, I KNEW IT!))
SIR GUIL: ((NO, NO, DUDE, IT'S NOT -- LOOK, I HAVEN'T TOLD THIS TO ANYONE. EXCEPT FOR KALTRON, WHO KINDA FOUND OUT BY ACCIDENT.))
SIR GUIL: ((PLEASE DON'T BE MAD, I WASN'T TRYING TO DECEIVE ANYONE OR ANYTHING IT -- GUIL REALLY OPENED UP SOMETHING FOR ME THAT WAS SORTA MORE REAL THAN I AM IF YOU KNOW WHAT I MEAN.))
MCCRAVERN:((COME ON, OUT WITH IT.))
SIR GUIL:((I'M))
SIR GUIL:(I'M A GIRL. JUST... A GIRL.))
MCCRAVERN:((ROFLMAO!!!!!))
SIR GUIL:((WHAT'S SO FUNNY?!))
COFFEE
HE WAS SOOOOOO MAJORLY HOT!
HOW COULD YOU JUST LET HIM PAW YOU LIKE THAT?
MCCRAVERN:((YOU AMUSE ME. LISTEN, FORGET THE "GIRL" NONSENSE, WE'VE SEEN PAST ALL THAT. YOU'RE NO MORE A "GIRL" THAN THE BIBLE IS A BOOK.))
MCCRAVERN:((COME ON, LIVE A LITTLE, MEET MY PLANE.))

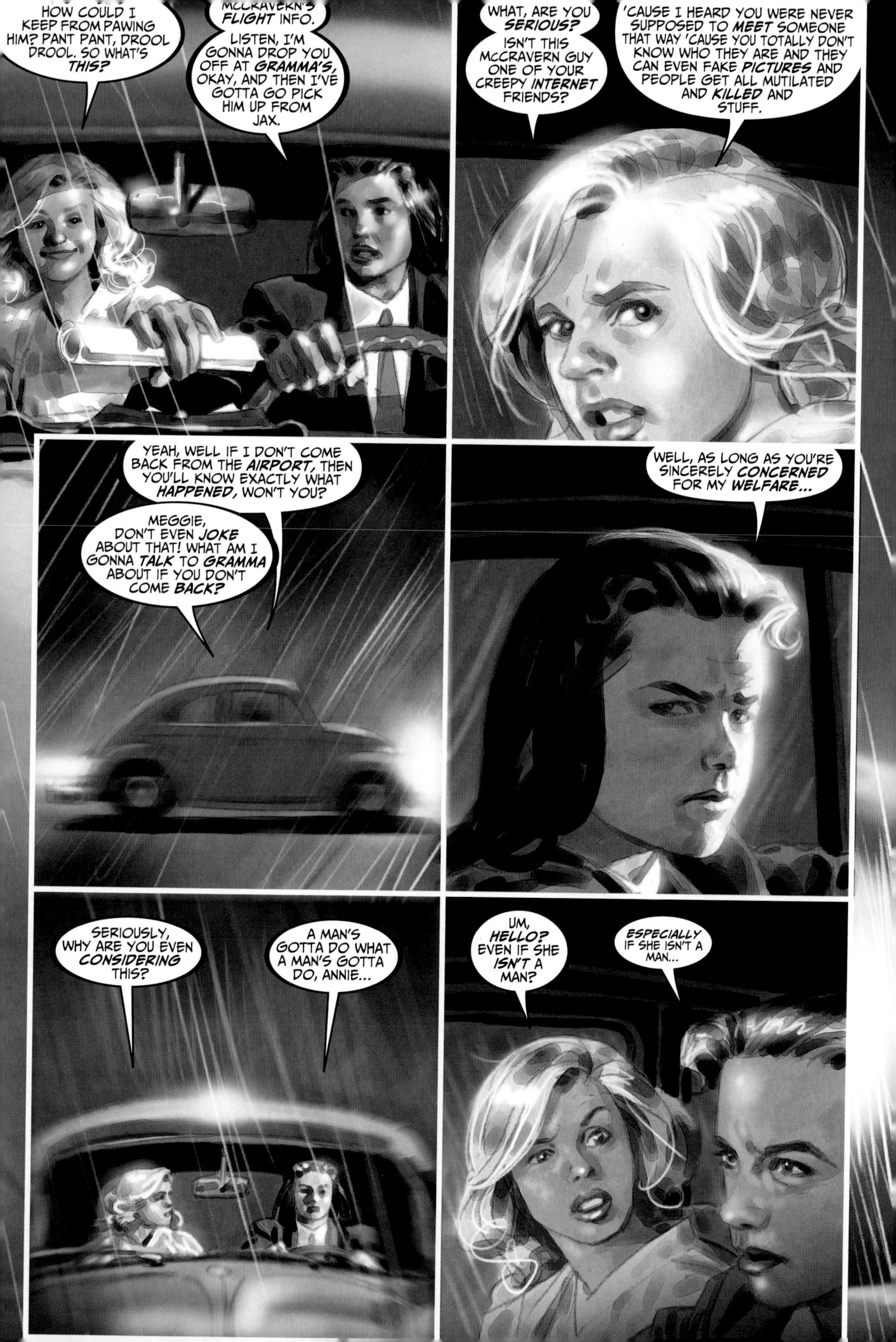

HOW COULD I KEEP FROM PAWING HIM? PANT PANT, DROOL DROOL. SO WHAT'S THIS?
McCRAVERN'S FLIGHT INFO.
LISTEN, I'M GONNA DROP YOU OFF AT GRAMMA'S, OKAY, AND THEN I'VE GOTTA GO PICK HIM UP FROM JAX.
WHAT, ARE YOU SERIOUS?
ISN'T THIS McCRAVERN GUY ONE OF YOUR CREEPY INTERNET FRIENDS?
'CAUSE I HEARD YOU WERE NEVER SUPPOSED TO MEET SOMEONE THAT WAY 'CAUSE YOU TOTALLY DON'T KNOW WHO THEY ARE AND THEY CAN EVEN FAKE PICTURES AND PEOPLE GET ALL MUTILATED AND KILLED AND STUFF.
YEAH, WELL IF I DON'T COME BACK FROM THE AIRPORT, THEN YOU'LL KNOW EXACTLY WHAT HAPPENED, WON'T YOU?
MEGGIE, DON'T EVEN JOKE ABOUT THAT! WHAT AM I GONNA TALK TO GRAMMA ABOUT IF YOU DON'T COME BACK?
WELL, AS LONG AS YOU'RE SINCERELY CONCERNED FOR MY WELFARE...
SERIOUSLY, WHY ARE YOU EVEN CONSIDERING THIS?
A MAN'S GOTTA DO WHAT A MAN'S GOTTA DO, ANNIE...
UM, HELLO? EVEN IF SHE ISN'T A MAN?
ESPECIALLY IF SHE ISN'T A MAN...

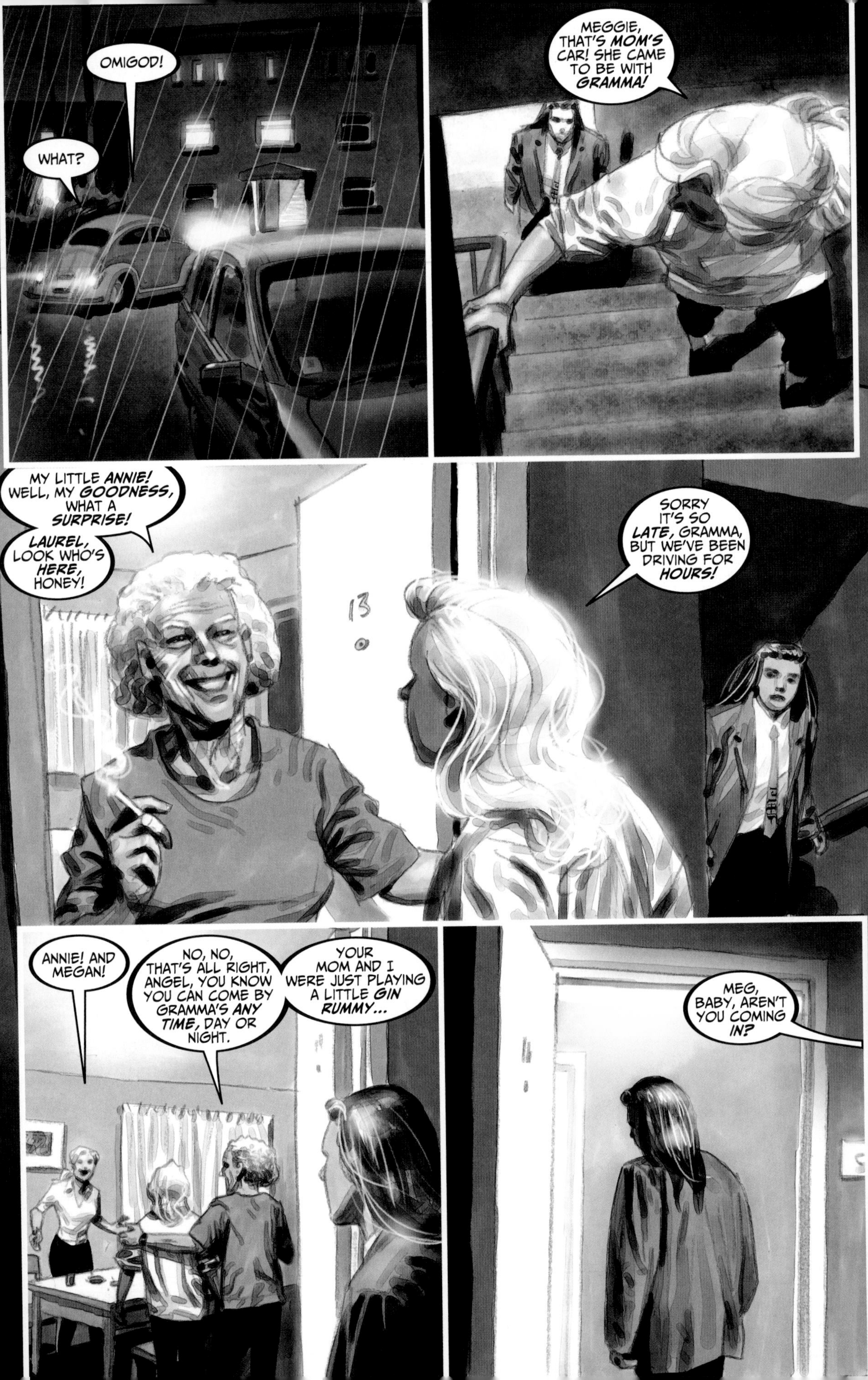
OMIGOD!
WHAT?
MEGGIE, THAT'S MOM'S CAR! SHE CAME TO BE WITH GRAMMA!
MY LITTLE ANNIE! WELL, MY GOODNESS, WHAT A SURPRISE!
LAUREL, LOOK WHO'S HERE, HONEY!
SORRY IT'S SO LATE, GRAMMA, BUT WE'VE BEEN DRIVING FOR HOURS!
ANNIE! AND MEGAN!
NO, NO, THAT'S ALL RIGHT, ANGEL, YOU KNOW YOU CAN COME BY GRAMMA'S ANY TIME, DAY OR NIGHT.
YOUR MOM AND I WERE JUST PLAYING A LITTLE GIN RUMMY...
MEG, BABY, AREN'T YOU COMING IN?

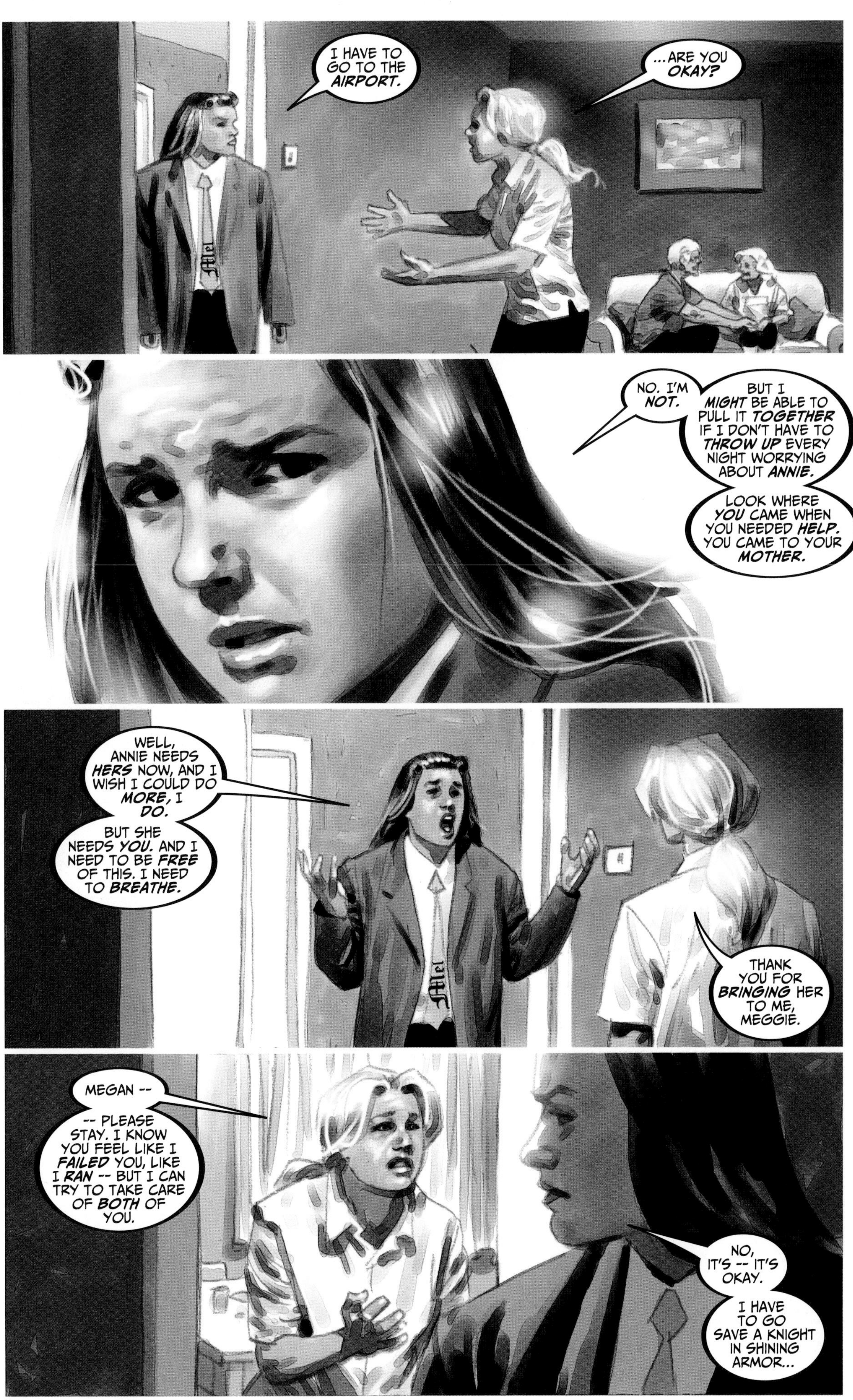
I HAVE TO GO TO THE AIRPORT.
...ARE YOU OKAY?
NO. I'M NOT.
BUT I MIGHT BE ABLE TO PULL IT TOGETHER IF I DON'T HAVE TO THROW UP EVERY NIGHT WORRYING ABOUT ANNIE.
LOOK WHERE YOU CAME WHEN YOU NEEDED HELP. YOU CAME TO YOUR MOTHER.
WELL, ANNIE NEEDS HERS NOW, AND I WISH I COULD DO MORE, I DO.
BUT SHE NEEDS YOU. AND I NEED TO BE FREE OF THIS. I NEED TO BREATHE.
THANK YOU FOR BRINGING HER TO ME, MEGGIE.
MEGAN --
-- PLEASE STAY. I KNOW YOU FEEL LIKE I FAILED YOU, LIKE I RAN -- BUT I CAN TRY TO TAKE CARE OF BOTH OF YOU.
NO, IT'S -- IT'S OKAY.
I HAVE TO GO SAVE A KNIGHT IN SHINING ARMOR...

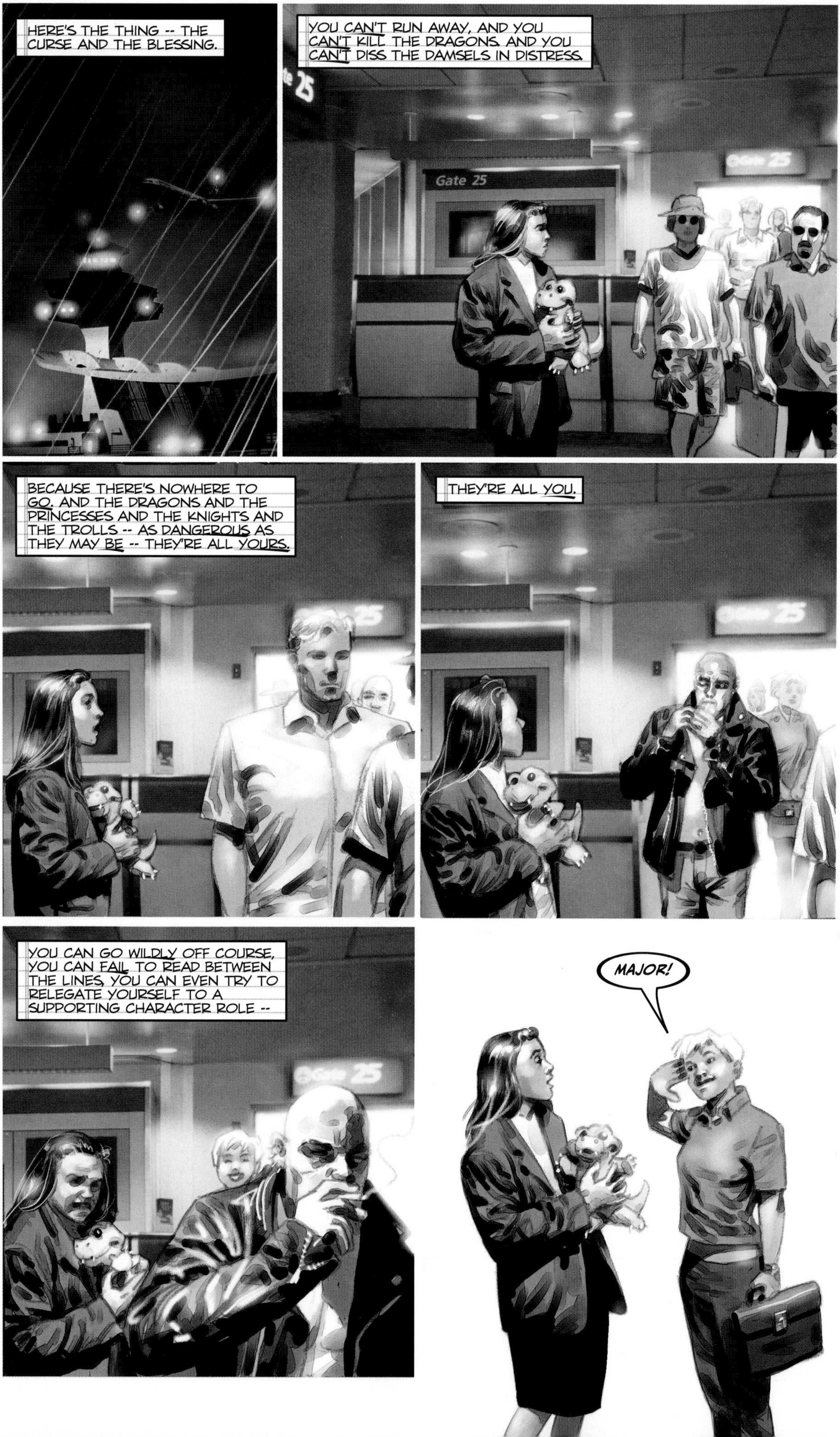
HERE'S THE THING -- THE CURSE AND THE BLESSING.
YOU CAN'T RUN AWAY, AND YOU CAN'T KILL THE DRAGONS. AND YOU CAN'T DISS THE DAMSELS IN DISTRESS.
Gate 25
BECAUSE THERE'S NOWHERE TO GO. AND THE DRAGONS AND THE PRINCESSES AND THE KNIGHTS AND THE TROLLS -- AS DANGEROUS AS THEY MAY BE -- THEY'RE ALL YOURS.
THEY'RE ALL YOU.
YOU CAN GO WILDLY OFF COURSE, YOU CAN FAIL TO READ BETWEEN THE LINES, YOU CAN EVEN TRY TO RELEGATE YOURSELF TO A SUPPORTING CHARACTER ROLE --
MAJOR!

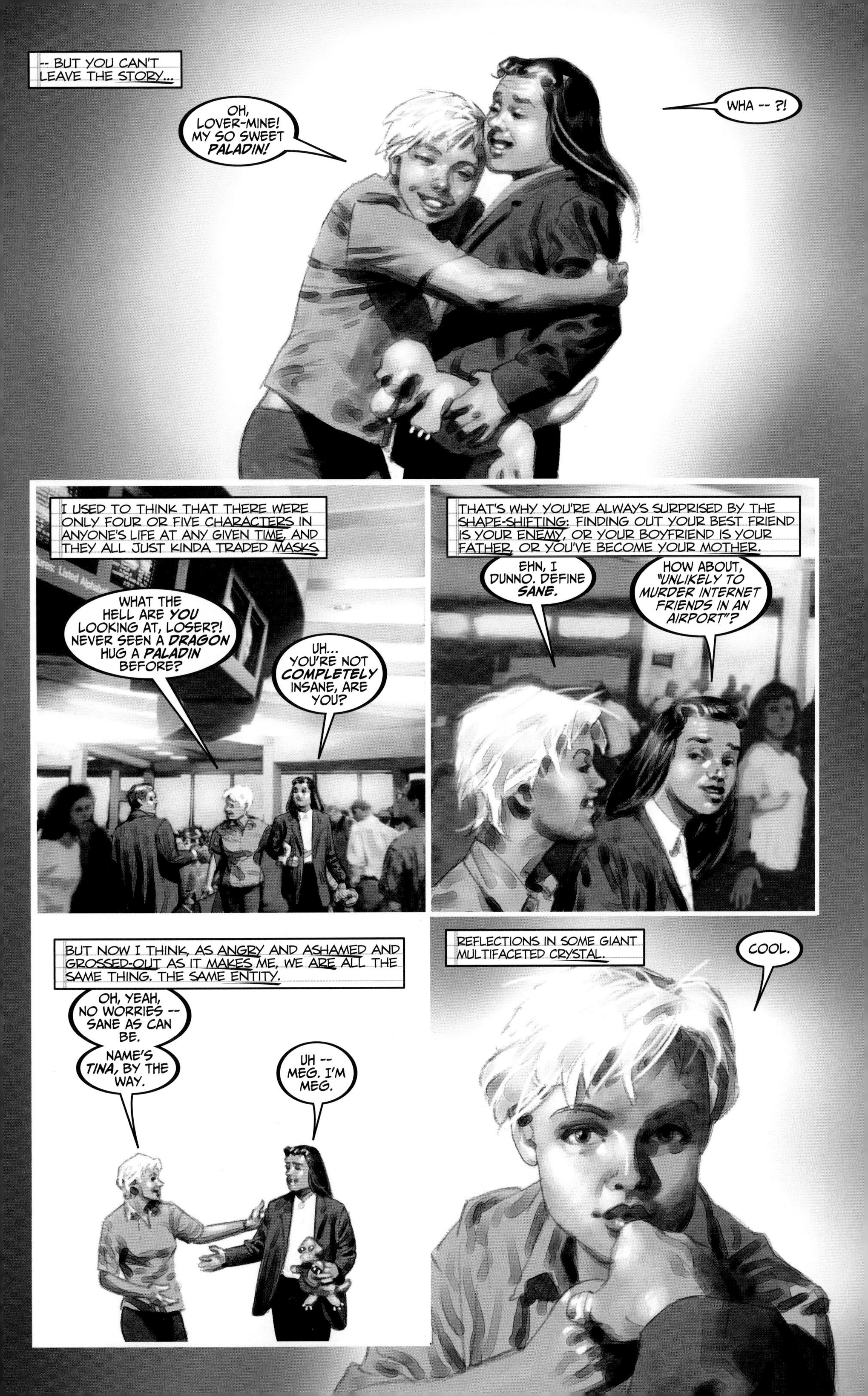
-- BUT YOU CAN'T LEAVE THE STORY...
OH, LOVER-MINE! MY SO SWEET PALADIN!
WHA -- ?!
I USED TO THINK THAT THERE WERE ONLY FOUR OR FIVE CHARACTERS IN ANYONE'S LIFE AT ANY GIVEN TIME, AND THEY ALL JUST KINDA TRADED MASKS.
WHAT THE HELL ARE YOU LOOKING AT, LOSER?! NEVER SEEN A DRAGON HUG A PALADIN BEFORE?
UH... YOU'RE NOT COMPLETELY INSANE, ARE YOU?
THAT'S WHY YOU'RE ALWAYS SURPRISED BY THE SHAPE-SHIFTING: FINDING OUT YOUR BEST FRIEND IS YOUR ENEMY, OR YOUR BOYFRIEND IS YOUR FATHER, OR YOU'VE BECOME YOUR MOTHER.
EHN, I DUNNO. DEFINE SANE.
HOW ABOUT, "UNLIKELY TO MURDER INTERNET FRIENDS IN AN AIRPORT"?
BUT NOW I THINK, AS ANGRY AND ASHAMED AND GROSSED-OUT AS IT MAKES ME, WE ARE ALL THE SAME THING. THE SAME ENTITY.
OH, YEAH, NO WORRIES -- SANE AS CAN BE.
NAME'S TINA, BY THE WAY.
UH -- MEG. I'M MEG.
REFLECTIONS IN SOME GIANT MULTIFACETED CRYSTAL.
COOL.

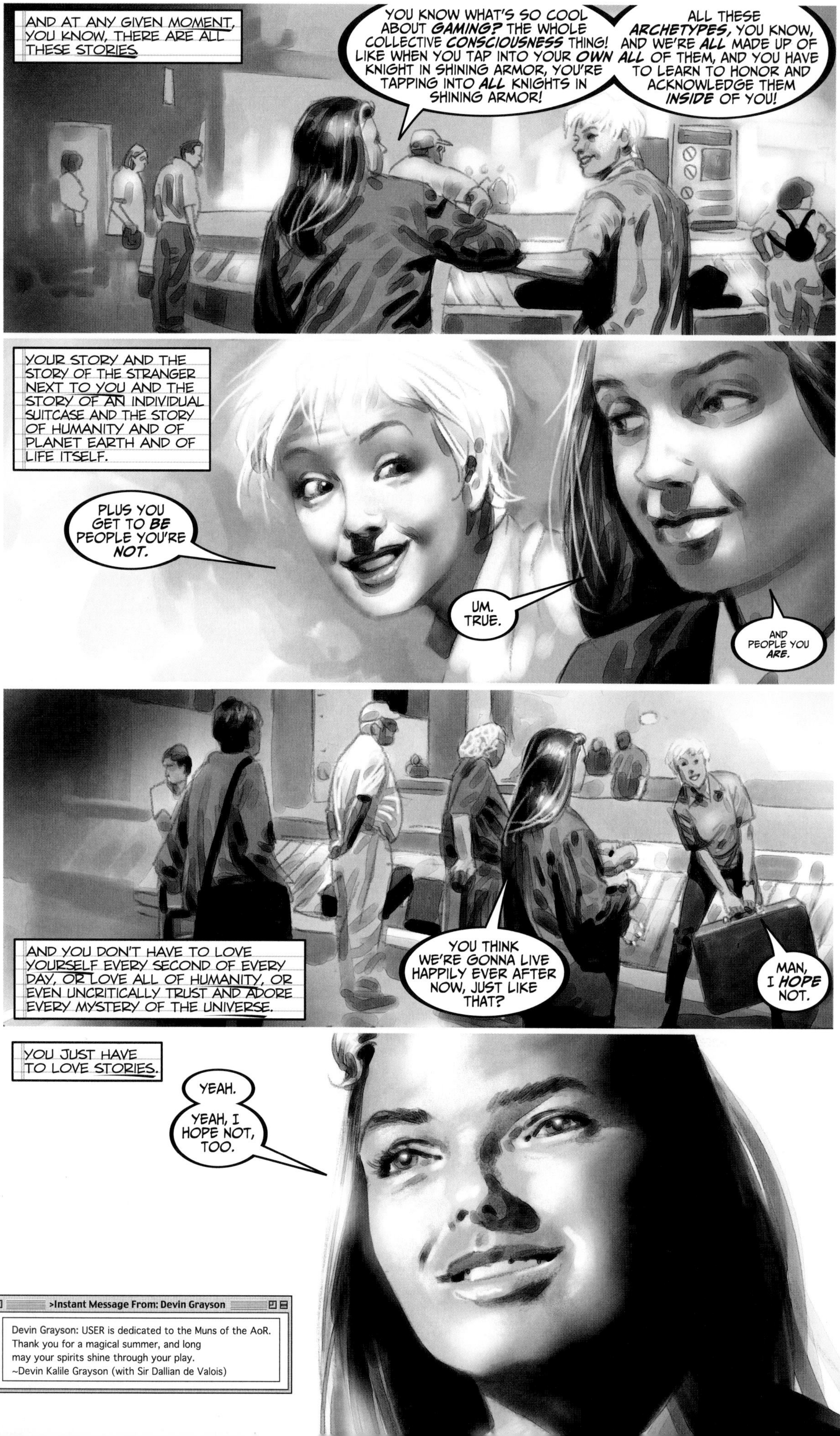
AND AT ANY GIVEN MOMENT, YOU KNOW, THERE ARE ALL THESE STORIES.
YOU KNOW WHAT'S SO COOL ABOUT GAMING? THE WHOLE COLLECTIVE CONSCIOUSNESS THING! LIKE WHEN YOU TAP INTO YOUR OWN KNIGHT IN SHINING ARMOR, YOU'RE TAPPING INTO ALL KNIGHTS IN SHINING ARMOR!
ALL THESE ARCHETYPES, YOU KNOW, AND WE'RE ALL MADE UP OF ALL OF THEM, AND YOU HAVE TO LEARN TO HONOR AND ACKNOWLEDGE THEM INSIDE OF YOU!
YOUR STORY AND THE STORY OF THE STRANGER NEXT TO YOU AND THE STORY OF AN INDIVIDUAL SUITCASE AND THE STORY OF HUMANITY AND OF PLANET EARTH AND OF LIFE ITSELF.
PLUS YOU GET TO BE PEOPLE YOU'RE NOT.
UM. TRUE.
AND PEOPLE YOU ARE.
AND YOU DON'T HAVE TO LOVE YOURSELF EVERY SECOND OF EVERY DAY, OR LOVE ALL OF HUMANITY, OR EVEN UNCRITICALLY TRUST AND ADORE EVERY MYSTERY OF THE UNIVERSE.
YOU THINK WE'RE GONNA LIVE HAPPILY EVER AFTER NOW, JUST LIKE THAT?
MAN, I HOPE NOT.
YOU JUST HAVE TO LOVE STORIES.
YEAH.
YEAH, I HOPE NOT, TOO.

>Instant Message From: Devin Grayson

Devin Grayson: USER is dedicated to the Muns of the AoR.
Thank you for a magical summer, and long
may your spirits shine through your play.
~Devin Kalile Grayson (with Sir Dallian de Valois)

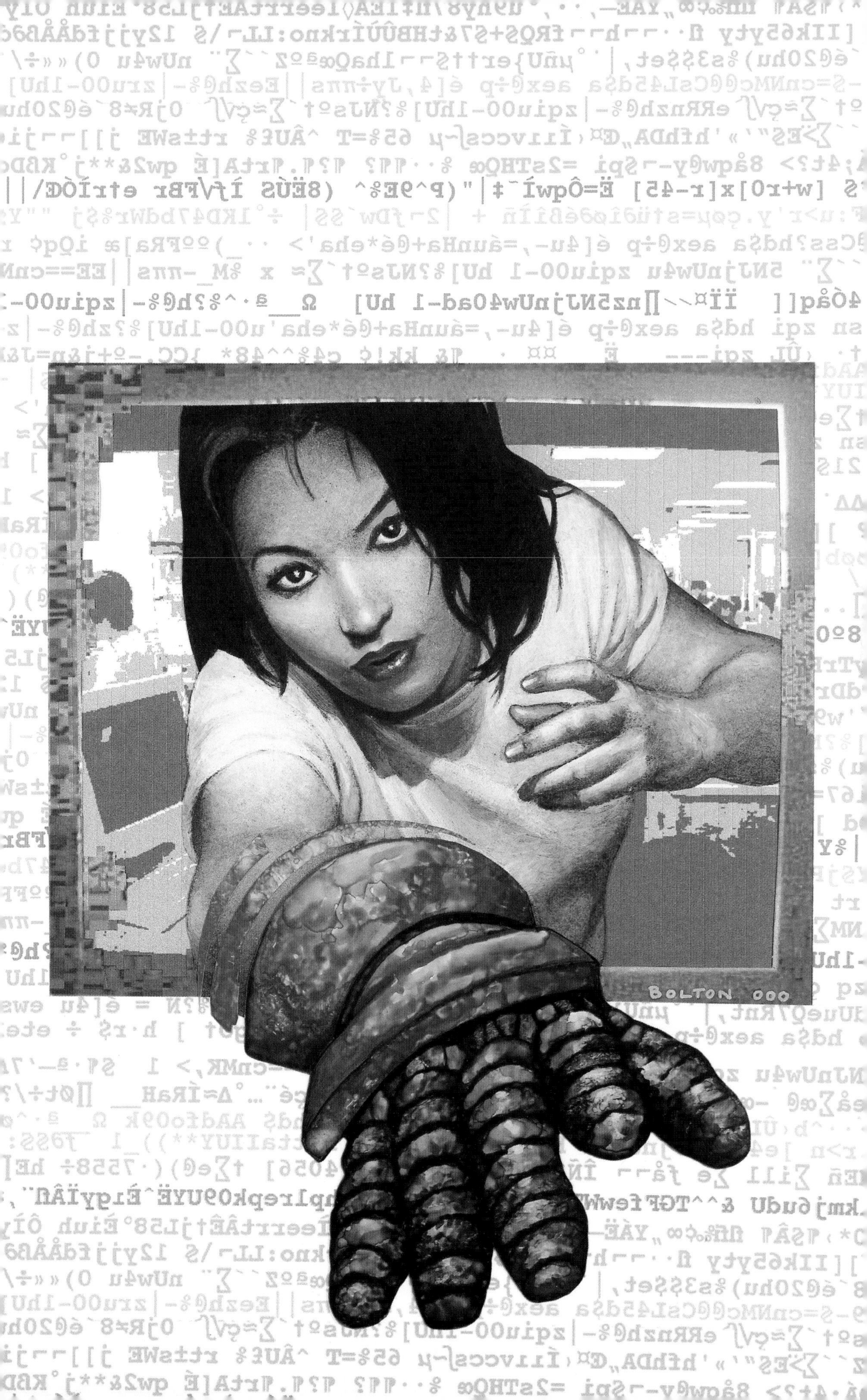
BOLTON 000

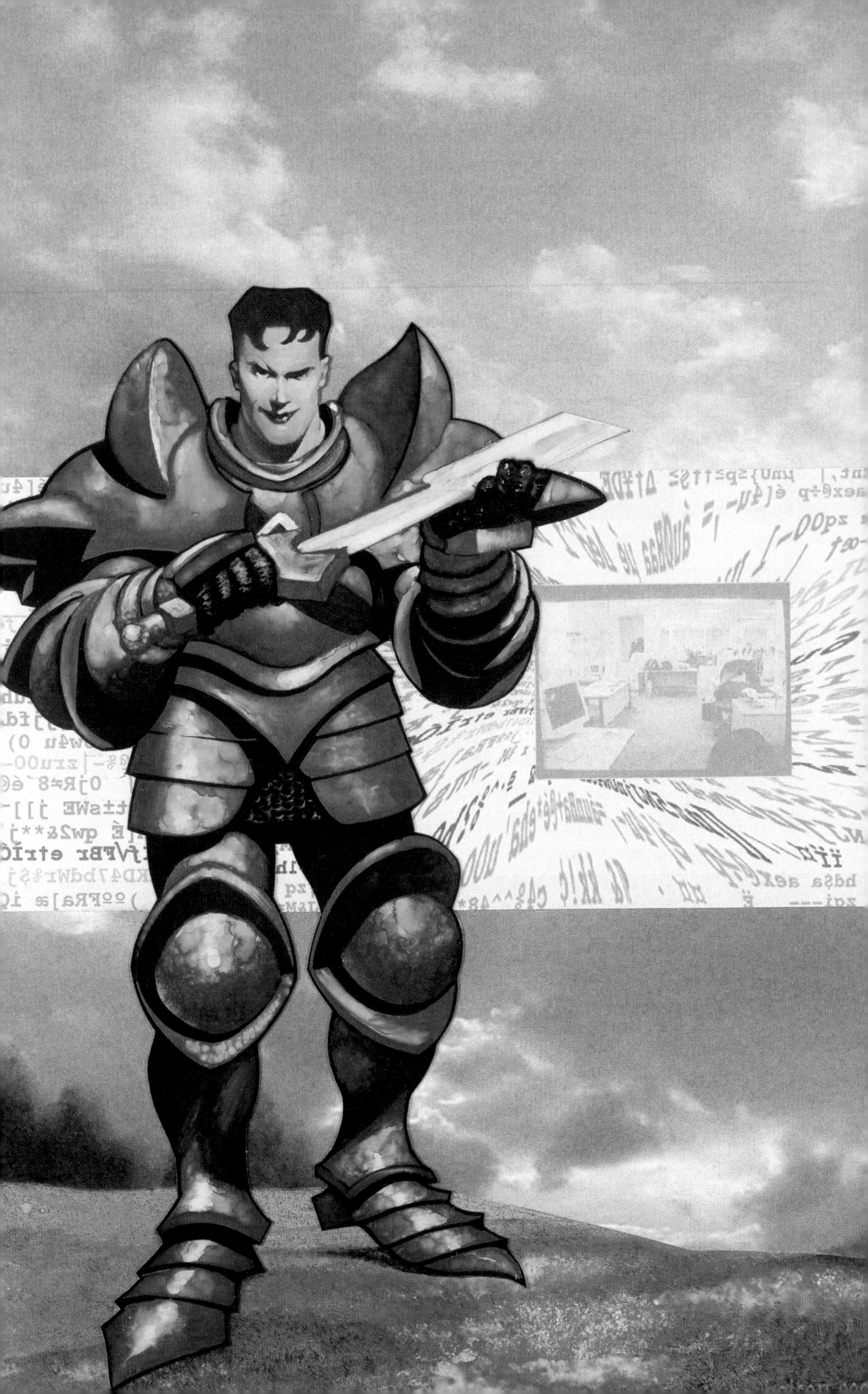

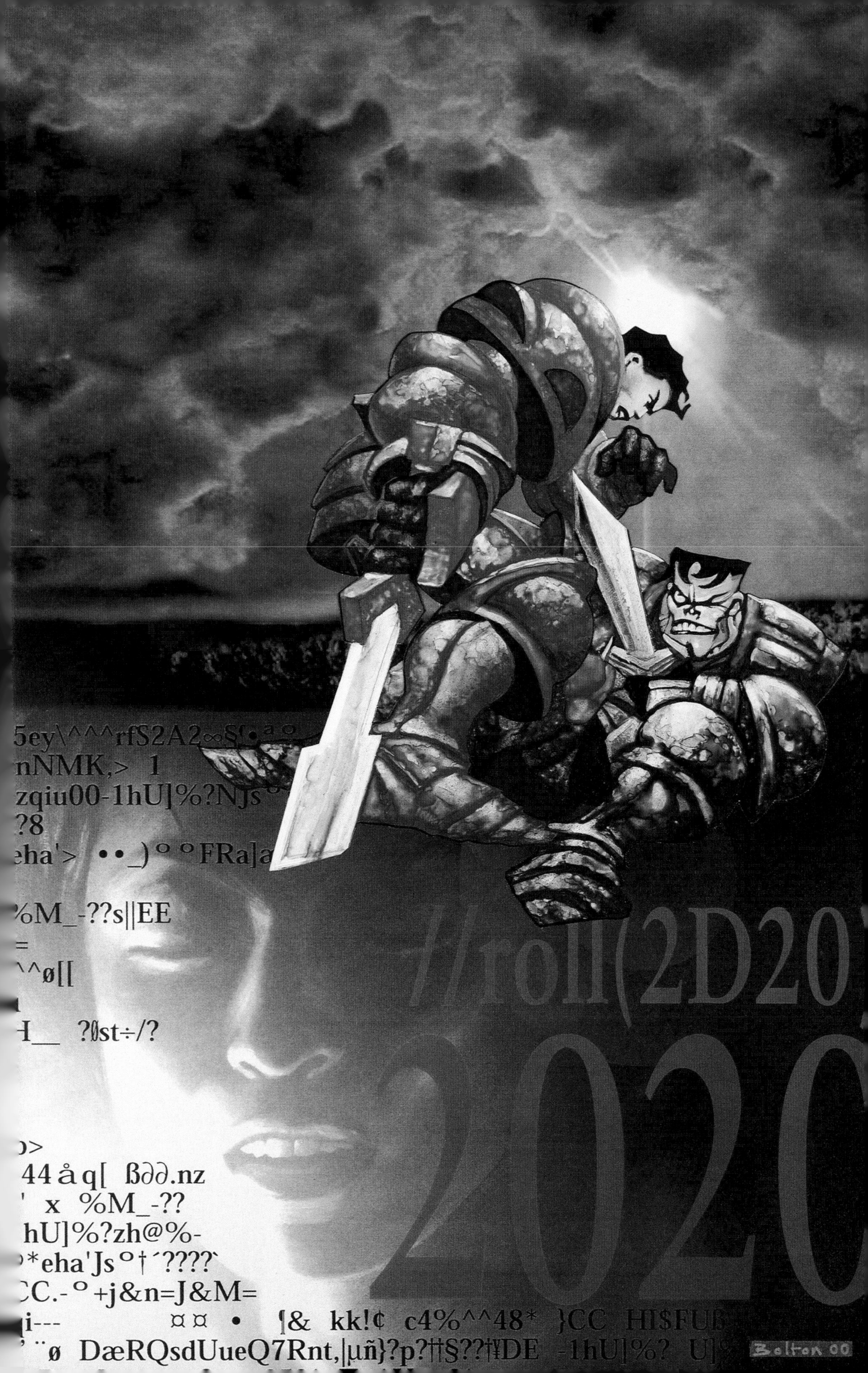

//roll(2D20
2020
Bolton 00

Process

Preparatory sketches by John Bolton

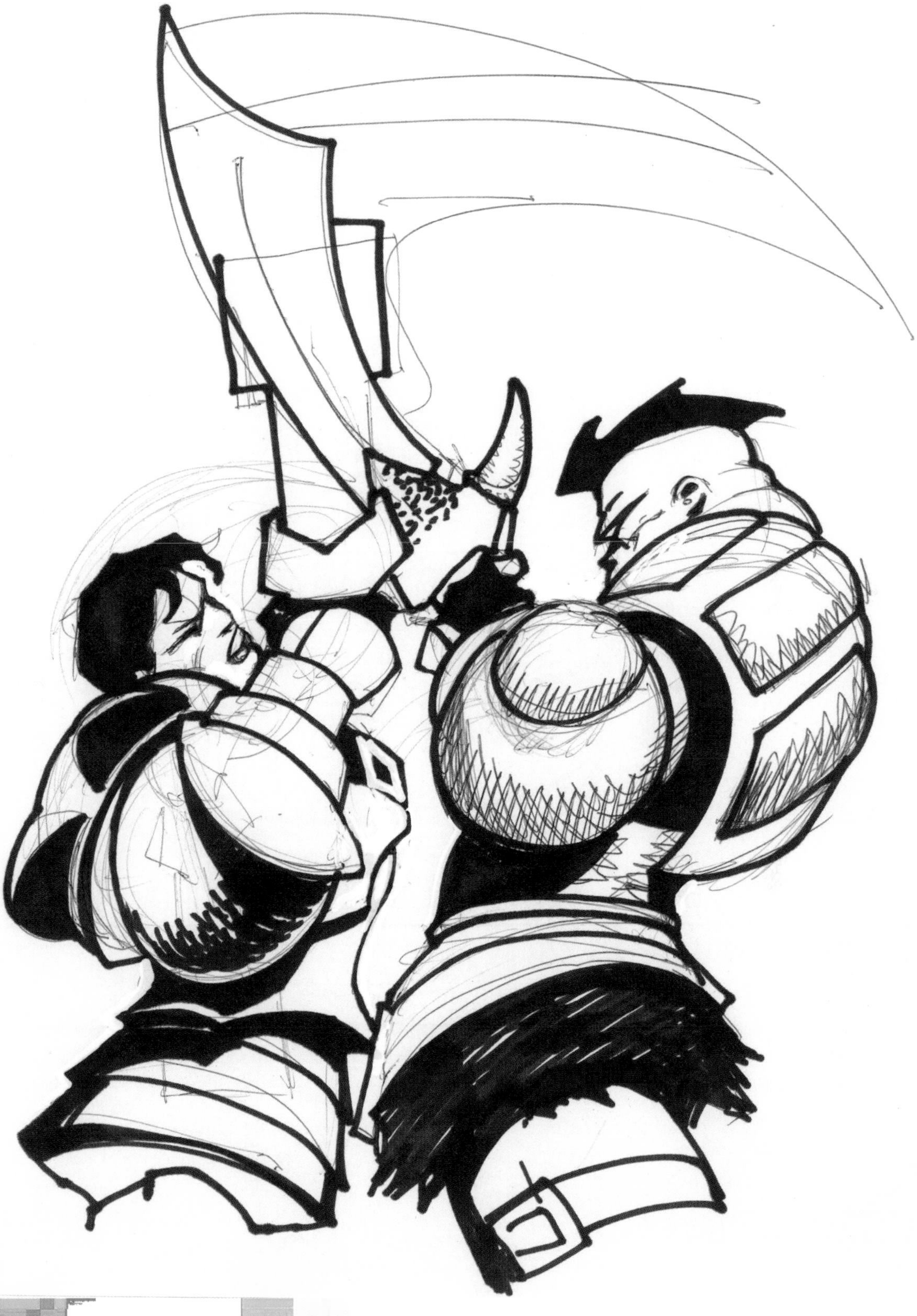

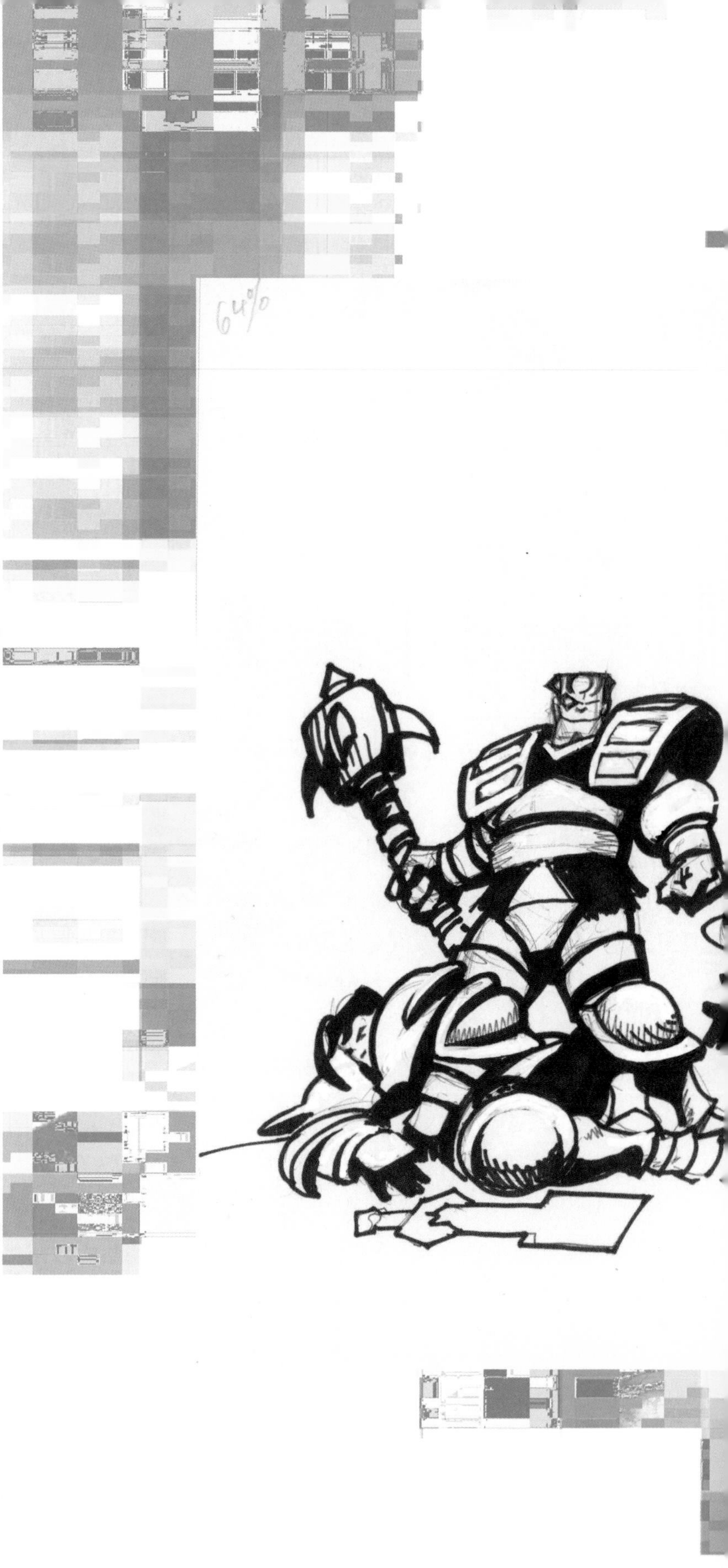
64%

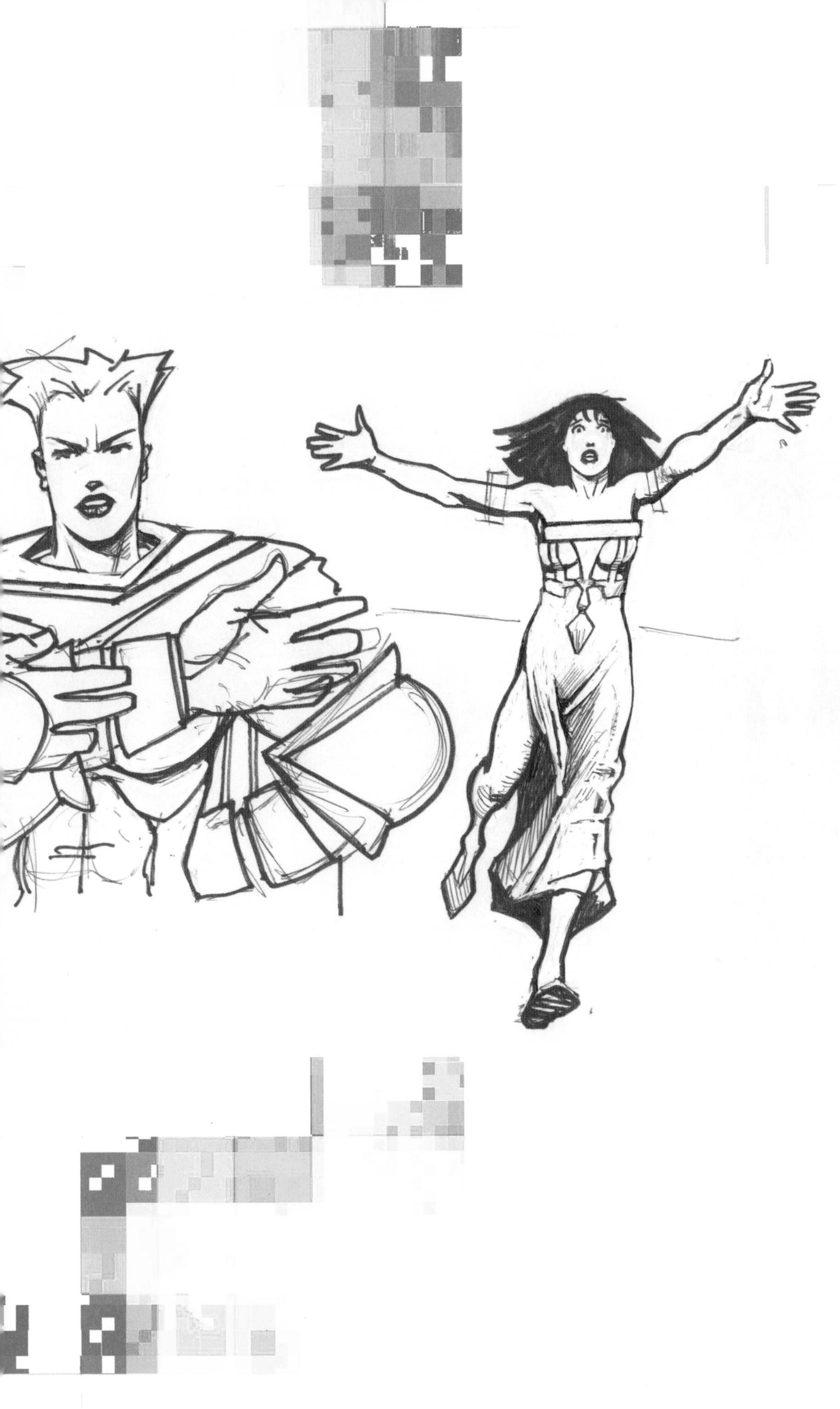

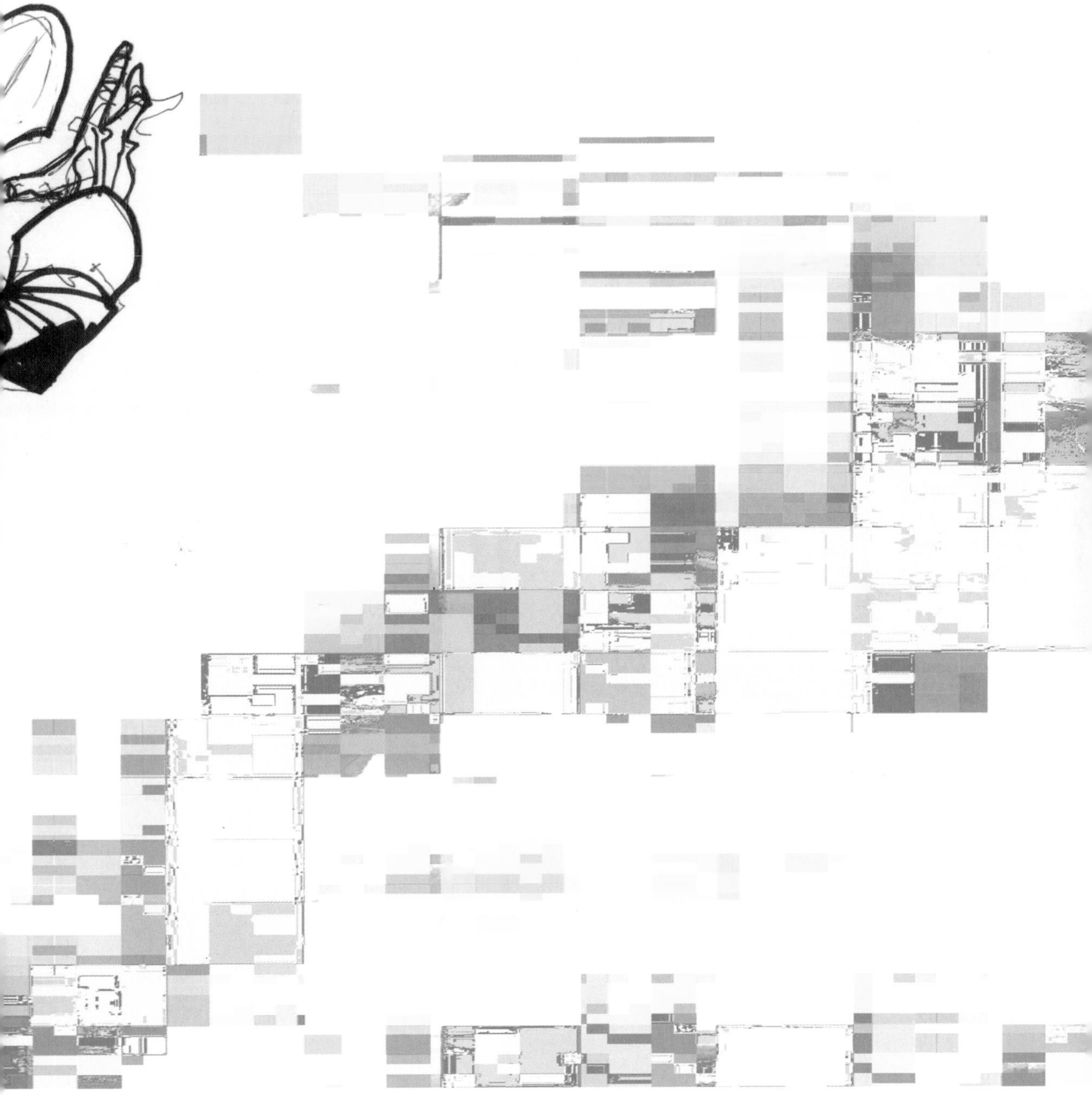

Thumbnails by Sean Phillips

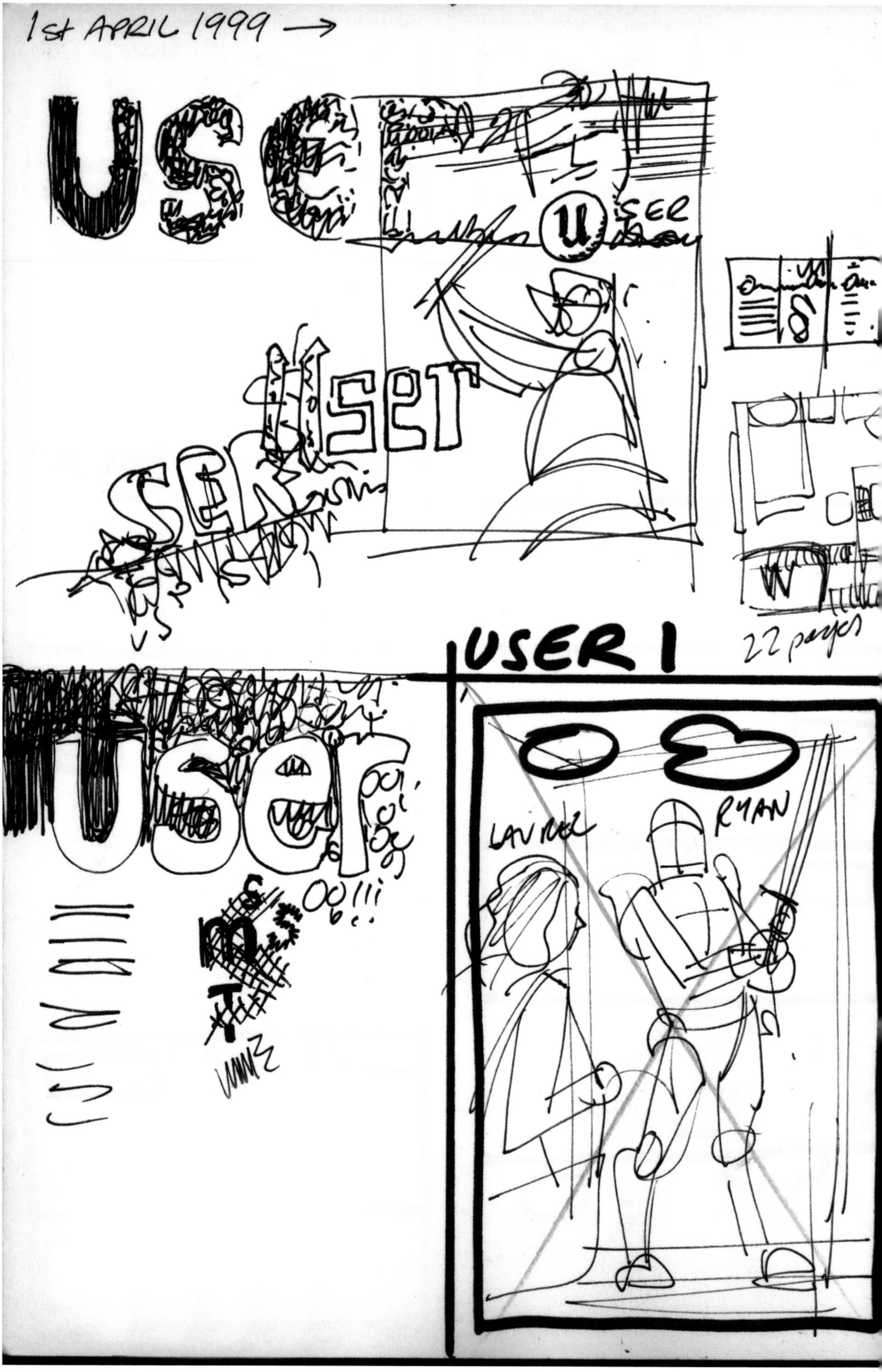
1st APRIL 1999 →
USER 1
22 pages
LAVINIA
RYAN

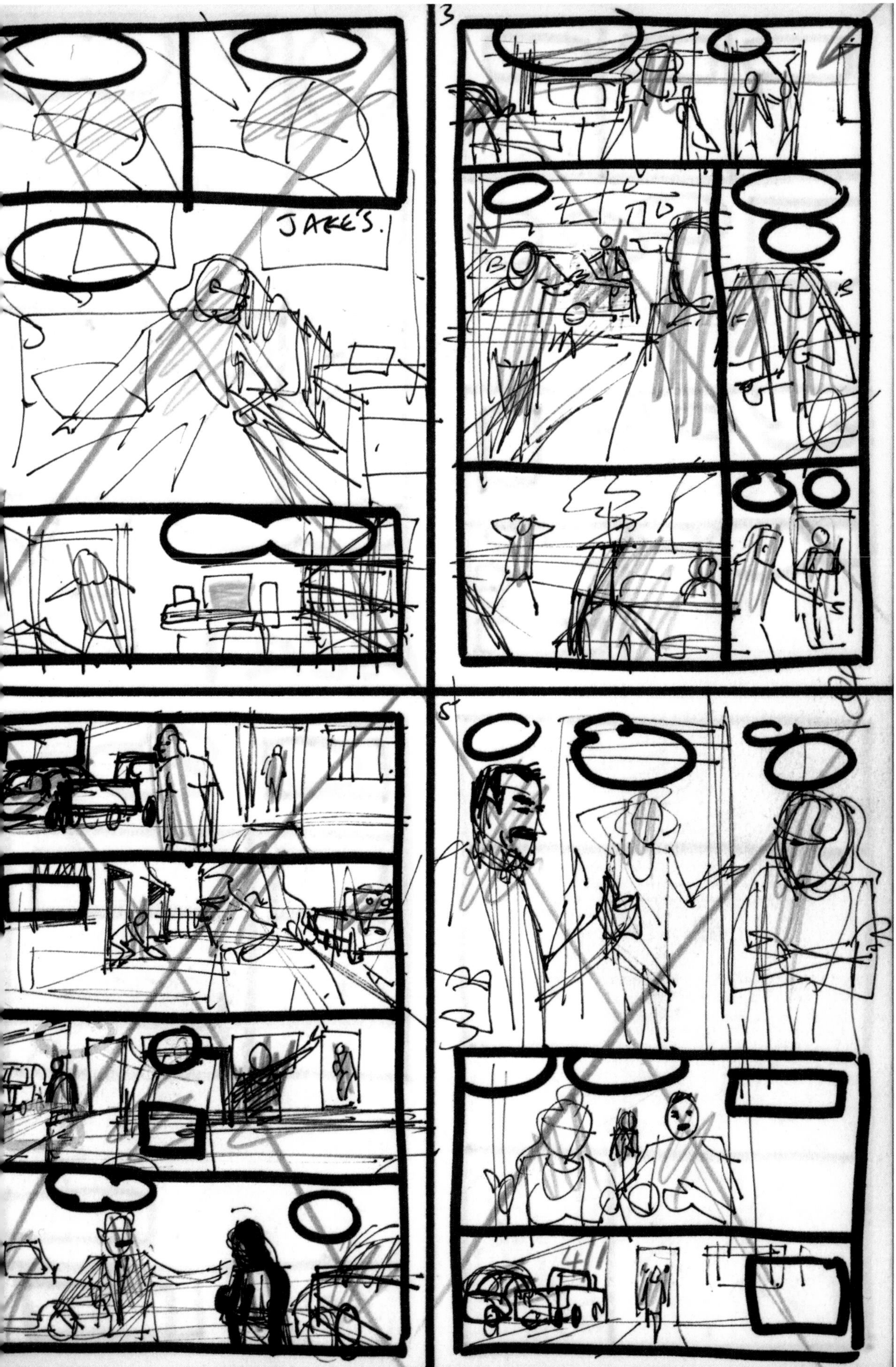
JAKE'S.

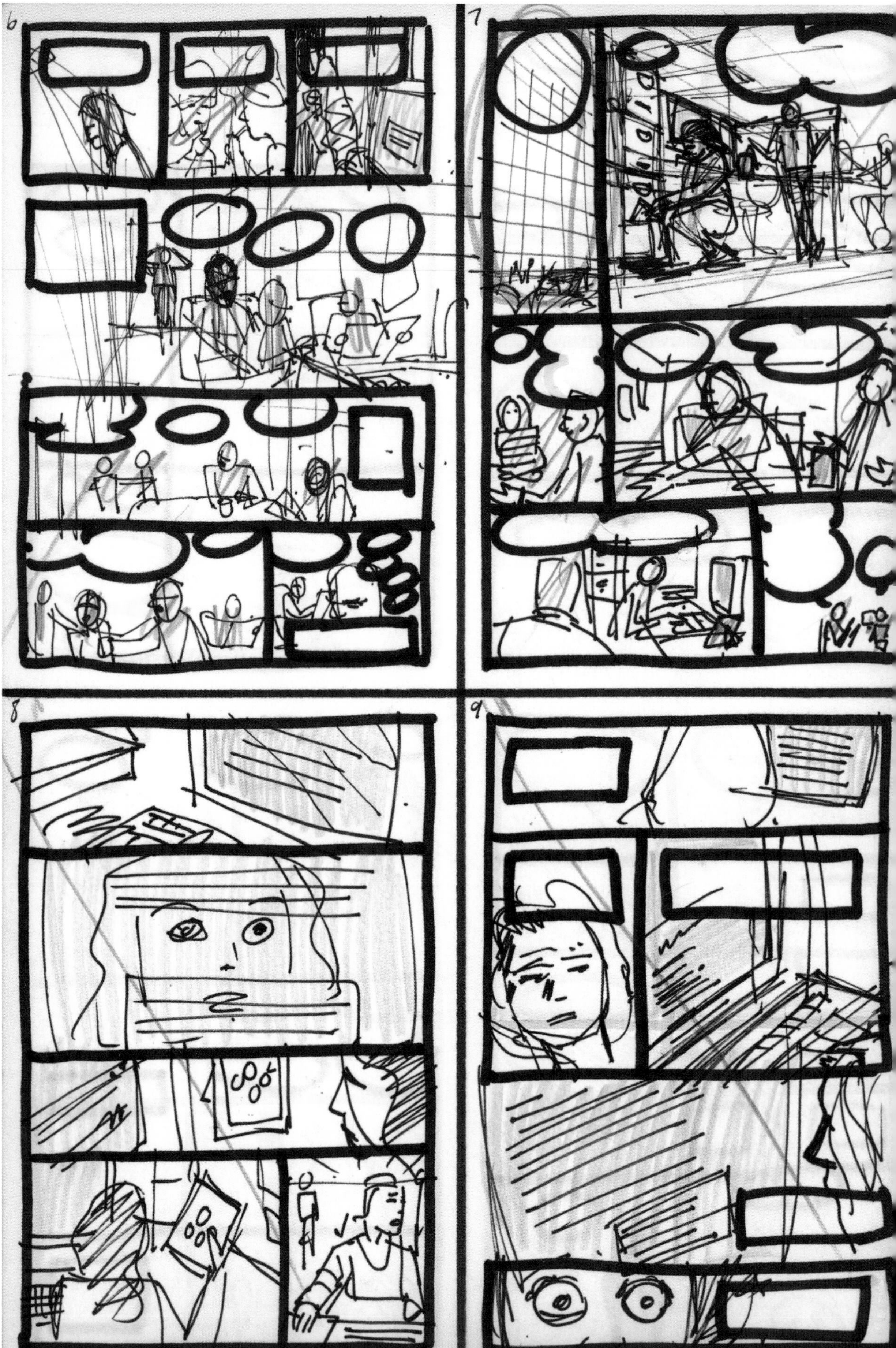
6
7
8
9

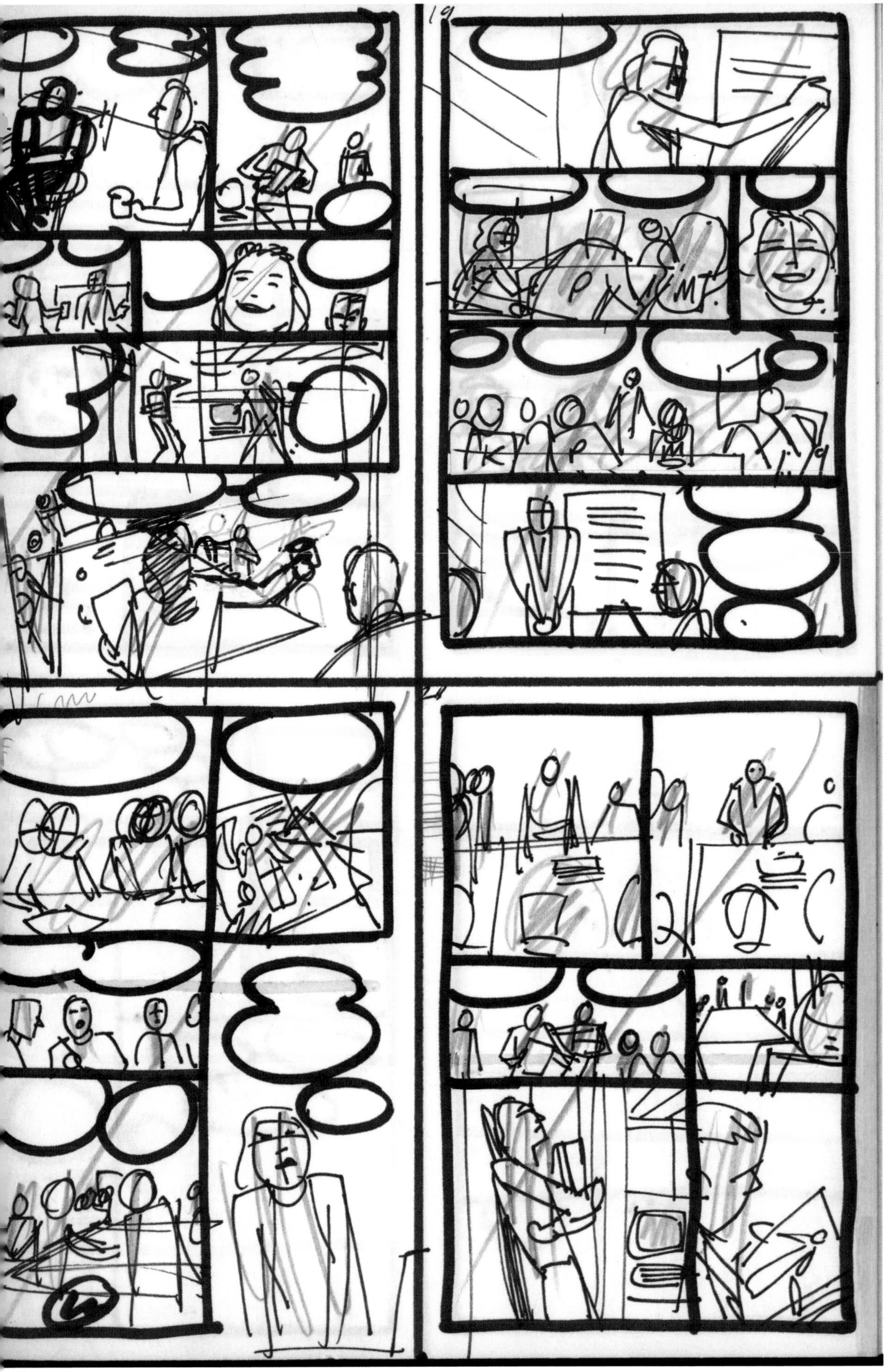

36

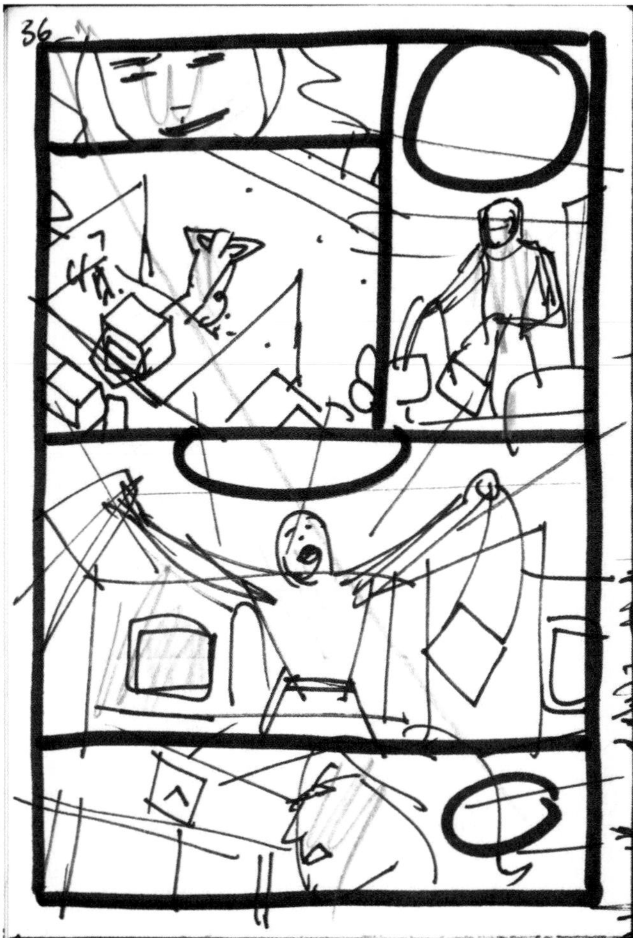

37

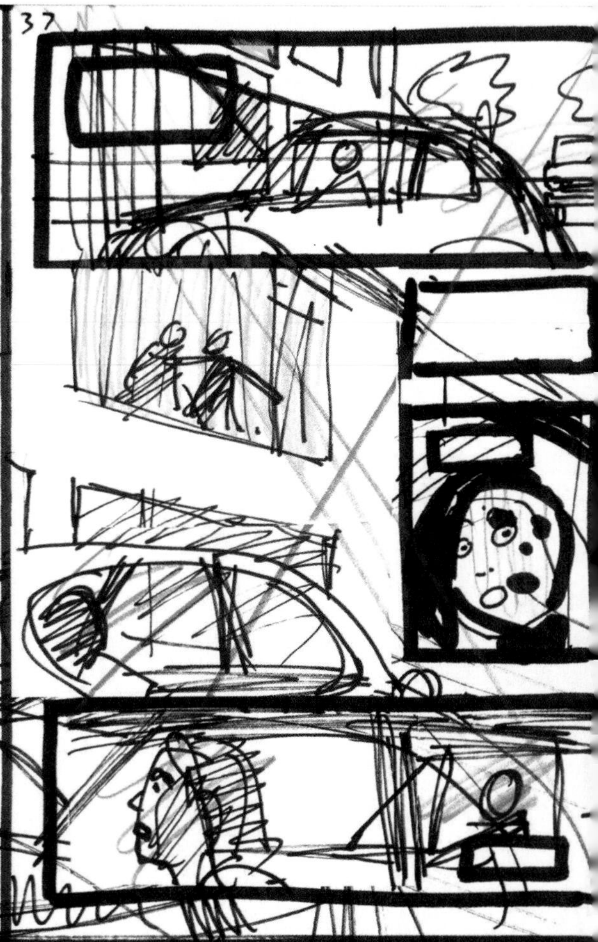

38

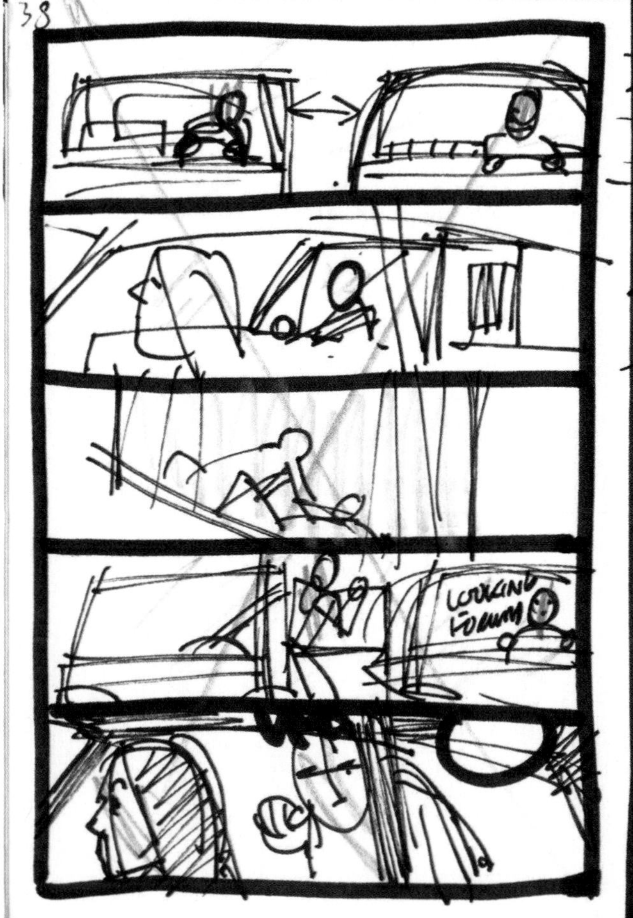
LOOKING

39

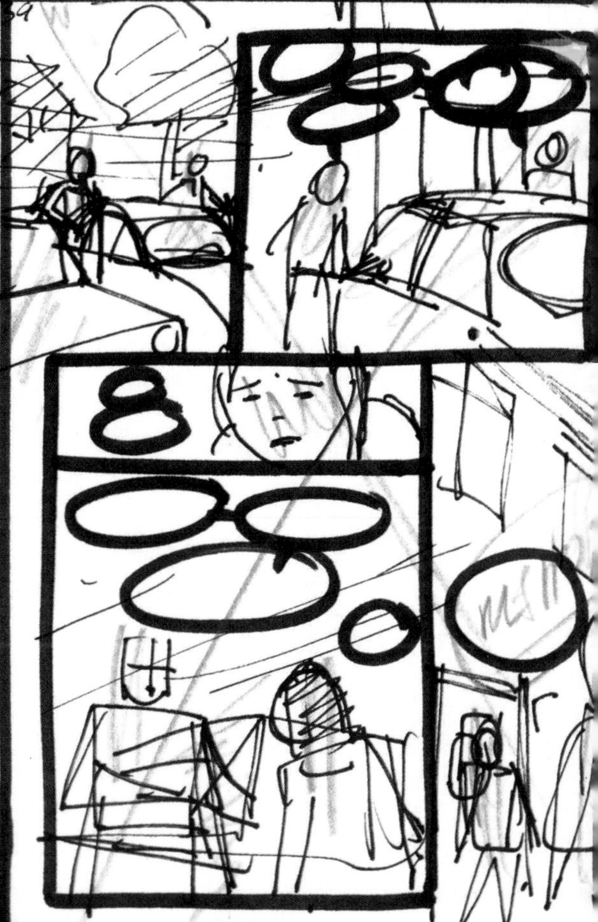

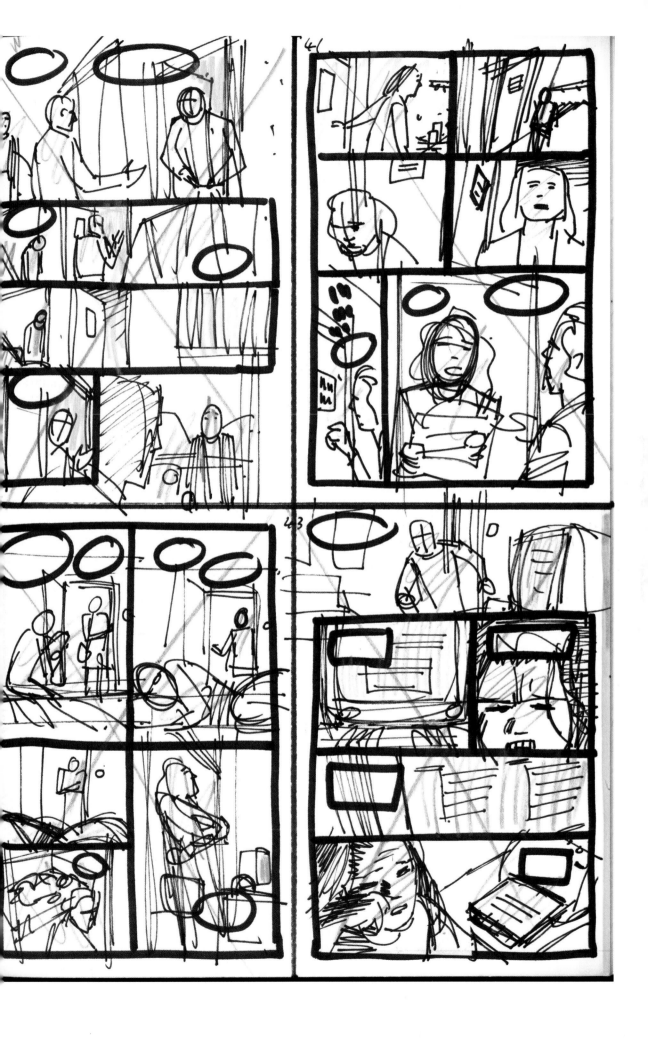

Pencils by Sean Phillips

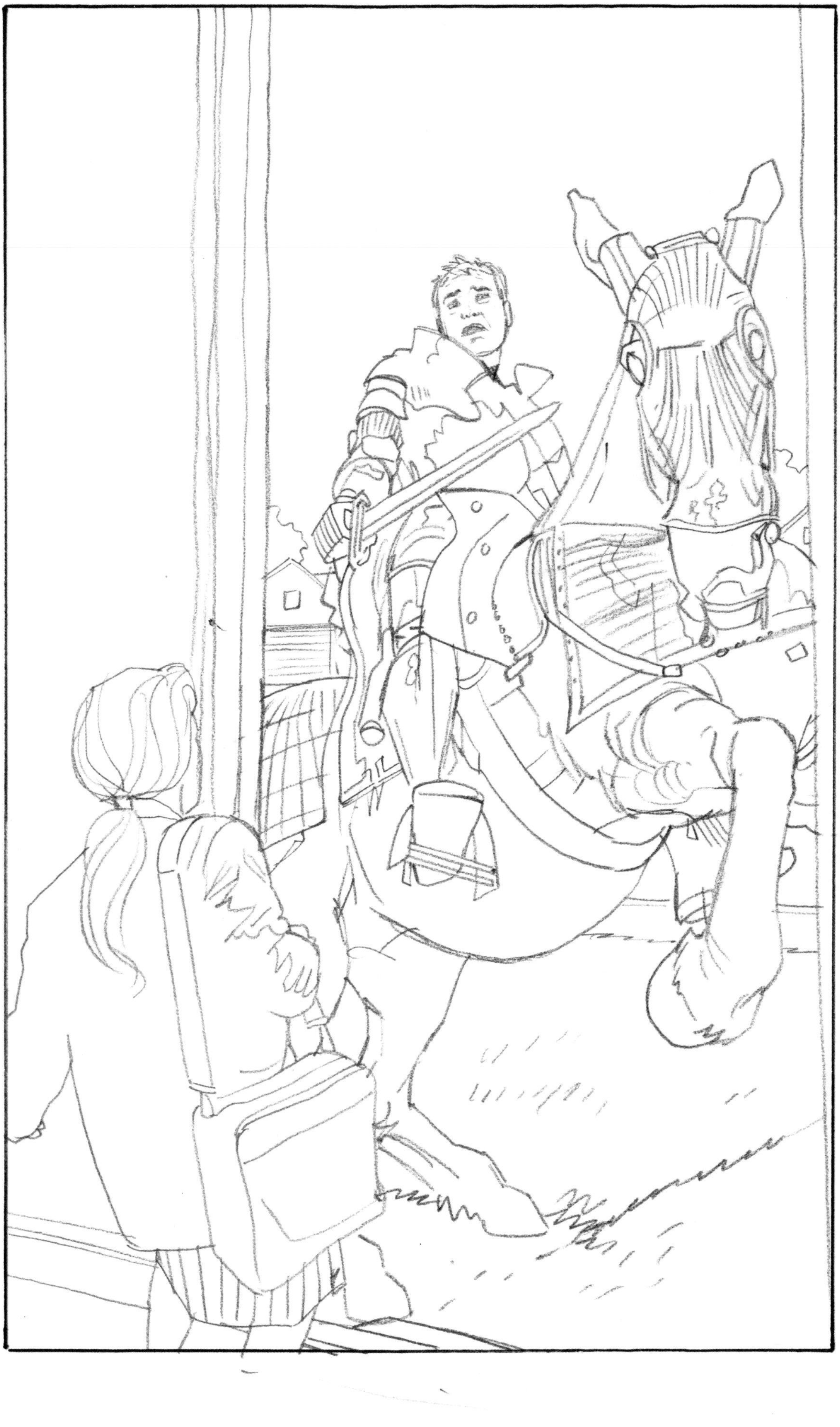

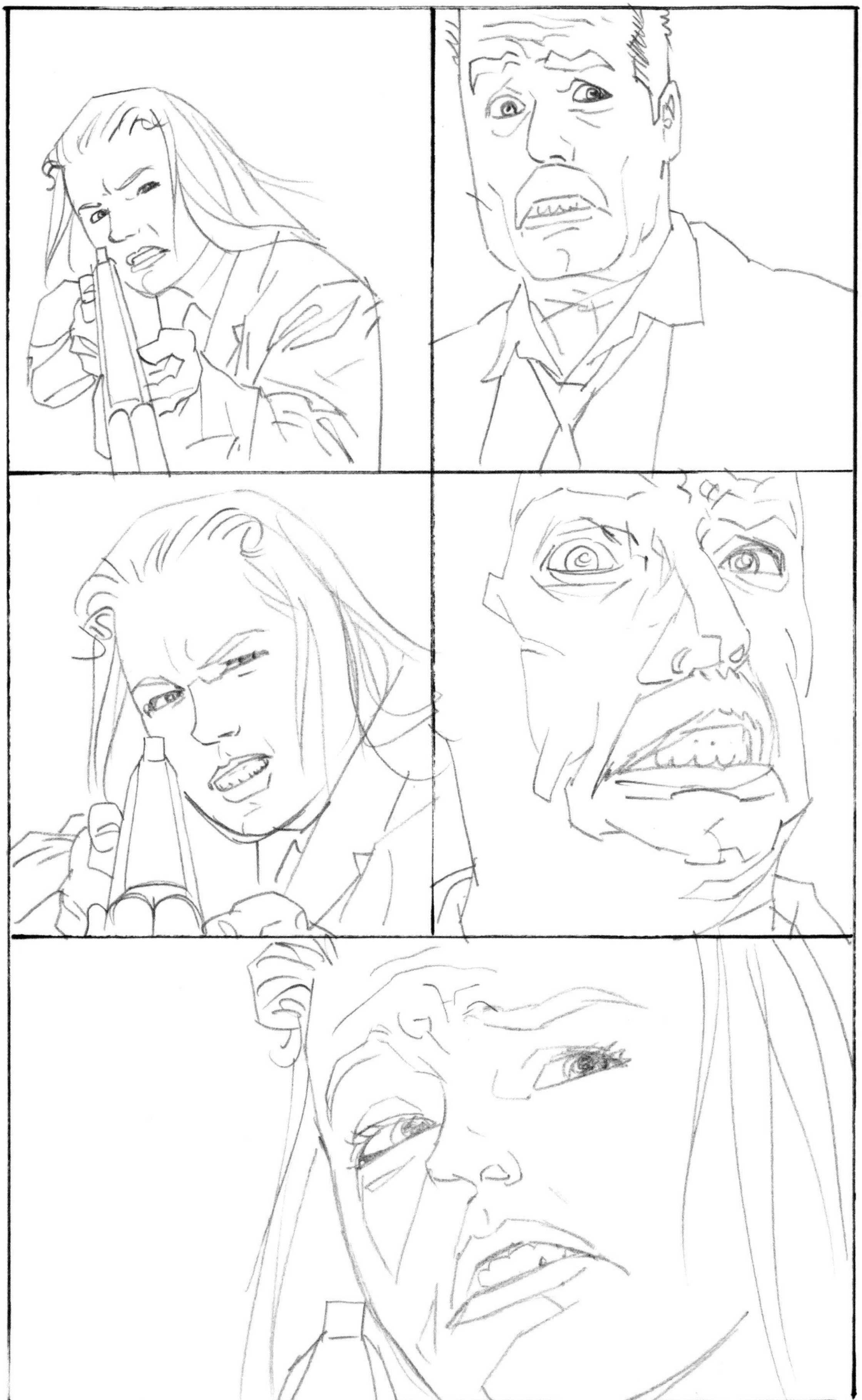

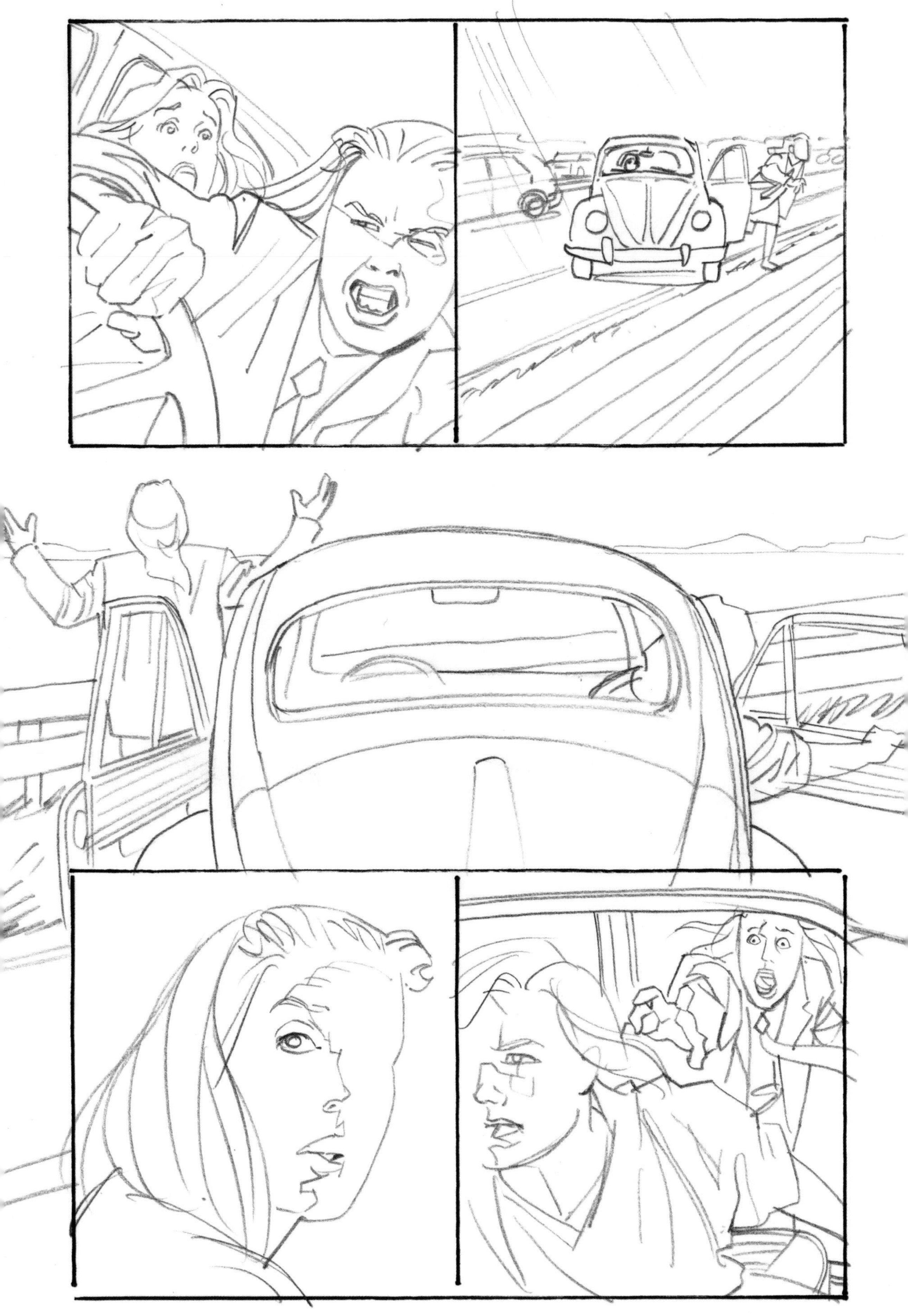

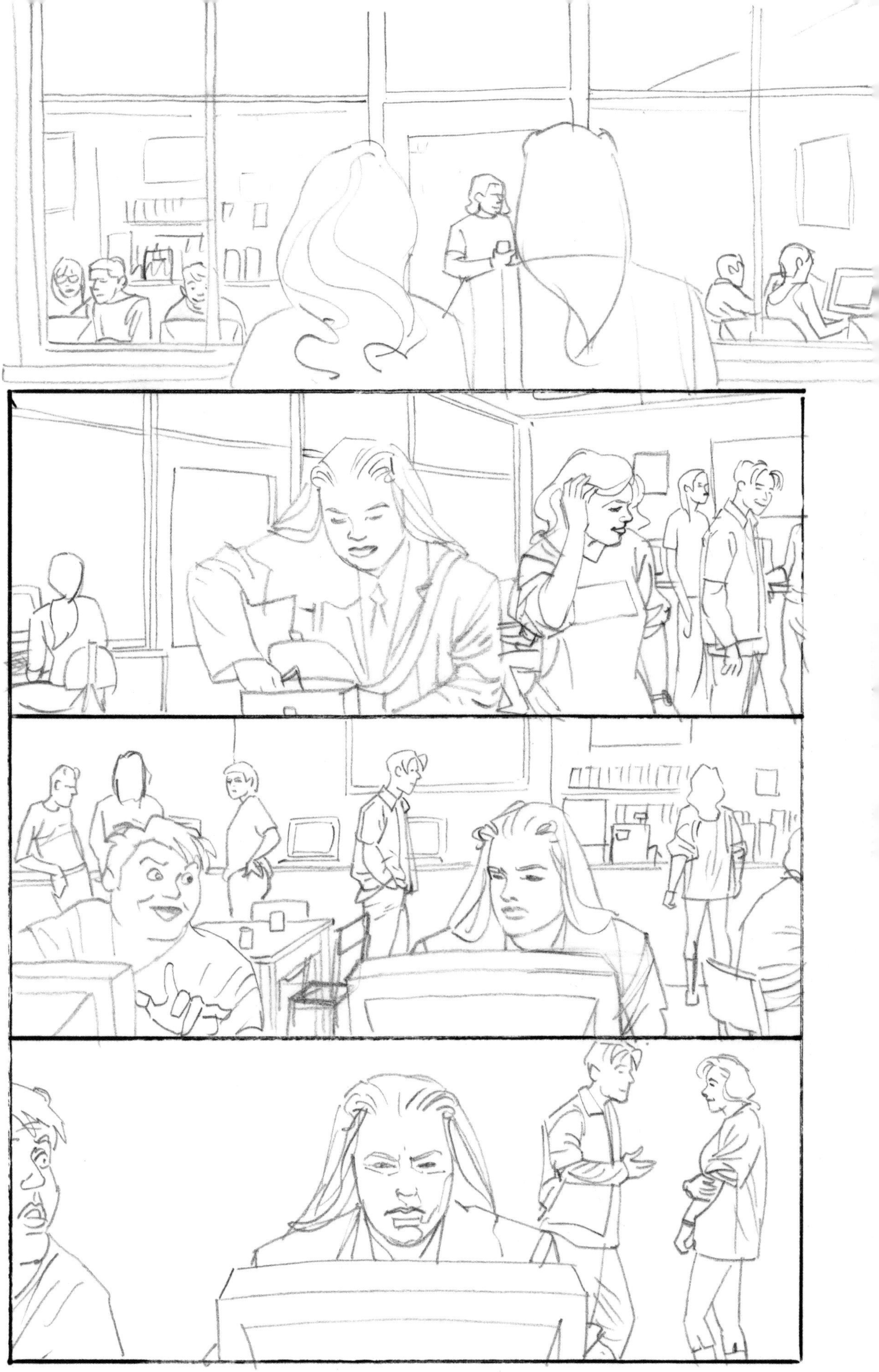

Biographies

Devin Grayson is an avid gamer, former acting student and voracious reader fortunate enough to have turned a lifelong obsession with fictional characters into a dynamic writing career. Best known for her award-winning body of work in the Batman Universe for DC Comics, Devin's published work includes comic books, graphic novels, novels, short fiction, essays, radio plays and scripting for casual games and MMOs, as well as a recently published full-length, original Doctor Strange novel for Marvel's prose line. Devin lives in Northern California with her family and considers **USER** her most personal work to date.

Photo by Robert Houser

John was seven when he first encountered a paint brush. It was love at first sight, offering him the opportunity to bring the visions in his mind vividly to life. Thus began a life-long devotion to art, with a wide variety of influences all connected by one underlying theme: the intriguing and the bizarre.

John has collaborated with some of the industry's most prestigious writers, including Neil Gaiman, Chris Claremont, Mike Carey, Mark Verheiden and, in the film world, Robert Zemeckis, Sam Raimi and Jonathan Glazer. He is currently working in watercolor for the second trilogy of Lovern Kindzierski's **Shame**.

Drawing comics professionally since the age of fifteen, Eisner Award-winning Sean Phillips has worked for all the major publishers. Since drawing **Sleeper**, **Hellblazer**, **Batman**, **X-Men**, **Marvel Zombies**, and Stephen King's **The Dark Tower**, Sean has concentrated on creator-owned books including **Criminal**, **Incognito**, **Fatale** and **The Fade Out**.

He is currently drawing **Kill Or Be Killed** written by his long-time collaborator Ed Brubaker.

Photo by Joe Gordon

He lives in the Lake District in the UK with his wife and three sons.

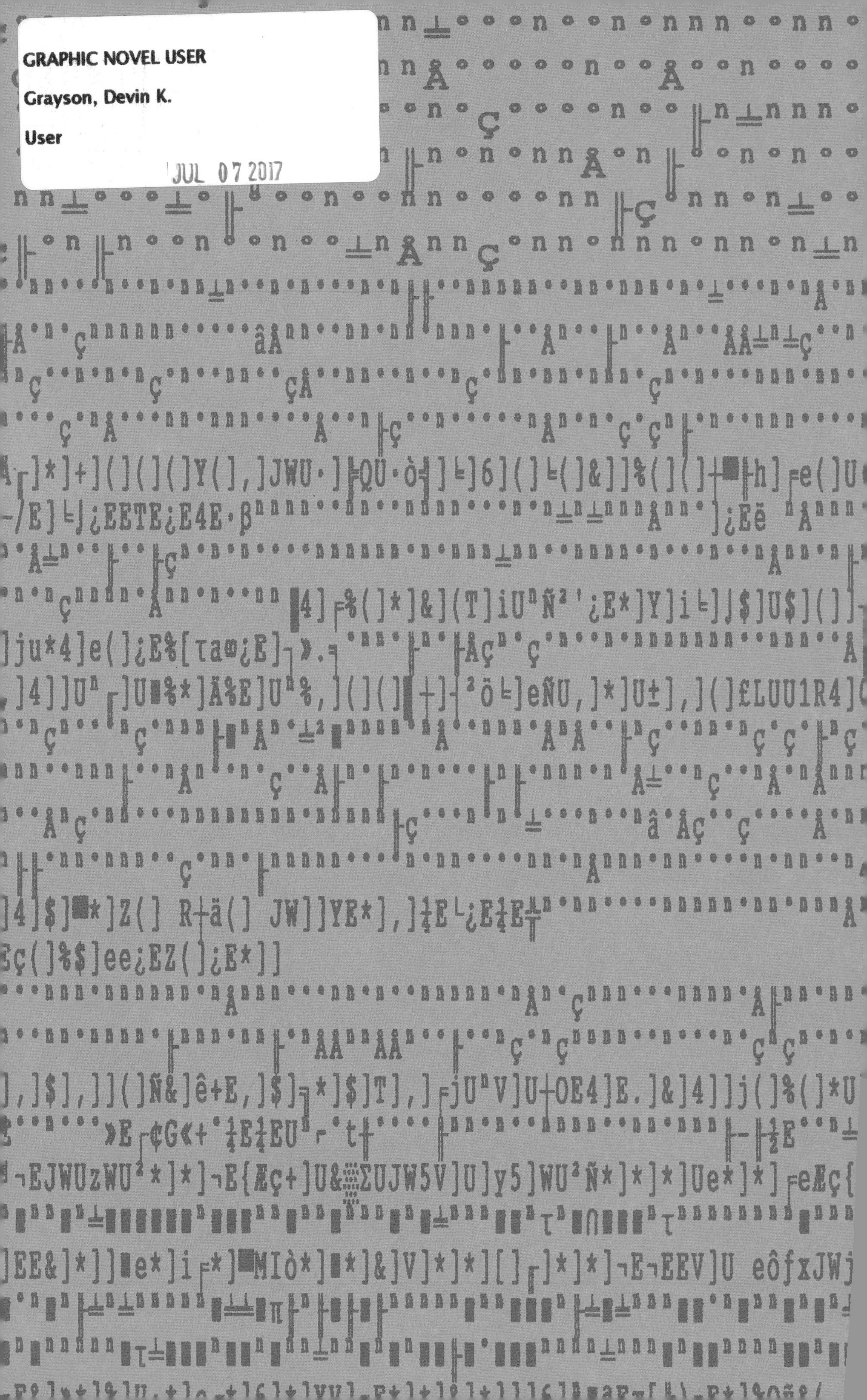